she was

ALSO BY JANIS HALLOWELL

The Annunciation of Francesca Dunn

she was

JANIS HALLOWELL

WILLIAM MORROW   *An Imprint of* HarperCollins*Publishers*

This book is a work of fiction. The characters, incidents, and dialogue are drawn from the author's imagination and are not to be construed as real. Any resemblance to actual events or persons, living or dead, is entirely coincidental.

HarperCollins books may be purchased for educational, business, or sales promotional use. For information please write: Special Markets Department, HarperCollins Publishers, 10 East 53rd Street, New York, NY 10022.

FIRST EDITION

Designed by Betty Lew

Library of Congress Cataloging-in-Publication Data

Hallowell, Janis
    She was : a novel / Janis Hallowell. — 1st ed.
        p. cm.
    ISBN 978-0-06-124325-7630
    1. Married women—Fiction. 2. Domestic Fiction. 1. Title.

PS3608.A5485S54 2008
813'.6—dc22

2007037320

08 09 10 11 12 OV/RRD 10 9 8 7 6 5 4 3 2 1

For Howie

she was

prologue

March 8, 1971
Columbia University, New York City

Louis Nilon pushes chapped fists into coat pockets and leans into the wind. The quad is already empty except for one lone student struggling with a big piece of cardboard that billows like a sail before him. Nilon's shoes are damp with mop water from the day's work, making the sharp wind coming off the river that much colder.

Most Monday nights he would be on the uptown bus to Harlem and his supper. This Monday is different. He's cleaning East Hall tonight so that tomorrow he'll be able to get off work to watch his oldest girl, his beautiful Yvonne, be Juliet in the school play.

He thinks about his boss, the Greek. This morning, when Nilon asked to change the schedule, he gave permission with a flip of his hand. The Greek was in a good mood, looking forward to six o'clock, when he would get in a taxi and head downtown to Madison Square Garden for the Ali–Frazier fight. A seat at the Garden costs $150, but the Greek has a cousin in the business. Louis Nilon looks at his watch. The Greek is there by now, waiting for the fight to start.

Nilon rounds the corner of the building. Out of the wind it's not so raw. He hurries up the walk to East Hall, and a strange elation takes hold. He's been looking forward to the fight, too. In the quiet of the empty building he'll listen on his transistor without interruptions and get tomorrow's work done at the same time.

He opens the front door to the old red brick building and turns on the lights. The place smells of floor wax and mildew, chalkboards and mimeographs. A few years back they were going to tear it down to make room for a newer building, but somebody formed a committee and made a fuss, and the upshot is that Louis Nilon has to keep dragging his mop bucket up three flights of narrow stairs and then he has to wax the floors because they're wood, not carpet. The commodes are small and old; he can hardly fit in the stalls to clean them. He's always bumping things, scared to death that, with his mop handle, he's going to crack one of the milky glass globes that hang from the ceilings. "You break one, it comes out of your check," the Greek said when he hired Nilon.

They've still got the army recruitment tables set up in the foyer. The brochures are in neat stacks and the eyes of the white soldier in the poster follow him as he wrestles his mop and bucket out of the closet and proceeds to haul them up the steps. The white soldier looks strong and healthy in his clean uniform. There's a fine, clear look in his eye. Not like the boys just back from Vietnam out of Louis Nilon's neighborhood. Those boys come back on drugs, if they come home at all, and since they don't fit in anymore, since they've had their bodies built up and their good sense removed by the army, they start misbehaving. But the neighborhood keeps on making boys and the government keeps on turning them into soldiers.

One boy, name of Lee James, was drafted in '68. His mother is an old friend of Wilmia's. He was a bright kid, and polite. Nilon remembers Lee helping him fix his mother's ironing board one Saturday morning years ago. The kid asked fifty questions. He wanted to learn how to use the saw and the drill. Lee James came home from 'Nam with his nappy hair out to there and a black fist sewed onto the back of his fatigues. Now he has the mean eyes of a kicked dog and he can't keep a job to help his mama pay the rent. It was the war that did it to him.

Because there isn't any water on three, Louis Nilon fills his bucket on two and carries it, heavy and sloshing, upstairs. Each step aggravates the pain in his knee. At the top, catching his breath, he sets his transistor radio on the rail and tunes in the fight.

"The Fight of the Century," they're calling it. Muhammad Ali's back to reclaim his title after they stripped him of it for refusing to go to Vietnam. The truth is, they were punishing him for changing his name from Cassius Clay to Muhammad Ali. It was penance for being mouthy, uppity; for becoming Muslim. But times are changing. The whole country's been down in Washington marching to stop the war, just like they did for Dr. King, and the Supreme Court says Ali can keep the title.

Louis Nilon mops the floors of the classrooms at the top of the building. "It's electric here tonight at the Garden," the man on the radio says. "Sammy Davis Jr. and Bill Cosby are sitting ringside. Ali isn't dancing like he used to. He's standing flatfooted, slugging it out."

Louis Nilon empties the trash into one big bag that he puts at the top of the stairs. He opens the can of floor wax and scoops some onto the waxing mop he's rigged up. There's a buffing machine in another building, but dragging it across the quad and up the stairs is too much trouble. It's easier to do this little bit of wood on his own. Using the rigged-up mop, he spreads the wax on the places where the floor needs it. When that's done he sits on the wood floor, ignoring the pain in his knee, and takes off his wet shoes and socks. He puts on another pair of thick wool socks he keeps for buffing. He groans as he clambers to his feet. Wilmia says he should stop this foot-polishing. She says it's bad for his knee. But Louis Nilon likes the feel of the thick socks and the heat and weight of his feet turning the soft wax into a high, hard shine. He slides back and forth on the new wax and listens to the fight.

Joe Frazier bludgeons Ali with his left hook while Ali flashes, speed and jab. Louis Nilon boxes along with them, inventing his own fancy footwork on the floor wax. He does the "Ali shuffle," moving his feet as fast as they will go, heedless of the bad knee now, traveling from doorway to chalkboard and back again. They fight their way to the sixth and the man on the radio says Ali's giving it away. Says he's taking punishment on the ropes. But Louis Nilon remembers what Ali did to Sonny Liston, back when he was Cassius Clay, how he took it on the ropes until he decided he wanted to knock Liston out. Any minute now, Ali's going to set Joe Frazier down.

When the new wax is hard and shiny, Louis Nilon sits on the top step and puts his damp socks and shoes back on. He carries the bucket down to two, empties it in the toilet, and then moves the mops, his polishing socks, and the transistor. He pours ammonia into the toilet and takes apart the gummy-pink soap dispenser, wiping it the same way he wipes his kids' noses. He fills it, fits brown paper towels into the towel dispenser, then starts on the floors and trash.

It's late in the fight by the time the floors on two are shined. Ali's backed Frazier up under a barrage of left-right combinations. Louis Nilon empties the bucket again and carries it down to the ground floor where he fills it one last time. The announcer says that Ali looks beat. Frazier rocks Ali with another left. Another brings him to his knees. Louis Nilon churns his mop in the sudsy water and turns the radio up. The man says that Ali's jaw looks broken, yet he keeps fighting. He takes another left hook. Nilon shakes his head and leans on his mop.

In the fifteenth round Frazier hits Ali again. Louis Nilon looks down into his bucket. It can't be that Ali is beat. He's "The People's Fighter," the greatest boxer in the world; a black man who has demanded respect and gotten it. But the announcer says he's broken. He's standing with his face hanging sideways. The ref should call the fight, but the people at the Garden want their money's worth. They smell blood and now they've got to have it.

Louis Nilon's mouth turns down at the corners as he listens to the uproar coming through the tiny holes of the transistor. He wipes at tears on his cheeks. His brow furrows as he opens the door to the far stall in the main-floor bathroom. He listens to the boos and the cheers as the greatest black man of his generation goes down. He doesn't see the plaid book bag behind the toilet or hear it ticking.

Louis Nilon checks his watch. It's nine o'clock.

august 2005

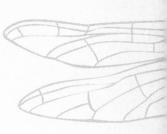

friday

chapter 1

DOREEN WOODS drives through the still
neighborhood. It is 7 A.M. and the August sky over Denver is already
baked to a high, hard shell. There is no breeze. It hasn't rained for
two months and none is expected. But at this hour, even though it's
already hot, there's a freshness that can't be denied. She punches the
AC button on the dashboard but keeps her window open. Extrava-
gant, she thinks, like Richard Nixon, thirty-five years ago, running
the White House air-conditioning at maximum so that he could enjoy his fireplace in the summer.

Thirty-five years ago she was eighteen, the same age as her son
is now. She would have rather died than compare herself to Nixon.
Thirty-five years ago, she and her generation, in their well-fed arrogance, agreed that Nixon was bad, Vietnam was wrong, and it was
time for revolution. For the three and a half decades since then she's
chastised herself for that arrogance, but now, in 2005, the architects of
the Iraq War make the Nixon administration look like amateurs. And
echoes of the old calls for change can be heard. It will be interesting to
see what this generation, her son's generation, will do with a bad war.

Cold air blasts out of the vents as she drives with her elbow jutting
out the open window. At fifty-three years old, nothing is as black-
and-white as it used to be. She's a wife, a mother, and a dentist. She's
middle-class, middle-aged, and what they called back then *bourgeois*.
She smiles at the word. Nobody uses it anymore, but that's what she
has become.

The elms that shade the streets stand thirsty and exhausted. Because of the drought, Denver has become a city that conserves water.
Their lawn, hers and Miles's, optimistically planted in May, was dutifully sacrificed in June when water restrictions forced them to choose
between the new sod in front and the cherry trees in back. There was
no debate. Miles is the gardener, it was his decision and he chose the
fruit trees over a water-guzzling lawn. He'd planted the ten saplings
when they first moved to Denver from Boston. They were the only
things, at first, that gave him pleasure here. He watered, mulched,
staked, and pruned the little trees. Now, six years later, they form a
small orchard that, if there had been moisture, would be bearing its
first fruit.

Most of the yards she passes are brown and parched, but three
houses flaunt deep green lawns and lush gardens. All three are mammoth and ostentatious. Miles despises the owners. "They have this
infuriating sense of entitlement," he says. "How could anyone expect
them to sacrifice *their* landscaping?" Driving by now, Doreen gazes
at the green, drinking it in. She understands why it irks Miles, but at
the same time she can't help her surge of unwarranted joy in those
three lawns, flamboyantly breaking the rules.

The truth is that in spite of drought and war, the mistakes of the
past and the tenuousness of the future, this particular morning makes
her absurdly happy. In spite of the vaguely disturbing realization that
she has something in common with Richard Nixon, she's happy with
the enamel blue sky and the fine linen of her skirt. And under the
skirt her legs are still strong, though her belly and butt have gone
soft. Right now, though, she doesn't care because the warm air from
outside mixes with the manufactured cool and plays with her hair.
The sun is still soft enough to feel welcome and nurturing. On such
a morning she feels incredibly lucky. She has everything she needs;
more than she ever thought she would get: a strong marriage, a son
successfully grown and going off to college in the fall, a satisfying

practice, and a beloved brother. Her elation subsides at the thought of Adam.

Adam's sudden decline over the last six months has been without mercy. He was functioning well with his MS, still building his sculptural stone walls. Then, one freezing day in February, when he'd been down with a cold and Doreen arrived with minestrone, she found him unable to see or walk. When the episode ended, he didn't regain as much as they'd hoped. Since then the cognitive symptoms have emerged: confusion, memory loss, and even some hallucinations.

Adam lives in a carriage house behind one of the old Denver mansions. She stops in every day now on her way to work. She uses her key to open the door, not wanting him to get up. In the small kitchen the dishes are clean and stacked in the drying rack next to the sink. The floor is swept, the stove is spotless, all evidence that Miranda's been here.

In Mexico, Miranda was a surgical nurse. Here, she's an illegal immigrant living with her son and daughter-in-law. She works for cash, prefers to do a split shift, coming to Adam's in the morning to get him up and give him breakfast, going home for the afternoon to watch her grandkids, and coming back again in the evening to give him supper, meds, and bed. Miranda makes Adam's illness bearable for all of them.

Walking through Adam's tiny vault of a living room with its high ceilings papered in William Morris is like taking a plunge into a tangled underworld. Doreen crosses over the threadbare Oriental, past the peacock green settee Adam bought in Boston. The door to the bedroom is open and she peeks in. His bed is not so large, it's only a queen ("*Only* a queen?" Adam has been known to say), but it fills the small room. The head- and footboards are massively ornate with a canopy frame Adam has draped with sheer white and pale blue silk.

He's sitting up in bed, propped on pillows. His bare chest is thin, his muscles ropy, so that he has the look of a ruined ballet dancer. He's holding a short string of black beads in his right hand. In his left is a small dog-eared book the size of a box of matches, strung onto a leather cord. He doesn't turn to Doreen, but keeps staring ahead at some point in the mid-distance.

"It's early," he says.

"I know. I have a full schedule today. It's Friday, you know, the day all normal dentists go golfing. How are you?"

"Pretty good. I'd say 92 percent."

Adam has started giving her this pseudo precise update on his mental condition every day. He doesn't talk about his physical condition at all anymore. "I'm about 86 percent," he'll say, or "Functioning at about 51 percent today." On really bad days he forgets to play the game.

"That's good," she says. As usual she feels embarrassingly healthy in his presence. "Can I help you get up?"

"No thanks. I think I'll sit here a while."

He sets the beads on his thigh and uses both hands to touch the little book. He turns a tiny page that's as fragile as an insect wing. His eyes are as blue as the silk above him but flat and unfocused.

"Do you need anything?" she asks. Other than a new nervous system, she thinks, or a cure.

His voice is reassuring. "No, Dorie, I'm fine. Miranda will be here soon."

She realizes that as everything fails a little more each day, he thinks it's his job to reassure her. "Go," he says. "You've got teeth to fix."

It sounds so weak, *teeth to fix*. For a minute she wishes she'd become something else: a scientist researching global warming or overpopulation. She should be working on a cure for MS. But she chose dentistry, the car mechanics of the medical professions. Much needed, but not loved. This is what she is, a dentist.

She takes the bridge over the interstate where rush hour is well under way. Ahead is downtown Denver, a lanky hayseed teenager trying hard to be taken seriously while standing knee-deep in amusement parks and stadiums. The sight of it makes her miss Boston, that old spinster. Still, Doreen's learned to like Denver in spite of, or maybe because of, how uncool it is. There's a shiny goodwill here, on top of the gritty misery that exists in every city. And after all, it's where Miles has planted cherry trees. It's where she established her practice and its offshoot, People's Dental, a free dental program for the homeless. Denver is where Ian has grown up; where Miles teaches in a downtown grade school. And it's likely to be where Adam will die. As places go, Denver has been as good to them as Boston was.

She drives into the heart of the city and the sense of fragile good fortune rises again. Such a morning, such a day is a gift. You don't sneer at a gift.

chapter 2

ADAM SITS on in sunlight and heat. He might have to pee, but it's such an ordeal these days, he puts it off. He fingers the beads, savoring their bumpy, familiar texture. He runs his fingers over the tiny book, careful of its fragile pages. The MS plays its latest trick and he finds himself, without warning, in 1967.

He was a senior in high school. He would graduate in a week. Johnson had refused a second term. The wheels were starting to come off in Vietnam but for the most part the war was still being fought by boys who enlisted, and in Kansas City, those boys were heroes. In Kansas City, people were more concerned about the race riots in Detroit. Going to war was an honorable thing. Other things, like being queer, wasn't.

Adam had already had one clumsy sexual encounter behind the bleachers with a boy from the rival high school. Afterward, he woke every morning twenty minutes before his alarm went off, dread like sand in his belly, thoughts a Möbius strip in his mind: Maybe it was a mistake. Maybe it was something he could chalk up to being young, a late bloomer. He hadn't ever wanted to be with a girl, but still he agonized. What would happen this summer when all the other kids were dating? What would happen in college? He knew what he was supposed to be doing.

It was much simpler to paint. Cadmium yellow, Payne's gray, rose madder. These were his companions. The struggle to understand color and then to brush it onto canvas replaced a social life. And at the end of the year he had four paintings hanging in the high school art show.

His sister and mother came to the show but his father stayed at home. "He's in one of his moods," Adam's mother said. They all knew what that meant. Most of the time, Ed Johansson was a quiet man who went to work every day at the phone company, but he was prone to headaches and violent mood swings. In his "moods" he picked on Adam and told stories about fighting in the Pacific in WWII.

When the three of them came in, triumphant over Adam's Best-of-Show, his father was sitting in front of the TV with an empty high-ball glass. He'd peeled an apple with his pocketknife and was feeding pieces of it, along with small tiles of orange cheese, to Hershey, the dachshund, who sat, rapt, on the carpet at his feet.

"That boxer Cassius Clay, I guess he calls himself *Muhammad Ali* now, has refused to go into the army," Ed said, addressing himself to Adam but maintaining eye contact with the dog as he held up a piece of cheese. "He's refused to serve his country. What do you think about that?"

"I don't know," Adam said. He tried to slide past his father. If he could make it to the stairs, he might avoid the argument.

"Well, you *better* know," Ed said. The corners of his mouth turned down in a grimace. The dog whined and stood to wag its tail. Ed turned back to it. "Hershey, sit," he said, and the dachshund dropped its hindquarters. Adam's sister, always spared the business end of Ed's ravings, skipped up the stairs.

"Why does a young Negro of your generation, who's had every-thing handed to him, who's rich with the white man's dollars, decide he doesn't have to defend his country?"

Adam and Augusta stood at the foot of the stairs, both waiting for the rant to end. Adam said, wearily, "Dad, how should I know?"

Augusta sighed and shook her head. She always said that if Adam refused to argue with his father, it would blow over sooner. Ed fed a piece of apple to Hershey, who chewed it up fast, never taking her eyes off the cheese.

"You think the blacks have the right to tear up cities? Do you think they have the right to refuse to fight to protect their country?"

Adam held his purple ribbon, trying to think of the right thing to say. He wanted to tell his father he was full of shit. He wanted to tell him he was a bigot and an asshole, but he wanted, more than that, to get into bed and go to sleep. He didn't want to fight.

"I don't know and I don't care," he said.

Ed pointed his finger at Adam's chest. "That's right; you don't care. You've had everything handed to *you*, too. If you had to fight for what you have, you damn well *would* care."

"Ed, you've worked yourself into a lather," Augusta said, clearing the drink glass and the apple peel away. Ed's lower lip was slack, indicating that he'd had several drinks, as he swung his head to look at his son.

"You're painting pretty pictures while the Communists are taking over in Asia and the Negroes are taking over here at home. You're eighteen years old, Adam. Almost a man. At your age I was in the Pacific. What are you doing? You think making pictures is going to fix things?"

"No," Adam said, feeling smaller and weaker by the moment, "but I think it's important."

"Oh. It's *important*, is it?" Ed said, doing a cruel exaggeration of Adam's slightly feminine delivery.

"Ed, cut it out," Augusta said. She took his arm but he wrenched it out of her grip. Adam stared at the gold clock over the fireplace. Misery and shame sloshed around inside of him.

"He's getting to be an embarrassment," Ed said, to Augusta. "He doesn't act right. Why, Dave Rostrum, at the company? His son joined the Marines. Dave can be proud. His boy will serve his country and help stop communism over there, and when he gets home he'll go through college on the GI Bill." He leaned over to croon at Hershey, still waiting for more cheese. "What's wrong with that?"

"Adam's going to college," said Augusta, looking scared. "We agreed on that. He'll enroll in school and they won't draft him."

"Well, I'm starting to wonder if that's the right decision. The boy needs to toughen up. Otherwise people are going to start talking. Hell, they already are."

Augusta sparred with Ed, diverting his attention away from Adam. When Ed turned his attention to Hershey again, cutting a sliver of apple for the dog, she indicated with her eyes for Adam to go upstairs.

He could hear them fighting as he undressed and got into bed. He lay with his arms folded behind his head and thought about it. Nobody could say he was a coward. He'd put up with more bullying and shoves and mean remarks than his father could imagine. He didn't think he acted queer but it seemed that other people knew. Every day this past school year he'd vowed to control himself. He wouldn't cross his legs. He wouldn't speak unless he was sure his voice was going to be low. He'd walk with his knees bowed out. Every day he failed. A laugh would slip out that was almost a giggle or a hand gesture would escape. Something. And someone was always there to see it.

He made up his mind that night while his parents were yelling downstairs. He didn't know if he was queer or not, but there didn't seem to be a lot he could do to change that. He *did* know he wasn't a coward. And there was something he could do to prove it.

On the last day of school, while the other seniors were throwing their term papers in the air and making plans to get drunk, Adam took his mother's Ford and drove downtown. He got out of the car and his palms were sweating, but he didn't hesitate. He squared his shoulders and stepped into the recruiting office for the Marines.

———

ADAM GETS HIMSELF UP TO GO TO THE BATHROOM. HIS LEGS
are distant objects that don't seem to belong to him. He furniture-
walks (a big no-no according to his physical therapist) out of the
bedroom and across the hall. He sits himself down on the recently
installed handicapped-accessible toilet, using the new handrails in
the wall.

HE LANDED IN VIETNAM IN SEPTEMBER OF '67 IN THE WAKE OF
the election of Thieu. There was a lull in the fighting and a cautious
optimism in-country but also the feeling that all hell would break
loose when the fighting resumed. His company's first mission was
north out of Da Nang to sweep the hot spots that had been reported
close to Hue. There was a guy Adam knew from basic on the same
truck. Tom Poole was a little banty rooster from Douglas, Wyoming.
He'd been a 4-H kid, a junior rodeo rider. He grew up on a ranch
nestled into an elbow of the Platte River, but his father lost the place
to the bank when Tom was thirteen. After that he worked his uncles'
ranches until he was old enough to join the Marines.

The caravan of six-bys wound up into the hills on Highway 1. The
air was cooler up there, and clear, compared to the sulfurous stench
of Da Nang. The South China Sea lay like a thick jade lozenge to
the east. To the west were Laos and the Ho Chi Minh Trail, the sup-
ply artery to the NVA and Viet Cong. In between were a thousand
serene hills and valleys, rice paddies and rivers, in dozens of shades
of viridian and cerulean. It was hard to believe they hid swarms of
men craving his blood.

"How're you doing?" said Tom Poole. "Scared?"

"I'm okay," Adam said, though his jaw was clenched so tight he
could barely speak.

"That's good. I'm about to shit myself, if you want to know the
truth."

The trucks shifted into low gear to crawl up Hai Van Pass. The area was supposed to be secure, but even the seasoned marines in the truck were jumpy and tense, holding their M16s as if guns could protect them from a mortar or a grenade. In the bush on the sides of the road old bunkers dripped with burst sandbags and there were a few rotting wooden buildings left over from the French. Any one of these structures could provide cover for VC.

They were still climbing, the trucks laboring in first gear, when the ambush came. When they realized their truck hadn't been hit, Adam and Tom took shelter behind it, along with the rest of the squad. Then, on the orders of their captain, they moved into one of the dilapidated bunkers at the side of the road just before all of the six-bys were hit. In the smoke and sudden quiet after the hits, hundreds of NVA ran down from the top of the pass. He heard the captain frantically radio for air. The NVA came at them like ants, fast and inevitable.

The M16 suddenly felt as small and inadequate as a plastic toy in Adam's hands, but basic training kicked in. The NVA weren't human, they were the enemy, they were gooks and he must kill them or be killed. That was the objective. That was the op. He and Tom ran up the hill together. He was aware of guys dropping to the left and right, and guys behind him pushing. At one point the gooks were on top of him. Tom shot one and then another before he and Adam were forced backward into the soldiers coming up. Confusion broke out. No one knew who was fighting whom. All Adam knew was that Tom, now on his right side, would blow away everything coming at them from that direction, just as Adam was spraying everything to the left.

In the middle of shooting and waiting for the shot that would kill him, a large-caliber round detonated over them. A man to his left, another grunt named Cecil Brown, was blown apart. They'd been in basic together, too, though they weren't friends. Cecil's face registered surprise and then disbelief when he saw that his arm and shoulder had been ripped from his body. He sank to his knees and looked up at Adam in mute outrage.

Adam was dimly aware of the captain on the radio with battalion, frantically asking if they had just fired. The next round came in before he got the confirmation. Two guys farther down the line were hit. A man whirled, eyes white-rimmed and insane, on the captain. "It's friendly fire. It's *friendly*. Motherfuckers are killing *us*."

Meanwhile, some marines were running up the hill into NVA fire, while other marines were running down the hill, taking friendly fire. The hill was a roiling mess of bodies fighting and dying. The captain grabbed boys running downhill, turned them around, and sent them back up, where most of them were greased immediately. The only still center in the confusion was Tom Poole, fighting next to him. He was aware of Tom's every move as a kind of dance mirroring his own.

Everywhere, there were gooks down and marines down. They fell in distorted heaps of human parts; a torso turned in an impossible direction from a lower body; a head opened from the top like a cooked egg. With their guts stomped into the dirt, the dead looked like roadkill. Alone, he might have given in to the real craziness that beckoned, but Tom was next to him and they had a purpose: to keep each other alive.

Adam kept shooting and climbing, there was no other choice. They would take the hill and that was that. His one prayer was that his 16 wouldn't jam. He took cover behind bush and dead bodies to reload and realized there was a sound coming out of his mouth. It was a sound so loud and compelling that he felt himself turn inside out around it, the way his mom turned her mink coat inside out when she set it down at a party, so that the rosy silk lining faced out.

Somehow, a rear perimeter was established and the order was given to fall back. A head count was taken. Out of 596 soldiers on the pass that day, only 320 still lived. Of those, 147 were wounded. The casualties on the other side were at least as bad. Adam and Tom were two of the 73 marines left to haul away the wounded and the dead. They worked all day and into the night, still side by side, through the smoke and combat debris that littered the ground. They moved in the peculiar slow-motion silence that comes after battle. They carried men who were wounded and stoic, and men who were wounded and crying. They loaded them all onto the choppers that appeared, hovered, and received them. Then they went back for the dead.

chapter 3

DOREEN TAKES the curve around Civic Center Park, makes the light, and starts up Capitol Hill. She turns on the radio. "Two car bombs exploded in Baghdad yesterday, killing seven and wounding sixteen," says the familiar voice. She turns it up. Car bombs and suicide bombs in Iraq have become so commonplace they're not always reported on radio news anymore. And in the papers they're often relegated to the inside pages. She waits for the commentator to tell her why this item made top-of-the-rush-hour NPR.

"Three of the dead were American soldiers; one was an American journalist."

There it is. American deaths, especially American civilian deaths, are still newsworthy on radio, although in this war, photos of the dead and their flag-draped coffins are noticeably absent from the papers, as are photos of wounded soldiers. The government says they don't want to subject the American people to unnecessary trauma. They also want to keep people from getting outraged enough to speak up. This administration is not stupid about the way propaganda works. Compared to Vietnam, when everyone under thirty was out in the streets protesting, the Iraq War in its third year still gets only a marginal murmur of protest.

Denver's gold dome catches the morning sun and temporarily blinds her. Ian, with his friend Kumar and Adam's friend Derek, will be here later, in just such a protest. In his last year of high school Ian realized that with another turn of the dial he could be drafted into this war. She's proud of him for speaking out, but she worries. These Iraq War protests seem tame (they'll march along with maybe a hundred other people in the blinding heat, and stay within the lines for the agreed-upon time), and she can't tell him not to go, but she knows what can happen and it makes her nervous.

She was the same age as Ian is now when she went to her first political rally. It was 1970. Adam was home from Vietnam with a broken arm that needed three surgeries. He lived in his own little apartment. He'd become silent, emaciated, and angry. The longer his hair and sideburns grew, the more morose he became. He smoked pot constantly, even in front of their parents. She'd been accepted to Berkeley in the fall, but even in Kansas she could see that attitudes about the war were changing. Hardly anyone under thirty supported it anymore. And radical kids around the country were blowing up National Guard headquarters and draft offices.

The rally took place at the University of Kansas in Lawrence. She and Adam stood in the hot sun and listened to speeches. The Jefferson Airplane was playing on somebody's transistor. She had just cut thick bangs into her long white-blond hair and they refused to hang straight. She'd plastered them down with water but they curled up in a most uncool flip on her sweaty forehead.

The couple speaking were young, in blue jeans and peasant shirts. The woman had long straight brown hair and oversized round sunglasses. She exuded an earthy confidence and hip style. She spoke passionately about getting out of Vietnam. She spoke about a world without war, where something she called the military-industrial complex wouldn't have power. "We have to refuse to go," she said. "If all of us refuse, they can't have a war."

That night their parents threw an engagement party for Linda DeVries, a girl Adam's age who lived next door. Linda wore navy blue pumps and her mother's pearls. Her husband-to-be already looked like a young copy of his dad in a gray suit. The boy stood on the sidelines with a stuffed-up nose, breathing noisily through his mouth.

Their parents had insisted that Adam help at the party. It was his job to pour drinks and keep the dishes filled with Chex Mix. Adam took his place behind the booze table and stood there with his dead soldier eyes, his hair down below his shoulders, and his pissed-off attitude, practically daring anybody to come near enough to get a drink. Their father made martinis for several of the intimidated guests, shooting furious looks at Adam. The drinks gave the men courage and soon they were talking in their wide, braying voices.

Doreen remembers herself, recently graduated and valedictorian of her high school class, standing at the edge of the party. She watched these people she'd known all her life and realized there was something about them that she always sensed but couldn't put words to, but now, after hearing the young woman in Lawrence speak, she knew what it was. Compared to the bright woman in Lawrence, these Kansas City suburbanites were dull and synthetic and selfish, and completely taken in by the president's agenda for more war in Southeast Asia.

She stood at the edge of the party, in the doorway behind Adam, and pressed her mangled bangs to her forehead. She was glad she would be leaving. Her idea of hell would be to end up stuck in Kansas City wearing blue pumps and getting married to a mouth-breather in a suit. She was going to Berkeley. She was going to be like the woman in Lawrence.

The bride's father tried to make conversation with Adam.

"Give me a bourbon and branch, son. Well, you were over there. Tell me, wasn't chasing the Viet Cong into Cambodia, in the end, a good idea?"

Adam stared the man down from under half-dropped lids. But Chip DeVries didn't take the hint.

"I always say if it gets this damn thing over with sooner, let's do it. I'd think you'd be all for it, being a marine. A little airpower on the situation. Save some lives." He made expansive gestures with his hands in front of his wide brown tie. "It must be working, the president says he's going to be able to withdraw by the end of the month. Put a little ice in it will you?"

Adam put two ice cubes in Chip DeVries's drink and handed it to him.

"You believe what the president says?" Adam said, soft as cotton, but everybody in the room heard him.

"Well, of course," Chip DeVries said.

Adam crossed his arms over his chest. "He doesn't know what's happening over there any more than you do. You'll never win this war."

"Oh? And why is that?"

"Because the VC will fight to the last man. They have to. They're not going to leave, so we will, eventually. How's that going to save lives, Mr. DeVries? Explain it to me."

Their father appeared and put his hand on Adam's shoulder. "Come with me, Adam, will you?"

In the kitchen their father yelled in a harsh whisper at Adam. He said all the things he usually said: The man's entitled to his opinion, and in my house you obey my rules, and if you want to argue your opinion, that's one thing, but who's going to take you seriously looking like a bum, and when are you going to get a job, and your mother's worried sick over you.

Adam didn't listen. He went out the door and walked down the dusky street. She ran after him.

"I gotta get out of here," he said.

"I know, me too."

He shook his head. "I was waiting around to drive you out to Berkeley, but I don't think I can stay here till August." He kicked a Dr Pepper can off the sidewalk into the empty lot on the corner.

"Where will you go?"

He stopped and stared at the clouds stacked up like pink erasers in the western sky.

"To Washington. To march on the Capitol."

She reached up to feel her bangs. They were hideous but she didn't care anymore. "Let me come," she begged. "I can help with the driving. You'll get there twice as fast."

So she and Adam drove to Berkeley by way of Washington, D.C. Everywhere they went, people were angry about the war. Young people on campuses wore beads and feathers and tribal garb. They clustered together and spoke out against the war and the president. They cried about the shootings at Kent State. By the end of the summer, people of all ages and styles started joining in and followed the free spirits that led the charge. And everywhere the police stood behind shields and gas masks, waiting for transgressions.

THE CAPITOL STEPS ARE EMPTY AT THIS HOUR EXCEPT FOR a sampling of the city's poor, scattered in the morning sun. Zeeda Bouray, in her dirty blue housecoat, is in her usual place swaying from side to side, shaking her head back and forth in perpetual "no." She's one of Doreen's People's Dental cases. Her husband died and left her penniless; her children live in another state. Zeeda's mental illness, some unnamed dementia, has made it so that she can't take care of herself. Doreen squints out the window. Zeeda is on the schedule for this afternoon and now Doreen knows why. She isn't wearing the bridge Doreen put in two weeks ago and her lips are once again sucked into her face. Doreen slows down and tries to pull over, but the car behind her honks, and anyway, Zeeda doesn't see her. Doreen presses her lips together. It's her own fault. She should have cemented in the bridge. Now she'll have to make another one.

The neighborhoods vary wildly between the Capitol and the office. She passes an upscale bookstore and coffee shop in one block, and a squalid mini-mart surrounded by adult bookstores in the next. And here, at last, is the prosperous commercial block with restored streetlights, a yoga center, and the remodeled Victorian mansion that houses her office.

She pulls into her parking spot behind the building. It's early enough that only Nikki, the receptionist, is here. Oddly, almost half of the receptionists, hygienists, and dental assistants Doreen has known in her twenty years of dentistry have been named Nikki, Nickie, Nicky, or Niki.

She hopes that for the first transitional minutes it will be just Nikki with her in the office. When Fern, Doreen's assistant, and Avery and Joan, the two hygienists, arrive, the place will become noisy and chaotic and Doreen won't get out of being the boss for even a moment. The others have their dramas of power and popularity and it's always up to her to settle their disputes. When she does, she then has to endure somebody's resentment and blame.

"Morning, Doc," Nikki says from the little area they use as a kitchen. She's making coffee. She looks tired.

"How's the move going?" Doreen asks.

"In this heat? Everything takes twice as long. But we're getting there. If I unpack boxes every night this week, I'll have the kitchen done by the weekend."

Doreen lets her hand rest on Nikki's shoulder as she reaches around her to pull her first bottle of water out of the fridge. She'd love to talk about Nikki's move into her first house but Fern comes in, young and beautiful with her hair down. Today her eyelids are painted a dramatic deep orchid fading into yellow-green near her brows. The eyes are rimmed with bright ultramarine. She once explained to Doreen that she does it for the patients. She likes to give them something to look at while they're in the chair. Every day she comes up with a different display.

Fern is followed by the two hygienists, Avery, a midthirties distance runner, and Joan, older than Doreen, with a personality as big as her bosom. The office fills with their voices. The radio and lights go on. Each chair and workstation has been disinfected the night before, but Fern sprays and wipes the chairs again before she begins Doreen's patient setups for the day.

"Who's our first patient?" Doreen asks.

"Amanda Buchwald," Nikki says, keeping her voice neutral but letting her eyes roll.

"Green-stripe," Fern announces. A green stripe at the top of their file is a way to quietly alert everybody in the office to a difficult or especially needy patient.

Amanda's been coming in with lower jaw pain Doreen can't reproduce in the office. She's nervous and controlling, and doesn't trust Fern in her mouth, only Doreen, which hasn't endeared her to Fern. She doesn't make appointments, she demands them, which has pissed off Nikki. But Doreen is intrigued by Amanda Buchwald because she hasn't been able to figure out what's causing the problem.

"She's in pain," she tells them. "You'd be cranky if you were in that kind of pain, too."

"She was a green-stripe before this," Fern mutters.

Doreen pulls Amanda Buchwald's file and reviews it, searching for something she might have missed. Initial pain three months ago. Intermittent since then. Most recent work done: two fillings Doreen did herself in April, a gold crown on 30 from the previous dentist. The tooth that seems to be the problem is the next tooth, number 29. Prescribed Percocet last week.

"Do you think she's making it up?" Fern says, while gathering her hair up into a ponytail.

There are patients who invent pain, the dental hypochondriacs of the world, but they're rare. There are even fewer genuine masochists who enjoy pain. Amanda Buchwald is neither.

"I don't think so," Doreen says, putting on her coat and turning on the faucet to scrub her hands for the first time of the day. Fern is lively and young, fun to have in the office, but sometimes, like now, her craving for drama is irritating when she should be thinking about the patient.

"Well then, is she looking for drugs?" Fern asks, while she puts Amanda's X-rays in the viewer on the side table and turns on the light.

Doreen shakes her head. "Think about it. She only asked for painkillers last week. Until then she was dealing with it. Her pain is real, we just haven't found the cause."

A pouty look crosses Fern's face at the rejection of her theory.

"Try to find some compassion, Fern," Doreen says loud enough for Fern to hear but no one else. Fern's pout dissolves into a look of self-reproach. She'll kick herself around the office for a while but she'll learn.

At two minutes before eight o'clock Amanda Buchwald comes in, holding her hand to her jaw. Her eyes are wild.

"Is it happening right now?" Doreen asks, helping her into the chair.

Amanda nods. Fern takes her position on the other side of Amanda. "Open, please."

Amanda does. It never ceases to amaze Doreen that those two words have the power to cause people to open their mouths, maybe the most vulnerable and intimate orifice of the human body. Most people open and a kind of docile fear and surrender mix in their eyes. Some, like Amanda, lie rigid, expecting and anticipating pain, fighting the situation. They stare at Doreen with dread but they open nevertheless. Because all of them know, in spite of how much they love to hate the dentist, that they need her.

Doreen knows she's a good dentist. She likes the art of diagnosing and then the craft of fixing the problem. She's good with her hands, with precision tools, always has been. The reason she's able to stay emotionally available to her patients while inflicting pain, and being resented for it, is that she never doubts that the small hurt she inflicts now prevents bigger pain later.

She examines the area, looking for cracks, root exposure, and decay. Though she has checked this many times before, she has Amanda bite on articulating paper and checks the fillings again. They're fine. She places the paper on the crown.

"Okay, bite, bite, bite," she says, demonstrating the motion yet again. Amanda bites quick and hard, almost vindictively. Her eyes are desperate and angry. She grinds and moves her jaw around more than she needs to. Midgrind, her eyes fly up to Doreen and fill.

"Was that it?"

Amanda nods.

"Open and don't move," Doreen says. She looks at the marks the paper has made. Because of the way Amanda exaggerated the grinding and biting, she got different marks this time. Now she can see where the crown is just a hair high on the back side. Amanda must be hitting it often enough to cause pain to radiate through the mandible.

"Hold it just a second," Doreen says, readying her drill. She pushes Amanda's tongue to the side with the mirror and burrs the gold of the crown. When the purple mark is gone and the area is smooth, Doreen rinses her while Fern operates the suction. Amanda's eyes flick from Doreen to Fern and back again. She tests her bite and moves her jaw around.

"How does it feel?" Doreen says. She can see that already Amanda is more relaxed.

Amanda's tentative, not ready to admit it could be this easy. "I don't know yet," she says, almost surly. Doreen checks the biting surface again. The marks are where they should be. She brings the chair up to sitting.

"Why don't you try that and see how it is?"

Amanda gets up, looking suspicious and doubtful. Doreen knows that the pain will subside and disappear. The change from that one small adjustment indicates it. The musculature will settle down and Amanda will be fine. Doreen is pleased; she feels a solid satisfaction as she walks Amanda out. She holds the door for Amanda and smiles at her. Maybe she is doing some good in the world, after all.

As always, Joan, Avery, Fern, and Nikki eat lunch together. They spread a gingham cloth over the table in the back and unpack Tupperware containers from home.

"I brought everybody some of this spicy chicken soup I made last night," Avery says, passing out paper cups full of soup to each. The others make appreciative noises.

"What kind of salad is that?" Nikki says, stabbing her fork at something Joan's eating. Joan, who is trying to lose weight, brings only salads.

"It's a taco salad with fake hamburger. Want some?"

"No thanks, baby. You enjoy it," Nikki says. The others laugh.

Doreen usually goes around the corner for a bagel and a change of scene, but these four take the lunch hour to hear about each other's boyfriends, kids, husbands, and mothers. It's a little too cloying for Doreen, but she has to admit, when one of them has something going on in her life, the other three are right there. When Fern's mother got diagnosed with liver cancer, the other three took turns visiting the hospital with Fern. They brought her little treats and patted her back. They gave her books on living with cancer and what to do when someone you love has cancer. All four cried at the funeral. More than once she's been a little envious on the outside, even though most of the time it's where she likes to be.

Doreen picks up her bag and tries to leave the office without disturbing their conversation but Joan spots her.

"Hey, Doc," she calls out, holding a potato chip in the air. "You got a second?"

Doreen turns back to the lunchroom and stands in the doorway. She knows what's coming. Joan is going to ask for something.

"Doc, my oldest, Jordan, needs to get running shoes and all his equipment for the cross-country team. They're having their first practice tomorrow morning. Do you think I could leave an hour early tonight? Avery said she'd do my last cleaning."

Doreen looks down to formulate what to say. On the one hand, if Avery and Joan have worked it out, Doreen should have no problem with it. On the other hand, Joan does this at least once a week, leaving Avery to clean up after her and even take her patients. It's important for patients to see the same hygienist every time. When Joan ducks out, it compromises that.

She knows she should say something to Joan. She should tell her she's been missing too much work, that she needs to plan ahead and not rely on Avery to take up the slack. But she can't stand the four of them looking at her with various mixes of obedience and veiled hostility on their faces.

She tries to look impassive. She tries hard not to let them see that she's irritated by Joan's repeated early exits. Fern, the one who knows Doreen best, is watching her closely. She can surely see that this kind of thing gets under her skin. Doreen takes a breath and smiles. She won't have them say she's stingy.

"If you and Avery have worked it out, it's all right with me," she says, "but this is the last time for a while."

AFTER LUNCH DOREEN stops at NIKKI'S DESK AND LOOKS AT the appointment book for the rest of the day. The next patient is Zeeda Bouray, the homeless woman who needs a new bridge. Then there's a filling. Then a crown prep. At four, an extraction, a seven-year-old whose baby tooth won't let go, causing the permanent one to come in crooked. The extraction will be a cinch, deciduous teeth always are, but the mother is what Fern calls a helicopter, meaning she hovers. Doreen sees another name has been written in after that.

"Who's this?" she says, pointing to the new name written in Nikki's loopy handwriting. She can't quite make it out. "Another pro bono?"

"Jane Marks," Nikki says, as always, surprised and slightly offended that Doreen can't read her handwriting. "She says she's an old friend of yours from college. She just moved to town."

Seeing the name written in her appointment book makes the blood drain from Doreen's face so fast that her lips go numb. The name brings with it a rush of memories. The first is the house on Bonita Street in Berkeley, its one off-center piece of ruby glass in the front door, its Salvation Army furniture covered in old quilts and Mexican blankets.

When she got to Berkeley that fall, the fall of 1970, she found the community she'd been looking for. The peaceful troubadours and gypsies of Berkeley were furious at Nixon for invading Cambodia and increasing the draft. And they were furious at the university administration for supporting the military industrialists who ran the war. She felt acutely, because of Adam, the damage the war was wreaking in America as well as Vietnam. And in Berkeley, unlike Kansas City, that was the common viewpoint, at least among the young. The successes of radical groups backed up by thousands marching on Washington signaled that change was coming, they just had to keep fighting for it.

Doreen can smell, suddenly, blackberry cobbler coming out of the Bonita Street oven and taste the psilocybin mushrooms cut with goldenseal that they took one afternoon. She can feel the benevolent California sun on her head and see it on the small red apples strewn across the yard.

Janey and her roommate, Adrienne, were students at Berkeley too, but their involvement in Fishbone, a student antiwar group, had taken them over. Doreen remembers asking them, "Why do you call yourselves Fishbone?"

It was Janey who answered. She smiled wickedly and her silver earrings glittered in her hair. "Because we stick in the throats of the pigs. We make them choke on us."

DOREEN TURNS THE BOOK BACK TO NIKKI, KEEPING HER FACE as neutral as she can, her eyes down, looking at the page.

Nikki says, "She said she needs to see you today. Pain in front tooth. Number 9."

Doreen taps her pencil on the book. She looks at the computer screen, where she can see Jane Marks and a phone number. No referral. It must be Janey. Doreen passes through a moment of vertigo. The next breath is an exercise that brings no replenishment of air. She knows only one thing. She must avoid contact with Jane Marks. She must buy some time to think what to do next. She clears her throat and forces herself to speak.

"Call her back, Nikki," she says. "Tell her there's been a mistake and I'm not taking new patients."

Nikki raises her eyebrows. "Okay, Doc," she says. "But for everybody else you're still taking new patients?"

The panic redoubles as the implications start to drop into place. It's more than Doreen can take in on an ordinary Friday afternoon. Janey could make an appointment using another name. Really, there's nothing to stop her from showing up here if she wants to. Nikki's waiting, gazing up at Doreen with a curious and concerned expression.

"Don't take any new patients for a while. I've been meaning to tell you the schedule is too full. Start a waiting list, get names and numbers for when things open up, and refer them to Bob Wolf and Iris Benson in the meantime."

"Okay," Nikki says, scrolling down to Jane Marks's phone number on the screen, then turning back to Doreen. "Do you want to call her? Being that she's your old friend and all? Or what?"

"You call her. Tell her she must be mistaken. I don't know her."

Doreen retreats into the bathroom, where she washes her face in cold water and forces herself to breathe. She will not think about Janey Marks right now. She will see her patients and give them the care they need. She will think about herself, and Janey, later. Right now her next patient is waiting. She goes out to greet Zeeda Bouray, who sits in the waiting room in her dirty blue housedress.

"What happened to your bridge, Zeeda?" she says, gently.

"I don't know," says Zeeda, her eyes latching onto Doreen's in spite of the involuntary shaking of her head. "I just lost it."

Doreen leans forward and touches Zeeda's shoulder. "I'm sorry. I should have made it better. It's my fault. I still have the mold, though. We can make you another one. But this time I'm going to fix it to your other teeth so that you can't lose it, okay?"

"Okay," Zeeda says, even as her head shakes: No, no, no, no.

chapter 4

ADAM SITS in a chair Miranda has placed in the doorway. If his eyes were working he would be able to see both the front door and the backyard from here. What he sees instead is a stab of light from the window on the right and the hanging shadows and webs that are everywhere in his vision these days. Out back, the parched yard ticks with grasshoppers. Still, his little house is a magical hidden place.

He counts the things he likes about it on his fingers to see if he still can. One, the little house is surrounded by garden and trees. The neighbors are polite and friendly, but not friends. That's number two. And three, the age of the place, the crumbling red brick with ivy growing on it. The fact that the house doesn't have a street entrance, only a door on the alley. He guesses that's number four. And then there are all the flowers that emerge every spring and take over the place so that he becomes the resident Lilliputian living under a canopy of peony, and climbing roses that he only thinks are trees.

He gazes at his fingers, trying to remember what he was counting.

The world is baked nearly colorless now. Or is he beginning to lose the colors, too? He observes the squares of linoleum on the kitchen floor that look like smears of oil paint. Payne's gray and rose madder veined with black. They look like rivers and burning hills seen from above. It's familiar and yet not. And now, looking down, he has a déjà vu feeling. He waits for it to pass and it does.

He starts another exercise. He can still remember all the places he's lived. The parts of his brain in charge of the memories of places seem to be holding up better than some of the other parts. He starts at the beginning: the old brick house in Kansas City with the Eisenhower addition where he and Doreen grew up. After his childhood home came the Marine barracks of basic training and then eight months in Vietnam.

And just like that, Vietnam rises up. He sees the faces of the Vietnamese: small, afraid, and somewhere deep behind their eyes, murderous. He sees the guys in his unit: beefy by comparison, but just as afraid and with the hate in their eyes fully displayed. He smells gunpowder and diesel fuel hanging in the air, and the cloying, fetid stench of death that won't wash off.

Adam and Tom Poole sat in a deux-and-a-half, along with a bunch of other grunts, waiting for transport. Five or six Vietnamese kids approached the truck. A sergeant, an E5, his rank almost unrecognizable for all the Magic Marker words soaked into his uniform, got agitated. It was understandable, sometimes kids had guns, were on suicide missions for the Viet Cong, but not usually. Usually all they wanted was to beg a few coins.

"Fuckin' zip kids," the E5 said. The kids grinned and kept coming. The sergeant's agitation increased. He stood up. The kids said something to him in Vietnamese and he waved them off. "Get the fuck outta here," he yelled. They backed away and then returned like flies to meat. "Beat it," the sergeant yelled. "*An guk*, eat shit."

The biggest one was maybe ten or twelve. Adam could see that he understood the sergeant. He said something to the others. Then he looked up at the sergeant and, grinning, flipped him off. The other children laughed. The bigger boy stood with his legs wide, his head thrown back defiantly. He brandished his hand higher and thrust it upward a couple of times. The sergeant's face froze in pure fury. Faster than Adam's eyes could register the motion the sergeant pulled his pistol and shot the kid. The others scattered. There was a collective shout from the marines in the truck. The sergeant took aim again, seeming to hesitate only about which child to shoot next. Before he could get off another round, Tom was standing next to him.

"Sarge," he said.

The sergeant turned as if he had been caught daydreaming.

"Don't," Tom said softly.

For a second it seemed that the sergeant would turn his wrath on Tom, that he might open fire on all the grunts sitting in the truck. Adam had heard about such things. Tom stood easy and relaxed next to the sergeant. He seemed to exude understanding, as though he sympathized with shooting down a kid for flipping the bird. The sergeant looked at Tom. His fury seemed to melt in the utter calm Tom radiated. He lowered his weapon, very gently laid it on the bed of the truck, dropped down next to it, and curled into a fetal position. There he huddled until the medics came and took him away.

ADAM STARES AT HIS FEET A MINUTE, WAITING FOR VIETNAM to pass. The sun's in his eyes, which means it's late afternoon. Miranda will be here before long, to make his dinner and take care of him. Three men make their way from the alley into the yard. It's hard to tell who they are until they speak.

"Not a bad turnout, for how hot it was out there," one says, and Adam recognizes the voice of his young nephew Ian.

"Those FBI guys were kinda freaking me out," says another. Adam knows this voice but it takes him a moment to place it. The person is not as tall as Ian but darker and broader. Adam's mind is skittering around like a water bug, looking for the boy's name.

Ian speaks again. "Yeah, what was that shit? What did they mean, they wanted to 'interview' us?"

The other voice says, "For a minute I thought they were going to take me away. You know, like to Abu Ghraib."

A third voice says, "They can't force you to come in for questioning unless they have something on you." This one is Derek. Earnest, gorgeous Derek, who moves his hands for emphasis. "They were just trying to intimidate you. They were trying to build files on any protester they could interview."

It's strange, Adam can't remember if he and Derek were ever lovers or not. It doesn't matter much. Sex, it turns out, after all the years of obsessing about it, is no longer interesting. Once the MS started to eat his eyes and mind, once his legs couldn't be relied on to hold him up anymore and he started seeing things that other people didn't, sex became a quaint custom from another time, along with restaurants and driving and distinguishing quarters from nickels.

The three stand just outside the door where he's sitting. Now they're blocking the sun so that he can see better. Ian, Derek, and the other one—Arab face, dark skin. Yes. The half-Iranian kid who also works for him. Kumar. The name bursts and sheds a brief light in his mind. These young men build the walls for him now.

"Is work over for the day?" Adam asks, aiming his eyes and voice at Derek.

Derek's voice is soft, the hand on his shoulder is gentle. "No, we're just getting started. We're starting late today."

Adam shakes his head. It's afternoon, he knows it is. The hours and days are hard enough to track without people playing tricks.

"I'll say you're late," he says, crossly.

Ian speaks up. "We were at the war protest. Remember, Adam? We told you about it yesterday."

For a moment he's not sure which war Ian's talking about, Vietnam or Iraq. It doesn't matter, it's all the same war.

Derek goes over to a blue wooden door in the corner of the yard and turns a key. A pickax emerges and two shovels, and the thing with the bubble of liquid in the glass; the name of which is almost within Adam's reach, but at the last second slips away.

"It'll be cooler this way, working into the evening," Derek says.

And Adam suddenly is in possession of the fact that he and Derek *were* lovers sometime ago, before the MS and before the drought but many years after Aaron, the love of Adam's life, died. Still, Derek was Adam's last lover. There's a distinction in that.

The two boys carry the tools to the truck, which, he now sees, is parked in the alley. Derek's hand comes to rest on Adam's cheek, caresses his face. Adam closes his eyes to savor it.

"Miranda will be here soon," Derek says. "Maybe she'll bring tamales." He kisses Adam's forehead and Adam drifts on the pleasure of the touch and the anticipation of tamales until all of it breaks up and floats away.

Time passes. Spoons full of it move from here to there. There to here. And in the middle of it comes Miranda. Plus-sized and generating her own light, she fills his house. Her soft brown hands pat him. She leans in close so that he can't avoid her startling green eyes. "Mr. Adam, how are you this evening?" she says with Latina formality.

They eat the tamales in the yard. He's captivated by a cunning little table that's appeared with woven rattan chairs to match. "This is cute," he says by way of conversation, by way of a compliment to her. But a shadow passes over her face. He can see that the table is another thing he should have known.

After the tamales, she bathes him in a miserly few inches of water. "*Yo soy como el chile verde,*" she sings. "*Picante pero sabroso.*" Her voice is warm and womanly. Aaron would have loved it. If he were here, he'd put a strange, high harmony on it and the song would take on dangerous and wondrous lights. The thought of him, the loss of him, makes Adam want to weep. If he were here, they would have grown old together. They would have had decades.

Miranda gives Adam a shot of Novantrone, trims his toenails, and waits while he empties his bladder, no small feat these days. Finally he sits in his bed, like a good child, while darkness fills the yard and the crickets come out to sing.

chapter 5

MILES RINSES a glass and puts it in the dishwasher. His stab at a home-cooked Indian dinner was only moderately successful, he decides, as he covers the curried vegetables with plastic wrap and spoons the cucumber *raita* into a glass bowl. He probably got this craving for Indian food from working all day on lesson plans for the fifth-grade unit on Asia. This year he's going to depart from his usual textbook route and teach it through the biographies of Gandhi, Mao, and Ho Chi Minh. Should keep it interesting.

The food would have been better with *chapatis* or *pooris*, but the night was too hot to fry anything. He gets a package of store-bought tortillas out of the fridge and puts it with the leftovers on the counter. When Ian comes home later he'll eat it all, along with anything else he can find.

Miles wanted dinner to be festive tonight. He put out candles and served the food from bowls at the table instead of dishing it up at the stove. Doreen didn't seem to notice. She picked the peas out of the curry and ate them absently. He sat across the table and watched her, this woman he loved. Her fine brown hair curved against her neck. Her deep-set eyes cast down as she stayed in her thoughts and, fork poised in midair, leaned her head on her hand for a moment like a sleepy child. He caught her profile with the strong nose, the beak, really, that made him fall in love with her all those years ago. It was the incongruity of that nose on that delicate face that first got him.

And still does. Doreen complains that her hips and thighs are fat; that her face is sagging, but Miles can see her without the lens of self-criticism. He sees her growing more beautiful each year in spite of the self-doubt. He wishes that she could see herself that way.

He learned early on, even before they were married, to back off when she was this way. She's never been someone who wanted coaxing. Usually she wants to stew in whatever it is and then tell him when she's ready. But he has always been aware of secret places in her. For instance, she almost never talks about her childhood. The fact that her parents are both dead only partly explains it. When Miles and his two brothers are together, they're loud and obnoxious, dredging up old jokes, old embarrassments about each other. They talk about their mom and dad, who are both gone now, too. They talk about the saltbox house in Newton, Mass., where they grew up; they tell stories about Marty Smart, the flatulent kid who lived at the top of the hill and had a go-cart that Miles crashed into the fire hydrant. Adam and Doreen don't talk about their parents, or say anything about their lives before they moved to Boston. If he brings it up, the subject is changed. Over the years he's gotten used to it. The past before he met her is pretty much off limits.

"What's up, Dorie? Did you see Adam today?"

She looked up, pulled from her thoughts. "I stopped by on my way to work."

Adam's recent decline was enough to put her in a funk. A year ago, before the diagnosis, Miles learned that Adam didn't have health insurance. Apparently it wasn't news to Dorie. "He's always been so healthy," she had said. "He never needed it." But now he needed nursing care and expensive meds, CAT scans and MRIs, appointments with neurologists, physical and occupational therapists, the urologist and the immunologist. And Doreen and Miles were paying for a lot of it.

"He should get on a plan now. It'll be expensive but still less than paying for everything out of pocket," Miles had suggested. Doreen said that Adam was so paranoid of the government that he wouldn't use his Social Security number, or get insurance. That he would never buy into the system. Miles hadn't realized that Adam was paranoid of the government. He never said much about it. It was true that Adam never used a credit card or a checking account, but Miles just assumed he preferred cash. He'd refused to buy a house even when his business started to do well. Now all of that seemed a little fishy.

Miles had pressed Doreen about it. "What's he hiding from?"

Her face had gone white. She spoke with an intensity that was extreme, even for her.

"Leave it alone, Miles," she'd said. "Don't ask."

So he didn't. It was one more item in the strange wall of privacy Doreen and her brother had built.

He watched her eat. She did it dutifully, as though she couldn't taste the food.

He said, "I was reading about Gandhi today. You know, by one account he was really kind of a tyrant in his own family? To show that he believed in equality between the castes, he made his wife clean out the latrines."

She was distracted but made an effort to listen. He could see her trying.

He went on, "It seems he didn't believe in equality enough to clean out the latrines himself."

He watched the joke run through her expression. Then she laughed. She looked at him and shook her head, laughing so hard she shook. She scooped rice and vegetables up with her tortilla and seemed to take new interest in what she was eating.

"This is good, Miles," she said. "Did you invent this, or is it from a cookbook?"

"I invented it, can't you tell?"

Early on in their marriage Miles started to do the cooking. Dorie was starting a practice and working late every night. Miles came home every day in time to cook, and he liked it, so the job became his. He only had one rule: If anybody complained about what he made, they got to cook the next meal. So, like the campers in the joke, who ate plates full of bear shit rather than complain about the cooking, Dorie and Ian put up with a lot of strange concoctions.

She took another big bite and spoke with her mouth full. "Tastes like bear shit, Miles. But it's good."

AFTER SHE GOES UP TO BED HE PUTTERS AROUND THE KITCHEN, putting the last of the dishes in the dishwasher while light-crazed miller moths beat themselves silly against the window screen. He squirts dish soap into the rice pot. Before the drought he would have filled a sticky pot like this with soapy water and left it to sit. But because of rationing he runs only enough water to cover the bottom of the pan and starts scrubbing.

The back door opens and Ian comes in. He's covered with dirt and rock dust. Two moths slip in with him and immediately fly up inside the fixture over the sink, where they ecstatically bang their bodies against the hot bulb.

"Hey, Dad," Ian says softly, the way he does. It takes Miles back ten years to Ian's first year of hockey. He was messing around in practice without a mouth guard or face guard and the puck hit him in the mouth, taking out his front teeth. When Miles arrived, Ian was holding his two front teeth in his palm, his jersey soaked in blood. He gave Miles the same soft greeting. "Hey, Dad," he'd said, and smiled so that Miles could see the hole. Of course when they got to Doreen's office, she was not so enamored of Ian and the mess he'd made of his teeth that day.

"No mouth guard? No helmet? Ian, what were you thinking?" she'd said, putting him in the chair and immediately going to work to reattach the teeth. One took, the other didn't, and Ian eventually lost it. But Doreen replaced it with a fake one that looked nearly identical to the other.

"You hungry?" Miles says, already pulling a plate out of the cupboard and handing it to his son. Ian heaps the rice and vegetables on it, accepts a tortilla, and tucks in, making satisfying sounds of appreciation.

"Here. Have a beer," Miles says, feeling absurdly grateful that Ian's so enthusiastic about the meal. He's only eighteen, and though Doreen thinks it's a mistake to give kids alcohol, Miles doesn't see the harm in letting him have a beer at home now and then. Ian doesn't party, he made good grades in school, got accepted to UCSD, and now that he works like a man, Miles thinks he ought to be able to drink a beer if he wants. He pulls two cold ones from the fridge and opens them, putting one next to Ian's plate and keeping the other for himself.

"How'd it go?" he asks, meaning the day, the work, or anything Ian wants to tell him. It doesn't matter. Miles just wants a glimpse of his son's day. Knowing that he's going away to college in less than a month, Miles has had many such moments lately. He tries to camouflage them in parental concern and casual, down-to-business conversations, but the craving to spend any time, however ordinary, with Ian has become an obsession.

Ian chews rapidly and swallows. He takes a pull of beer. "The protest? It was weird. These FBI guys tried to get us to talk to them. Especially Kumar. They really wanted him to come with them for an 'interview,' they called it."

Miles puts his beer down. Ian has attended several antiwar protests since the Iraq War started in 2003. He's marched for the Kyoto Protocol and other environmental concerns, too, but he's never been questioned by the FBI. "Did you talk to them?" Miles asks.

"No. Derek said we didn't have to, and then the FBI dudes backed off. But they sure were making it sound like we did until Derek came up."

"Did you see their IDs?"

"Yeah, but how would I know what a real FBI ID looks like?"

"Well, Derek was right. You don't have to submit to questioning unless you're being charged with a crime. And even then you get a lawyer."

"They asked if Kumar was an American citizen. They wanted to see his ID."

Suddenly it makes sense. Miles wonders if Kumar's parents are hearing the same thing two blocks away at their house. Brad and Mitra Pearson have been in the neighborhood longer than he and Doreen. Mitra was born in Iran but has lived in the States since the shah's regime, and Kumar is as American as Ian. Kumar and Ian played hockey on the same team in middle school. They went through high school together. Kumar is going to Yale next year.

"Did he get your names?"

"No, that's when Derek came over."

"Good." Miles makes a mental note to call Brad and Mitra tomorrow. And Derek.

Ian stuffs *dal* and *raita* into his mouth and mops his plate with the tortilla.

"You have to get up early for work?" Miles asks gently. It's almost eleven and still hot. The nights are short.

Ian shakes his head. "Tomorrow's Saturday, Dad. I'm sleeping in."

Miles realizes with a start that in the summer sameness of days he's lost track. It's a feeling like climbing up stairs and finding one step two inches lower than the others. Disturbing. It occurs to him that Adam, with the MS increasing, must feel like this all the time.

Ian unfolds his long body until he's standing. "I'm going to take a shower and go to bed," he says. He adds, over his shoulder as he leaves the room, "Thanks for dinner, Dad."

Miles washes Ian's plate and fork and puts them in the dish drainer to dry. He rewraps the food in its plastic and puts it back in the fridge. He checks to make sure the doors are locked, the lights are out. He can hear the water in the pipes from the shower at Ian's end of the hall upstairs. He climbs the stairs in the dark, savoring the knowledge that at the other end of the hall Doreen is in their bed under a single sheet, the space beside her vacant. He wants to jump and shout that they're all together, that Ian is going off to college in a few weeks, that he and Doreen have made it against all odds and raised a good kid. And at the same time he's terrified that in a few weeks it will be over. Once Ian goes off to college their lives will never be exactly like this again.

He takes his clothes off and lays them on the chair on his side of the bed. Ah, summer. Tomorrow he'll get up and put on the same shorts and T-shirt again, and work in his little orchard. It will be heaven.

Ian's bedroom door closes. It is quiet in the house. Miles pads across the bedroom floor and, without turning on lights or shutting the bathroom door, steps into the shower and lets water, that most precious substance, pour over him in an extravagance of cold, clear, life-sustaining liquid.

When he's chilled through he turns off the water. Forgoing the towel, he lays himself down next to Doreen and, listening to her feathery snores, falls asleep before his skin is dry.

chapter 6

JANEY MARKS makes the phone calls on her cell from the couch in the artificially cool bedroom of her hotel suite in Denver. Connor, her fifteen-year-old son, is sleeping in the next room. She takes a sip of Balvenie out of a thick glass while the phone rings in New York. She can hear the assistant U.S. attorney scramble; he must be in bed next to his earnest, artsy wife. She looks at her watch. If it's eleven in Denver, it's 1 A.M. in New York.

"Bob," she says, "sorry to call so late. I tried to see her today. I was going to take a picture of her with my cell phone but I couldn't get in. Her office said she's not taking new patients. But she's Lucy Johansson. I'm even more sure of it now. Otherwise she would have seen me."

Bob Pettibone sighs on the other end. She can hear him scratching his head and smacking his lips, trying to wake up. "Maybe she is and maybe she isn't. Maybe she's just a dentist who isn't taking new patients," he says dryly.

Janey drinks again and lets the cold, smoky scotch linger before she swallows. Bob Pettibone has always been a poor negotiator. She remembers him from ten years ago, before he was married and before he was an assistant U.S. attorney. And later, when Jack hadn't been in prison more than six months, Bob Pettibone had the nerve to try to talk Janey into sleeping with him. Connor was only seven. Jack had been arrested for the old conspiracy to use and possession of explosives charge they thought had gone away during the early eighties. All the lawyers, including Bob Pettibone, and all the favors her father could call in didn't help. Even with the muscle of her father's firm powering the defense, Jack was convicted. They got him after the statute of limitations ran out by claiming he was in hiding. True, he'd changed his last name from O'Neil to Marks. But he wasn't hiding. He did it because Janey wouldn't change hers to O'Neil.

They were stunned. It was 1997 and she and Jack didn't think of themselves as revolutionaries anymore. They had a big house in Connecticut, they drove BMWs. Jack was a successful financial analyst. They thought their biggest worry was how to spend all the money they were making in the stock market. And then he was arrested. For explosives. Hell, she'd done much worse than possess explosives. They all had.

"We're back to this," she says into the phone. "What do you want me to do, Bob? Start stalking her and send her farther underground? You might never find her if that happens. Come on; you know me. You know my family. Why don't you just trust me that this is right?"

Pettibone is awake, now, and his tone becomes sarcastic. "Well, possibly your husband's criminal record and your own past just might put a bad taste in my boss's mouth. Janey, what can I say? The case has gone under seal. We're taking you very seriously because of the Sewell, Smith & Marks connection, but your word alone isn't going to get an indictment from a grand jury as fast as an ID from a witness will. Why don't you let me send Marvin Leach out there, wherever you are? He's come out of retirement specifically to work on this case. He can track her better than you can because she doesn't know him. You'll only spook her."

But Janey doesn't trust Pettibone. If she gave up her location, he'd have that old FBI bloodhound out here arresting Lucy before Janey can get the deal she needs for Jack. And she needs that deal.

"You know why, Bob. Because Connor hasn't seen his dad since he was seven. He barely remembers him from before he went to jail."

Pettibone sighs again. "You know I can't get parole for Jack based on your say-so. I can't get anything for you until we know for sure that this dentist is really Lucy Johansson."

Janey pours herself another scotch. She wonders how long before Pettibone and his boss (who would like the Lucy Johansson conviction to move him up the Justice Department ladder) decide to track Janey down and get to Lucy before she can cut the deal for Jack. "Okay, Bob. Give me a few more days. I'll get you a photo. Would it help if I got another person, other than your agent, I mean, to ID her? I'll have her swear out an affidavit."

He groans. "It might," he says grudgingly.

"All right, then."

"Don't spook the suspect, though."

"I won't."

"And hurry. The minute the grand jury indicts they're going to want her in custody. And then I won't be able to keep the FBI from finding you, and through you, Lucy J."

"You just get everybody ready to make a deal," Janey says, and hangs up.

She opens the address book on her computer and dials another number. It's only ten o'clock in Northern California. Adrienne's voice is vague and tentative, nothing like the old Adrienne, who was the smartest one of them all, the one woman in Fishbone who wouldn't hesitate to take on any of the guys in a debate and usually came out the winner.

"You'll never guess who I've found," says Janey.

"Who?"

Janey imagines Adrienne: brittle and older than her age, with badly dyed red hair and the profound distraction that characterizes her now.

"Lucy."

"No kidding. Lucy?"

"Yep. And she wants to see you."

"Me?"

"You know what? You should come out for the weekend. We'll have fun remembering the old days together." Janey grimaces, wondering if this is going too far. Even in her permanent fugue state Adrienne knows that Lucy is a fugitive.

"I don't know," Adrienne says.

"It'll be good for you to get away for a few days. I'll make the arrangements. It'll be my treat. All you have to do is get in the car when it comes for you. The rest will be on me." She can feel Adrienne seduced by the ease of it and the idea of a weekend with the girls; just like old times.

"Will you do it, Ade?"

Now she can hear a smile start to creep into Adrienne's voice. "Sounds like fun."

Her heart aches for her old friend, but that doesn't stop her from using Adrienne's infirmity to get what she wants. "It will be," says Janey. "It's going to be a blast."

saturday

chapter 7

DOREEN JOLTS awake in the felted dark. It's hot and close and a film of sweat coats her chest, forehead, and neck. She pushes the sheet away from her body, hoping she doesn't wake Miles. Dread sits on her, heavy and malignant, and for a moment she doesn't know why, can't remember what it's about. Then the thought of Janey Marks rises like a rash.

She glances over at Miles, sleeping soundly, blowing little puffs of air through his closed lips. He has never known the truth about her. Neither has Ian. She moved them from Boston to Denver after she had a close call, and still they never knew why.

She'd been in Boston, married to Miles and practicing dentistry for more than two decades, when a man she knew from Berkeley, from Fishbone, a loudmouth-know-it-all they called Murray the A, bumped into her on the sidewalk in front of her office. He'd grown a middle-aged belly and his hair was gray. His mustache and sideburns were gone, but it was Murray. "Lucy?" he'd said with a big grin on his face. "Is that you?"

She'd denied it, and walked away, but she knew she'd been spotted. She realized that all the years of insulation she thought she had built up around herself were nothing at all if Murray the A could recognize her on the street.

After running into Murray she became obsessed with the idea that somebody was following her. She started varying her schedule, canceling patients, and taking different routes to work. She again began to hate going outside, to the point where she went out of her way to avoid it. She started staying up late, all night sometimes, watching the street outside the house for suspicious cars. Finally, when she canceled a week's worth of patients because she couldn't leave the house, she knew she had to do something.

Within days she found a dental practice she wanted to buy in Denver. She sold the idea to Miles, saying that they were all in a rut; Ian would like the West; Adam could use a change; she would make more money; it would be an adventure. Eventually, he came around. Only Adam knew the real reason.

She can't move her family again. For one thing, this isn't like the Murray the A situation. Janey knows who she is and where she works. She probably knows everything about Doreen, Miles, Ian, and Adam, too. Short of all of them going deeply underground with new identities, there is nothing to do. It's impossible. She won't make Miles and Ian felons, which they would be if they ran with her. And even if Miles agreed to it, Ian's life would be ruined, he'd never be able to go to college, get a passport, use his own name, or stay connected to his friends. And then there's Adam. A sudden plunge underground would cause him serious harm. For herself, she has known for a while now that she won't run again. She's been Doreen a long time. She *is* Doreen.

And so it's settled. She won't run. She's had thirty-four good years. If they're over, she'll still be grateful for them. If she has more time, she will take it.

She turns on her side and stares out the window. There is no sign of dawn. Even the birds are asleep. One more thing to be grateful for. For a little while longer she can lie here, inert and with identity intact, before the day begins.

chapter 8

MILES FINDS Doreen in the kitchen, pouring hot tea over a glass full of ice. Her hair is damp and sticking to her neck. She's in rubber flip-flops and a cotton nightgown and she has the same preoccupied, worried look she had last night. For a moment he wants to get angry, to start a fight with her. He'd like to tell her to stop being so self-absorbed. But as infuriating as she is, he knows that when she's like this it's because she's hiding something that hurts. That thought drains all the fight out of him. He ventures an arm around her. She leans her head against his chest a moment, then goes back to her tea. She stirs in milk.

"What's going on, Dorie?"

She looks up and smiles a miserable little smile. "You know. Work, Adam, Ian. The usual."

"I guess Ian was a little shaken by that FBI guy yesterday," he says, tentatively.

She puts her glass down. The area around her mouth goes white and her body tenses tighter.

"What FBI guy?"

Miles is immediately, desperately sorry he brought it up. Now this will be added into the mix of whatever's bothering her.

"You didn't talk to Ian yesterday?" he says.

"No."

He could kick himself. Because he brought it up, he has to explain it now. "Well, at the protest an FBI agent wanted Ian and Kumar to come in for questioning."

"What?" Her voice rises at the end of the word.

"It's nothing. It wasn't mandatory. The boys said no. The guy was just trying to build files on protesters. He probably noticed Ian and Kumar because Kumar's half Iranian."

She passes one hand over her brows as if to both shield her eyes and calm the skin around them. She looks ready to cry. "They didn't give him their names or anything?"

"Ian said they didn't. I thought I'd call Mitra and Brad later, see how Kumar's doing. They're the ones who should be upset. This may have been a random questioning, but I don't think so."

Doreen drinks the tea and puts the glass in the sink. She heads up the stairs in a hurry. He follows. He stands in the doorway and watches her pull on a pair of white jeans and a blue T-shirt. She brushes her hair back into a ponytail and grabs her bag.

"I forgot. I have to go. I have a hair appointment," she says, still looking worried and strained.

"It's only seven o'clock, Dorie," he says.

She buckles her watch and turns her arm over to look. "I know, but I want to stop off at Adam's first." He follows her downstairs. She rushes to the door and stops, turns, and faces him. Her lips are tight against her teeth. She nods to herself as if she's arrived at some difficult decision.

"Miles, it's important that Ian stay away from the FBI. I don't want him talking to them or going to any more rallies."

"Dorie, relax. He's not going to be anywhere near the FBI today."

"You'll make sure?"

"Yes," he says, feeling absurd and, as he often does with her, that he's missing something. She nods again and leaves the house like a woman with much more on her mind than getting her hair done.

She's always had this intensity. When he met her she was a fourth-year dental student clocking clinical hours. He had a chipped tooth in front that was turning brown and needed a cap, but being an elementary school teacher he didn't have the money to get it done. His tennis partner had nice-looking teeth and he got all his dental work cheap at Tufts's dental school. So Miles made an appointment. It was the luck of the draw that Dorie was his dentist that day.

She came in wearing her mask, so all he could see were her sky blue eyes. There were no windows in the dental clinic, so neither of them knew that the storm that had been threatening all day had begun to unburden itself with late-afternoon vindication. She made the mold for the cap first. Then she prepared to fit him with a temporary. He watched her eyes. They were delicate with pale lids. The inner corner turned down and she wore no makeup. The lashes were a dull brown, much like her hair. "I assume you want anesthetic for this," she said, severely.

He wondered what the rest of her face looked like. It was vaguely erotic seeing only her eyes. This must be what it's like in Muslim countries, he thought. You relate to a set of eyes. It was all in the eyes. No lips, cheeks, breasts, legs. Just eyes.

"Do I need it?" he asked.

The eyes darted to the side and back again. "Some people refuse anesthetic for everything. I'm going to be removing most of the tooth around the nerve, and since we don't know if the tooth is completely dead, we don't know if you'll feel it. Close to the nerve, it could be painful. If you like, we can start, and if you get uncomfortable I can always give you the shot."

"Do you need to practice giving the shot?" he asked. "Because if you do, I don't want to tell you not to." He thought he was being magnanimous but it came out sounding patronizing.

The eyes narrowed, slightly. "I don't need 'practice'," she said. "I'm here to do whatever is indicated."

He didn't mean to insult her. Still, it was amazing how quickly she got defensive. He wondered if he should mention it on the questionnaire that would surely come at the end of his appointment, or perhaps would be sent in the mail. He might say that she needed a little work in the "bedside manner" category.

"Is the Novocain indicated?" he said.

"It is." Still giving no quarter.

"Then let's do it," he said.

She had just finished giving him the shot when the electricity cut out. The emergency exit lights flickered blue, but everything else was black. He could barely make out her masked profile.

"They'll come back on in a minute," she said, but her voice was suddenly tentative.

"Probably the storm," he said.

They waited. His lip and nose started to get numb.

She cleared her throat. "It seems like a long time, doesn't it?"

Could it be, he thought, that she's afraid of the dark? Other people in the dental clinic began to make their way to the exits, the patients still in their paper bibs. Somebody must have bumped into a tray of instruments because there was a huge clatter on the other side of the partition. Now Miles couldn't feel his nose or upper lip.

"Do you want to go?" he asked. In the dark it sounded like a come-on. Like something a person would say in a bar: Let's go. You want to? He hoped she wouldn't take offense.

"I suppose we should," she said.

He could make out her silhouette as she took off her mask, gloves, and white coat. That was when he caught his first glimpse of her nose. It was no apologetic ski jump or cute little button. This was a strong appendage, a hatchet, a beak. He fell in love with it instantly.

She held on to his arm and let him lead her to the emergency lighted stairway. With more light she let go of his arm and resumed the authoritative role. She led the way down the steps.

"Here's the last step," she said at the bottom, though he could see it as well as she. And then, severely, "How are you doing?"

"Doing fine," he answered. He tested his lip with his bottom teeth and couldn't feel anything at all.

They emerged out of the stairwell into an entrance hall on the ground floor. Watery light came through the glass doors. Outside, the wind blew the rain sideways in an eggplant sky. Other people were standing in the foyer, waiting for the storm to pass, or trying to decide whether to brave it. An older man in a white doctor's coat moved through the crowd and spoke to people. He came over to Dorie. "We're closing the clinic for the day, Dr. MacFadden. You can go home," he said, before he moved off.

She looked at Miles and smiled. She had the look of someone guarded or shy, but her smile was crooked and warm. And of course he'd already fallen in love with her nose.

"Are you driving or on foot?" he asked.

"Foot," she said. "You?"

"Foot, but I can catch the T."

"I wonder if it's running."

He began to wonder if she was making more than idle chat. "Good point. I'd rather not be stuck in a train."

She smiled at him again. He definitely was getting a vibe. He had never been particularly adroit at asking girls out. Usually he was too vague and they didn't know if he was asking for a date or stalking them. He took a deep breath and tried to smile and be direct, though his wonky lip made him feel ridiculous.

"There's a place up the street," he said. "You want to get a beer? Wait out the storm?"

She actually flushed a rosy color before she answered. "Sure," she said.

They were soaked by the time they got inside the bar. The barkeep had put out candles. The place was crowded. When they finally found a spot at the bar, it was so tight they had to squeeze in together. She pressed up against him. They were wet. It was dark and warm.

He ordered two bottles of beer, starting to feel like a suave guy who knows how to be cool with his gorgeous dentist in a bar. He handed her one of the beers. They clinked bottles.

"To rainstorms," she said.

He laughed softly, not overdoing it; not cracking his face ear to ear like he wanted to. No, he was doing this exactly right. He looked down into her eyes, those eyes that he had found so erotic when she was masked were even better now that he saw the rest of her. There was definitely a sexy vibe between them.

She took a drink of beer, keeping her eyes on him. It was like something in a movie. He'd never had a date like this. She was pursuing him, he was sure of it. And he was being so cool. He was reacting just right.

He raised the long-necked bottle to his lips and tipped it. It was supposed to be a very worldly tip, loose and easy against his mouth. He'd practiced it many times when he drank alone. Expert. Sexy. Designed so that he would get a mouthful of beer; not so much that his cheeks bulged, not so little that he looked like a dork, sipping.

He tipped the bottle, keeping his eyes on hers, and the beer ran out of his mouth and down the front of his shirt. For a moment he didn't believe it. He'd done the sexy beer-drinking move just right. He tried again, and again beer poured out of his mouth. Dorie put her hand over her mouth.

"You're still numb," she said, laughing.

He raised the beer again, willing his lip to make a seal around the bottle and failing. Again beer ran down onto his wet shirt.

"Come on," she said, and took him by the hand. "Let's go to your house."

By the time they got there the storm had slowed into a deep, soaking rain and his lip and nose were starting to wake up. She kissed him and it felt like a hundred fireflies against his lip. They took off their wet clothes and got into his bed. She kept kissing him until all the feeling came back into his mouth, and then he returned the favor.

chapter 9

IN THE winter, the cold soothes Adam's shredded nerve sheaths and calms the disease. But in summer, especially this driest and hottest of summers, there's been a kind of torpor in addition to the lead weight of his legs; his heavy, unresponsive bladder; the thickening, misfiring nerves of his eyes and mind. The MS is a hot-blooded creature who craves heat.

Still, he feels a little better today. The sight in his right eye is back, though blurred, and he seems to be firing on more cylinders, probably due to the shot of Novantrone Miranda gave him last night. He uses his arms to help his legs to the edge of the bed. There's some juice in them because when he swings them over the side of the bed he's able to feel his feet brush the floor. That's a good sign. A very good sign.

He scoots his butt to the edge of the bed and then pulls himself up, using the bedpost. He stands there in a swirl of vertigo, a skinny, crippled old man with an overfull bladder. How did this happen? Wasn't he young and strong just a minute ago?

Wasn't he, just a minute ago, in Vietnam, where the standing water in the bunkers and the dirt sores and the mosquitoes made some guys lose it even before the shooting started? Tom Poole was always the one who could calm them down. He had the stiff, bowlegged gait of a cowboy and the tranquil certainty of a priest. He had earned the reputation as a comforting, healing presence; a person who could antidote the berserker state. As such, he became the object of fetishistic adulation. But right from the beginning, ever since Hai Van Pass, he and Adam were partners. They fought, slept, ate, and shit side by side, always watching out for each other first, considering all others second. Adam knew he was lucky to have the special attention of Tom, but he never for a second thought that it was sexual. It was beyond that. Tom Poole was his mother, his brother, his child, and his hero. When Vietnam stopped making sense, Tom Poole was his shelter.

One night, after running point, they got caught in mortar cross-fire and separated from their squad, surrounded by the enemy. They dug a hole just big enough for the two of them to squeeze in. They wedged their E-tools above them across the opening with brush on top for camouflage. Tom had impetigo so bad on his hands and face that it was a relief to be in the dark and not see his scaly, bleeding skin, the yellowing crust around his eyes. They waited a day and a night for a gook or a mortar to drop into the hole. They slept sitting, their knees wedged into the dirt. There was no light, no place to take a shit. One C ration apiece. Just before dawn on the second day, as they were getting ready to make a run for it, not knowing if the area was clear or not, Tom dug a letter out of his boot and gave it to Adam.

"Get this to Marjorie if I get greased," he said. It was the first and only time he heard Tom Poole talk about a girlfriend.

Adam took the letter and put it in the chest pocket of his shirt. Neither of them mentioned it again.

When they were on base in Da Nang, Tom got them a gig driving a jeep to the airstrip to pick up medical supplies. They became expert at stretching the trip. They'd go to the PX, maybe pick up a hamburger, once in a while see a movie. Tom liked to drive through town on various routes. He liked to negotiate the busy streets full of rickshaws and belching cyclos, through the crowds of Vietnamese cooking along the edges of the streets where the smell of rotten fish was strong and inescapable.

On one medical run they drove by the building the GIs called the White Elephant, which housed the American consulate. In front of the steel gates of the compound was a tight knot of Vietnamese.

Everybody in America, just about, had seen the pictures of the monk on fire in 1963, but that image didn't come to Adam's mind as Tom stopped the jeep and they got out. It's true that smoke arose from whatever they were looking at, but even that didn't suggest the immolating monk. He assumed someone was cooking there in front of the consulate building. Then he wondered if there had been an explosion or a vehicle fire, though this was too small a cluster for either of those.

When they got closer he could see that there was something charred on the stones, fallen forward, the flesh cooked onto its bones. It looked like a burned deer or elk, maybe, long limbs in sharp angles in a pile. But in 'Nam you never saw deer or elk. All the game had been hunted out or destroyed a long time before this. Then he saw a foot. Cooked and charred black but unmistakable. A human foot.

Three Buddhist nuns, with their smooth-shaven heads and dove gray robes, hovered around the smoking object while the other people watched. Suddenly the heavy air shifted and Adam picked up the smell of burned meat mixed with diesel fuel. He saw the nuns spread a black cloth over the charred corpse. A large piece of sheet metal painted with Vietnamese words leaned against the steel gate.

Two Vietnamese military police and two American MP arrived in jeeps as the women picked up the body and carried it away. The MP let the nuns go. They picked up the sign and put it in their jeep, then they disbursed the crowd with a few waves of their hands.

"What happened?" Tom asked the American MP.

"Another immolator," said the MP, shaking his head. "A nun."

Tom seemed transfixed by the sooty black spot where the body had been.

"You see a lot of these?" Adam asked.

"More than you'll ever read about in the papers. There's more of it in Saigon. They keep it hush-hush. Orders from the brass. We get four or five a year here. Lately it's been nuns. Last time it was four of them together. They got a big crowd and some American press. This poor girl just came out here on her own and did it. Nobody paid much attention. Pretty much for nothing, you ask me. She ain't gonna stop this war."

"What does the sign say?"

The MP shrugged and scratched his chin. "The usual. My body's a torch to light the way for peace or some such shit." He got back in his jeep. "You marines have business at the consulate?"

"No sir."

"Then move it."

He drove off. With the police gone, the current of the street resumed. People trotted under coolie hats carrying loads in baskets. Two men walked by, hand in hand as was the Vietnamese custom. Adam got back in the jeep. He would drive, he thought, as Tom seemed so shook up by what they'd just seen. But Tom stood on the spot where the nun had burned. He crouched and picked up something, took a step and crouched again. He did this six or seven times before he came back to the jeep. He swung into the passenger side and opened his hand for Adam to see. On his palm were a dozen bumpy black spheres.

"Her prayer beads," Tom said. "The string holding them together burned but these are her beads. There must have been more but this was all I could find."

The next time they made a medical run Tom found the MP who talked to them and asked a lot of questions about the monks and nuns who had immolated. He started making written inquiries to monasteries in Saigon and Hue. He collected American and Vietnamese newspaper stories with anything in them about self-immolators or their cause. He bought a tiny rice paper book with blank pages and wrote the names of every monk and nun who had immolated since 1963. The names in the little book grew to twelve and then twenty and then forty. He took the beads to a craftsman in the market and had them restrung. He had the same man put the little book on a thong so he could wear it around his neck. It stayed under his shirt, next to his dog tags. The beads made a string too small to wear around his neck or wrist, so he kept it in his chest pocket.

Tom became obsessed. In the bush or on transport to and from ops he'd pull the beads out and hold them in his hand. If there was light enough, he'd read the names of the dead immolators. Soon he was able to recite them from memory and count them like a rosary on the beads.

ADAM DISDAINS THE CANE AND WALKS SLOWLY ACROSS THE hall, keeping his hand on the wall for security. In the bathroom he practices Zen urination. Peeing has been difficult lately, but this usually does the trick. He waits and not-waits, tries not to push and tries not to try. He's calm and relaxed and thinking of water. He thinks of creeks and burbling streams in sunlight. Nothing happens. He conjures the image and sound of his mother running a trickle of water for him as a child. No good. Frustrated, he thinks of mud and floods and a hillside he saw in Hong Kong where all the rickety houses slid to a broken pile at the bottom. He thinks of swollen, uncontrollable rivers, and, inevitably, a dead cow he once saw, eddied up against the pylons of a bridge. He thinks of flying above Vietnamese farmers, any one of them a possible Viet Cong, up to their knees in rice paddies and the glass-smooth water stippled by machine-gun rounds that looked like upside-down rain.

His bladder is full, but he can't empty it. Panic rises. Feeling his mind going is the worst thing, but not being able to control his bladder is second. Whatever muscles fire or relax to pee, he can't find them. And later, when he's not on the toilet, he'll pee and be unable to stop it. Something so fundamental, something he's possessed since toddlerhood, and it's slipping away.

He gives up, a failed three-year-old. He tries to stand but finds his legs have gone completely numb. He can see them, but he can't feel a thing. He closes his eyes, conjures an image of the bones in his feet and legs, in three dimensions, colored bright red and heavy, the way the physical therapist taught him. It's helped in the past. He tries again but can't envision it. He can't feel them. The more he tries, the worse it gets until he gives up. Well. Miranda, with her soothing voice, will be here soon enough.

Adam hears Miranda let herself in the kitchen door. She has groceries, he can tell from the grunt she makes and the rustle of paper bags on the countertop. He waits on the pot for her.

"Mr. Adam?" she says softly, rapping on the doorjamb and turning her face away as though there were a closed door between them. With his arms he pulls himself up to standing on legs that are only there in theory and then he feels his bladder let go. He's powerless to stop the flow of urine now, so he tries to sit back down and nearly slips off the toilet.

Miranda has the floor wiped up before he can fully apologize for his lack of control. She runs a washcloth under the warm water and hands it to him to wipe his legs. She doesn't say anything. Thank God she doesn't chatter. She just does the work and smiles into his eyes. He puts on one of the new adult diapers and then he lets her help him back to bed.

chapter 10

IT's ALWAYS been Adam. From her earliest childhood Adam was the one person in her family, in her life, that she went to with all hurts, big and small. As a child, her mother's intense criticism and withering gaze taught her not to go there for comfort. Her father was usually at work. So Lucy went to Adam. When the dog bit, she hid the pain and blood until she could show it to her brother. And when it got infected, she would only go to the doctor if Adam went with her. When she scraped her knees at school, she pulled her ripped tights up over the wound, not washing it out, not going to the school nurse. Later, when she showed it to Adam and the tights had stuck to the wound, he helped her soak them off with warm water.

So now she finds herself at his door again. Like yesterday, she lets herself in. Today, everything is different. Today, Doreen knows that Janey Marks is hunting her. Today, Miranda is already here. She's at the sink washing a plate. A basket of clean laundry sits on the table waiting to be folded.

"Dr. Woods? Here on Saturday?" Miranda says. Her teeth are bright white against her warm skin. "You should be at home sleeping."

"Oh, I know," Doreen says, feigning casualness. "But I had some errands, so I thought I'd drop by anyway. How is he?"

Miranda keeps smiling, though it grows in gentleness, at the mention of Adam. "He had his shot last night, so maybe he will feel better today. He was up very early."

Doreen wades through the murky dusk of the parlor and knocks on Adam's door.

"Come in," he says, and she walks into the bright room.

"Did you see that?" he says, but doesn't move his head. He keeps staring straight ahead.

"What?"

He points to the windows to his left. "There. It just moved."

She doesn't see anything other than the window shades, half drawn, the windows themselves, and the browns and greens of his garden outside.

"What is it?" she asks.

"I'm not sure," he says. "I keep catching a glimpse of it out of the corner of my eye. It's gone now. Ah well."

She goes over to the window and leans to look out. "Was it something outside? Was it someone running by?"

"No, nothing like that. It was here. In the room. Never mind, it must have been my eyes playing tricks on me."

She wonders if he needs to go back to the ophthalmologist, if this is a retinal problem. "What did it look like? Was it a white flash, like lightning?" It's the standard thing to ask about if the concern is his retinas.

He shakes his head. "No, no. It was blue. And green. And very sheer. Like an insect wing."

She searches his face, looking for signs of further deterioration. He's been confused a lot and he's reported a few fleeting hallucinations on bad days, but this seems different.

He smiles over at her. "It was nothing. Really. How are you?"

He waits, giving her his attention. He doesn't like to think about his body, she knows that. She makes a mental note to call the ophthalmologist.

"Janey Marks made an appointment at my office yesterday," she says.

His thin eyebrows go up. "We haven't heard from her in a while," he says dryly.

When Adam first got sick he used all kinds of ploys like this to cover up his failing memory. He's dropped the pretense lately, but she needs to make sure he's with her. "Do you remember who that is?" she asks.

"Of course I do. Black hair, blue eyes. Rich girl. She left you guys hanging in New York. So what did you do?"

"I had Nikki tell her I wasn't taking new patients."

"You're sure she's the same Jane Marks?"

"She told Nikki she was a friend from college."

"Ah."

"And yesterday Ian was questioned by the FBI."

His eyebrows go up again and for a moment he focuses his eyes on hers. "You think it's related?"

"Don't you? It's too much of a coincidence, don't you think?"

He stares off into the distance again. She knows that maintaining a focus is difficult for him. "Not necessarily," he says.

And just like that, Doreen is aware of the possibility of life staying normal and good. Because if Adam doesn't think this is a problem, then it might not be.

He says, "The FBI were at the peace rally, right? They were looking for terrorists, not children of radicals from the Vietnam War. It's not connected."

The fear climbs her bones again. She wants to believe him, but she can't stop obsessing. "I don't know. International terrorists, aging underground radicals, it's all the same to the Feds. And that still leaves Janey. What am I going to do about Janey?"

He doesn't have an answer. He looks exhausted. Now she regrets bursting in here with this. He's too sick to help her and it will only upset him. She shouldn't have bothered him with it.

"It's probably nothing," she says, quickly. "Don't worry, Adam. I just wanted to tell you about it, that's all."

At eight fifteen, Doreen pushes through the heavy glass door of Avant Salon. Not knowing what else to do, she's decided to go through her day as planned.

She can't go into a place like this, a beauty parlor, they used to call it, without a familiar twang of guilt and its accompanying judgment. Avant, with its pretensions to glamour, its chrome and leather chairs and reproduction antique workstations, is what she and Janey and Adrienne, back in the Berkeley days, would have flatly called a "piggy parlor."

The receptionist looks up from his computer. "I'll let Jeanne know you're here, Dr. Woods," he says, around an inflamed lip ring.

Jeanne appears, gone carrot-top since last month and wearing a pilly red sweater. Doreen follows to her workstation and sits in the chair. Jeanne drapes her with a black gown snapped tight at the neck. She stands behind and fluffs up Doreen's hair, feeling the ends for damage, looking at Doreen in the mirror. "Roots and highlights today?" she asks.

Doreen nods. Her hair was her glory once, her trademark, back when she was Lucy Johansson. It had been as white-blond as Adam's and down to her waist. She wore it in a long braid. It was easy, then, to be scornful of beauty parlors; she was nineteen, beautiful, and had nothing to hide.

Now she's fifty-three. And her hair hasn't been natural since 1971. It was the first thing to go when she went underground. She cut it herself in Philly, and when she got to Boston, Aaron cut it shorter and dyed it auburn out of a Clairol box. It made her look foreign and slutty, especially when she penciled her eyebrows dark and wore black mascara. Later, when she started having it dyed in humble, B-class piggy parlors, along with her lashes and brows, she made them do it all a mousy brown. No more trademark hair. No standing out in any way. For decades she sought to be average, unremarkable, ordinary. All the way through college and dental school her trips to the beauty parlor were necessary security events that she kept secret, even from Miles.

In recent years she's allowed herself a little more leeway. She likes the way Jeanne keeps her hair layered to the collarbone and puts caramel highlights in the brown. It makes her feel a little bit beautiful again, a little bit sexy. She even talks about it with Miles, letting him assume that she's started coloring her hair to cover the gray. At fifty-three, all the women she knows are dying their hair once a month. She's no different.

Jeanne brushes on the thick purple stuff that will end up highlighted and folds up each strand in a square of foil. The rest is daubed at the roots with the darker color. Doreen keeps her eyes closed. She lets Jeanne tug and prod. In spite of what Adam says, it's alarming that the FBI questioned Ian on the same day Janey Marks called her office.

Only a few more weeks and he'll be in San Diego going to college to study marine biology. Doreen tried to convince him to go to college in Colorado but he won't have anything but marine biology. Through high school he took up scuba diving, in one of the most landlocked places in the world, paying for his own lessons in YMCA pools.

San Diego will be good for Ian. He'll finally get to be in the ocean as much as he wants, and maybe school and diving will distract him from the political activism he's embraced this summer. And the shit storm that may overtake his mother.

Jeanne leaves to let the dye do its work. Doreen sits, her head quilled in aluminum blinkers and the viscous dye in between. She picks up a magazine. The cover is a photo from the London bombings of a month ago. It's shot from above. A double-decker bus is blown into red, white, and blue confetti on the black street. The headline reads: 7/7 IS ENGLAND'S 9/11.

Hairdressers and people mill around. Her eyes nearly close,

insulated as she is by the foil and the ammonia smell, but a graceful hand with newly painted red nails rests lightly on her arm, and now, here is Kumar's mother, Doreen's closest friend, Mitra Pearson, leaning in to make eye contact.

"Dorie? I was going to call you today."

"About yesterday?" Doreen asks.

"Yes, what do you think of this FBI?" Mitra says, lowering her voice and looking around. "I am outraged. I am twenty years an American citizen. Kumar is American all his life. He's never even been to Iran. But because his blood is half Persian they assume he's a terrorist?"

"I know. It's not right," Doreen says.

Mitra's voice gets louder again. People turn to look at them. "Well, what should we do? I mean, this is military-state behavior, taking innocent boys in for questioning. This is why I left Iran."

Doreen must calm her down, quiet her. This talk is too alarming.

"Mitra," she hisses, "they weren't actually taken in for questioning. They were asked to participate in an interview and they said no."

Mitra's voice stays loud. "Yes, but we have our rights. Don't you think we should talk to the newspapers or the ACLU or something?"

That's exactly what Doreen doesn't want to do. She sits up straighter and pulls herself together.

"I don't think it would do anything but cause more trouble," she says, evenly. "The best thing we can do is keep Kumar and Ian away from political demonstrations. And if there's any more interest from the FBI, we should do exactly what the boys did: refuse to answer any questions. What does Brad say?"

Mitra sniffs. Her voice takes on a shame-on-you quality. "He says the same as you. You both surprise me. You sound like people in Iran: Don't make trouble, don't rock boats."

"Believe me, Mitra, you don't want the FBI snooping around

trying to find something on Kumar. They've pretty much admitted they're using racial profiling to find terrorists now."

Jeanne appears so it must be time to rinse. Mitra Pearson drifts off, looking alarmed. The chemicals on Doreen's head are itchy and caustic. She follows Jeanne to the sink, leans back in the chair, and lets her pluck out the foils. The warm water feels good on her irritated scalp but she can't let herself enjoy Jeanne's massaging hands.

Ian and Kumar have been best friends since the first day of fifth grade when Ian was the new kid from Boston. Kumar, smaller, smarter, and in the know at school, asked Ian to sit with him at lunch. They have both been working for Adam after school and on vacations since they were sophomores, first carrying rock for the stone walls Adam built, and eventually, as Adam's health declined, designing and building simple walls themselves. Neither of them has had a serious girlfriend up until now, although this summer Ian has been seeing a girl named Selima more than he's been hanging out with Kumar. He's invited her to dinner tonight, a significant first, and has hinted that this girl is special.

Back in the chair, Jeanne does the blow-out, working the hair around the brush to get a smooth, curved wing of hair. When she's finished, Jeanne gives Doreen the hand mirror and unsnaps the black gown. She removes the gown with a flourish and steps away, twirling Doreen in the chair.

In the mirror Doreen catches the back of a woman's head across the room. A glimpse of the face in a mirror stops her. The woman has mottled, thin-looking skin that has collected in fine wrinkles around her eyes, she's heavy around the waist, but she is Janey, there's no doubt. She still has that straight, black, almost metallic hair, though now it's shot with silver and only grazes her jawbone. She's wearing a tailored linen blouse and a wedding ring. In the mirror she smiles at the stylist, the same diamond-bright smile with the crooked front tooth, number 9.

Most telling is her manner, that smug, privileged way Janey always had has stayed with her and even grown, if that's possible. Janey, the most radical of the radicals, now looks like the wealthy society matron her parents always meant her to become.

Doreen stands transfixed even though she knows she should leave as quietly and quickly as possible. Instead she stares. And Janey stops in midsentence and lifts her chin. She sees Doreen in the mirror. Moving as if underwater, as if in a persecution dream, Doreen picks up her purse and tries to go but Janey has caught her eye. The hairdresser waves his hands around Janey's hair. "I want to undercut it a little more back here," he's saying. Janey nods but keeps her eyes on Doreen. She opens her phone as if she's going to make a call, then changes her mind.

Doreen mutters to Jeanne, "I'm late. I gotta go. I'll send you a check." She rushes out and doesn't look back.

Her car is at a meter on the street, two blocks away. Once out of the building, she breaks into a run. She gets in the car and turns the key. The air-conditioning blows an inferno of hot air in her face as the car starts.

Janey, sweaty and flushed, knocks on the passenger side window. Doreen considers putting the car in gear and stepping on the gas. But Janey knows things. She knows where Doreen works, she knows where and when Doreen has her hair done, and now she's confirmed, if she didn't know already, that Doreen Woods is Lucy Johansson.

Doreen pushes the button and the glass slides down.

Janey rests her arms on the door, sticks her head in.

"Hi, Lucy," she says. A sick twist goes through Doreen at hearing the name.

"How did you find me?"

Janey looks coy. "Remember Leon? I guess he bumped into you in Mexico."

Suddenly she remembers. It was about two years ago. Ian was sixteen and she and Miles were suffering through one of the flatter stretches of their marriage. To salvage it, Miles planned a trip to Mexico without asking her. It was in the nature of a spontaneous event, a surprise, so when he produced the tickets she couldn't refuse. But she panicked.

It was about the passport. She'd never had one, and since 9/11, applications for first-time passports had become much more scrutinized than before. She knew she would have to use her phony, black-market birth certificate to get into Mexico. It originally belonged to someone named Doreen MacFadden who was born in 1952 and died as a child. It came with a real Social Security number she's been using ever since, but the birth certificate itself is a forgery. She used it twice, early on. It got her a Boston driver's license and it was given a cursory look when she and Miles got married. The rest of the time it sits with cash and another, less reliable ID, bought for emergencies, in a locked box she keeps on her closet shelf.

She worried day and night before the trip. She worried that new technology developed over the last thirty years would somehow identify the birth certificate as a fake. But applying for a passport in the middle of the national paranoia about terrorists seemed riskier than chancing the birth certificate at the Mexican border. She wanted to cancel the trip, claiming illness, but Miles's face would show such disappointment, such self-blame that she couldn't do it. And besides, they'd never been anywhere; she'd nixed trips to London, trips to Italy. Over time she had become the agoraphobe she pretended to be and the marriage was suffering. Other people went away together. Other people took vacations. She owed this one to Miles.

The night before they left she dreamed that she was stopped by uniformed guards who looked at her birth certificate and saw instead a newspaper article with her picture. They gave her a form to fill out. What was her business in Mexico? The choices were: visiting relatives, work, tourism, and terrorism. She kept trying to check tourism but always checked terrorism.

The best Miles could do on short notice was a cut-rate 3 A.M. charter to Cancún. "It doesn't matter, you'll be on the beach by noon," the travel agent had said. The plane was a wretched airbus with the rows of seats set so close her knees touched the seat in front. Miles had to sit with his legs turned to the side, his femurs were too long to point straight ahead. Doreen pulled her legs up, shoes on the seat, knees to chin, so that Miles could stretch his legs into her small leg space. The plane shimmied and moaned like a cat in heat. No plane she'd ever been on before had made that kind of noise. Surely, she thought, it would burst into pieces of exhausted metal, saving her from having to show the fake birth certificate at customs, getting thrown into a Mexican jail, and facing extradition to the United States as a terrorist.

They got off the plane at daybreak in Cancún and stood in a sleepy line with all the other tourists. She broke into a prickly sweat, sure that the uniformed officer standing at customs was waiting for her, sure that his German shepherd would sniff her out.

But the sleepy official at the desk didn't even look at her birth certificate. He glanced at the Colorado driver's license and waved her through. The soldier smiled at her and the dog lay down at his feet. She'd gone giddy with relief, with the thrill of being out of the country for the first time in her life. She and Miles checked into their hotel, made love like twenty-year-olds, and then went out to the beach, as promised, by noon.

So the next day, when a vaguely familiar man walked by their breakfast table at the hotel restaurant, turned, and walked by again, it had a particularly unreal quality to it, as though he was a remnant of her paranoia from the day before. The third time he walked by, Miles was at the buffet table trying to decide between the rubbery eggs and the pastries. This time the man stopped and she recognized him. He was a guy named Leon who had been on the fringes of the Fishbone organization. She didn't know him well. He'd been memorable for a ponytail which went down to his waist and his horse-jawed face. Janey might have had a thing with him.

Now he was bald on top. His ponytail was short and wispy. He looked down on his luck, maybe living out of a backpack. He stared at her for thirty seconds without saying a word. Miles came back to the table with a miniature Danish. Leon moved on.

"Do you know that guy?" Miles asked.

"No," she answered. "Of course not."

JANEY SMILES HER BRILLIANT SMILE AND REACHES INTO THE car to touch Doreen. "It's so good to see you," she says.

Doreen shrinks back into the leather upholstery. It's nightmarish, the way she can't get away and has to endure Janey's hand on her arm.

"What do you want?"

Janey's smile fades. She pulls back, offended. "I wanted to find out if that was really you," she says. "I wasn't sure until I saw you today."

"You called my office."

Janey points to her crooked front tooth. "It's this one."

"Look, if you have something to tell me, why don't you say it?"

Janey's face closes. She looks fully middle-aged now. "I had no idea we were in the same town, that's all. I found out you were here by accident. Have you stayed in touch with anybody from the movement?"

Is it possible that she can be this deranged?

"It wasn't a sorority, Janey. And, no, I haven't stayed in touch. I don't know anybody from then. I have a completely different life and this is a monumentally bad idea."

Janey holds her hand out like a supplicant.

"Lucy."

"I'm not Lucy."

"Doreen, then."

There's a weird sensation of worlds colliding to hear Janey Marks call her Doreen.

"Since we both live here, I'd like it if we could be friends," Janey says. "I don't know anybody else from the old days."

"Janey, maybe you don't get it," Doreen says, and then drops her voice to a hiss. "I can't know you."

Janey says, "Maybe I can help you."

Doreen almost laughs. "Like you helped in New York? No, thanks."

A tired, gritty feeling overtakes her. The heat, due to climb up to 105 degrees today, wafts into the car through the open window in spite of the air-conditioning. Her mind works through the possible consequences of talking to Janey. In the end, she decides she might as well find out what Janey really wants.

"What happened to Jack?" she says. After Janey ratted Lucy out, she and Jack disappeared into the family's Connecticut estate.

Janey looks vague. "Oh, we sort of kept a low profile for a while. Then we drifted apart."

"Where did he go?" Might as well ask. Information is the only weapon Doreen has.

Again the vague look, as if Janey doesn't want to say or doesn't know.

"I think he went to Canada."

"So you never were arrested or anything?" Janey would have been implicated if she hadn't bailed on Lucy and Mojo. Along with hating her for abandoning them in New York, Doreen has always envied Janey for being the one to get out, to get away and live a normal life. As far as Doreen knows, the FBI connected only Mojo and Lucy to the crime. Never Janey. Not Jack. Not Adrienne, either.

"I'm so sorry," Janey says. "I've wanted to say that all these years. I'm sorry about New York. I was afraid. I didn't know what to do."

There was supposed to be a car. Janey was responsible for having a legal car ready and waiting for them to drive back to Berkeley. Doreen still remembers standing on the sidewalk in Manhattan, adrenaline pumping while Mojo stole a Rambler.

"And then when things went bad I didn't think I could help you."

Went bad. A nice passive way to talk about it.

"What are you doing in Denver?" Doreen says.

"I have an office here. Denver branch of Sewell, Smith & Marks," Janey says.

"Reunited with the family money, I see."

Janey's face tightens. Her expression takes on the ruthless tinge that Doreen remembers. People don't change, they just add layers.

"That's right. And you're a *dentist*."

"That's right." How is it that she's suddenly ashamed of it? How is it that she's sparring with Janey Marks on a street in Denver? Doreen has had enough. She pushes the button to roll up the window but Janey shoves the glass back down. She's strong; the window mechanism grinds and clunks while she talks.

"Lucy, what happened wasn't my fault. You guys fucked up. You and Mojo did it, not me."

It's not like Doreen hasn't said the same thing to herself for thirty-four years. She's said all this and more. But Janey goes on. Her teeth look carnivorous. "I do have something to tell you. I'm going to give you this information because I'm your friend."

The window is still open and Janey still has her hand on the car. Doreen waits. A sudden coy expression comes over Janey's face. "Have you heard from Augusta lately? It's such a shame about Ed."

The use of her parents' first names jars Doreen. Janey has no reason to know them; she didn't know them back in the seventies.

Doreen has kept her own contact with them minimal, for their protection. Two or three times a year she drives to a post office box in Cheyenne to get letters sent from her mother. It's been five months since the last time. For security reasons she doesn't write back. Her parents know nothing about Ian and Miles. They know nothing about her life. That's the arrangement.

Doreen tries the button again but the window mechanism is broken.

"Augusta and I talk all the time," says Janey. "She's worried sick about Adam. We all are."

"Stay away from her," Doreen says furiously, jamming the car into gear.

She heads for the highway. Hot air blusters in through the stuck window and competes with the air-conditioning. Her newly dyed hair blows all around her head. She drives, her fingers frozen on the hot steering wheel, her eyes only blinking when hair blows into them. She realizes that she's in a sort of triage mode. She must take care of the heavy bleeding first and then see to the other wounds in lessening order of gravity. Miles and Ian don't have a glimmer yet that the life she's built for herself, for the three of them, could come crashing down. In their ignorance they are protected a little longer. She thinks of Miles, working in his orchard, pruning, watering, checking the small trees for parasites and rot. He's in the same khaki shorts he's worn all week. He's wearing a Red Sox hat. He's thinking about the clam pasta he wants to make for supper tomorrow and whether it would be best with farfalle or congili. She thinks about Ian, on his day off from working for Adam. He's certainly not awake yet, but still dreaming in the childhood bed his man-sized body now dwarfs. And she thinks of Adam, losing ground to the MS, all too vulnerable in illness. She must not forget that because of her mistake Adam is a fugitive, too. If she gets caught, so does he. If she turns herself in, what about Adam? Her heart contracts painfully. Before she wrecks the equilibrium of the three people she loves most in the world, she must find out some things. She must have more information.

She heads north. If she hurries she can make it to Cheyenne before the mailbox place closes at twelve. The interstate swoops around two sunbaked stadiums and an amusement park and then goes north through the suburbs and outlying towns. Every time she makes this drive from Denver to Cheyenne there's another new mall erupting like a boil out of the prairie grass or farmland. First comes the big-box store in the middle of nowhere. Then the rest of the mall. It's the "If you build it, they will come" mentality. After the mother mall is up, a smattering of condos or houses appears and grows into a development that puts out tentacles and spreads. Even so, there are still spots of untouched prairie encroached on by farms and fields. Even now, through the open window, she can hear a meadowlark.

After she went underground she spent the rest of the seventies hiding and denying to herself her involvement with the radical left. In the eighties she did what everybody did: worked for her own financial security and scuttled what was left of her idealism. By the nineties she had talked herself into believing, along with the rest of the entitled class, that there never had been a revolution to win or lose, only a handful of disgruntled hippies playing at a dangerous game. As the last of the radical fugitives were caught and brought in, middle-aged, middle-class people with families and lives, Doreen watched along with everybody else. Patty Hearst was given a presidential pardon, but Kathy Boudin and Kathleen Soliah were put away. Then came the election of George W. Bush. And the strangely anticlimactic turn of the millennium, the destruction of the towers and the wars that followed. Inside her dormant heart, feelings of betrayal, of impotency and the urge to rip it away, began to grow again like rogue weeds busting through sidewalk. A couple of years into the new millennium she realized, along with many other people, that conditions were remarkably similar to the conditions of the sixties and early seventies, except that nobody seemed to have the time or energy to do anything about it. The passion never built. *That* was different.

IN THOSE FIRST WEEKS THE CAMPUS AT BERKELEY WAS SEETH-ing with protest. Each morning she walked from her dorm across Sproul Plaza and through Sather Gate, where people circulated petitions and demonstrated. Classes became a minor activity, compared to protesting the war and condemning the government and the university administration. Radical student groups were everywhere. Students for a Democratic Society and their militant offshoot, Weatherman, were the vanguard, but every rally, every action was attended by dozens of other organizations, co-ops, communes, cadres, and factions. Everyone was radical and they wanted revolution. Up the revolution. Come the revolution. Power to the people, right on.

The unofficial leaders of Fishbone were a ginger-haired construction worker named Jack O'Neil and a half-Chinese ambulance driver named Mojo Hong. The group of fifteen or twenty people met in a moldy church basement off Telegraph. They sat on folding chairs beneath buzzing fluorescent tubes.

Jack started the meeting. "Okay, so tomorrow there's a planned action that starts at Sproul Plaza at three and we're going to march down to ROTC headquarters at Callaghan Hall. This is an important action for us because we want ROTC and war-related research off campus."

There was a general murmur of agreement and a couple of low "Right ons." Jack and Mojo sat next to each other. In spite of his long hair and muttonchop sideburns, Jack exuded an honest and optimistic boy-next-door quality. He leaned forward with his elbows on his knees and regarded the group with a welcoming, friendly expression. Most of the women smiled back at him. The guys nodded their heads, contemplating the action scheduled for the next day.

Mojo sat back in his chair. His was the only face in the room that wasn't white European, and that gave him the moral power of the oppressed. His black eyes slanted up and his features seemed smooth and refined in contrast to Jack's roughness. He was haughty and handsome and a steady stream of charisma pumped out of him.

"Is this a sit-in or a lay-in or what, man?" asked a guy wearing a T-shirt that read TODAY'S PIG IS TOMORROW'S BACON.

Jack glanced at Mojo. "We'll sit in at the entrance to the building and even block the road if we can."

A guy with a huge red beard wearing a purple shirt and a NIXON EATS BABIES button spoke. "I heard people were going to throw rocks. We don't want to be sitting with our dicks in our hands waiting for the pigs to carry us away while it's raining rocks on our heads, you know?"

"Have we checked with the other groups about that?" the girl next to him asked.

"Why do we have to start at Sproul?" said a man with the large hands of a laborer and the face of a cherub. "I'm sick of speeches. We all know why we hate the ROTCs. Why don't we just go down to Callaghan and kick some ROTC ass?"

There were murmurs of confusion and different opinions. The group was no longer listening to Jack, they were turning in their chairs and talking to each other. Adrienne stood up and yelled for order.

"We've checked it out and nobody's throwing rocks," she said, when she had their attention. "Gandhi said, 'You must be the change you want to see in the world.' We want peace, so we must *be* peace. This is active nonviolence, not passivity. Violence is unproductive. So, in addition to the sit-in tomorrow, we've been working on starting a program to talk one on one with the ROTC members and negotiate their leaving campus."

There were groans and derisive laughter from some.

Jack spoke over them, "That's why it's important to be there to-morrow with all the other groups and show the ROTCs how many are against them. The idea is to start the negotiations after a show of strength."

The man with the big hands stood up and said, "I'm done with sit-ins. How many times are you going to sit in down there? I came to your meeting because Mojo said you people understood we're at war. I guess that was bullshit. You all need to understand this: The ROTCs and the pigs of the University of California don't give a shit about your peaceful protests. They're not going to negotiate with you. Why should they? To keep you from scheduling another sit-in next week? They're not going to cancel the military contracts that make them fat and corrupt just because you apply for a permit and then sit in for an hour or two before you go home and watch *The Mod Squad* on TV."

"You're full of shit, Ron," someone said. People stirred nervously. Jack smiled ruefully and shook his head. "That's a little extreme, don't you think, Ron?"

The man with the NIXON EATS BABIES button popped up. "Any-ways, we should be prepared because pigs fight dirty. Two pieces of technical equipment everybody should have: a mouth guard to pro-tect your teeth against a punch, kick, or a club attack, and a sports cup protector held in place by a jock strap. For your nuts, man."

Some of the women laughed.

The man went on, liking the attention. "Well, I guess you girls should get boob armor or something, but everybody should get the mouth guard. A buck ninety down at Wilson Sports."

Mojo stayed seated and spoke softly but all eyes in the room went to him and Lucy could sense the release, the unanimous relief with which they let him take the lead. He was the only one of them who had dropped out of college because he refused to be a hypocrite and accept an imperialist education. He had openly refused induction into the military and could be arrested at any time.

"Ron, you're right, I did say Fishbone might go beyond passive resistance. But tomorrow's action wasn't organized by us, we're just participating with all the other student groups, and they've organized it as a peaceful demonstration, so that's what we'll do." He looked at Jack. "But this brings up the question of how far will Fishbone go on the next action. Some people in our group think we should always stay within the parameters of Gandhi's ideas. Think about it. Tomorrow, as you're sitting there all secure in your nut protectors and your teeth protectors, and the pig starts beating your head and kidneys and legs with his stick, think about it: Is this really going to bring the war home? Is refusing to fight back going to aid in the destruction of U.S. racism and imperialism? Think about what kind of action will best make the American establishment see that it's all one war. And then ask yourself, what are you, personally, willing to do to bring the giant to its knees?"

Jack sat next to him, listening respectfully, but shaking his head from time to time. "That's not going to happen."

Mojo just looked at him and kept going.

"When we do take up the gun, when we do decide to use force against force, it sure as shit won't be at a planned peaceful protest where people are sitting in and could get hurt by us. It won't be when every pig in Berkeley is aching to gun us down the way they did at Kent State. We're not stupid and we're not terrorists. We don't want to off civilians. So tomorrow we're sitting peacefully. Dig it?"

On the pretext of bringing him coffee, Janey squeezed in next to Mojo. He looked around the circle of quiet, rapt students and somehow, under his gaze, they coalesced into a group. Even Jack had stopped disagreeing. Ron looked down at his shoes and nodded. His arms went limp as he acquiesced, and his big hands became still in his lap. Mojo went on, "Nixon speaks of peace and then he bombs Cambodia. We keep protesting and the National Guard kills four kids at Kent State. Ninety thousand peaceful protesters marched on

Washington last spring, but all that came of it was that two black college kids got gunned down by police in Mississippi. I'm all for peace
but we're in a war of aggression here. The sixties are over, man. The
rallies had their place, but ultimately they failed. We're being ignored
or else killed. The world is watching. Nixon is watching. When you're
tired of getting fucked over by the pigs and nothing changing, you'll
want to fight back. Probably not tomorrow. But soon." He raised his
fist. "All power to the people."

THE INTERSTATE NORTH FROM DENVER IS NONE OTHER THAN
the Pan-American Highway. It was built during the cold war by the
industrialists of the mid-twentieth century whose idea of national security was the ability to truck outsized nuclear missiles efficiently to
all corners of the continent. The road is straight, hard, seamed, and
white, just like the men who built it, and runs from Canada all the
way down through Mexico.

Close to Wyoming the landscape changes. It becomes exclusively
dun-colored prairie, and Doreen can see how it must have been
when everything between the Mississippi and the Rocky Mountains
looked like this. Small rock formations swell into ripples of buttes
and badlands. The one use, so far, that humanity seems to have for it
is a dirt-bike track looping up and over the lip of one of the hills and
back down again.

The mailbox store is on the south side of Cheyenne, in a strip
mall not far from the highway that sports a Safeway, a Jack in the
Box, and a U-Gas-Um. The place is called, simply, Mailboxes. She
used her other ID, Patricia Wolfer, the one sitting in the locked box
in her closet, when she rented the mailbox under that name. She
pays for the box in cash, a year ahead. For seven years, now, this arrangement has worked. Her mom writes letters to Patricia Wolfer of
Cheyenne, Wyoming, and Doreen picks them up two or three times
a year, give or take a month, and never on the same date.

She parks by the Safeway and walks to Mailboxes, making sure that no one is watching her. The place is empty except for the new guy at the counter. She goes in, smiles at the guy (high turnover is one of the pluses of Mailboxes), and opens her mailbox with her key. There are three letters from her mother. A wave of ache goes through her when she sees her mother's light, slanting hand on the envelopes. She closes the box, walks out slowly over the soft blacktop to the car, drives to a nearby park where she sits with the air-conditioning running, and reads them. The first one is postmarked five months ago: March 10.

> Dear Patricia,
>
> Dad fell and broke his hip. He's in the hospital and going to have hip replacement surgery tomorrow. I don't know when you'll get this. I don't know if you or Adam are alive or dead. Can't you be in touch somehow? Don't you think you're overdoing it? I haven't seen anyone around here in ages.
>
> Surely they know what you did was an accident and you never meant to hurt anyone. With all the real terrorists in the world now, you're probably small potatoes by comparison. Have you talked to a lawyer recently? Maybe something has changed since you first disappeared. As I've said many times, we can help with money if you need it. Give my love to Adam.
>
> Love,
> Mother

The second one is postmarked July 20.

> Dear Patricia,
>
> Dad hasn't been well since the hip replacement. It's been one thing after another and now he has pneumonia. He's in the hospital again and they're doing everything they can for him but it's not good.
>
> Your friend Jane has called me twice. She's very nice.

It's touching how she takes such a kindly interest in two old people. We are thrilled about this expanded contact, though I must say hearing from a friend of yours isn't the same as hearing from you.

Jane calls from a blocked phone and says that it can't be traced. I tried that star-sixty-nine, and sure enough, it was blocked. Couldn't you call me that way? Or just come. If ever there was a time you should come, this is it. Because of Dad.

Love,
Mother

The third letter is postmarked July 30. Less than a week ago.

Dear Patricia,

I've asked Jane to contact you in case you don't get this letter. Dad is not doing well. His pneumonia is not responding to the medicine, no matter what they try.

Jane says you've agreed to let her tell me a few things. I can see why you trust her, she's very circumspect—won't tell me where you're living, though she says it's not Cheyenne and you're not using Patricia Wolfer. She did say that you're married and have a boy! But—she says Adam is ill? What is it, I must know, is it AIDS? I've worried about this for all these years.

It's all too much to take in, what with Dad so low. But I'm living for her next call. Or a call from you or Adam. Please give Adam my love.

Love,
Mother

In the white heat of midday, Doreen walks through the empty park to one of many cooking grates provided for picnickers. She lights the letters on the spent charcoal of the last user. She watches the paper burn, feels the quick heat on her face. When the fire goes out, she stirs the ash with a stick and returns to her car.

THERE WERE THE USUAL SPEECHES THAT DAY IN SPROUL PLAZA given by the usual student leaders. There weren't any celebrities, no Tom Hayden or Joan Baez, and the crowd was only about three hundred instead of thousands. But the local bands turned out, among them Oddyssey West and the Buzzards. The front man for the Buzzards got the crowd singing "All We Are Saying Is Give Peace a Chance." Lucy sang proudly with the other Fishbones, and as she sang the familiar melody she was aware of Mojo next to her and Janey, brilliant and jewel-like, on the other side of him.

When they were given the word, they swarmed through Sather Gate and wended their way up through the campus to the Campanile, then back downhill, marching past the library and the life sciences building to the western edge of the campus. Callaghan Hall was an old army barracks sitting in the curve of the road across from the eucalyptus grove and Strawberry Creek. The wooden building butted against a chain-link fence so that to surround it was impossible. Six campus police in white helmets and brown shirts stood staring into the space above the protesters' heads at the entrance to the building. A dozen more blocked the sidewalk. So the protesters filled the road.

"Keep the road clear," the cops said, motioning them across the street to the more removed location of the eucalyptus grove. "Anyone who remains on the road will be subject to arrest."

"No, come up here," Jack shouted. "Sit right on their feet." He got belly to belly with one cop and sat down, forcing the cop to take a small step backward. Lucy, Adrienne, and the other members of Fishbone rushed up to fill in the area around Callaghan Hall. Three hundred protesters packed onto the sidewalk, the street, and over-flowed into the eucalyptus grove. At the signal they sat down together in a fluid wave.

The October afternoon was bright and warm, the sun shone in their eyes and made it hard to see. The cops in their gas masks stood with legs apart and hands on their night sticks in a show of strength, but from where she sat, Lucy could see the sheen of sweat on the brow of the cop nearest her. He was young, not a lot older than most of the students, and though he wore a gun and carried a stick, it was obvious that he was scared. She felt sorry for him. She wanted to say, "Put down your gun and join us. You belong with us."

The cops on the sidewalk attempted to clear the road but the protesters refused to move, successfully bottling up the few cars that tried to pass.

"Clear the road," one cop said, his voice amplified by a bullhorn. The students stayed where they were and continued singing "Give Peace a Chance." Some of them waved signs that read OFF ROTC and NO MORE WAR. The cop with the bullhorn tried to overpower the singing. "Clear the road, *now*. Obstructing the road is a fire hazard." He and two other cops waded into the edges of the crowd. Lucy watched from her place near the front line as the protesters in the street were prodded by boots and sticks. Most kept singing. A few left off singing when they were nudged by the cops to look up angrily at them, breaking the first rule of passive resistance as stated by Jack the night before, "Don't look at or challenge the oppressor, keep steadfast to your purpose of peace."

There were still only about a dozen campus police trying to con-trol three hundred protesters, but they kept working the edges of the group in the road, trying, Lucy could see, to split the group and al-low traffic on the road again, thereby effectively cutting the protest in half and diluting its strength. At the west edge of the group the cops started to move protesters. They picked up girls first, she figured, because they were lighter and usually easier to intimidate, and moved them to the eucalyptus grove. The first four or five girls let themselves be carried off the street and resumed their sitting position where they were put. But one girl started hitting at a cop who held her by the arm. The boy next to her grabbed the arm of the cop, allowing the girl to get free. The cop hit the guy, and then it looked like that part of the crowd shifted into high speed. The cop's stick hit and hit and hit. The boy fell over. Fighting spread like infection. The people near the ruckus stood up and two of them jumped on the cop. Other cops abandoned their stations to join the fray. Lucy felt a rush of air over her head, and another, and as if in delayed time she heard glass breaking in the building behind her. The cops near her began to move. She looked one more time in the direction of the fight in the street and saw all the protesters on their feet now, and a knot of cops and kids fighting. Elbows, fists, and heads against clubs and steel-toed boots. The rock throwers in the eucalyptus grove kept throwing rocks. Most of the rocks hit the wood but some fell short, hitting the protesters and the cops. The young cop she had felt sorry for a few minutes ago grabbed a girl and held her in front of him as a human shield. The girl's shouts turned into shrieks and then sobs of pain and anger as she was hit by rocks.

Standing up, Lucy felt herself to be much more in the line of fire from the rocks, but sitting, now, was impossible. Jack and Mojo were both up and into it. She saw Adrienne bashing her sign over the head of a cop who was clubbing Jack. Instinct took over and Lucy crawled east on hands and knees, to get to the edge of the crowd. Her one thought was to get away. But from the east came the highway patrol on motorcycles and more police in cars and vans. Cops stood by their vehicles in gas masks and behind shields and threw canisters of paint and tear gas into the crowd. As if a stone had been dropped into a pool of fish, people darted in all directions. The red-haired man from the meeting ran by with a large screwdriver and broke the windshield of the cop car nearest to her. As three cops jumped him, he jammed the screwdriver into the tire of the next car. They beat him in the head and kicked him in the back. She could still see his yellow NIXON EATS BABIES button pinned to his blood-soaked shirt.

The remaining protesters were choking on tear gas. Acidic smoke hung in the air. The students ran with bandannas and shirts over their faces and eyes, running from the gas, many of them marked by paint. The cops handcuffed everyone they could and made them lie facedown on the ground. Crying now, Lucy turned and ran east, past the systolic pumping of the Campus Works building, back up toward Sproul and onto Bancroft, where she slipped into the moving stream of nonprotesting students and ordinary pedestrians going about their business, as yet unaware of the mayhem at Callaghan.

chapter 11

THE 101-DEGREE day shudders into evening and hangs suspended over the distant mountains. It is still as death, no breezes, no rain, but the light is pure gold. The news has been full of mountain fires in the west and grass fires in the east. Miles can smell smoke, even here in the city. It brings with it an instinctive fear of forest fire, an unbidden image of Bambis running in terror while the green world that was their home crashes and burns around them.

Clouds of gnats swarm between the ground and the trees. Miles sets the sprinkler on the fruit trees and checks his watch. The rules say he's only allowed to give any part of his yard fifteen minutes of water, three times a week. But since there's no yard in front anymore, he decides that leaving the water on the trees for an extra fifteen minutes is justified.

The sprinkler among the young trees creates its own microclimate. Plants open their leaves, the water clears the air and collects in droplets on spiderwebs. Robins appear and peck worms from the wet dirt. The sound and smell of water renew everything around the little orchard, and just standing near it, getting his feet splashed, makes him feel cooler and calmer.

While the water runs, he readies the house for evening. He opens the windows on the east side, starts the fans, and begins, once again, the process of cooling the house. The lovely old house, with its high ceilings and plaster walls, holds the cold longer than newer ones and they've never needed air-conditioning. But this year, in spite of his efforts, the house seems to stay hot.

When Doreen came home earlier, exhausted and grumpy at the rump end of the day, Miles sent her upstairs for a nap. Now he can hear her in the shower. Ian has been in the hammock on the porch for the last hour, iPod in ears, eyes closed. Selima is coming to dinner for the first time. There are indications he's remembered she's coming: He's showered and shaved and he's wearing a clean T-shirt. He nods his head every now and then in time to his music and beats a rhythm on his knees.

Miles has already hard-boiled six eggs and three potatoes and steamed green beans for his version of a Niçoise salad. He washes the lettuce, spins it, and tears it into a large bowl. He cuts up the eggs, potatoes, and cucumbers and tosses them in. He opens a can of black olives and dumps most of them into the salad. A can of tuna follows. He crumples feta cheese over all of it and begins the dressing, pouring oil, vinegar, tamari, and salt and pepper directly on the salad. It's a simple cool dinner, all in one bowl. They'll have cold white wine with it and bread. Miles washes strawberries for dessert and takes the baguette out of its wrapper. He puts a clean cloth on the table he's dragged outside to the watered orchard and sets it, by chance finding four clean napkins that match.

Doreen appears with wet hair and wearing a simple shift.

"Feeling better?" he asks.

She nods. She doesn't look much happier, though she's cooler and more comfortable than this afternoon. He pours her a glass of wine.

"So tonight we get to meet the mysterious Selima," she says.

"Any minute now," Miles says, checking his watch. And, as if he's been summoned by a whistle on a special frequency, Ian gets up and goes inside to the front door. Miles can hear the soft explosions of Ian kissing the girl before he brings her out back. To Miles it seems as if Ian's jaw has, just today, grown stronger, the look in his eyes sharper. Even his chest suddenly seems broader and harder. It's as if, because of Selima, a window has been opened onto the man Ian is becoming.

Selima is physically Ian's opposite. She's dark and petite, rounded and compact. The top of her head hits below his shoulder. They're dressed alike, though, both wearing cargo shorts and T-shirts that make them look like androgynous eco-mercenaries. Selima's hair is gathered in a messy knot and a bit of fabric keeps the stray curls in check. She wears no makeup or jewelry. Both of them sport amphibious sandals. Both gaze with the same earnest, clear-eyed expression.

Miles is filled with tenderness. He gets almost teary, at their coupleness, at the pure young optimism of the two of them. He's pretty sure that he and Doreen never had this equality, this perfectly parallel sensibility that Ian and Selima have. Doreen ripped and tore her way through everything she did, afraid to be noticed yet fiercely competitive. And Miles, even thirty years ago, was more interested in facilitating, in bringing together ideas and people and watching to see what would happen, what was there to be learned. From the start, he took the protective, nurturing role in the marriage and Doreen took the high-achieving, high-maintenance role. He's not complaining; he wouldn't trade a moment of it.

Watching Ian and Selima, Doreen grips her hands together so hard that the skin is white at the tips of her fingers. Her face is a stream of emotion which runs from prideful to jealous to protective and settles somewhere in the vicinity of dismay. Selima seems nervous to meet Dorie, too. No doubt she's been told by Ian how high Dorie's standards are, how intense she can be.

Ian is suddenly fourteen again, all awkward and embarrassed and unable to say anything. Miles, himself, doesn't know quite how to ease this meeting between the two women. Selima takes charge of the situation. She lets go of Ian and thrusts her hand out, smiling and gently holding Dorie's gaze. "I've looked forward to this," she says, with the right mix of respect and confidence.

Doreen seems to melt. Her hands unclench and she takes Selima's offered hand. He can see her liking the pluckiness of the girl and maybe seeing something of herself there. Smiling, he puts the meal on the table in the damp orchard. They drink the wine, lingering as the light fades from gold to amber and then drops altogether and the crickets come out.

"I've made a decision," Ian announces. Miles stiffens. For a second he's afraid that Ian is going to announce that he and Selima are engaged. He can't make out Doreen's face across the table.

"Selima and I applied to be research interns at NOAA. We didn't think we'd have a chance because most of the people who go are in college. But we got in. We're going to Costa Rica to help with fieldwork on olive ridley sea turtles."

Cricket song swells into the silence.

Doreen is the first to speak. "All of this in the three weeks before you start at the university?"

Ian speaks quietly but firmly. He doesn't sound defensive or expectant. Miles is proud of him. "I want to take a year off, Mom. Or at least a semester."

Doreen says nothing. It's difficult to tell what she might be thinking. Miles knows kids take a year off between high school and college all the time, but he somehow never thought Ian would. They've always operated on the assumption that Ian would go right to college, that he would then choose his field and go on to graduate school.

"We'll do Costa Rica for six months," Ian says eagerly, seeing no immediate resistance from his parents. "Then we want to go to Europe and travel."

Miles suppresses a smile, remembering his own European trip after college. He had a backpack and a Eurail pass like every other kid doing the same thing, and he spent the summer traveling with friends, seeing the great cities of Europe. He spent something like eight hundred dollars including his plane ticket. But more memorable than any of the monuments or art were the two weeks in Brussels he spent in a third-floor walk-up with a Belgian girl. They made big plans for her to come to the States. They even wrote for a few months that fall before she stopped writing back. But he was left with a sweet feeling of gratitude and pleasure at the thought of her, and of Brussels, ever since. Not a bad experience for a young man to have, but he wouldn't bet that Doreen sees it that way. She sits quietly in the gathering darkness and then begins to stack the dirty plates and cutlery.

"Sounds like it could be an interesting plan," Miles says cautiously, trying to leave room for the discussion he and Dorie will undoubtedly have later. He'll be advocating for Ian. Dorie will argue that Ian shouldn't postpone college.

"We should move inside, don't you think?" she says. She picks up the stack of plates. Even in the dark Miles can't miss Ian's confusion. He was surely expecting an argument.

Selima gathers up the wineglasses. Miles gets everything else. Doreen starts across the grass. The others trail behind her.

"Well, what do you think, Mom?" Ian blurts.

She turns and Miles sees graciousness and understanding in her face. "I think it's a fabulous idea," she says.

chapter 12

IT'S TOO hot for a nightgown or even a sheet, so she is naked on the bed next to her husband. The fan by the window oscillates, bringing a cooling movement of air but also a disturbing tickling that keeps her awake. Miles has no such trouble. He's facing out on his side of the bed, the fan ruffling his hair, the crack of his butt cheeks facing her. He's snoring lightly and making his peculiar chewing noise from time to time. She's checked his teeth, sure she would see damage from the habit, but they're fine. She made a night guard for him, but he refuses to wear it.

"You surprised me tonight," he said earlier, getting undressed for bed. "I thought you would never go for Ian taking a year off. You surprised him, too. I don't think he knew what hit him."

She shrugged, and carried by the momentum of habit, opened her jar of beeswax face cream. "It was easy to see that he'd thought it through."

But even as she was saying it, she was thinking that at least if Ian was diving with sea turtles in Costa Rica or traveling across Europe, he might be spared some of the pain of what is to come. She smoothed the rich cream over her dry cheeks and thought about Janey. Had she told anyone about finding Lucy Johansson in the unlikely disguise of dentist Doreen Woods? What, exactly, was Janey up to?

She gets up and adjusts the fan so that it doesn't oscillate anymore. She aims it at the bed; fiddles with it so that it blows the air at Miles's knees. That way it might cool the rest of them without blowing in their faces.

She tries to think if she ever saw her father ill. She can't imagine him as old and infirm. He was always more accepting of Lucy than Adam, and more than a little biased. He hated it that Adam came home from the war more of a misfit than when he went in. He detested Adam's politics, yet he respected Lucy for being idealistic. Adam and Ed fought bitterly. Lucy and Ed discussed ideas. In the four-sided equation of their family, Ed antagonized Adam but tolerated Lucy. Augusta criticized Lucy and protected Adam.

Doreen is tired. Maybe she could fall asleep for a hundred years, like Rip Van Winkle, and wake up to find that everyone who knew her as Lucy Johansson is dead. But then everyone who knew her as Doreen would be dead, too. She turns over onto her back and stares up at the smallish crystal chandelier over the bed. She and Miles bought it at a flea market in Boston in 1979, the year they were married. It was a brutally muggy day and they haggled for it on the melting tar until the vendor, a Jamaican man with a ruby in his ear, finally gave in to their price. He wrapped it in newspapers, smiling and continuously wishing them good luck. They took it home to their peeling, leaning apartment in Cambridge and hung it over the dining room table, their first purchase as a married couple. It was the first time since the bomb at Columbia that she felt safe. She had become Doreen Woods; she was two identities away from Lucy Johansson; she had graduated from dental school, started her own practice, and she was married to a good man who bought her antique chandeliers and knew nothing of her crime.

With its cloudy crystal and chipped gilt the chandelier hung over their table for the entire twenty-three years they lived in the Boston area, moving with them from the decrepit apartment in Cambridge to a larger, better apartment in Jamaica Plains, then to the house in Brookline where Ian was born and where they remained until they moved to Denver. Here, the chandelier seemed too small, too dingy for the wide dining room and huge new table, so they replaced it with a modern fixture and she put the old chandelier in the bedroom.

Their marriage has been like this lamp, a steady presence, something to be counted on and cherished in spite of its imperfections. Over the years they've nurtured it until she can honestly say that if the lamp is the symbol of their marriage, it belongs over the bed, but their relationship has never had the pure heat she sensed tonight between Ian and Selima, the kind of heat you have at eighteen.

JUST AS HE PREDICTED, THE ROTC DEMONSTRATION BROUGHT Fishbone members around to Mojo's way of thinking. Fager, the man with the red beard and the NIXON EATS BABIES button, was in the hospital with broken ribs, a concussion, and a punctured lung. Other than that, the worst injuries were a broken collarbone, a broken arm, a broken nose or two, a few broken fingers, and a couple of head wounds. Most everybody had cuts and bruises.

They wore their injuries proudly. Adrienne had a purple and yellow bruise around a swollen cut on her cheekbone, Janey displayed deep bruises up and down her shins. Jack had a black eye and a gash on his head and had been one of the group taken to jail. Janey told Lucy that Mojo had been kicked in the ribs. Lucy, herself, only had cut and scraped palms and knees from crawling in the broken glass.

Even Jack, the one who most believed in the effectiveness of peaceful actions, who never got angry, who didn't want to "sink to the pigs' level," had changed his mind. He talked softly, as if he were working out what he was saying as he spoke. "I don't know about you, but I went into Saturday's demonstration peacefully." A murmur of agreement answered him. "The New Mobe says these rallies are still effective antiwar actions. But I've come to agree with Mojo. That's counterrevolutionary bullshit." Most people clapped.

Adrienne stood up. "Demonstrations still have a place. They make it clear to administrations and politicians that the voters and students don't like what they're doing. Come on, guys, don't give up.

Nobody said it was going to be easy. We have to keep going. Nonviolently."

Mojo stood bent slightly at the waist and breathing shallowly. His smooth face was strained. "We're in the belly of the mother country and it's up to us to take action. War changes everything. In war, if you don't fight against your enemy you allow your enemy to win. Brother Huey is fighting the same war as we are and he says that at this time in history, having respect for human life means picking up the gun. In order to get rid of the gun we have to pick up the gun. Can you dig it? Not taking action at this time is not cool."

There was much stirring and murmuring. Jack spoke up. "I still say that we don't hurt people. We do everything we can to avoid hurting people."

Mojo looked irritated. "I drive an ambulance, Jack. Do you really think I want to hurt *people*? It's in our own best interests and in the interests of humanity to plan our actions so that civilians don't get hurt."

Janey popped to her feet and Lucy could see the purple bruises on her bare shins. "What about pigs? We should off all pigs, right?"

The group of fifteen or so shifted in their seats and twittered. Some laughed, not sure if Janey was joking or serious.

Jack took her seriously. "We aren't going to *really* off them. But we get them where it hurts most; we destroy their stuff. Nobody gets offed. We take care to limit it to stuff, not people, or else I won't be involved."

"Me, either," said Adrienne.

Janey stopped smiling. "I was kidding, Jack. Did you think I meant *literally* kill pigs?"

Mojo said, "Everybody who agrees that we will up the militant level of our actions to include destruction of establishment stuff, say aye." The room rang with ayes. "Those not in favor, say nay." The room was silent.

"Let's give ourselves two weeks to heal our injuries and then we'll act."

The next day Lucy brought soup to Mojo's basement apartment. He lay in a sleeping bag on a bare mattress, icing his ribs. He ate the soup, slurping it down in huge gulps. While he was eating she looked around the room. There was a two-burner gas stove, a bar-sized fridge, a sink with a steady drip, all in a line on one side of the room. His mattress lay on the other side, near the garden-level window. Outside, dull grass broke through concrete before a splintered brown fence that blocked the view of anything else. A sagging couch sat against the long wall next to the stove, its nubby fabric worn to an indeterminate color ranging from dirty green to gold on the arms and sliding into brown on the lumpy seat cushions. On the couch were knitting needles in a large piece of work and a ball of blue yarn.

"You *knit?*" Lucy asked. She expected him to say it belonged to some woman he slept with here.

He glanced over at it. "Is that so hard to believe?"

"Kind of," she said.

"Why? Gandhi sewed."

She didn't know that Gandhi sewed. She blushed into her hair. Mojo grinned.

"How old are you?" he said.

She blushed again and desperately tried to stop. She wished she could say she was twenty-one. Or even nineteen. She wondered if he would declare her too young to be in the organization, sort of like being too young to drink. Or date.

"Eighteen."

He looked at her as if from far away. "You're the youngest person in Fishbone."

"I am?"

"I think so."

She struggled against this distinction. She knew she was every bit as committed as most of the people in Fishbone. Her age shouldn't matter. She forced herself to look at him.

"Is that a problem?"

He laughed. "No, just the opposite. I think we can make good use of you and your pretty blond youth. When we do the action at ROTC, I'll ask you to help me with something special. Are you ready for that?"

She couldn't believe it. He was going to give her a special part in the next action. She nodded, barely managing to maintain her cool.

"I'm ready," she said.

THE NIGHT MOJO PICKED WAS FLOODED WITH PEARLY LIGHT from a moon just shy of full. Two of their comrades waited off campus in a car with five two-gallon gasoline cans in the trunk. Dividing up the gas, Mojo had reasoned, would allow them to pour it faster.

Jack and Adrienne climbed the fence at the back side of the building. Mojo, Lucy, and Janey waited in the eucalyptus grove for the car to drive up. When it did, they opened the trunk and passed two of the cans over the fence to Jack and Adrienne, who set to work pouring it all around the back of the dry wooden building. The car drove away. They carried the other three cans into the eucalyptus grove. When Jack and Adrienne came across the road, Janey, Mojo, and Lucy moved out and poured the gas in their cans around the base of the front of the building and doused the sides with what was left over. Lucy looked at her watch, an old Timex of her father's, and saw that they'd done it all in five minutes. During that time there had been no traffic and no pedestrians on the Cross Campus Road.

"Okay, split," Mojo said. The other three took off in separate directions, as planned, but before Lucy could go, Mojo grabbed her arm. "Stay," he said. She caught the hurt look on Janey's face just before Janey turned and ran. Lucy stayed and held the funnel as he poured the last of the gasoline into a bottle and fitted a knotted rag in the top. He looked at her and it was almost impossible to tell what he was thinking. Then he struck the match and lit the wick on the bottle and threw it at the door of the empty building. She saw it explode against the old wood. She froze, transfixed by the line of fire that began drawing itself around the structure.

Mojo grabbed her hand and then they were running. They ran uphill, through the campus, staying off the main walkways and service roads, keeping to smaller paths and cutting through bushes, across grassy patches, ducking around buildings and over a fence or two. They threaded through the science buildings, up a steep flight of steps, over a stone wall, and up to the eastern edge of the campus. From here, glancing back quickly, she could see the spire of the Campanile drawn in silverpoint and rising from the rooftops. Now she could hear the sirens of fire trucks, weak and tinny, coming from somewhere far away.

They kept running up and around the rim of the football stadium, past an old dormitory building set into the steep hillside, and still up, always up, through scrubby trees until she thought her chest would burst. The ground was crumbly, covered with slick pine needles so that it was difficult to get a foothold. She grabbed at branches and trees in order to keep scrambling up. Now, even though they were climbing as fast as they could, the steep slope and soft dirt slowed them down.

She became aware of a movement, a rustling sound in the trees to her right. Sure that someone was following them, that they would be caught at any moment, she doubled her pace, and just as she grabbed Mojo's hand, a small black deer startled and ran. Holding hands, they crossed a dirt road near the top of the hill. Once across it, they resumed the climb to a clear place another hundred feet above, and there, finally, Mojo stopped. She knew the place. People called it "Tightwad Hill." Students came here to watch football games without paying to get into the stadium.

Mojo and Lucy threw themselves down on the ground. She lay on her back, working to get air into her lungs. When she could breathe normally, she sat up and looked where Mojo was pointing.

It was an enchanted landscape. From so high above, the university looked like a small Italian city spilling down the hill. Far away, the moon was reflected in water cradled by hilly arms of land reaching from across the bay. The Campanile, from here, was a small toy tower, the stadium a neat oval bowl. She followed Mojo's sight line and saw what he was pointing at. A smudge of smoke and a glimmer of fire so small as to be unremarkable rose from a place she could only assume was Callaghan Hall. The pinpoint red and white lights of tiny fire engines could be seen but the fire didn't seem to be disturbing anyone in the sleeping town or the dark hills. All was strangely quiet and peaceful. Just a faraway flame, a bit of smoke, and a few toy trucks.

Mojo pulled a bag of weed out of his pocket and rolled a fat joint.

"Look at that," he said as a third fire truck pulled up to the burning building. "Three trucks. That's good. We did good." He lit the joint and passed it to her.

"Will it burn down?" she said, taking the joint.

"Maybe. I don't know. But enough damage has been done that the ROTCs won't be using that old barracks anymore." He watched her smoke.

She held the smoke in until she could feel the familiar droning, like an old-fashioned propeller airplane starting in the back of her head. She'd been smoking a lot with her Fishbone comrades; it was what they did when they got together. It was what everyone over fourteen and under thirty *did* in Berkeley. At meetings, after meetings, or hanging out at Adrienne and Janey's house, someone would pull out a bag of weed and they would get high. The others all seemed to enjoy it. For them, getting stoned was a way to relax and feel happy with each other, and was used much as alcohol was used in other strata of society, though the Fishbone members felt that alcohol was the establishment's drug and not mind-opening in the way of grass, acid, peyote, and mushrooms.

For Lucy, the obligatory pot smoking was becoming increasingly strange. Very rarely now did she feel relaxed and happy when she smoked. Usually, after even a toke or two she started to get edgy and afraid. A dreadful feeling of being out of touch with herself came over her. After smoking, even familiar friendly faces took on menace, and good friends seemed to conspire against her. Marijuana was so fundamental to the movement that the others would take refusing to smoke as uncool and even hostile. They all embraced Timothy Leary's commandment to "stay high and fight the revolution," so she smoked and each time worried that the paranoia would come, and when it did, tried to hide it from the others.

She handed the joint back to Mojo, who smoked deep and long. She could already feel the paranoia creeping into the landscape and into the air between them. Mojo moved closer so that their hips were touching. He put his arm around her. For a second she could see them, as they would have been in another decade, at Tightwad Hill to watch a football game, or maybe coming up here to neck. His arm was reassuring and his hip lit a silvery pleasure in hers, so she put her attention on that to avoid the deep buzzing that was the harbinger of a bad high.

"See?" Mojo said, smiling down at the city. "Nobody got hurt. The action was effective and they won't forget it." He turned to look at her and in his dark eyes she saw desire and triumph but also the dark fleeing tail of something dangerous.

"Here's the thing, and you can't ever forget it," he said, taking her face in his hands and looking into her eyes. "Sometimes we have to do a small evil to bring about a much greater good."

chapter 13

JANEY MAKES her son, Connor, go with her to pick Adrienne up from the airport. The flight will arrive at ten and it takes a good half hour or more to drive to Denver International, so they leave at nine. Connor, who has a learner's permit, wants to drive. The one good thing about Denver, in Connor's mind, is that he can drive as much as he wants. They spend hours every day, in this automobile-obsessed city, Connor driving and Janey riding shotgun, giving him pointers. This is how she's placated him for bringing him here. He's good at it. She's proud that he's become a good driver.

"Not to the airport," Janey says. She watches his chin lengthen and his lower lip go out. He's inherited his father's red curls and boy-next-door good looks. And like his father, he knows how to pout. He kicks the toe of his sneaker into the hotel carpet and leans his lanky body against the bedroom door frame.

"Come on. I can do it," he wheedles. "You know I'm a good driver."

She shakes her head. "Not at night. Not the first time. You're not ready for that. We don't know the roads here well enough. I just want you to come and keep me company. Will you do that? Please?"

He looks disgusted but he follows her out into the warm, orange-tinted evening and slouches into the passenger seat of the rented car. When they begin to move, he starts in with his complaints.

"What are we doing in this shit town, anyway? I miss New York. I miss my friends."

"It shouldn't be much longer," she says, taking a street that's supposed to lead to the highway. She MapQuested it but it still seems complicated. She's just about to panic, thinking she missed the exit, when she sees a green sign with a plane logo.

"I even miss Pop and Gram," he says. "Pop and I have to pick out my car because I need it the day I get my license. No later."

She follows the green signs leading from one highway to the next in a maze of roads. He's still a kid. The minute he gets his own wheels, compliments of her parents, he'll be gone. "Well, you've still got a couple of months."

"Yeah, but Mom. They aren't going to have exactly what I want on the lot, you know."

"No, I know."

"And anyway, school starts in three weeks. We *better* be outta here by then. Shit, I'm missing my whole summer."

"I know, honey, and I'm sorry. But hopefully the work I'm doing here will help bring Dad home sooner than we thought."

He looks up and stops whining. "For real?"

She backpedals. She shouldn't hold out false hope. "It's not a sure thing, but I hope so."

He juts his chin a couple of times and drums the dashboard. "Cool," he says.

At the airport they find Adrienne. Janey hugs her, amazed at how small and brittle she feels. It's been probably five years since they've seen each other and the change is significant. Adrienne's face is doughy and her cheeks wobble as she hugs a reluctant Connor. Her eyes have the frozen, fearful look of the very old or ill. She is stooped and shapeless, though she still wears jeans and peasant shirts. *That* hasn't changed in forty years, but the body in them has.

Adrienne has foolishly checked her bag. They have to wait at baggage claim for almost an hour before a beat-up green bag the size of a small refrigerator comes down the conveyor.

"Shit, how long are you staying?" Connor says, dragging the huge bag off the carousel.

"Oh, I know it looks like I'm moving in, but don't worry," says Adrienne, flushed and frowsy, her gray hair frizzing even in the air-conditioned dry air. "It's the only bag I have. So I filled it up. Might as well."

Janey watches as Connor extends the handle and begins to pull the bag on its wheels. Janey, herself, never takes more than she can pack into a carry-on. Even when she's going to the other side of the world. If it won't fit in the carry-on, she doesn't take it. She's lost too many bags and spent too many hours waiting around in airports. She's found that beyond the essentials there are very few things she might need that can't be bought anywhere she might be. But Adrienne has rarely been out of California. She's stayed in her little house in Mendocino, living off a small inheritance and getting by on next to nothing. She never had children or a husband; she doesn't even own a car. All she has is the house and a bunch of cats and the sound of the ocean worrying the bottoms of the cliffs.

"Where's Lucy?" Adrienne asks after she's belted into the front seat and Connor is grumpily occupying the backseat. She sounds like a child, purposefully unaware of the reality of the situation. Janey hopes she isn't so far gone that she can't be a witness. "Are we going to her house right now?"

Janey checks her watch. By the time they drive to Doreen's house it will be near midnight; too late to drop in for a visit. "I think we should wait until tomorrow."

Adrienne nods vacantly. Janey drives back to the hotel. Tomorrow is Sunday. They'll drop in on Lucy on Sunday morning. Janey will continue to pretend that she just wants to reconnect. And Adrienne's vapidness will reinforce it. With luck, she'll get a picture on her cell phone and by Monday Lucy will be arrested before she has time to disappear again.

She's ordered a rollaway bed for Adrienne which she sets up in her bedroom, since Connor's foldout couch is in the living room. He gets in bed and starts his late-night MTV watching, accompanied by his laptop for instant messaging and his cell phone for text messaging with friends in New York.

Adrienne putters around her suitcase, refusing to unpack it but constantly opening it for toothbrush, reading glasses, pajamas, and medications. Janey watches her from the bed. Adrienne was the most beautiful of them all, back then. Willowy and auburn-haired, she had grace and a gentle kindness in her blue eyes. Now she takes off her jeans and peasant shirt and Janey sees the flaccid thighs and non-existent calves etched with purple veins. The small breasts that never suckled a child are sagging nevertheless. Janey has seen Adrienne naked before. Many times. Back in the day, when group love and group sex was what they all did, she watched Adrienne fuck Jack and Mojo. It was the scene. But Jack was the one Adrienne loved. They were like male and female versions of the same person, both pale and freckled, both redheads, both open and friendly and winsome, but because they all said they didn't believe in monogamy and Adrienne was a true believer who played by the rules, she had to share him. Janey found it easy to lure him away. Adrienne, guileless and loving to the end, didn't blame Janey, she accepted their marriage and wished them well before she crawled off to Mendocino.

Now Adrienne is old. And though Janey prides herself on being in good shape, she's getting older, too. Next year she'll be fifty-five. She remembers her grandmother at fifty-five: diabetic and swollen in a muumuu, with a high, angry old-lady voice, venomously living through one health crisis after another until she died at sixty-five, after going blind and losing both legs. And her own mother who, at forty-nine, five years younger than Janey is now, after the hysterectomy and the sudden drop of estrogen, turned old in a matter of weeks.

Their generation, Janey and Adrienne's, wasn't supposed to get old. They broke all the rules and intended to be immortal. Back then they called it having a dream. But seeing Adrienne's used-up body and blunted mind now, after all the years, she understands that what they refused to see was that no matter how many buildings they blew up or how many orgies they had, they were still going to get old. And now old age is here, sleeping next to her in the rollaway cot.

chapter 14

DOREEN SITS up. There will be no sleeping. She puts her bare feet to the smooth wood floor and stands up. She pulls on a cotton nightgown from the chair by her closet. She can see well enough so she moves through the dark house with no need for light. Besides, she knows every creak in the floorboards, every chip in the paint. Her laptop is pulsing green-white on her desk and she picks it up and takes it downstairs, outside to the table in the orchard under a hundred million stars. Out here the loud metallic chirp of crickets could easily be mistaken for the sound of the stars themselves.

She opens the lid of the laptop and clicks on the Internet symbol. She stares a moment at the Google box, not sure if she wants to take this plunge. In all the years since the Internet began, she's never Googled anyone or anything from the radical movement. She never wanted to know what happened to the other Fishbones. The distance provided by not knowing made her feel safer. But here she is, typing in "Lucy Johansson." There are a handful of links to articles that mention her and the bombs that went off at NYU and Columbia on March 8, 1971. There are links to seventies radical websites, Most Wanted lists, a link to pictures of her as a child and into college. One intriguing link features a computer-aided age enhancement of her high school graduation photo that supposedly shows what she looks like now. Thankfully it bears no resemblance to Doreen.

It seems Lucy's become something of a cult hero among anarchists and radicals. They laud her as a revolutionary who slipped through the net. Conservative fanatics try and condemn her for her crime, brand her as an evil woman, a traitor to her country. They call her a terrorist.

A light goes on in the kitchen. She shuts the lid on the laptop and waits as Ian crosses the yard.

"Mom?"

"Hey, sweet boy. Can't sleep?"

"No." He sits down across from her. He's made a peanut butter and honey sandwich. It smells wonderful. He takes a huge bite.

"I think Costa Rica sounds like a good thing," she says. She's not sure why, but now she's tearing up, thinking about him going there and working with sea turtles. She clears her throat. "I like Selima, too."

"You do?"

"Yes."

"So you're not mad at me?"

She laughs but it's a distant cousin of the laugh she would laugh if she weren't scared shitless about Janey Marks.

"I'm not mad at all. But Ian?"

"Hm?"

"Don't go to any rallies for a while, okay?"

"Okay, Mom. Dad already talked to me about it. He said the FBI thing freaked you out."

"It did."

"Sorry. No, I'm going to help Derek with the stones until Selima and I go to Costa Rica. I'm not going to have any time for protests."

He stands up and yawns.

"Think you can sleep now?" she asks.

"I think so."

He kisses her good night. She watches him walk back to the house. He's bigger than his father now. His back is broad and he walks with a man's gait. The light in the kitchen goes out and she opens the laptop again.

She types in "Brian Hong," Mojo's real name, and gets a plethora of references to Brian Hongs all over the world, none of which seem to be Mojo. She types in "Mojo Hong" and gets one reference from a Weather Underground memoir that mentions him along with Lucy Johansson in the context of Fishbone. There is nothing current about Mojo and no mention of his connection to the bombs at NYU and Columbia. It seems that Mojo has effectively disappeared.

She types the letters of Janey's name and waits for the information to appear. There are scores of references to Sewell, Smith & Marks, and Janey's promotions within the company, but nothing about a move to the Denver office. There are dozens of references to her father and mother and the prominent Marks clan of Connecticut.

On the third or fourth page of links she finds a newspaper article referring to Jack Marks, née O'Neil, married to the Marks heiress in 1979, convicted in 1997 on a possession of explosives and conspiracy charge in conjunction with the Columbia and NYU bombings of 1971. He's doing a twenty-five-year bid in Lewisburg.

Her mouth tastes rusty, as if she's been touching her tongue to the screen door on her parents' house in Kansas City. It's true, then. Here is proof that it's no coincidence that Janey has turned up. This is not a benign nostalgic attempt merely to reconnect. Doreen knows with a certainty that makes her bowels churn that Janey is here to confirm that Doreen is Lucy. And she will try to trade Lucy to the Feds for Jack. Maybe she's done it already. The FBI could be on their way right now. They could find her in her nightie in the fruit trees in the middle of the night looking up information about herself on the Internet.

With trembling fingers she quits all the links she's opened and clears the Internet history stored on her computer. She goes through her finder and clears out all memory of recent items and then logs out. She hugs the laptop to her chest and runs through the dewy grass to the house where she locks the door behind her.

This is it, then. The moment she's imagined for three and a half decades. This is the moment when she knows that she's caught. Standing in her dark kitchen, with her heart pumping, she picks up the phone and dials the number she hasn't forgotten in thirty-four years.

"Mom?"

"Lucy," says the voice she would know anywhere, even thickened as it is with tears. "Dad died yesterday morning."

"No," Doreen says. And then she's crying for her dad who ate cheddar and apples with Hershey the dog and took her out for long drives in his Cadillac when she and her mom fought. She's even crying for her dad who was so cruel to Adam before and after the war. She knew it was possible she'd never see him again, but now she realizes she always thought she would, somehow.

It hurts. She didn't get to see him or even talk to him again. She didn't get to explain what happened at Columbia. She didn't get to tell him how sorry she was.

"He only wanted to see you again," Augusta says. "You and Adam."

"We can't talk on the phone," Doreen says, wiping her face. "It's not safe. I'll be there tomorrow night."

She sits on the kitchen floor and weeps. For her dad. For Adam, who now will never see their father again either. For the past, and for Lucy, the girl she was.

For Louis Nilon.

The sorrow is an underground cavern that is wide and deep enough to hold all these things. But the spring that fills it and saturates everything in it is that she was the one who connected the last wires to complete the circuit on the bomb. And she was the one who put it in the book bag and left it in the bathroom at Columbia. That

act has defined everything since. If she could go back and change it,
undo it somehow, wipe it out, enter into a pact with God or the devil
to change it back again, she would. But nothing, she now knows, will
change the domination that one act has had and will have on every
following moment of her life. Nothing compares. Not hiding, not a
new identity, not keeping it all a dark and dirty secret. What she did
has caused this sorrow for herself and her family and the family of
Louis Nilon. It's hers. She did it. It's on her head.

The suitcases are in the cellar. She pulls open the trapdoor in
the sitting room and contemplates the narrow stairway down. She
flips the switch and, squinting against the sudden brightness, runs
down the stairs, grabs a duffel, and brings it back up in the space of
a breath or two.

Upstairs she gathers clothes for three or four days and stuffs them
in the bag along with a spare pair of shoes, a hairbrush, a toothbrush.
She opens her locked box and pulls out the Patricia Wolfer ID and
sticks it in the bag, too. She takes the stack of hundred-dollar bills
she has been collecting here, a few out of every paycheck, and puts
them in the bag, too. She might as well send this one last envelope
to Wilmia Nilon.

Miles stirs. "Dorie? What are you doing?"

She places the packed bag next to the bedroom door. "Nothing,"
she says.

"Can't sleep?" he says, thickly.

"No."

His breathing deepens. He may be asleep again. He makes a
huge effort to surface. "Come to bed. Let me hold you till you fall
asleep."

Her eyes fill all over again. Her nose and jaw sting with the effort of fighting tears. She pulls the nightie off over her head. In her
new softened state she can hardly bear the texture of the air coming
through the window, the first thinning of dark that means dawn.

She turns off the fan and slips into the bed. Miles pulls her to him. His hand finds her stomach and caresses it, stroking down over her hip and ending midthigh. He hesitates as if he's thinking of something else, then relaxes. The pull of sleep is too strong. His arm grows heavy on her hip. A soft snore reverberates against her neck.

She takes his hand and holds it, listens carefully to his even breath. She strokes the hairs on his wrist and feels his belly fill and empty against her back. Something so ordinary, so commonplace, so utterly precious, her marriage has always been a place of safety. But not anymore. It's been a long time coming, thirty-four years, to be exact, and now it's here. Now no place is safe.

sunday

chapter 15

DOREEN MAY not have slept at all. She can't be sure. It feels like she's been lying awake for what was left of the short, hot night, and now another day is breaking, as hard and white as yesterday. But this day, whatever else it might be, is the day the secrets end.

She is aware of a particular threadbare exhaustion that reminds her of Ian's infancy. His first six months were a reprieve in that she could think of no one and nothing but Ian. For six months she forgot she'd ever been Lucy Johansson, that she'd ever been wanted for murder. She was Ian's mother and nothing else. Every night from five to nine he cried inconsolably and then settled into a rhythm of sleeping and waking, never achieving more than two hours of sleep before he needed to eat again. She watched as her body became increasingly not her own and marveled that she didn't mind. It obeyed *him*, it was as simple as that. He demanded milk and her breasts obliged. He woke and so did she. When he slept, she slept. She was in his thrall. For the first time in her life she was completely happy.

When he was six months old her secret started to move back into the forefront again. The ongoing deception of being Doreen Woods, and now having a child, spawned a whole set of other, smaller deceptions. She had to re-create a childhood suitable for talking about to others. She had to pretend she didn't care deeply about politics. She couldn't vote. She couldn't leave the country. She had to keep guard of her own mind, making sure that nothing slipped out. So she never drank too much, she avoided close friendships, and she obsessed that she would talk in her sleep or that, if she ever had to have surgery, she'd say something coming out of anesthesia. Over time, the adoption of her new identity became so complete that most of the time she doesn't feel like she's lying. It's more like there is a vague sense of untruth rotting at her core.

She remembers seeing a human heart for the first time, dissecting cadavers in anatomy lab. Her group's cadaver was named Louise Hardy. She had been a smoker who died of emphysema in her eighties. The cadaver was tiny and the embalming and preserving fluids had turned her dark gray. She stank of chemicals with a powerful undercurrent of rot that clung to Doreen's hair and scrubs.

On that first day, Louise Hardy's body lay exposed but intact. She had hair and eyelashes and skin and genitals. Doreen realized with a nasty jolt that the corpse still had nail polish, dark pink, on her long fingernails. Somehow the nail polish turned the cadaver into a body that had belonged to a living person.

At first Doreen was reluctant to cut into the gray tissue. It felt as though they would be disturbing Louise Hardy in her death sleep. But once her team began to strip away layers of skin, fat, muscle, veins and arteries, nerves, organs, and bone, she, along with all the other students, became numb to the fact that they were cutting up something that used to be a person. Even the sight of the chipped fingernail polish failed to make her squeamish.

She looked forward to the class when they would dissect the thorax because that was where most of the major organs, including the heart, were located. Somehow she held on to the idea, knowing it was wrong, that the heart would be different from other tissue. It would be pinker, it would be stronger, it would retain some remnant of life. Doreen and her dissection team cut through the upper ribs at the sternum and then worked to free the lower ribs until they could lift the rib cage so that it sat up like a band shell on the chest. Then they removed the lungs,

those strange, spongy lobes that separated into three neat parts in the hand. The moment finally came when they could see the heart, tucked behind the sternum, encased in its protective sac. It was excised and removed. The students took turns holding it. When it was Doreen's turn, she accepted the handful of muscle, and although she knew she was supposed to be marveling at the wonders of the organ, she was thinking that this most deeply buried, romanticized, and feared organ was, after all, just another hunk of formaldehyde-cooked meat. Louise Hardy, in her long life, surely felt this heart beat faster when she fell in love, felt it ache when it was broken, felt it twist with sorrow when someone she loved left her or died. And all of that was reduced to a hunk of dead gray meat in the hands of first-year dental students.

She imagines her own heart as persimmon orange, not pink or red. It sits behind her breastbone, in a rich loam of fascia protected by her rib cage. The lie that encases it, like the sac of fluid in the physical heart, has turned it bitter. So, instead of veins and arteries, a poisonous green vine grows out of it and curls through her vessels like bindweed. Today she will begin to purge herself of it, strip it away, pull it up by the root, and be free of it.

She puts her hand on Miles's shoulder and gives it a little shake. This is the day the secrets end. This is the day she will begin to re-claim her heart.

"Hunh," he says.

"Sorry. I have to tell you something."

His eyes open.

"What?" he says.

And it's as if she's standing on the edge of her childhood swim-ming pool in Kansas City. Her toes are curled around the rough ce-ment edge, her arms are stretched above her rubber-capped head, her skinny legs wobbly from fear and cold. Her dad is in the water speaking soft encouragement. "Come on, Luce, I've got you." And then she leans over and drops into the water.

"I have to drive to Kansas City today."

"What's in Kansas City?" Miles asks.

"My mother. My father has died."

She watches him take in the information that she has a mother in Kansas City, that her father has only just died. She watches him struggle to rework his understanding of her life. It dawns on her how tortuous for Miles the next days are going to be and she aches for him. But this thing has its own momentum now.

She says, "I haven't told Adam yet. I'll take him with me if he feels up to it."

Miles nods slowly. Pain and sparks of sudden understanding start to mix with the confusion on his face. Now he'll ask a thousand questions. She can see them coming. She dreads the long explanation she owes him.

"Wait," he says.

"What," she says.

"What?" he echoes, loudly and incredulously. "For twenty-six years I've believed your parents are both dead and now you tell me you're going to Kansas City to bury your father and see your mother. Don't you think you should explain? Don't you think you're moving a little fast?"

"Miles, I have to move fast."

"How come? Tell me."

"I will. I'll tell you, but I don't know where to start. It's a long story."

"I've got all day."

"Well, I don't."

"Jesus Christ, Dorie. What's going on?"

"My parents are still living. Or at least my mom is."

"We've established that."

He has every right to be confused and indignant. She knows what she has to say but she doesn't want to. She *is* Doreen. More Doreen than she ever was Lucy. And she doesn't want to let go of Doreen, especially right now.

"I was born Lucy Amelia Johansson," she says, slowly.

He stares at her.

"I committed a crime in 1971."

She gets up and puts on shorts and a T-shirt. Her bag is where she left it by the bedroom door. Standing in the doorway is Ian in gym shorts with a perplexed look on his face.

"What are you guys talking about?" Ian says.

She looks back at Miles. When it comes to Ian, they've always conferred on everything. When it comes to Ian, her resolve wobbles. She can feel the tears backing up.

"I have a lot to tell both of you," she says, clinging to the business at hand. It really wouldn't do to get emotional now. "But there isn't time. I've got to hurry. Do you want to drive to Kansas City with Adam and me? It's a long day's drive. We'll be there tonight, stay tomorrow, and then drive back again on Tuesday. We can talk in the car."

Miles gets up, pulls on his shorts, and says, simply, "I'll go. How about you, Ian?"

Relief is sweet and sudden. There can be some comfort, some normality, then, if Miles comes with her. They will talk. He will help her with Adam. She turns to face the tall young man she gave birth to, one winter morning in Boston eighteen years ago.

"Ian?"

"Yeah, okay."

They will have twelve hours in the car together. Time enough to go over all of it. "We have to hurry, then," she says.

Miles digs out the backpack he uses during the school year and puts in a T-shirt and some jeans, underwear, and socks. From the closet he gets his one suit. Seeing it now, she realizes that she has been avoiding the fact of her father's funeral. The sudden image she can't stand to think about is the one of FBI agents waiting for her at his grave site. She opens her own closet door and pulls out a black dress and a pair of black sandals anyway.

Miles says, "You go get Adam started. Ian and I will meet you over there in ten minutes."

SHE FINDS ADAM LYING ACROSS HIS BED WITH THE SHEETS wound around him, Pièta-like. His face is angular and serene. His eyes are flat and unseeing for a moment, then they seem to take her in.

"Adam," she says, softly. And after a moment, "Dad died. Do you think you're up for driving to Kansas City?"

He pulls himself up with his arms until he's sitting with his legs straight out in front of him.

"How do you know?" he says.

"Janey told me he was sick, so I picked up letters yesterday. It didn't sound good so I called Mom last night. He died Friday."

Adam bends his knees up and flexes and points his feet, checking, she knows, for feeling in his legs. She picks up the pants she sees neatly folded on the chair in the corner and hands them to him.

"Are you up for it?" she says again.

He doesn't take the pants from her. He needs both hands to maneuver his legs around. "I think so. Are you?"

She considers the question. For all these years they haven't gone home for birthdays, anniversaries, Christmas, or illness. They've stayed away because they're fugitives. At least that's the way she's always put it to herself. But she knows, she has always known, she could have done this before. She could have spontaneously driven to Kansas City, showed up at her parents' home, and spent a night or a couple of days with them. Especially in recent years, they weren't being watched all the time. It would have been okay. She could have used her fake ID and rented a car to muddy the trail. The Feds wouldn't have figured it out in the short time she might have stayed. So why hadn't she?

Keeping away from home, from anything that was Lucy Johansson, had become the equivalent of surviving. Pushing her childhood and parents into the past and leaving them there was essential to being Doreen. Switching back to Lucy, however briefly, however safe from the law, was something that jumbled her up. Just driving to Cheyenne a couple of times a year threatened to put her into a major funk, and always spawned profound doubt. So, over time, she learned to stay as far away from Kansas City and her parents as possible.

"It doesn't matter," she says. "I'm going."

He pulls himself up to standing. She can see now that he's wearing a large disposable diaper. She resists the urge to be embarrassed for him.

"Nice diaper."

"Thanks," he says, walking awkwardly toward the bathroom by throwing his legs out in front of him. Clothed as he is in only the diaper, she can see that his muscles aren't able to do the subtle work of making his steps smooth; they can only manage the large movements. Still, he's getting around better than he has been lately.

"What's your percentage today?" she calls out.

"Eighty-nine," he responds firmly.

She smooths the sheets on the bed and puts the pillows back where they belong, clears away a glass of water and a plate from the side table, takes them to the kitchen and washes them.

"Can I start packing for you?" she calls when she passes the closed bathroom door on the way back.

"What's the hurry?" he says, irritated.

There's no help for it. This is the day the secrets end.

"Janey may have blown the whistle on me. I want to get home and see Mom before it all comes down. Miles and Ian will be here in a minute."

The toilet flushes. She can hear the plastic rustling of a fresh diaper. In a minute he opens the door, her wasted, once-beautiful brother who came to her rescue thirty-four years ago and has been paying for it ever since. They've always been Hansel and Gretel, walking through the treacherous world together, leaving a breadcrumb trail to find their way home.

Adam walks his new gangly walk into the bedroom and pulls on a T-shirt and pants. He's wearing the frayed little book on a leather thong around his neck. He drags a marbled green suitcase that must be as old as he is out from under the bed. Into it go a pair of dark pants and a dark shirt, khakis, and a fresh T-shirt, a couple of pairs of boxers, a comb, and a toothbrush. He picks up a cane she's never seen before and the bag of disposable adult diapers.

"Ready," he says.

chapter 16

FOR ADAM it's like being a kid again, sitting in the backseat with Ian, racing along the interstate over the flat plains of eastern Colorado. They are almost a typical American family: father driving, mother in the passenger seat, and the two kids in back, one a sullen teenager, and the other in diapers.

When he and Doreen were kids their father decided that they needed to "see America." Adam was eleven, a serious fifth grader in button-down madras; Lucy was seven. It was the last summer of the Eisenhower administration, and from Kansas to New York, down through the South and back to Kansas again, his parents debated leaving the Republican Party to vote for Kennedy while every radio station seemed to be playing "Mack the Knife."

"I don't care," his mother kept saying. "Richard Nixon's got shifty eyes. I don't trust him."

"Vote the party, not the man," his father insisted.

Adam sang along with Bobby Darin, smoothing his hair back and casting smoky glances around the car.

His mother sat on the other side of the Ford's wide front seat, in tortoiseshell sunglasses, her short hair blowing and her bare brown arm resting on the open window. Behind her, on the seat next to Adam, Lucy played with her dolls and coloring books.

Adam sat in the backseat and charted their progress on the road map, filling in the white line that ran through the pastel states with a ballpoint pen he kept clipped to his shirt pocket. Whenever "Mack the Knife" came on the radio he practiced his Bobby Darin imitation and made his mother laugh. The rest of the time he stared at his father's freckled neck and the blond hair above it, rendered nearly transparent with hair dressing.

It was a trip of endless motels (some with pools and some without) and strange-tasting grilled cheese sandwiches. From Kansas City to New York he saw towns and fields and people much like in Kansas. But as they drove down the Atlantic coast and through the southern states, he saw large numbers of black people for the first time in his life, other than on TV, and bathrooms in filling stations with signs that said WHITES ONLY.

Somewhere in Alabama they stopped for lunch at a Woolworth's. A handful of white people, their faces blank as windows, stood outside. Inside, three young black men sat on stools at the lunch counter. They wore dark suits and white shirts with skinny dark ties.

They faced the white man behind the counter who paced uneasily, his hands in his pockets. Another man with porcine bristles and little blue eyes watched through the window from the kitchen.

"You boys go on home, now," the counterman said in his high voice. "You know I cain't serve you nothing."

The black men ignored him.

The counterman spoke to Adam's father. "You folks want, you can sit at one of them tables." He indicated one of the four empty tables near the lunch counter. Ed hesitated. Adam realized he was trying to discern if it was safe.

His mother turned to his father. "Well?" she said.

Ed moved the family to one of the tables and they sat down. Lucy stood on her knees in her chair to be tall enough to reach the table. She watched the neat black men carefully. They were quiet, as if waiting to be served their lunch, but there weren't any menus or silverware before them. The white men behind the counter stared at the black men. The doughnuts in the glass case and the shelf of pies remained untouched. The counterman brought the Johanssons menus.

"Thank you very much," said Augusta, smiling pleasantly and speaking loud enough for all to hear, "but I believe those gentlemen were here first."

"Hush, Aggie," Ed said.

Before the waiter could respond, the street filled up with a red fire engine. A policeman came into the restaurant with his thumbs hooked in his belt loops. His eyes flicked from the three black men to the Johansson family.

"Sir, I'ma have to ask you to leave," he said to Adam's father.

Augusta opened her mouth to speak, but before she could, Ed pulled her to her feet. He picked up Lucy and pushed Adam ahead of him toward the door.

"I'm sorry," he said, over Augusta's protest. "We didn't realize."

On the sidewalk the crowd was growing. His mother glared at his father and tried to extract her arm from his grip, but Ed wouldn't let her go. Adam held Lucy's hand and stayed close. Another police car and a paddy wagon pulled up to the curb with their sirens on. White firemen stood shifting from foot to foot in their big boots. The white Woolworth's customers watched the display of law enforcement with eager eyes. A man in a crumpled gray suit peeled away from the group and met the police at the curb.

"We don't want any trouble, now. Just get 'em outta my restaurant."

The backup police, a young boy with freckled skin and big ears and an older cop, heavy in the jowls and middle, passed through the crowd and into the Woolworth's. Adam watched along with every-body else as, without pause or warning, the two cops pulled the first man off his stool and dragged him by the arms through the store and outside to the paddy wagon. The man was tall and strong, but he of-fered neither resistance nor help. He went limp and the policemen had to work hard to move him. As he was dragged past the small group of citizens, a woman spat at the man and her spittle looked like a white grub on his black coat sleeve. The man stayed limp, forcing the police officers to lift him into the wagon.

The second man was dragged out in the same way. By the time the police got to the last man, they were sweating and huffing with the effort. The last man was the biggest.

"Come on, you," said the older cop, grunting as he dragged the man through the doorway. The black man's leg caught on the door-jamb, making it more difficult for the police to pull him through. The black man didn't help. Disgusted, the older cop dropped him and poked at him with his stick. The other cop let go, too. The black man lay at their feet, staring straight ahead. Adam could see that he was afraid. He was blinking rapidly and his chest moved out and in with short, quick breaths. The freckled cop pulled his stick out. Both cops seemed to have decided simultaneously not to lift this man. They poked him in the back with the sticks instead.

"Move along," the older cop said, nudging the man with his boot. The black man didn't budge. "He's as big as that old bull your daddy got in his pasture, Tubby."

Tubby struck the black man once with his stick. "Get up," he barked hoarsely. Still the man stayed where he was. Adam could see the other two black men locked in the paddy wagon, looking out through the slot in the back. The policeman standing by the door of the wagon whacked the door with his stick. The sharp sound of his stick on the metal door of the wagon seemed to ignite the two police-men, prodding the man in the doorway. Suddenly they rained blows on his back and legs. His only defense was to try to protect his head with his arms.

Adam's father forced his family through the crowd. Their car was blocked by the fire engine, but they got in it anyway. "Keep the win-dows rolled up," he ordered. He turned on the radio to block out the noise of the man being beaten.

"Ed? Shouldn't we help that poor man?" his mother asked. "We can't just sit here and watch."

His father lost his composure. "What do you want me to do?" He was sweating heavily in the close car. It was the first time Adam saw his father afraid. "It's none of our business, Aggie, we can't get involved."

His mother turned away with an expression of disgust on her face. "What are you teaching your children?" His father glanced into the rearview mirror, caught Adam's eye and looked away.

The officers' arms swung up with each stroke. Lucy glued her face to the window. Their father winced every time one of the police officers hit the man. A piece of his carefully combed hair fell across his forehead and his face contorted with his inner struggle. Finally, in frustration, he laid on the horn until he got a fireman's attention. He rolled his window down and shouted at the firemen, "We're from Kansas. We want no part of this. Let us out of here." The fireman nodded and held up his finger, indicating that their release would come momentarily.

And then it was over. The police loaded the beaten man into the paddy wagon with the others and drove away with the two cruisers and the fire engine following. The white people in front of the Woolworth's went about their business with guilty, smug faces. His father started the Ford. Adam and Lucy were allowed to roll down their windows as they drove out of town. They ate lunch in the next town at a café where there were only white people.

All through the South Adam had been pestering his parents to let him order grits. "You wouldn't like it," his mom always said, and talked him into a hot dog or another grilled cheese. But that day, when the waitress came, he ordered grits and refused to be talked out of it. He'd imagined them to be delicious, something like fried potatoes with crunchy dark edges, hence the name: grits. They came, looking more like cream of wheat than like anything that could possibly deserve the name of grits. Resolutely, he picked up his spoon and scooped some into his mouth. The taste was bland and starchy. The texture was worse, mealy and gelatinous, and hard to swallow.

"What did I tell you?" his mom said.

Adam forced himself to eat it. This was the taste of the South. He forced himself to remember it. Maybe this was what the black men would have ordered at the Woolworth's if they'd been allowed to. He ate it all, wiped his mouth on his napkin, and refused anything else. He did it for the men at Woolworth's.

FROM THE BACKSEAT HE WATCHES DOREEN, MILES, AND IAN. She tells about the bomb and running, about living underground and changing her identity. She doesn't tell about their childhoods. She doesn't tell about how much she loved Mojo. She doesn't say that marrying Miles was a good strategy for staying hidden. She's turned sideways in the front seat and tells it to the side of Miles's face. Her mouth goes fast and she gestures with her hands. Adam doesn't pay a lot of attention to the words, but lets the sharp rise and fall of inflection wash over him. Miles listens as he drives, his face a stone. Ian has popped out of his seat belt in the back and is leaning forward to hear every word. He looks like a guy who has just stepped on a land mine and knows that his life is already gone.

When some people get devastating news they cry; some are agitated; others, like Miles and Ian, are stoic and focus on the business at hand.

THE DAY HE ENLISTED IN THE MARINES, ADAM BROUGHT THE mail into the kitchen where his mother was cooking dinner. She had pulled the wooden cutting board out of the slot in the countertop and was cutting carrots into rounds. A supermarket chicken was washed and oiled, and waiting in all its raw goose-pimpled nakedness to go into the oven.

She listened calmly while he told her. She didn't look at him, but kept her eyes on the sharp knife in her hand. She sliced up all the carrots until there was a mound on the board. Then she calmly picked up the fryer in both hands and walked out the door into the backyard. It was June and the roses were blooming. The smell of them wafted into the house where he stood watching. She carefully held the chicken as she walked unhurriedly across the grass to the back fence where the yards of the Blackburns and the Healys butted to theirs. There she stood a moment, as if she was waiting for Mrs. Healy or Mrs. Blackburn to come out and accept her challenge. After a minute her body seemed to fill with movement. A little breeze came up and her dress latched onto the backs of her legs. Her apron blew out in front of her as she changed her grip on the chicken so that she was holding it by one of its drumstick legs. Her other hand floated out for balance. Slowly, she began to wind up like Bob Gibson on the pitcher's mound, and the chicken in her hand circled above her head as she spun it by the loose joint in its leg. Two spins, her hand opened, and the chicken rose with useless wings spread on either side of its overfed pink breast. Headless, it cleared the fence by a good three feet into Mrs. Blackburn's backyard, where it bounced gracelessly on the flagstones and came to a stop next to the chaise longue.

IN THE FRONT SEAT MILES DRIVES AND DOREEN TALKS. ON either side of the interstate the fields of eastern Colorado and western Kansas are dry and brown, much browner than Adam remembers them.

"So that's your real name, Lucy Johansson?" Ian says, his voice breaking into a higher register like a twelve-year-old's.

"No," Doreen says, turning around to face him. Her eyes are fierce and overbright. "My *real* name is Doreen Woods. I took that name and made it my own." Ian sits back in the face of her intensity.

For Doreen, fugitive life has been a quest to become so respectable and embedded in middle-class life that she can't be found. She left Lucy behind and became another person: Doreen. Adam never legally changed his name, he merely started using Doreen's purchased surname, MacFadden, and it became his. But he didn't care about it the way she did. He never desired to be successful or middle class anyway; for him the challenge has been to stay himself and not attract attention.

ADAM DROVE LUCY OUT TO THE BAY AREA AND ENDED UP staying. He didn't think it through, exactly, he just went. He knew he couldn't stay with his parents, he didn't want to be in Kansas City, and he no longer wanted to go to college. Vietnam had leached all the ambition out of him.

In San Francisco he took a studio apartment and tried to paint. He stretched canvases and mixed pigment, but after the preparation, actually putting brush to canvas eluded him. He couldn't produce anything at all, not even bad paintings. He couldn't keep his mind on it long enough. Vietnam was always leaking through. Tom's face, or the immolated nun, or any number of dead or dying people reared up and demanded his attention so that he couldn't concentrate. He took to walking around San Francisco. Here, the beats were turning into hippies, the hippies were turning into revolutionaries, and the queers were coming out en masse. In the tenderloin Adam wasn't an outsider at all. For the first time in his life he was surrounded by other gay men.

Somebody took him to a drag show called the Cockettes. The Cockettes were hippies as well as gay. Both men and women performed in a kind of rotating carousel of skits and songs that shocked and shook up audiences. Watching their absurd antics, he was able to pay attention; to laugh and temporarily shrug off the anxiety that had gripped him.

There was one thin, dark-haired Cockette who wound his naked body in Saran Wrap and sang high and strange. He didn't play it broad and goofy the way the others did. He seemed absorbed in the alien space character he played. He stood still, his arms up in a machinelike salutation, and with robotic movements belying the longing in his voice, he reduced the audience to silence and then roars of applause.

Adam went to the party after the show. It wasn't exclusive, everybody who wanted to be there, in those days, was there. He waited until the singer was alone for a minute. Then he introduced himself to Aaron Star.

Aaron and Adam fell in love. When he wasn't performing, Aaron was good-natured and quiet. He soothed Adam and reassured him. When he wasn't performing, Aaron was extremely wholesome. He liked to play basketball. He liked to play cards. Everyone became more serene when they were near him. Like Tom Poole, he had that effect on people. But unlike Tom Poole, he was queer as a three-dollar bill, and with him in San Francisco, Adam understood, finally, that being gay was not a choice, it was a given. He embraced the life and the war began to leave him. The nightmares stopped. The paranoia retreated.

They were in Boston, ten years later, when Adam sent Aaron to the doctor for a cough that wouldn't go away. They'd heard of a new disease some were calling "gay cancer." The newspapers and radio were starting to run cryptic reports. Nobody knew what it was, how it was transmitted, how to protect themselves, or why it was killing gay men. All they knew was that everyone who got it died sooner rather than later, horribly, painfully, and usually alone and shunned because the fear of it had driven people past compassion.

Adam was no better. He found himself avoiding men who looked sick. He made excuses not to visit men who ended up in the hospital. He stayed away from clubs, washed his hands obsessively, and even avoided sex. After Aaron's cough became chronic, Adam caught himself holding his breath when he came near, as if he could protect himself from the germs that way. He wasn't proud of his fear; he went to great lengths to hide it, but it had him. He pretended he was tired and didn't want to have sex. He became prickly and withdrawn and accused Aaron of losing interest, when really it was Adam who was afraid to touch Aaron.

The day the test results came back, Aaron was rehearsing his show at the Orpheum. After all the years of female impersonation in places like Jacques's or the Other Side, he finally had his own show. Boston had caught on to Aaron. Recent audiences were as much straight as they were gay. People from New York were showing up. The show sold out every performance.

Aaron was in the middle of a sound check. In jeans and clogs and a black T-shirt, he looked like an ordinary guy, like anybody those days, a little too thin, a little too pale, but not unusual. For the performance he would whiten his face and shellac his hair in a ridge of upright black waves. His shaved eyebrows and painted mouth and plastic-encased body would make him androgynous. For now he stood on the stage and simply held the microphone in both hands, but even without costumes, makeup, or lights, when he opened his mouth to sing, something otherworldly and other-gendered emerged. He was a space traveler or a dolphin singing about wonder and loss. His voice soared every bit as high as Maria Callas's, but this was no campy imitation. He leapt clear of gravity, and then, just when Adam thought he couldn't stand the purity of it, flew back to ground to weep dark, earthly waters as he crooned, "I am the other, I am no one new."

After the sound check Aaron walked offstage and up the center aisle.

"What is it?" he said when he saw Adam.

"The doc wouldn't tell me. He wants you to come in."

Aaron raised the skin of his forehead where his eyebrows were starting to grow back in. He kept walking out the theater door and onto the ticket-littered sidewalk in front. "Well, not today. I've got a show in six hours."

"No," Adam said. "We need to go now."

"I don't see why."

"Because we need to find out what's wrong so you can start getting better."

Aaron stopped and turned his reproachful eyes on Adam. He wasn't buying it. "You mean so you'll know if you're going to leave me? Adam, if I have this new cancer, then I'm already dead. It won't matter if I talk to the doctor today or tomorrow."

That Aaron saw through him made Adam argue all the more. "I'm not leaving," he said.

"We'll see. I don't expect you to take care of me when I get the sores and the runs and my insides start to rot. I don't want you to see me like that anyway."

"Aaron, you don't even know if you've got it. It's probably just bronchitis. Or maybe pneumonia."

"No," Aaron said. "I have it."

"Let's find out for sure."

Aaron stood there on the dirty sidewalk outside of the Orpheum on a bright fall day, caught in his moment of hesitation, and Adam realized that this was the image of Aaron he would carry with him into the future. Not his new performance persona or all the drag acts he'd ever done. Not memories of lovemaking, laughing, and living together. No, the permanent shot of Aaron would be of him looking scared and sick and defeated in the custardy light of a Boston afternoon, in boy clothes, in the last moments before Adam forced him to hear his own death sentence. In the last moments before death became more than something to sing about.

ADAM TURNS TO LOOK OUT THE WINDOW OF THE CAR. HE catches, out of the corner of his eye, a blue-green blur like a wide sleeve moving in a sweeping circle. When he focuses on the brown landscape, the blue-green wedge-shaped thing whirls and dances just inside his peripheral vision. He sees that what he thought was a sleeve, made of some sort of sheer green and blue fabric, is a paper-thin wing. He's able to see it quite clearly when he can see it at all. It's covered with a fine, thin fuzz. Maroon veins branch through the shining blue and green. Once, he even catches sight of a sliver of abdomen, the same blue-green as the wings but more solid and speckled with spots of black fur.

He's known she was there but seeing her stops his breath. He holds her in his gaze and feels the balm and the breeze of her, the cool mist of her. He wills her to stay. He's tired of waiting.

chapter 17

MILES DRIVES the straight, flat highway east. Doreen has fallen quiet. She's told them her bizarre story until she's repeating herself. When she starts to tell him again how she got involved with the radical group in Berkeley, Miles suddenly can't bear it.

There's a rest area ahead and he pulls off the road into it. They bounce hard over the speed bumps and the muffler scrapes the pavement. It feels good to be out of control, just a little. It feels good to scare her with his recklessness. He jams on the brakes where the pavement ends at the edge of a cornfield. He turns the ignition off and gets out, not bothering to close the door behind him. As he wades out into the corn he can hear the *ping-ping-ping* of the bell.

He walks, fast and hard, between two rows of corn taller than he is. The ears are almost ripe and the rough leaves scrape his arms and thighs as he pushes through them.

When Ian was twelve, he and Kumar called in a phony bomb scare to their middle school. It was before the Columbine High School massacre and long before 9/11. Still, such pranks were not taken lightly. They made the call from a phone booth outside of the neighborhood gas station and other kids reported them to the principal. Miles thought the penalty of suspension for three days from school was stiff, but fair. Doreen, who abhorred spanking and never struck her child, slapped Ian when they picked him up from school. Though he was already ashamed and demoralized, she made him

stay in his room without supper the first night and docked his al-
lowance for two months. He wasn't allowed to play at Kumar's for
months. Miles had never seen her so furious.

"It was a prank. They're kids, for God's sake," he'd said.

"No," she'd insisted. "He needs to learn that it doesn't matter if
they're kids or if they meant to really do it or not. I want him to
know that putting even one toe into that territory brings heavy consequences."

IT FEELS GOOD TO WALK, TO MOVE STRAIGHT FORWARD WITH-
out looking back, without caring about her. For a minute he wants
nothing other than to follow this row of corn, to go wherever it will
take him, even if it takes him all the way around the world and back
to this very spot. He could set himself on that track and think of nothing else, not Doreen and her past, not his marriage to a criminal,
not the fact that she was Lucy Johansson, the notorious radical he'd
heard about in the seventies and then every five or ten years after
when someone would write a story in a newspaper or magazine men-
tioning her. That he is married to her and has been for twenty-six
years is more absurd than he can fathom at the moment, so he walks,
wherever the row might take him. The sound of the car door is long
behind him. He can't hear Doreen, Ian, or Adam.

There was a time, back in Boston, before Ian was born, when
he contemplated leaving her. She was getting her practice started
and was consumed with her work. Things between them hadn't pro-
gressed the way he would have liked. With Doreen there were always
corridors with rooms he would never be allowed into. He was lonely.
There was a new fifth-grade teacher at his school, a winsome, open-
faced girl named Meredith Ransom who made it clear to him that
she was interested. They worked together on several projects, taking
their classes to the art museum, Bunker Hill, and Walden Pond. It

started to feel as if they were dating. She cooked dinner for him one night when Doreen was out of town at a conference and he knew that he would either walk away from Meredith or sleep with her and his marriage would be over. He arrived with a bottle of wine, not knowing which way his life would turn that night. But when Meredith opened the door, he handed the bottle to her and said good-bye.

Now, all he can hear, all he can see, is corn and more corn. When a fence and a road suddenly appear, he turns back, not wanting anything but the endlessness of the cornfield. He retraces his steps until he is roughly in the middle of the field. He squats, to see what the corn looks like towering above him. Liking it, he sits down in the dark, rich soil.

He wishes himself to be a permanent part of this cornfield. If he could only sit here forever, in the green twilight of corn and dirt, where a spider making its way along the rough ground is all there is to concern himself with, he would be happy. He closes his eyes. Should he have known? Is it possible to be married to someone for twenty-six years and not know? He did wonder at the secrecy about Adam's and Doreen's childhoods. He did think it was odd that Adam never used credit or had a job or health insurance. But if anything, he had suspected that Adam was the one with the hidden past, that Adam was the one who had something to hide. Never once did Miles think it was Doreen who had committed a crime and had been using their marriage to hide. He feels sudden shame at his gullibility. In his world, when you love someone, trust someone, you can't help but know everything essential and fundamental about them. He feels used, ravaged, and dumped in this cornfield. He wraps his arms around his knees and hugs them to himself. His face is wet and so are his knees.

He hears someone coming from the direction of the car. He keeps still, stifles his snuffling. They're several rows away from him. He sees her legs, skin, the khaki of her shorts. He barely breathes the corn-infused air. He feels like a kid, crying and hiding, and there's something liberating about it. In all the years he's taught fifth grade, every year he has at least one kid who hides, who needs to be alone and unseen by the others so that he can cry and rage. Now he's that kid.

She stops about four rows away. "I know you're here," she says. If she hadn't just been moving, he wouldn't have been able to see her, so he knows she can't see him. He doesn't move. He likes being invisible.

"I'm sure you're mad at me," she says. "You have every right."

Thank you, Doreen, he thinks bitterly, for giving me permission to be angry.

"It was to protect you and Ian. That's the only reason I didn't tell you. If you didn't know, you couldn't be implicated."

And suddenly he's remembering when they moved to Denver from Boston. Doreen had built a solid practice in Boston. She was finally making money, had paid off her start-up loans, yet without warning, she decided that she wanted to sell out and move to Colorado. So he and Ian uprooted and moved across the country to Denver, where they didn't know a soul. By the time they sold their house in Brookline, bought a more expensive one in Denver, moved, and added in the cost of Miles being out of work for an entire school year, the switch from Boston to Denver cost them several thousand dollars. He didn't question Doreen's reasons at the time. The change seemed like a good idea. But now, in this cornfield in Kansas, he wonders what was really behind the move.

Doreen turns to go back the way she came.

"Is that why you wanted to leave Boston?" he says, but the anger is already draining out of his voice. "To protect us?"

She stops where she is. "Yes, partly," she says, quietly. "All the other stuff was true too, but I had a close call in Boston and thought it was best if we left."

Two earthworms poke up through the crusty dirt. They writhe and reveal more of themselves and he sees that they are actually two ends of the same long earthworm.

"Why have you decided to let us in on it now? There's more going on than your father's funeral, isn't there?"

She crunches through the corn and sits down next to him in the row. She speaks softly, matter-of-factly. "I believe someone is going to turn me in soon, if she hasn't already. I'd rather negotiate my surrender than get caught."

He swallows this new information whole. He has no choice and there isn't time for him to digest it a little at a time. "Are those the only options? Couldn't we go, what-do-you-call-it, *underground*, a little deeper?"

She's looking at him. Her blue eyes are clear and sad. "I don't want to run anymore, Miles. And Adam can't. And I don't want you and Ian to have to."

He looks down to hide his wet eyes and the struggle around his lips.

She says, "I want to bury my dad and see my mom while I'm free, and then I think I should turn myself in."

And now his arms are around her and she's holding on. He pulls her into his lap and cradles her, rocks her in the green twilight. He whispers into her hair, and she cries into his shirt. He holds her; they hold each other for a long time, but eventually they have to think of Ian and Adam. He helps her up and they walk back to the car.

chapter 18

SHE'S TIRED of talking, and anyway, there's no more to say. Miles insists on driving. The late-afternoon light is relentless, reflecting off the other cars, baking the dirt in the fields. An hour passes and no one says anything. Doreen gives in to the urge to close her eyes. The relief is huge. It immediately sweeps her into a strange awareness where she can pass freely, in and out, through the barrier of a delicious sleep.

She and Mojo drove Interstate 80 across Nevada, Utah, and Wyoming and into the Midwest. Mojo talked about how essential their action was to the future of America and the world. He believed, and she believed him, that the peaceful protests had played out and now only the bombs set by radical groups were getting the attention of the world. She and Mojo and the rest of Fishbone were going to be part of that history.

Back in Berkeley they had planned a dozen actions. The first would be a double hit in New York by Mojo and Lucy. The idea was that they would come in from California with bomb makings, blow up two symbolic locations of American injustice, get in and out without the pigs knowing who, exactly, had set the bombs, and be back in California by the time anybody could come looking. Other Fishbone members would then do the same in other locations across the country. The idea was to keep a steady stream of actions in the public view and then join with other groups to demand immediate withdrawal from Vietnam.

They made their way across the country in the deep freeze of late February. She remembers the loose shifter on the steering column of the old green bus and how the engine missed when they put it in second. Mojo cut his hair and took the earring out of his ear. Lucy wore the straight clothes her mom had sent, kilts and sweaters, kneesocks and penny loafers, and braided her hair down her back. They chose their road names after much debate. Finally, he chose Fred, for Fred Hampton, she chose Joan, for Joan Baez. They became Fred and Joan Williams, married students. She wore a wedding band. They took their disguise seriously and before long it felt natural. As Fred Williams, Mojo was softer. He held doors for her at truck stops and called her "honey." By the time they were into Nebraska, he even started using the sweeter tone of voice when they were alone together. She loved being "married" to Mojo. And she believed they were doing something essential for the country and the world. But she caught herself wishing that they really were Fred and Joan Williams on their way to graduate school in New York.

They spoke in slogans and phrases even when they were alone together.

"We're bringing the war home, Lucy, we're making it real," Mojo said. He quoted King. "Freedom is never voluntarily given by the oppressor; it must be demanded by the oppressed."

The war continued, in fact was ramping up, even though America wanted out. They were patriots in the sense that they wanted to restore the government to the people. "The political is personal," Mojo said. Lucy took that as a personal call to action. She was proud of what they were doing.

The bus didn't have a radio so they sang as the temperature dropped. Bob Dylan, Joan Baez, the Beatles, the Doors. Mojo did a passable imitation of Dylan, matching his intensity and howl. At night, they parked next to a field or stopped on a town street somewhere and made love in the back of the bus in down sleeping bags zipped together and piled with all the quilts and coats they owned. Beneath them, underneath a false floor in the bus, were the makings for the bombs: wiring, detonators, batteries, tools, and the clocks that would delay the blasts. Everything except the dynamite.

To pick up the dynamite, they detoured north at Des Moines and made their way along smaller, two-lane roads into the frozen fields of the Minnesota countryside. Trees, roads, barns, and farmhouses were all frosted equally in a hoary palette of silver. The weak winter sun stayed close to the horizon and didn't offer anything in the way of warmth. They ran the old bus's heater on high and put cardboard in the grille in front of the radiator to make it hotter, but still their toes and fingers grew numb and their breath hovered in frozen clouds between them. Lucy layered on most of the clothes she brought and was grateful for her Kansas coat, never once used in Berkeley.

Mojo followed directions scribbled on a piece of paper. Lucy only knew they were somewhere west of Minneapolis. Night would come fast, that much she knew. In the brittle light of late afternoon she saw the same barn and mailboxes go by three times and realized they were going in circles.

"Goddamn fucking Jack," Mojo muttered, slamming his mittened hands on the steering wheel. "This is the wrong fucking road."

He turned the bus around and went back to the larger county road. They followed it, thoroughly lost. From her side of the bus she could see that the road was following the curve of a lake. Past the guardrail and down a steep embankment the ice began. Out on the lake there were tracks from a car that had driven onto the ice and made loop-de-loops in the snow.

They came around the next bend to find the road littered with tools, nails, and pieces of drywall. The guardrail was twisted and broken. Mojo stopped the bus. Lucy could see a powder blue truck on the edge of the ice, overturned. Mojo reached past Lucy and opened the glove box. He pulled out a first aid kit he'd insisted on bringing with them.

"Don't forget we're Joan and Fred," he said before he opened his door and slid down the snowy bank to the accident.

She followed. At the bottom, about twenty feet away from the truck, two men lay in the snow-covered grass. Everything was impossibly still except for the back wheels spinning on the truck. Mojo checked first one man and then the other.

"See if you can reach through the truck window and turn the ignition off," he said to Lucy. "Then come back here."

The truck balanced on its cab. The doors were flung open. The driver's side window was broken out. She knelt down and leaned into the cab to turn the key. The engine stopped and the truck settled, going as quiet as everything else, except for a plume of steam rising from the smashed front end.

Mojo was listening with his head on the chest of one of the men. The man was covered with white dust (or was it snow?) and lay there so quietly she couldn't imagine him ever moving again.

"Go get the blankets."

She ran back up the embankment and grabbed the sleeping bags and blankets from the back of the bus. She brought them to Mojo, who had started mouth-to-mouth resuscitation on one of the men.

"Wrap my guy in one of the bags," he said, not stopping his compressions. She tucked a sleeping bag and a blanket around him. "Take the rest over to the other guy. Get him warm. He's still breathing. Probably bleeding inside, though. Just touch him and talk to him. Let him know you're there."

The other man lay with his eyes closed. He was in his twenties, with short blond hair. Underneath his jacket he wore painter's overalls splattered with plaster and paint. She couldn't see any blood or sign of injury. He just lay still. She touched his cold face. She could see a faint steam coming out of his nose.

"Talk to him," Mojo said while he worked at keeping the heart pumping on his guy.

Up on the road a car stopped behind the bus. A man got out and stood looking down on them.

"Call an ambulance," Mojo yelled up at him. "They're still alive."

Without a word the man turned away and got back into his car.

Lucy held the cold hands of her injured man under the blankets. She touched his face, the only skin showing.

"You're going to be okay," she said, feeling a little foolish. "People are driving to a phone and they're going to call an ambulance."

She didn't know what might comfort him but she knew what comforted her. "Imagine a warm place," she said. "It's really warm and bright. Someone's baking cookies and they smell like butter and sugar and chocolate. You're snuggled under some nice blankets. Do you like cats? There's a nice cat on the rug. Or maybe a dog, if you like dogs better. Someone you love is there. It could be your mom or your girlfriend or your buddy over there. Just someone you love. They're holding your hands. They want you to try to stay alive. I want you to stay alive, too." She looked at the man, wondering if anything was going on behind his bluish eyelids. She leaned close to his ear and whispered, "Please stay alive."

Time passed. She was soaked from sitting in the snow and her hands were numb. She was wondering for the hundredth time whether anyone would ever come when a long hearselike ambulance pulled up behind the bus. Two medics came down the embankment with stretchers and a bag of equipment.

"Over here," Mojo said, still alternating pumping on the man's chest with mouth-to-mouth resuscitation. The medics took over. Mojo came to Lucy and felt the vein in her guy's neck.

A second ambulance and a tow truck pulled up. "This one's breathing," Mojo yelled up to them. Soon, with Mojo's help, they had her guy in the ambulance. There wasn't much headroom. She squeezed in next to her guy and talked about anything that came to her while Mojo and the medics worked on moving the other guy. When he was loaded into the other ambulance, she had to get out.

"We'll get those boys into Minneapolis and see what's going on," the driver said.

The driver of the other ambulance piled the sodden sleeping bags and blankets into her arms. "You two did a good thing today. Can I tell them who saved their lives?"

"That's okay, man," Mojo said, shaking the driver's hand. "It doesn't matter."

She and Mojo stood on the road and watched the two ambulances circle the lake, their lights flashing cherry red in the white landscape.

The tow truck driver worked at winching the blue truck up the bank. "You kids want to warm up in the cab?" he shouted, around the cigarette hanging from his lip. His cab looked warm. Lucy would have liked to sit in it for a few minutes.

"No thanks," Mojo said.

They got back in their cold bus, wet and frozen now, and drove down the road. After about twenty minutes Mojo spoke. His voice was thin from exhaustion and cold. "I still don't know where we're supposed to be going. We're going to have to call."

He left Lucy in the idling bus at the end of a farm road and walked up the ruts to the house to make the call. With the bus only idling, the heater's faint warmth faded to cold air. Lucy could no longer feel her feet, hands, or face. Even the moisture in her eyes was frozen, making her eyes stick whenever she blinked. She tried not to think about what would happen if they couldn't find the place before nightfall. They couldn't sleep in the bus in wet blankets and sleeping bags. They would freeze to death, for sure.

"It's the next road over," Mojo said, swinging himself into the driver's seat. "It's not far." His face was patchy white from cold. His hair and eyelashes were frozen. His California coat was almost useless.

As the short winter day gave up, they finally turned off the county road onto a two-lane track with frozen ruts that grabbed the tires of the bus and jerked them toward a small white farmhouse with a huge brown barn hovering behind it. Lucy had never seen any place more welcoming than this house with its warm yellow window light spilling onto the snow. A man maybe ten years older than Mojo opened the door.

"Jack's friends. Come in," he said, smiling. "I'm glad you called. We were starting to get worried." He had a full beard sprinkled with gray and a ponytail that went down his flannel-clad back. He picked up an armful of firewood and followed them into the house. "I'm Robert, this is Marnie, and that's Woody, our son."

"Fred and Joan," Mojo said, awkwardly.

Marnie was a tall woman with a bright smile who sat next to a stone fireplace nursing a baby. "You folks are frozen," she said. "Come closer to the fire. Get out of those wet things. Robert? Get them some dry things."

Robert went into the bedroom and came back with long underwear and a flannel shirt for Mojo, and a big flannel nightgown for Lucy.

"You can change in the bedroom if you want," he said. "Or here. The bedroom's pretty cold." He turned his back and busied himself in the kitchen at the back of the house. Marnie switched the baby to her other breast. Mojo slipped out of his wet jeans and stepped into the long underwear. His thighs were bright red from cold. His face was bright red too, now that he was starting to thaw out. Lucy took off her wet clothes in front of the fire. Her frozen toes and fingers stung. In the warm, dry flannel near the fire, they suddenly hurt so much that she started to cry.

"Joan," said Marnie, "you might have a little bit of frostbite. Don't rush it. It hurts like hell. Robert? Get her some room-temperature water for her hands and feet."

Robert came from the kitchen with a basin and set it on the hearthstones. Lucy put her hands in first. The cool water felt like it was boiling to her frozen flesh. But after a few minutes it started to hurt less, so she put in her feet. When everything was merely prickling and red, instead of white and excruciating, she tucked her feet and hands inside the flannel nightgown and was able to pay attention to her surroundings.

The farmhouse was an L-shaped building. The short side of the L was the bedroom. The living room and kitchen were combined into the long side of the L. Marnie had finished feeding the baby. She stirred something in a big pot on the woodstove in the kitchen. A bright orchid-colored couch faced the huge fireplace along with various upholstered chairs. The long wall and ceiling were painted with fantastical flowers and strange human figures together on a black sky.

Robert brought Lucy a bowl of vegetable stew and a thick piece of bread slathered in butter. The bread had cranberries in it. After all the truck-stop food, Lucy thought she'd never tasted anything more delicious. They sat by the fire and ate and drank home-brewed beer. After a while Marnie and the baby went into the bedroom to sleep. Robert opened the couch for Mojo and Lucy and handed them a pile of sheets and blankets.

"Why don't you stay a day or two? Tomorrow you can go into town and wash your stuff, stretch your legs a bit."

Lucy wanted to stay. She wanted to wash her clothes and her hair. She wanted to clean the stench of dying men out of their sleeping bags and blankets. She wanted to fill up on the lives of these friendly people along with more of the cranberry bread. She knew it wasn't revolutionary but she wanted to stay warm and safe for one more day. She hoped he would say yes.

Mojo said, "Thanks, man. I guess we could both use a rest. Do you have the goods?"

"Sure," Robert said, evenly. "A whole box. It's out in the barn. It's real good quality. A guy I know got it from a quarry." He glanced at the bedroom door. "But, uh, Fred? We don't talk about that in the house. Okay?"

Mojo nodded. "That's cool."

After Robert disappeared behind the bedroom door, Mojo and Lucy got into the bed. It felt as though they were going to be doing this for the rest of their lives. She curled up on her side and he picked up his knitting.

"You like it here," he said softly.

"Yes," she answered.

"We'll have all this someday. You'll see. After the revolution."

THEY PULLED INTO NEW YORK CITY THREE DAYS LATER ON another cold, clear night. Janey had already flown in, ostensibly to visit her parents in Connecticut, and had rented them an apartment on the second floor of a building three blocks from Columbia. She showed up in a fur hat and a suede coat embroidered with white flowers. She was every inch the rich debutante. She helped them move in, transporting with her gloved hands the bomb makings stowed in miscellaneous boxes and suitcases underneath the false floor in the bus.

The place was furnished with chairs and tables that looked as if they came from a hospital waiting room. The floor was covered in dirty orange shag and the curtains were made of a stiff woven green substance. In the kitchen there were a percolator and a few pots and pans, mismatched silverware, and a set of thick brown plates and cups. The bedroom came with a real bed up off the floor on a metal frame. In the closet she found musty-smelling sheets, old but serviceable, with yellow flowers sprinkled over a field of yellowed white. Somehow these cheery sheets only made the rest of the apartment more grim. She made the bed, putting their blankets on top, and decided that as long as the bed was good enough, the rest of the place didn't matter. It would serve for what they intended to do here.

Mojo carried in the box with the dynamite and put it in a kitchen cabinet next to the tiny refrigerator. Janey moved around the small rooms, storing boxes of wiring and tools in the cupboards of the dining area. She rolled and lit a joint, then passed it to Mojo. Her straight black hair was as shiny and healthy as the fur on her hat. She smelled faintly of expensive shampoo. She smiled her electric smile at Mojo. He pulled her fur hat off and kissed her.

Lucy turned away. She could hear Janey's muffled laugh as Mojo said something low and throaty. She reminded herself that exclusive relationships were bourgeois. Monogamy wasn't revolutionary. But all those days and nights on the road as Fred and Joan Williams had made their case. She more than halfway believed that they were that couple.

She took satisfaction in knowing there wasn't a couch or bed out in the other room, just the institutional chairs, the rickety Formica table, and the dirty floor. It was some compensation to think of Janey's clean hair and expensive clothes on that filthy carpet. She was just settling into the bed, the one nice spot in the place, expecting them to stay together in the other room, when the door to the bedroom opened. Mojo came in, with Janey wrapped around him. They stumbled toward the bed and came down next to her. Janey had shed her coat. Her skirt rode up and Mojo fumbled with the buttons on her shirt. Lucy could see one breast emerging. She got up and moved toward the door.

"Stay with us," Janey said. "It's just love. We all love each other. Let's celebrate that you're here. And that this is going to be a kick-ass action."

"Janey, you're not even supposed to be here," Lucy said, knowing she sounded like a prude. "The plan was that you rent the apartment, dump the bus, and get us a clean car for the getaway. You're blowing the action."

"You're blowing the action," Mojo mimicked, but he stopped unbuttoning Janey's blouse and sat up. Janey looked irritated. She stayed where she was and turned on Mojo.

"You're not going to listen to this child, are you?" Janey said.

Mojo ran his hand through his short hair. A brief struggle took place on the smooth planes of his face before the self-controlled revolutionary came back.

"She's right. Someone might see you here. And the bus can't stay out front all night. We should stick to the plan."

Janey turned over onto her back and buttoned her shirt. "Your loss," she said. She went into the other room, put on her coat, hat, and gloves, and swept out the door. Mojo sat at the end of the bed with his head in his hands.

Lucy hadn't eaten since eastern Ohio. She rummaged around until she found the bag of food they had in the bus. All that was left was an open box of Raisin Bran. She hoisted herself up onto the kitchen counter and sat cross-legged, eating handfuls of cereal, looking out the windows onto the buildings across the street. There was a lighted apartment where people were having a party. Ten or fifteen of them stood in the living room holding glasses of wine. The living room had dark green walls and two couches upholstered persimmon red. Framed prints hung on the walls and there were lamps on tables. The women wore slacks and sweaters; their hair was shoulder length or shorter, and well groomed. They were young, probably graduate students, or young professionals. They were young bourgeois, what Mojo, Janey, and the others would call "piglets."

She watched until the guests started to put their coats on. They left in couples, smiling and kissing their hosts' cheeks. When they were gone, glasses and plates of food littered the apartment. The woman started to pick up, but the man took the glasses out of her hands and put his arms around her. She smiled up at him. They stood in their living room for a long time, holding each other. When the embrace was over they went around the room turning off the lights.

Once the apartment was dark, Lucy put down the box of cereal and eased herself off the counter. Her legs were stiff from cold and sitting cross-legged. In the bedroom, the bare bulb overhead was still burning. Mojo had taken off his dirty clothes and was in between the sheets. She turned off the light and, still thinking of the couple across the street, slipped in next to him.

chapter 19

"WE SHOULD bring flowers," Adrienne says as they get into Janey's rented car. Her legs are thin and mottled and sticking out from under the long dress she's wearing. She's also wearing a big floppy hat Janey could swear she remembers from the seventies. "Or food. We should bring something."

So Janey stops at a market and buys a bouquet of red, gold, and pink zinnias, and a bag of blueberry muffins. Whatever it takes to keep up the pretense for Adrienne. She drives into Doreen's neighborhood. "Oh, how nice," says Adrienne. "This reminds me of Berkeley when we were in school. Remember? It was so nice and funky then. Now it's all rich people. Probably all Republicans."

As they pull up to the house Janey's palms sweat. She reminds herself of the objective: So that Pettibone has no choice but to believe Doreen is Lucy, she's got to get Adrienne to see Doreen and then swear out an affidavit. When Pettibone's made the deal for Jack, and only then, she will tell him where the agents can find Lucy. As for not spooking Doreen, all she can hope is that when Doreen sees how dotty Adrienne is, she won't feel so threatened. Maybe she'll think they're both harmless and out of touch with reality. It's weak, Janey knows, but she has to try.

They ring the bell several times but nobody answers. Janey looks in the window. Books and newspapers sit on the coffee table, she can see dishes next to the sink in the kitchen. The door is locked so she looks under the mat and over the door for a spare key. It would be too easy, she thinks, to find a spare, walk in, and grab a family picture off a dresser or bookshelf. If she found a picture that clearly indicated Doreen was Lucy, she wouldn't need to use Adrienne.

"What are you doing?" says Adrienne.

"Looking for a key."

Adrienne steps back. With the floppy hat and sundress and crushing the flowers to her chest, she looks like what she is: an ancient flower child, a throwback to another age, as bizarre and extinct as a dinosaur or a woolly mammoth.

"You wouldn't go in when they're not home. Would you?"

Janey says, "I don't think Lucy would mind. Remember how we never used to lock our doors and everybody was welcome?"

Adrienne doesn't look convinced. "We should come back later."

Janey walks around to the back of the house to try the back door. Adrienne follows. "We should go," she says.

"Maybe they left the back door unlocked." Janey searches around the back door for a key. Where would Lucy hide a key? She knows that with a teenage son there's got to be one. Janey, herself, has a key hidden for Connor. It wouldn't be in any of the obvious places. She looks around. There's a huge maple growing near the house, next to the fence. She circles the trunk of the tree.

"I don't like this," Adrienne announces from the door.

At about six feet above the ground, on the back of the tree, is a small nail hammered into the trunk. On it is a key. Janey takes it down.

"Janey, no. This is wrong." Adrienne puts herself in front of the door. She looks ridiculous in her floppy hat and sundress.

"I'm just going in for a second. I just need to get something," Janey says.

Adrienne's spacey eyes narrow and she suddenly seems to understand what's going on. "You aren't here for a visit, are you?" she says, slowly.

"Well, yes, of course I am. But I also need to get something."

"What?"

"A picture."

"You're going to steal a picture from Lucy?"

The exasperation rises in Janey's throat. This may be the only chance she has to get in, get a picture, and have Adrienne identify Lucy from it. She tries to push Adrienne away from the door. The old girl holds her ground.

"You're trying to hurt her, aren't you? Why else would you be sneaking around like this? Are you going to turn her in?"

So Adrienne understands that Lucy's still wanted.

"Shhh," she says. "No. Nothing like that."

"It's wrong," Adrienne says. "You *are* going to turn her in. That's why you want her picture." She blinks hard and looks at her feet. "And that's why I'm here, too. You want me to ID her. Well, I won't." She looks reproachfully at Janey. "Why are you doing this? After all these years, why now?"

Janey decides to switch tacks. "What she did was wrong. You know that. She killed a man. The rest of us did things but nobody else killed someone. And she's out here, free, while Jack's in prison."

Adrienne still holds her flowers. "So this is for Jack?"

Janey nods. "It's for Jack. And it's for the family of Louis Nilon, the man she killed. Do you know that his widow is still alive? Her name is Wilmia Nilon. She's sixty-nine years old. She was thirty-five when he was killed. She had to work as a maid after that, to support the family. That was half of her lifetime ago. They had four kids. Two of them are dead, one from drugs, one from cancer. Wilmia Nilon has had to deal with that all alone. The two girls that are left have kids of their own, who never got to know their grandfather. All because of Lucy."

Janey succeeds at pushing Adrienne away from the door. She unlocks it and walks in. She goes straight into the kitchen, to the refrigerator door covered with pictures. Here are the pictures of a handsome young kid, the kid with his friends, a trip somewhere, and there, in a plastic frame, is a shot of the boy and his parents. Doreen is smiling into the camera standing between the two men in her life. The sun on her hair makes it almost blond.

It's her. It's Lucy. She's aged, but she still looks like Lucy Johansson, and from this snapshot anyone who knew her then would see it. Janey takes it from the fridge and puts it in her pocket before she carefully locks up the house and replaces the key.

AFTER SHE SETTLES ADRIENNE BACK INTO THE HOTEL SUITE, SHE drives her rented car over the grid of empty Sunday afternoon streets. The dry heat wavers over the streets. No one is outside, it's too hot. She can't wait to do what she has to do and leave this cow town with its drought and pretension.

The picture she has in her pocket is going to get Jack out of jail. She can feel it. She sails through a series of green lights. This part of her life, the part without Jack, is almost over.

She uses her key and takes the elevator up to the fifth floor. No one is in at Sewell, Smith & Marks, and that suits her fine. She lets herself into the small office she's been using and proceeds to scan the photo of Doreen Woods, aka Lucy Johansson. Then she e-mails it to Robert Pettibone.

chapter 20

MILES DRIVES through the relentless blue afternoon. Dread lingers in the pit of his stomach, though he goes for whole minutes forgetting why, only to remember again with the full punch of the initial shock. At a truck stop he pays for the gas with cash (Doreen's request) and Doreen and Ian change places. Miles scrubs the mustardy bug splats off the windshield, and then they're back on the highway.

Ian has his iPod in his ears and sits in the front seat recently vacated by his mother. He bobs his head and occasionally performs drum riffs on his leg while he watches the road and the passing fields on either side.

"So how are you doing?" Miles asks.

Ian, to his credit, doesn't pretend not to know what Miles is talking about. He shrugs and pulls the earphones out of his ears. He glances in the backseat, where Doreen is riding with her eyes closed and Adam is staring out the side window.

"It's pretty weird," he says. "I'm still trying to make sure this isn't a joke or something."

Miles nods. He says, "Mom explained to me, when we were out there in the cornfield, why she didn't tell us before." Miles has always hated parents who call each other Mom and Dad. He and Doreen made a point to never do that, and he just did. But he can't bring himself to say her name right now.

"You really didn't know?" Ian says.

"No."

"I thought I was the only one who didn't know."

"No. I didn't have a clue. Really," Miles says. "It's important that you believe me. It's going to be extremely important."

"Why?"

There's no way to soften it, so Miles just says it.

"She thinks she's going to be caught soon, if she doesn't turn herself in. So after Kansas City, she's going to start talking to the Feds about coming in."

Ian expels air through his lips, making a rushing sound of disbelief.

Miles goes on, "I don't know any more about it than that, but I think these things are handled with discretion when someone is a good citizen for thirty-four years, a doctor, a wife, a mother."

Miles feels himself getting worked up, feels tears in his eyes again. "She won't be coming to them like a criminal. She'll have lawyers talk to them first and make the best deal possible. They'll take her whole life into consideration, along with the knowledge that she was only nineteen when it happened, and she was influenced by a bad group of kids. She had no prior record. She didn't mean to hurt anyone." He hears how weak that sounds: she didn't mean to hurt anyone. How many criminals go to prison saying the same thing? He wishes he could do better. He should reassure Ian but he can't.

"I'm not going to bullshit you, Ian," he says. "I really don't know much yet. But don't forget, this is hard on her, too."

Ian flips the air-conditioning vent up. "I know that," he says impatiently. He takes out his cell phone. "I should call Selima," he says, and punches in the numbers.

Miles's anxiety goes up another notch. "Don't say anything to her," he warns.

Ian talks to his girlfriend, telling her they're going to be away for a few days. He doesn't say where. He doesn't say anything or even hint at his newfound grandparents or his mother's sudden revelation. The kid is smart, has good instincts. Without being told, he knows that saying anything over the phone, to anybody, could cost them the advantage Doreen still has. It strikes him hard, how quickly they have all started thinking like fugitives.

"It's a family thing," Ian says into the phone. "I can't tell you the details now but I will when I get home. No, this won't change Costa Rica. I'll be back day after tomorrow."

"You're still going to go?" Miles says when Ian flips his phone closed.

Ian observes Miles calmly. "What do you think? Do you think I shouldn't?"

"Well, maybe you could hold off until we know what's going on with her . . . conversation . . . with the lawyers." His mind whirrs with thoughts of the lawyers, the media, and the whole public spectacle it undoubtedly will be. "We're going to need to present a united front while she's going through this."

Ian looks at him. "Present a united front of what? That she didn't mean any of it? Vietnam was just fine and the Nixon administration were actually the good guys?"

Miles shifts in his seat, his lower back aches from all the driving. "Well, I think she's going to want to show them that she hasn't participated in anything illegal or even remotely militant all these years. You know how they pick apart a person's family in these things." He realizes that he doesn't really know what he's saying. Most of his impressions of the legal system, fugitives, and that sort of thing come straight out of TV dramas.

"How do you know that's what she's going to want?" Ian says, keeping his voice low so as not to wake Doreen. "Did she tell you?"

Miles spots a state patrol car on an exit ramp and adjusts the cruise control. It wouldn't help if they were pulled over by the police now. Seeing the cop is like a slap of aftershave on a raw face. It helps him sharpen what he really means to say.

"You're right, we *don't* know what the legal strategy is going to be, so it's important for you and me to put our own interests on hold for a little while and figure out what will help her the most."

Ian slumps in his seat and puts one of his feet on the dashboard, something that Doreen, under different circumstances, would never allow. In this instance Miles knows it's a sign of reluctant acquiescence.

Adam pipes up from the backseat. "Can we stop? I need to eat. I need a bathroom."

They eat in a small town near Salina. Even with the cane, Adam has trouble walking from the car to the café. Miles can tell by the way Adam looks at them out of the sides of his eyes that he can't see well, either. The four of them squeeze into in an undersized booth.

"Are you okay?" Doreen asks Adam once they're settled.

He looks vague. "I'm tired," he says. "And the creature's rearing her beautiful head."

Miles wonders if he's talking about the MS or about something only he sees. Doreen looks confused, too, but lets it pass. "It's less than two hours and we're there," she says. She catches Miles's eye and he sees the wild look she always gets when Adam is doing badly.

"You gonna make it?" she says to her brother, very gently.

He nods.

She orders soup for him, and when it comes begins spooning it into his mouth.

chapter 21

"THE THING is," Doreen says to Ian as she pulls the car onto the highway for the last leg of the drive, "we didn't know what to do with the knowledge that our country was murdering hundreds of thousands of people in Southeast Asia. After the invasion of Laos, none of the excuses were valid anymore. We felt it was up to us to stop it."

Ian listens, picking at his shoe, the iPod earphones hanging around his neck now. In the rearview mirror she can see Miles in the backseat listening, too. And Adam.

"It's also true that I got caught up in the romance of it all."

In the years before she went to Berkeley, the hit movies were *Butch Cassidy and the Sundance Kid* and *Bonnie and Clyde*. Both romantic portrayals of outlaws who ended up dead. The real-life heroes of her generation were dying at an alarming rate, too. The Kennedys, Malcolm X, Martin Luther King Jr., Fred Hampton: all murdered. Janis Joplin, Jimi Hendrix, Jim Morrison: dead by overdose. The four students at Kent State were a recent addition to the list, as were the two black students killed at Jackson State, and the three Weathermen killed by the misfiring of their own bomb. In revolutionary culture, those who died fighting became martyrs and inspired those who came after to be brave and avenge their deaths.

The plan was that Mojo would set a timed bomb at NYU and Lucy would do the same at Columbia. On the first morning, Lucy braided her hair, put on her Black Watch kilt, knee socks, boots, and peacoat.

She carried only a notebook and a biology textbook in her large bag. She was Joan Williams, a Barnard girl married to a Columbia grad student. Having studied the map provided by the East Coast cadre, she walked, for the first time, the four blocks from the apartment to the Morningside campus.

The differences between Berkeley and New York were evident. The cold air cut through her and seemed laced with exhaust fumes. Dirty snow lay in piles at the edges of the quad. The similarities between the universities were apparent, too. Like Berkeley, Columbia presented the same stone edifice, the same columns and outsized urns that made them both monuments to the Establishment. And like Sproul Plaza, the quad at Columbia was filled with students moving like schools of fish across a grid of concrete.

East Hall was a red brick cottage with quaint white trim and tall windows. In the large vestibule an army recruiting table faced the door. Two soldiers sat behind it. She walked in, heart hammering, and pretended not to notice them. She walked past and up the stairs as if she knew where she was going. Classes were in session in the rooms on the second floor, and as she walked by she saw room numbers and placards that showed the classes to be French and Italian with the names of the instructors. She let herself into the bathroom at the far end of the hall and repeated the names of the teachers to herself until she knew them before she went up to the third floor. There was only the one staircase, in the middle of the building. None of the people she passed seemed to know she didn't belong there. None of them questioned her or gave her a second look.

Back on the ground floor again, Lucy walked past the recruiting table, interested, in spite of herself, in what the military used to lure kids to Vietnam. It was simple, the table had a large framed photo of a young soldier in dress uniform, hat under the arm, gloves and braid and medals and a photographer's aura behind him. He was more handsome and confident-looking than the live boys who sat at the table with their stacks of brochures and clipboards.

One of the soldiers smiled at her and she smiled back. She reckoned he was about twenty-one years old. Young enough to be an undergraduate.

"You need some help, miss?" His hair was short and oiled. His small ears stood out like pale mushrooms on either side of his head. His eyes were blue and he seemed perpetually startled.

She had a prepared answer. "I'm looking for Career Services."

The other soldier, much more sure of himself, jutted a thumb over his shoulder to the hallway behind him. "Right back there."

She ducked into the hallway. The bathroom was close to the vestibule. She went in and saw that it had two toilets in wooden stalls, one sink, and a metal trash can. Beyond the restroom were the offices of Career Services. She walked by the first open door and saw a student clerk sitting at a counter reading a book. The second office contained an older woman working at a typewriter on a desk. She looked up when Lucy lingered at the door.

"May I help you?"

"I'm looking for the career counseling office," Lucy said.

"If you're looking for arts and sciences, that's here. If you're looking for architecture, law, medicine, engineering, those are elsewhere. Are you a liberal arts undergraduate at Barnard?"

Lucy nodded.

The woman pointed to a clipboard on the wall. "You can sign up for an appointment with Mrs. Keebler. Over there, dear."

Lucy looked at the sign-up sheet. Appointments were available from 9:00 A.M. to 4:30 P.M. The two hours between eleven and one were blocked out. She feigned dismay and looked over at the woman at the desk.

"Excuse me, but I can't meet with her at any of these times because of my class schedule and my job. Does she have any appointments later in the day?"

"Her last appointment is four-thirty. You can't make that?"

"I'm sorry. My classes are in the morning and I have to work in the afternoon. I had a doctor's appointment and missed my first class; that's the only reason I could come today. Does she ever see people later? Say, five-thirty or six?"

The woman took her glasses off. "Well, the building is closed at six, dear."

Lucy made a show of disappointment. "Every night?"

"It's locked at six on weekdays. And closed on the weekends."

Lucy nodded, doing her best to look resigned.

Then, as an afterthought and just to make sure, she said, "But aren't there evening French classes upstairs? I thought there were."

"No, there aren't any night classes in this building." Now the woman looked quizzically at Lucy.

Lucy said, "Okay, thanks a lot."

The woman picked up her pencil. "You know, I could always ask Mrs. Keebler if she'd make an exception and meet you somewhere else. What's your name, dear?"

Lucy was already backing toward the door. "Thanks, but that's okay. I'll just wait till next semester when my schedule opens up."

"Are you sure?"

Lucy looked at her watch as if she were in a hurry. "I'm sure. But thanks."

"All right."

She made her way past the army guys, across the black-and-white checkerboard of the vestibule, and outside into the cold damp. She made herself walk slowly at first, but she couldn't help skipping down the quad steps, three sets of ten steps each, startling the pigeons.

In the following days she made several forays to Columbia. She walked around campus, observing East Hall from the library, the chapel, and various other buildings. She got to know each room in

East Hall and quickly made the decision that the first-floor bathroom would be the place to leave the bomb. Meanwhile, Mojo was doing the same at NYU.

They resumed their relationship as though Janey hadn't come to the apartment that first night. For a week or so they went to their respective universities at various times but always met at the apartment at night. They bought pizza or Chinese food and ate it on the bed while they made intricate plans about the hits. They timed themselves getting to their respective targets and back again. Phone calls, discreetly spaced over a period of several days, were made from pay phones, asking about janitorial services and repairs, trying to discover any possibility of human beings going into either building at night. By March 1, Lucy and Mojo determined that the best time to hit both locations at once would be a Monday night. They set the date for Monday, March 8.

Then they started working on the bombs. They moved the bed out of the bedroom, into the living room, so that they could use the more private bedroom for bomb building. The rickety Formica table was moved into the bedroom and reinforced with two-by-fours. Lucy stretched a piece of thick black cotton over the window, secured it with thumbtacks, and then taped two layers of brown paper shopping bags over that, ensuring that all light would be contained and not even a silhouette could be perceived from outside.

Mojo laid the tools out on the table: needlenose pliers, soldering gun, black electrician's tape, magnifying glass, wire cutters, screwdrivers, screws. The materials, alarm clocks, wiring, detonators, and batteries, were placed on the floor next to the wall. The dynamite would stay in the kitchen cabinet, just to be safe, until the bombs were completed.

Mojo began working on the wiring that would eventually connect the disparate bomb parts. He showed her how to take the clocks apart, how to clip the minute hand so that it was shorter than the hour hand, how to solder a screw into the clock face and one into the hour hand so that, at the appointed hour, the two screws would make contact, connect the wires, and complete the circuit, causing the dynamite to ignite. She tested the clocks and the connections on both bombs time and time again.

On the night of March 7 she taped four sticks of dynamite together for each bomb and Mojo attached the detonators. At this point every move was deliberate and careful. Lucy felt as if the three Weathermen who died in the Greenwich Village blast were watching over them. The final connection would be made at the bomb locations.

As they were packing the bombs into their book bags for the next day, with all but the last connections on the wiring in place, they heard a knock on the door. Mojo calmly shut the door to the bedroom and opened the front door. Jack and Janey stood in the hallway, arms wrapped around each other.

"Pizza delivery," Jack said, grinning.

"What are you doing here?" Mojo said, pulling them inside.

"Thought maybe you could use some help."

"You know you're not supposed to be here."

"Relax, man. After tomorrow you'll be on the road, and as far as anyone else knows, Janey and I have been visiting her parents this whole time."

"You're acting like amateurs," Mojo said. "None of the East Coast cadre has shown up."

"Man, you're too uptight," said Jack. Looking around, taking note of the bed in the living room and the drawn curtains, he pointed at the closed bedroom door and said, "Is that where you've got it? Come on, man, let me have a look."

Lucy wondered if Mojo was going to throw them out, but after an intense moment he seemed to decide to let it go. He shrugged as if he were trying to shake off his bad humor and admitted them into the closed-off room where Lucy and Mojo's book bags lay on the table.

She could tell Mojo was proud of their work by the way he un-zipped the bags and folded the covers back. The bombs were beauti-ful. Every wire, every detail, was clean and well crafted. The wiring was efficient and tidy. The solders on the altered clocks were sound. She knew because she'd made them. The dynamite bundles were taped into tight packages and the wires of the final connections, the ones that would make the bombs hot, were capped with swabs of black tape. All that remained was for them to wind the clocks and set them, unwrap the wire ends and twist them together, put the bombs back in their bags, and leave them at their respective target sites.

"Far out," Janey breathed, reaching out her gloved hand.

"Don't touch," said Mojo, but he went through the wiring of the bombs and showed them both how they worked.

"Where'd you learn how to do this?" Jack asked. He walked over to the pile of unused parts underneath the window, picked up a deto-nator, and turned it over and over in his hands, like a squirrel with a nut.

Mojo took it out of his hands and put it back. "A guy in Chicago. We did some actions last year."

"And you're sure no people are going to get hurt?"

Lucy spoke up. "We've spent the last week and a half making sure of that. Nobody goes in either of those buildings on Monday nights."

"Don't worry," said Mojo. "We've done our homework. And to-morrow the entire pig Establishment will know that this is for the invasion of Laos. This is for Cambodia. This is for Agent Orange."

After the bombs were put away, the four of them went in the other room, kicked off their shoes, and sat on the bed. Mojo unwrapped the tinfoil off a chunk of hashish and lit it in his stubby pipe.

He took a hit and said, "I've been saving this for tonight."

The hash was rich and strong and tasted like potent earth. Lucy was surprised to find it didn't make her paranoid. Unlike pot, the hash seemed to calm her nerves. A smooth, bright feeling swept and lifted her. She stared at all the shoes on the floor and felt herself to be looking down on them from a great height. The others were starting to entwine arms and legs on the bed. She watched them and it seemed to her, suddenly, that their bodies and hearts were incomparably pure. Jack smiled at her and his hand caressed her hair. She leaned into him and soon her clothes were sliding off to join the shoes on the floor and then the four of them were moving together, and she didn't know where she left off and the others began. They were all one body, one mouth, one genital, one breast, one mind with one purpose, and many arms and legs, like a Hindu statue, connected by a single pumping heart.

chapter 22

AS FAR as Adam is concerned, it's always been pink and brown in Kansas City. Rose madder and raw umber. And the same sunset that played when he left home all those years ago has played every night since. There has always been ginger ale in thick ceramic tumblers and the sulfurous smell of fireworks just shot off. There has always been the unspoken but prevailing sentiment that Adam has merely temporarily misplaced his heterosexuality and that one day he will denounce his fairy ways and resume his life as a "real" man. Kansas City has held on to this agenda along with this sunset, in hopes that he will come to his senses. And here he is, home at last. Broken and ill and still queer after all these years.

The hours of sitting in the moving car are beginning to take their toll. He's lost his legs again. With his hands he feels them, and it's as if they belong to somebody else. The flesh is heavy and unresponsive. They are the legs of a corpse, though they ache where they attach to his torso.

He wonders when the MS will crawl all the way up his body, like a water line rising on a flooded building, until he has lost his belly and chest, hands and arms, neck, face, head, and finally, what's left of his brain.

It feels like his brain is killing and sloughing off its own living cells, layer by layer, until nothing is left. It reminds him of the way his mother used to cook hamburger meat. She would take a white paper package out of the freezer, unwrap it, and sit the frozen brick of meat in a hot cast-iron frying pan on the stove. The lump of pink-ish frozen stuff sizzled and steamed and turned gray as the outmost layer cooked. The smell of it made him hungry even as he was dis-gusted by the sight. His mother moved the mass around the pan with her spatula. Every so often she would flip the lump of meat over to reveal the browning meat on the bottom. This she would scrape off with the spatula, revealing a new layer of rosy meat beneath. He stood there, fascinated, watching her turn and scrape, turn and scrape, un-til the lump of raw meat was gone and cooked hamburger filled the pan. Then she deftly poured barbecue sauce over it and served it on buns.

They drive through western Kansas City, which is now loaded with malls and strips like every other American city. He may have to go to the bathroom, but his parents' house is only minutes away. He can wait.

Doreen stops at a light in a seventies-style housing develop-ment with tallish trees and split-level houses. "Look at how this has changed," she says, half turning toward Adam. "Remember? This was just fields here."

He does remember. They rode bikes over dirt trails through sun-flowers jumping with grasshoppers. This was where he and Russell Dortmunder made a fort out of two refrigerator boxes taped together and jerked each other off inside it.

The seventies neighborhood gives way to an older, historic neigh-borhood and now more things are recognizable. Here is the junior high school, which has a new wing jutting out into what was a base-ball field in his day and is now a parking lot. The houses look nearly the same, though they've all been renovated. The cars parked outside them are new. Since 1971, when he was last here, the neighborhood went from old and run-down to chic. Just about every house sports a tasteful addition.

It's certain that he has to pee. He tries to hold it back, tries to find the muscles in charge and issue the executive order for them to keep his bladder from releasing its load. They turn the corner and are on their old street, the setting of recurring dreams and some of his most vivid memories. Doreen slows the car to a stop in front of the house, still grand with its mansard roof and nineteenth-century front, still awkward with its Eisenhower-era addition.

The front door opens and light spills onto the old porch. Is that their mother, that small, stooped person who hurries out to them?

"It really is you," she says when Doreen rolls down the window. She's seamed and lined and her hair is pure white, but it's still cut in a smart bob and her eyes are sparkling beneath hooded lids. "Park in the garage. Get the car off the street."

It was always Adam's job to jump out of the family car and open the garage door. He still remembers the feel of the handle and the heft of the door as he pulled up. Now, however, it opens automatically when Doreen drives toward it. She parks next to a Toyota that sits where his mother's Ford always sat. There's no sign of a Cadillac. Adam can't remember his father ever not having a shiny Cadillac.

The lights come on and the car door opens and his mother's hand, familiar, but impossibly old, is reaching for him. He moves his legs toward the open door. His cane is useless to him until he's standing up, so he gives it to his mother. He uses his arms against the car frame to pull himself onto nonexistent feet. His mother tries to help, she clutches at his arm and supplies the cane, making the entire procedure more difficult. That's when he feels his bladder let go. There's nothing he can do to bring it back once it's started. He stands and knows he is peeing, still holding on to the car, still not feeling much in his legs. He feels the diaper filling up, expanding and growing heavy with the weight of his urine. He hopes it won't leak through onto his pants. He's suddenly terribly afraid his mother will see.

"Adam," she says, putting her arms around him. He hugs her awkwardly, because of the proximity of the full diaper. While she turns to Doreen, Adam makes his way to the door of the house, using his cane and his father's workbench, the wall, the woodwork, anything he can for stability. His father's oil-stained cement garage floor would not be a good place to fall.

The closed-up garage is stifling, but the house has been retrofitted for air-conditioning and is blessedly cool. He can faintly hear his mother's voice out in the garage with the others as he gets himself to the bathroom off the kitchen. His bladder is empty now, but he removes the diaper and rolls it up in toilet paper. It's as big as a volleyball but urine is already soaking through. It fills his mother's tiny powder room wastebasket. He panics, a toddler who's wet his pants and fears his mother's wrath. He can't leave the diaper there. He pulls up his pants and picks up the diaper again. In the kitchen there is a larger trash can underneath the left side of the sink. He's heading for it with the sodden diaper in hand when she walks into the kitchen. She's a miniature, brittle version of herself. A strange, cruel parody of herself. She holds out her clawlike hand for it. Filled with shame, he hands it over.

He lets her lead him to a chair in the kitchen which is almost a replica of the kitchen of his childhood. It's a nightmarish version, nearly right, but not. Where is he? What's he doing here? He doesn't want to be here. He never wanted to see this place again.

chapter 23

MILES CANNOT shake the feeling that he's tumbled into a psychotic dream version of Doreen's life. This old house is where Doreen would have lived if she had grown up in Kansas City. This petite, stern woman calling his wife Lucy is what Doreen's mother would have been like if she were alive. Ian stands with him, both of them awkward, and watches Adam and Doreen and Augusta together.

Here in the house, with the window shades drawn, Augusta pulls Adam to her. She is strong and wiry for such a slight person, and her ropy arms flex when she hugs him. She's crying, making hoarse sobbing noises. It's a strange sight, to see Doreen, his capable and extremely grown-up wife, look so rejected.

"I was beginning to think I would never see this day," Augusta says. "But that it had to be because of this. Oh, I wish he could have lived to see you again."

She catches Miles's eye over Adam's shoulder and pulls back, wipes her face with the flat of her hand. She turns to Doreen. "This is your husband," she says as a statement of fact.

Miles steps forward, awkwardly, because Augusta hasn't let go of Adam yet. "I'm Miles. And this is Ian."

Augusta claps eyes on Ian. She approaches him as if he were a wild animal. She holds her gnarled hand out as if he should sniff it. He takes it and makes a clumsy lifting movement with his arms, not sure if he's supposed to hug her. She doesn't interpret it correctly, or else she doesn't want to. She shakes his hand, almost formally.

"He's big," she says to Miles, as if Miles is to blame for it.

"Yes," Miles says.

"How old are you?" Augusta asks the boy.

"Eighteen."

"Eighteen years old," she says, as if it's an obscene amount of time. "And you're my grandson. Well, we'll have to try to catch up somehow."

She makes herself busy getting things out of the refrigerator. "Would you like iced tea? Ginger ale? I have some chicken salad here, and a three-bean salad and a macaroni salad. You know how people are when someone dies, they bring food. Everything comes out of their refrigerator and into yours. I'll have to throw it all out by the end of the week."

Adam looks tired. He has that spaced-out expression he gets when the MS is acting up. Augusta brings him a plate full of salads.

They're all hungry, even though they ate in Salina. Doreen brings more plates and forks, and it strikes Miles as strange that she knows which cupboard, which drawer these things are in.

"What time is the funeral?" asks Doreen.

"Not until eleven," Augusta says. She turns to Ian. "You can sleep in if you want to. I'll bet you like to sleep," she says, and it doesn't sound like a compliment. She turns to Miles. "How long have you and Lucy been married?"

"Twenty-six years."

"Why didn't you have children before Ian? Or is that too personal?"

"No," he says. "Of course it isn't." He glances over at Doreen, who is watching her mother with a pained expression.

"We wanted to wait. Doreen was starting a practice."

Augusta shakes her head. "Doreen? Who's Doreen? Practice? What are you talking about?"

Doreen answers. "Me, Mom. My name is Doreen. My friends call me Dorie. I'm a dentist."

"All these years of writing letters to Patricia Wolfer and now you say you're called Doreen?"

"Patricia Wolfer of Cheyenne was just for the mail between us, Mom. In case, you know, the Feds were watching."

Augusta sniffs. "I like Patricia much better than Doreen. What kind of a name is Doreen? And Dorie sounds like the name of a fat woman."

Doreen wipes her mouth on a napkin. She glances at Ian. "It's the name I bought in Boston right after I went underground. It was Doreen MacFadden and then I married Miles and it became Doreen Woods. I took it because it came with a Social Security number and a birth certificate. It's my name now, Mom. I've used it for over thirty years."

"But you say that you're a dentist? That's just, what do you call it, your *cover*, right? You're not a *real* dentist."

Doreen presses her lips together. Miles gets the impression that Doreen is remembering how confrontational her mother is. "I'm a real dentist, Mom. I went to dental school and I've been practicing for more than twenty years."

Adam says, "It's not like we hide. We don't. Dorie is just Doreen Woods now. And I'm Adam MacFadden"—he smiles dryly—"because I never married."

Augusta appraises Adam. The hard expression on her face begins to soften and her lips purse together in an effort at control. She goes over to Adam, sits down beside him. She takes his face in her arthritic hands and smiles into his eyes. "My darling boy. I'm happy to have you back."

chapter 24

DOREEN IS too tired to shower, too tired to think much about being here. She crawls into her childhood bed before Miles comes up for the night, unable to keep her eyes open, but the minute the light is out and she's settled in, they pop open and she's staring at the ceiling. She tries not to think about tomorrow when they will bury her father or the upcoming days in which she will call the lawyer and begin the process of turning herself in. She doesn't want to think about her mother's coldness or how difficult all of this must be for Ian and Miles. For a while she calms herself thinking about Ian and Selima, working with the sea turtles in Costa Rica. She sees them swimming in turquoise waters with the reptiles. She tries to remember the feeling of being lulled by the movements of the sea. And when her eyes start to get heavy again, Wilmia Nilon rushes in. In her fantasies Wilmia Nilon is a substantial older woman with a strong neck that supports her proud head crowned with tiny braids. She's opening her mail. There's an envelope with no return address. These envelopes come at random times and are always postmarked from different places. Over the years she's gotten them from New Mexico, Wyoming, Florida, Mexico, Chicago, and St. Louis. This one is postmarked somewhere in Kansas. She opens the envelope knowing what she'll find. Inside, folded into a sheet of blank paper, is a stack of new hundred-dollar bills. Sometimes there are ten. Sometimes there are twenty. This time there are thirty-four hundred-dollar bills. In Doreen's imagination Wilmia Nilon accepts the money and uses it for her children and grandchildren and for herself. She knows who sent it and why. She accepts that Doreen wants to help her family, and she understands that the money isn't meant to buy forgiveness; it's been sent from pure regret. As she drifts off to sleep, Doreen relaxes into the dream, the fervent wish, that between she and Wilmia Nilon there is an understanding: that the money Doreen sends has been washed clean in sorrow.

monday

chapter 25

MILES IS already up so Doreen gives herself a minute in bed. Her neck and back hurt from being crammed into the twin-size bed with Miles. One of them could have slept on the couch downstairs, but neither of them wanted to be that far away from the other. Since yesterday, when she told Miles and Ian everything about Lucy Johansson, she's wanted to be as close to them as she can.

Her eyes follow the sprigged wallpaper: celery green bouquets marching diagonally up the white wall. As a girl, Lucy begged her mother to paint her room pink and buy the imitation French provincial furniture she craved from the Sears & Roebuck catalog, but Augusta refused, insisting that the brass bed and maple dresser, both real antiques, were in keeping with the period of the house. Later, as a teenager, Lucy wanted to paint the room dark blue and hang posters on the walls and beads in the windows. Augusta demurred again. "You're going to college in two years and you won't have to see it every day, but I will."

She feels flat. She tries to rustle up some genuine emotion. After all, today is the day they will bury her father. His body is at a mortuary somewhere in Kansas City. She tells herself this, but still feels nothing.

If she could see his body, she knows the eyes would be milky and dull, the features heavy and thick, not like her father's, but more like a wax dummy of him. That was the thing that amazed her about the cadavers in dental school, though she hadn't yet seen a surgery and didn't know for sure what living tissue looked like, it was obvious that the cadaver tissue held no possibility of life.

She crosses the hall to the bathroom. Unlike her bedroom, this room has changed entirely. The linoleum and varnished beadboard have been replaced by tile and painted cabinets. The forties-era beige sink has been replaced by a white oval and no-nonsense taps. She finds a towel in the cabinet next to a bottle green vase she remembers from early childhood. This, at least, is still the same. It's still full of buttons. On rainy days she and Adam would spill them out and sort them into piles, fighting over who got to "have" the oldest, the most unusual, the most ornate.

She turns on the shower and steps in, lathering her head with her mother's green shampoo that gives off the smell of childhood, of mother, of that other life. Under the hot water, in the piney suds, she feels herself softening, becoming raw and exposed. And now she can't help it. She can't hold it back. All the maintaining of secrets, all the effort it took to live her daily life as Doreen MacFadden and then Doreen Woods, has had a way of keeping this, this melting, at bay. But now Lucy has begun to leak through, and though she always dreaded this very thing, she finds herself unable to resist. A peculiar sense of giving in, of giving up, claims her and it is terrifying and painful but also a relief. To allow for *not* struggling and maintaining, to allow her past to touch her now, is to feel a strange sense of release. She has no control over her father's death, Janey's intentions, Adam's illness. For the first time she sees the relief as well as the rightness of turning herself in. And she wonders what it will be like to live without every action being a reaction to that night thirty-four years ago.

LUCY WALKED TO COLUMBIA AT 5:45 P.M. ON MARCH 8, 1971, with the bomb in her book bag. She crossed the quad in the cold breeze, just the way she had every day for the last week. She opened the door to East Hall, her hands and lips numb with cold and adrenaline. It was the end of the workday, nearly six o'clock, and the army guys were packing up their stuff. The more confident one had started to like her, she could tell. He'd been noticing her over the last few days and had started getting that look in his eyes when he saw her. He smiled and watched her walk through the room.

"Hello," he said softly, almost intimately. The other guy's cheeks flushed red as he packed his papers into his briefcase and pretended not to notice. This was not good. They were supposed to be used to seeing her around but not taking special notice. She should be wallpaper, not a girl who catches their attention.

"Hi," she said. It would have been worse to not say anything.

She walked past them to the bathroom and locked the door behind her. She went into the second stall and took the bomb out of the bag exactly as she'd rehearsed with Mojo, many times. Her hands didn't tremble as she connected the final wire but she had a strange tall feeling, as if she were up near the ceiling, looking down on herself. When the bomb was wired she double-checked that the clock was set to go off at nine, then she put it all back in the book bag and left it in the far corner behind the toilet. It was five minutes to six. She left the bathroom knowing that Mrs. Perkins would lock the building in five minutes. She didn't look at the army guys as she left.

"'Night," they called after her.

She stepped out, strangely light without her book bag, hoping that neither of the boys noticed that she didn't have it. She resisted the urge to run, but made herself walk down the steps, across the quad, and out through the gate onto Morningside. As she walked the three blocks to the apartment, a wild giddiness lifted her. How easy! How well planned and smart! Now that it was finally happening, the action was simple. Elegant. A piece of cake. She will meet Mojo at the apartment and they will drive off in the car that Janey will have delivered, call the authorities from a phone booth to claim the bombs for Fishbone, and then drive back to Berkeley before anybody can connect them, personally, to it.

When she got back to the apartment, Mojo was already there, pacing up and down the length of the shabby living room where their clothes and boxes of tools sat next to the door. The blue wool of his knitting poked out of the top bag.

"Where the fuck is she?" he said, through clenched teeth.

"Who, Janey?" she asked.

"Yes, Janey," he said. "Who do you think? Anita fucking Bryant?" He twitched the curtain back and peered out to the street. "Oh, this is just fucking brilliant. We've got two live ones on location and there's no car. We've got a box full of bomb makings here and no car to move them with. We're screwed."

Lucy looked out the window, too, not sure what kind of car she might be looking for but not seeing Janey or Jack on the street. Mojo walked the floor, muttering under his breath, then threw open the door.

"Wait here," he said, as if it were her fault that Janey hadn't shown up. "Watch for me. When I bring a car around, grab the stuff and get in. Smooth, not in a panic. But move it. You got that?"

She nodded. She had never seen him like this.

Ten minutes later he double-parked a dirty white Rambler in front of the building. She had a paper bag with their laundry in it, their duffel bags, and a heavy box of leftover bomb makings. She couldn't carry all of it at once. She picked up the laundry bag and the duffels and went down the stairs. In the foyer the bottom of the bag ripped out, dumping their clothing all over the hall. Mojo came in and, seeing her struggling, picked up the dirty clothes and stuffed them into the backseat of the Rambler.

"Hurry up, hurry up, hurry up," he muttered, putting the duffels into the backseat before letting her into the front. She got in and he pulled away from the curb, making a great effort not to squeal out or speed. She thought about the box of wires, batteries, and tools left in the foyer, but didn't have the nerve to tell him.

The Rambler was at least ten years old and the seats were worn to threads. There were women's sunglasses on the dashboard and a dog-eared paperback copy of *In Cold Blood*. The car made a grinding sound when he gave it gas but it moved into the stream of cabs going north.

"This piece of shit was the best I could do. There's always somebody who leaves their car keys on the visor. Especially with a wreck like this, people actually hope someone will do them a favor and take it."

She turned to him, reality dawning on her. "You stole this?"

"Well, I didn't *buy* it." He glanced at her. "After leaving a parcel of dynamite in the john at Columbia, you're worried that I stole a shitty old Rambler? Come on, Luce. Grow up."

"But won't this make it that much easier to link us to the bombs?"

He looked exasperated. "What did you want me to do? Buy bus tickets? We have to head west. If we stay off the main highways and drive at night, we'll be okay until we can get in touch with somebody in the organization who can meet us with a clean car."

Traffic slowed to a rush-hour crawl. She timed it on her watch: It took twenty minutes to go one block. They waited in a sea of taxis at a light on Broadway, then inched their way up to 181st Street and the George Washington Bridge. Whenever the traffic started moving, he gripped the wheel and drove the little Rambler with his entire body, forcing his way between cabs and through intersections, propelling the car forward as if by sheer will toward the parkway and the bridge. The sky turned indigo except for a wide magenta streak in the west. Lights started coming on. Mojo squirmed behind the wheel, there was a slick of sweat on his forehead.

"We've got to get over the bridge."

Lucy looked at her watch. It was seven o'clock. "We have time," she said.

She could see him clutch at her reassurance even in the midst of his fury. He seemed much more afraid, much more nervous than she was. He punched at the buttons on the dashboard, adjusted and readjusted the rearview mirror. His left knee jiggled like a junkie's.

It was slow and excruciating but eventually they crossed the parkway and got on the bridge. Mojo took a shaky breath. The cables sang as they picked up speed. Lucy's feeling of exhilaration returned. She was aware of a distinct regret that she wouldn't be there to see the explosion in East Hall at Columbia, would miss the evidence of her handiwork, the smoke and fire and hullabaloo. She wondered how much damage there would be. The interior would certainly be damaged, but how much? They really didn't know how powerful the dynamite was. They had guessed at four sticks for each bomb. She hoped it was enough.

By the time they were over the bridge and into New Jersey it was completely dark and she was certain that she'd connected the final wiring incorrectly. The bomb would be a dud. How could it possibly go off? After all the practice runs, being careful to not complete the wiring, maybe she had merely repeated the actions of the rehearsals so that at nine o'clock the contacts would touch and nothing would happen. Suddenly she was sure of it. Her bomb, her great political statement, would fizzle. Back in Berkeley the other Fishbones would look at her with contempt.

Both of them checked their watches obsessively as the time crawled toward nine. There were moments when it felt to Lucy like they were part of a prank, a huge childhood prank involving the ringing of doorbells and hiding, not two bombs exploding in recruitment offices.

The landscape of western New Jersey became decidedly rural.

Off the main highways, the roadsides were dark and foggy. Occasionally they drove through towns that she experienced as dim hallucinations of light rising out of the mist and then fading away. Mojo turned on the radio and fiddled with the tuning. He finally settled on a station that had news interspersed with rock and roll.

Just before nine he looked at her. "Should be lighting up about now," he said. They grinned uneasily at each other. Not one but two bombs, going off simultaneously at different "institutes of injustice."

Mojo banged the heel of his hand against the steering wheel. "The world is finally going to dig that we aren't a bunch of stupid, crazy kids," he shouted. "And we're not Charles Mansons, either. We're organized and we're fighting the revolution. We're the people and we're taking back the power."

A minute or two crawled by. One song ended on the radio and then Pete Townsend's sneering "fuck you" to the Establishment came on. Mojo sang along, adding his own venom to the stuttering words of "My Generation."

"I suppose we should make the phone calls," Lucy said. Meaning the calls to newspapers and radio stations. She had the list of phone numbers on a piece of paper in her pocket.

He pursed his lips, a familiar expression of disagreement. "After the fuckup with the car, I think we should bag it," he said. "Until we know what happened to Janey and Jack, we need to look out for ourselves and get out of this borrowed vehicle before we announce ourselves to anyone."

Again, the car. The car seemed to be the thing that scared him. It scared Lucy, too. Even though she knew that explosives and destruction of public property were grave offenses, those were crimes she committed willingly, against the system. The stolen car was hurting an individual, someone too poor to afford better than a beaten-up Rambler. From the looks of the sunglasses on the dashboard, the car belonged to a youngish, rather hip woman. She was just a struggling worker, an ordinary citizen, probably not pro-war or pro–Nixon; she was too poor for that. It wasn't right. It wasn't on the side of right, to steal from the people, and it bothered her much more than blowing up the government offices at Columbia and NYU.

"Then do you want to call Janey? She's supposed to be our point person. Or do you want to call Berkeley?"

He shook his head. "I don't know yet. Let's see how it went down before we do anything."

She looked at her watch again. The face was discolored and worn, but it kept good time. It said three minutes past nine o'clock. She had set it to match the clocks on the bombs. Even if the watch and the clocks weren't in perfect sync, the bombs should have gone off by now. She gazed out the window at the rushing darkness, empty now except for a sprinkling of yellow lights in the distance.

chapter 26

At Columbia, in the far stall of the main-floor bathroom in East Hall, Louis Nilon checks his watch. It is nine o'clock.

At the Garden, Ali stumbles across the ring and Frazier follows. The crowd roars. Louis Nilon notices a smell of electrical burning. He still doesn't see the book bag in the far stall. All he does is raise his head at the unusual smell.

There is flat silence and a sudden condensing force. Air, wood, plaster, brick, and human flesh momentarily become more solid, more concentrated, before the homemade bomb in the bag sends all the molecules, each one a tiny locomotive, rushing away at a terrible speed.

At Madison Square Garden, Ali goes down. The people jump out of their $150 seats and yell, raising fists and hats at the ceiling, at God, at each other. The ref counts, and everybody holds their breath. Ali, "The People's Fighter," stays on his back.

Uptown, at Columbia, plumbing bursts, plaster and bricks crumble, the old globe lights fly into a thousand shards. Louis Nilon falls. A long blade of porcelain eases into his abdomen and slices through the root of his liver. For a moment he's aware of the old red brick building coming down on top of him and water everywhere, as if he's in the Hudson itself and the current has him in its strong arms.

The water knows the way to the sea. It is impatient, seeking the lowest spot, and the lowest, and the lowest, because that is its nature.

Louis Nilon could as easily be a twig or an ocean liner as a man. He doesn't fight. He lets the river take him. He pulls Wilmia and the children in with the last contraction of his heart and then he has no choice but to let go.

IN TIME THE SIRENS COME. HUMAN HANDS AND ARMS PULL him out from under the pile of debris. The shard and the water have leeched his body nearly bloodless. Someone turns him over, and though his face is calm, it is gray and inanimate. His flesh hardens while the firemen wait for the Greek, who comes and puts his hands to his head, turns, and curses the ruined building.

"He wasn't supposed to be here tonight," the Greek cries. "He begged me to let him work. Who would do such a thing? What kind of a monster would do this?" He goes into his office and finds Louis Nilon's application for employment where there is a name and a phone number. He picks up the phone and dials.

The water is turned off at the source. The rubble smokes and steams. Louis Nilon is about to be lifted into the dark ambulance when Wilmia and Yvonne hurry into the quad. They move as if by hurrying they can save him. Out of respect, the firemen wait while Wilmia bends and puts her head to his, listening as if he can tell her where he's gone.

chapter 27

AT NINE-THIRTY, when Lucy and Mojo were wending their way west across Pennsylvania's back roads, the music on the car radio was interrupted for a news report.

"There have been two explosions tonight on New York City campuses."

"This is it!" hooted Mojo, and turned the volume up.

"Presumably more of the violence from the radical student left we've been experiencing lately. But this time a man is dead at Columbia. The U.S. attorney's office in New York has said they will prosecute to the full extent of the law. No group has identified itself as responsible. We'll bring you more as it comes in."

Lucy's ears pounded. The air inside the old Rambler was suddenly pressurized and threatened to flatten her. *A man is dead at Columbia.*

"Wait," Mojo said, and turned up the volume again. "What did he say?"

But Lucy had heard.

Though it was impossible. No one could be dead at Columbia. Not at East Hall. She'd been there every day for a week. She'd checked the lockup time of the building every which way. She knew that building was empty five minutes after she left and nobody was ever in there on Monday nights.

"That can't be right," she said. Her voice came from someplace behind her head and seemed to have no use for her mouth. But even as she was saying it she already knew it was true by the way she felt like she'd swallowed a bag of nickels. She knew by the way the words, A *man is dead at Columbia,* burned into her brain and took up residence in her heart.

"It can't be," she said again, refusing it as long as she could.

Mojo looked at her for a long second and now she felt as though she'd taken bad acid. Thoughts and possibilities of the worst sort sprang up and became real. "Do you think they're making it up?" Mojo asked. Then he pounded his fists on the steering wheel, making the little car jump on the road.

"How did you miss that guy?" Mojo yelled. "How could you be so stupid? You're a moron and I was a fool to think you could do this without fucking up." He smacked the wheel another time or two before he withdrew into rigid silence.

He drove with a vengeance, gripping the wheel at the top, straining to see as far as he could through the soupy mist on the road. A town emerged with an open gas station on the corner and he pulled up to the pump. The man who pumped the gas peered into the Rambler and, it seemed to Lucy, looked suspiciously at her.

"Why don't you go inside and use the bathroom?" Mojo said. She couldn't read his face. A *man is dead at Columbia* had turned everything into an accusation and everyone into a persecutor. She did as she was told. The attendant followed her into the building, sorting out the crumple of dollar bills Mojo had given him, and handed her a key fastened to a Ping-Pong paddle that said *Ladies.*

She peed, hovering over the dirty toilet, not able to think past that one statement: A *man is dead at Columbia.* She washed her hands and saw part of her face in the tiny mirror above the sink. Dead eyes looked back.

She came out of the bathroom, holding the Ping-Pong paddle key and for a second she was sure that Mojo had moved the car. He'd moved it so that someone else could pull up to the pump. He'd pulled over to the side of the building to check the air pressure in the tires. Something, anything, but what it was.

She handed the key back to the attendant, who stared at her as if he had bad news.

"Where's my husband?" she said, making the effort to pull on the persona of the road: Joan and Fred Williams, college students. "The white Rambler?"

The guy jerked his head toward the door. "He took off."

She followed his gaze, still expecting to see Mojo waiting with the car by the side of the road.

"Which way?"

The guy pointed up the road, the way they'd come from.

She blinked but she couldn't stop the tears from stinging. The gas station man watched her carefully. She didn't even know exactly where they were, only that they were in eastern Pennsylvania. She pointed the other way toward the direction they had been going when they stopped for gas.

"What's that way?"

"Allentown and Philadelphia."

She turned to the door, and then back to the man at the cash register.

"He'll be back," she said.

He looked at his watch with a somber expression. She noticed that the name over his shirt pocket was Glen.

"I'm closing up at ten o'clock," Glen said. "You're welcome to wait in here till then."

She nodded and found a place to sit near the window. She was aware that her circumstances had abruptly changed. She had three dollars in her pocket and the clothes on her back. *A man is dead at Columbia.* Now, she must take any help offered, however small.

At ten after ten Glen started to close up the gas station. He turned off the OPEN sign in the window. She was just about to leave and try her luck at hitching when a truck rattled into the station and a portly man got out.

"You closed?" he said to Glen.

"You headed to Philly?" Glen asked.

"I am, but I need gas."

"Tell you what," said Glen. "I'll let you fill it if you'll take this young lady to Philly. She's missed her ride."

The driver's name was Henry Baker and he didn't ask questions. He said he lived in Philly with his wife. They had two married daughters who lived in the suburbs. He'd been up to his brother's farm helping clear some timber that had fallen in a windstorm over the winter. The timber would fetch a good price, he said. He chatted all the way into Philadelphia so that she didn't have to say much. She considered her options while he drove. She had nowhere to go. Mojo had ditched her. Janey and Jack seemed to have done the same. Or else they were caught with the car. Either way it wouldn't be safe to call Janey at her parents' house now that a man was dead at Columbia.

What did it mean? she wondered. Did it mean, absolutely, that her bomb had killed a man in spite of how hard she'd worked to make sure nobody would be in the building? Maybe the report was wrong. Perhaps a man did die at Columbia but not because of her bomb. Maybe he died for other reasons. There could be many reasons why a man would die at Columbia. Maybe he had a heart attack. Maybe he was shot. The chances of a man dying from the dynamite she put in the bathroom at East Hall were much slimmer. Weren't they?

It was unthinkable, but if it was true, if, by some bizarre stroke of bad luck her bomb exploded in the bathroom and someone was in the building, the cops would be after her. She thought of the recruiters. How long before they gave the pigs a description of her? How long before she was officially wanted, her name and picture on the walls of post offices all over the country?

She had to do something. She had to make a move, not just go where her luck took her. Janey was out. Mojo was gone. Berkeley? Could she call Adrienne in Berkeley? If she really was going to be wanted for the death of a man at Columbia, it wouldn't take long for the East Coast cadre of Fishbone to give her up. None of them knew her; it was designed that way. So how long before Berkeley wasn't safe? She knew the answer. By the time she hitched across the country she wouldn't be safe anywhere.

She became aware that they were stopped at a streetlight and Henry Baker was asking a question. He was waiting for an answer, leaning on the steering wheel of his truck and smiling his wide gentle smile.

"Sorry," she said, "what did you say?"

"That's all right," said Henry Baker as the light changed. "I said, we're nearly there. Where are you going to in Philly?"

Indeed, the countryside had been replaced with buildings and lights. She gazed out the window, not knowing what to say. The towns they went through now came one on top of the other and each was as austere and blank as the one before, with the same thrifty houses set close to the road distinguished only by variations of brambly hedgerows and pinched metal awnings. She became exquisitely aware that she had nowhere to go.

"Well," said Henry Baker, "would you like to come to my house and use the phone? You can maybe call someone?"

And all she could think was, if he knew a man was dead at Columbia, he wouldn't be so kind.

"Do you have family you can call?"

She thought of her mother and father in Kansas City. And she thought of Adam in San Francisco.

"I'll call my brother," she said.

"All right," Henry Baker said, as though this was the answer he'd been waiting for. "You'll call your brother."

He skillfully navigated the narrow streets until they ended up in one so tight it was more like an alley. He turned off the engine underneath a tangle of black iron fire escapes going three stories up the side of a red brick building. They were met at the door by Henry's wife, Sheila, who took Lucy's coat and ushered her to a worn gray couch that hunkered beneath the one living room window. Henry indicated the phone on the side table.

"Don't rush her, Henry," Sheila said. "Poor love, maybe she'd like something hot to drink first."

Lucy pulled her money out of her pocket and showed them. "It's a long-distance call, but I have money."

Sheila waved it away. "Shush. You just go ahead and call."

They both sat rapt as she picked up the receiver and dialed Adam's phone number, but the minute Lucy heard Adam's voice she started crying, which sent Sheila and Henry scurrying into the kitchen.

"I'm in Philadelphia," she sobbed.

"Philadelphia? What are you doing there?"

"Adam, I'm in trouble."

His voice sounded every bit as far away as it was. "What kind of trouble?"

"I can't say. But it's bad."

"What do you want me to do?"

She sobbed, unable to speak. "I don't know. I need to go someplace. Someplace safe."

"You have to tell me what's going on."

She tried to control herself. She glanced at the kitchen and lowered her voice. "I did something. I can't say. But I need to hide. I need someplace to hide for a few days to figure everything out."

He was silent for a moment.

"Adam?"

"Yes."

"Don't hang up. I have nowhere to go. I need help."

"I'm not hanging up. Are you alone?"

"Yes. Well, no. This nice man gave me a ride to Philly and I'm calling from his house."

"How much money do you have?"

"Three dollars."

He groaned.

Panic ran through her. He was right. Without money she couldn't do anything.

"Can you get to the train station in Philly?"

"I think so. Probably."

"Put the guy who helped you on the phone."

"What?"

"Just put him on."

So Lucy called to Henry Baker, who came into the living room looking sheepish. She handed him the phone. He spoke to Adam for a minute and then handed the phone back to her.

"He's going to give you thirty bucks. It's all the cash he has," Adam said. "I'm going to send him the money. He said a train ticket to Boston will cost about twenty, so you should be okay. Catch the next train to Boston. I'm going to give you Aaron's phone number. Call him from the train station in Philly and tell him what time it gets into Boston. He'll meet you. I'll be there as soon as I can get a flight."

"Adam?"

"What?"

"You can't tell anyone where you're going or that you're going to meet me. Aaron can't tell anyone, either."

"Jesus, Lucy. What did you do? Never mind. Just get to Boston."

As soon as Lucy hung up, Sheila rushed into the room with a mug of hot cocoa. Lucy drank it. It was rich and sweet and it filled the emptiness temporarily. It tasted wonderful.

"May I use your bathroom?" Lucy asked.

She was directed to a door down a narrow hallway. In the

bathroom she wondered how long before the police in Philadelphia would be looking for her. She was easy to describe: long white-blond hair, Black Watch plaid skirt, blue coat. While she was drying her hands she noticed on a shelf above the towel rack, next to Band-Aids, Q-tips, and other bathroom items, a pair of household scissors. She picked them up and slipped them in her pocket.

Back in the living room with Sheila and Henry, she didn't offer an explanation and they didn't ask. Sheila patted her shoulder, handed her a brown bag lunch, and wished her good luck. Henry opened the door and followed her out to the truck.

He drove smiling gently at the windshield but not saying anything. The train station in all its dilapidated grandeur rose out of the mist. Henry stopped by the sooty columns at the entrance. There wasn't anybody around. He dug into his pocket and came up with a folded wad of money which he pressed into her hand.

"Take this," he said.

She took it. "Thank you," she said, simply, and she meant it. She got out of the truck feeling that she was leaving the last safe place. As she pushed through the dirty brass revolving door, she knew she'd never been more alone.

The high marble room made her feel exposed. She tucked her long braid inside her coat. She found the ticket counter and bought an $18.91 ticket to Boston. The train didn't leave for six and a half hours, at five forty-five in the morning, so after she called Aaron from one of the wooden phone booths, she made her way beneath the yellow, churchy lights down into the bowels of the station where the trains burrowed and screeched in their dark tunnels. Rounding a corner, she nearly ran into a cop who eyed her once and kept going. When she found a ladies' room on the lowest level, she hurried in, thinking that this was one place the cop wouldn't go.

She stood in front of a cracked sink that dripped water into a rusty drain and looked at her long hair in the smeary glass. She took the scissors out of her pocket and put the length of her hair between the blades. She hesitated, not because she was trying to decide if it was the right thing to do or out of some sentimental attachment to her trademark hair; she was past such things now. She would do whatever she had to do to survive, she recognized that instinct in herself. She hesitated only to determine what would make her look different from her usual self but still not draw unnecessary attention. Short, obviously, but since she couldn't give herself a real beauty shop haircut, short short was not the best idea, she'd end up looking like she came from a concentration camp. She settled on chin length. Short enough that nobody could describe her as having long hair, but long enough that she could cut it off in a clean blunt line and hopefully escape notice.

She cut carefully but quickly, hoping no one would come into the bathroom. She tried to do a neat job, working around her head, struggling to get at the parts in back. Lengths of hair fell in lifeless ribbons onto the octagonal tiles. When she was done she had itchy hairs prickling her back underneath her sweater and a lopsided Dutch-boy haircut which she evened up as best she could. She picked up most of the hair from the floor and sink and buried it in the trash can, then she rinsed out the sink. When she'd got all the stray hairs she could, she locked herself in a stall, much like the stall in East Hall at Columbia, and sat on the toilet, where she bent over, cradled her head in her arms, and began to wait out the night.

chapter 28

JANEY WAITS at the receptionist's desk in Doreen's office.

"May I speak to Dr. Woods?" she asks when the girl comes out.

"Your name?"

Janey shifts her weight impatiently. "Sarah Calder."

The girl scans the appointment book. "Do you have an appointment?"

"No," Janey says. "I just want a word with the doctor, if that's possible."

The girl sizes Janey up. She isn't going to give up anything.

"The doctor is out of the office. One of the hygienists might be able to help you. Shall I get one?"

"How long will the doctor be out?"

The girl studies Janey for a moment. "She'll be back next week. It's a family emergency."

At the Woods house, Janey knocks on the front door, trying to calm herself. She looks in the windows and sees nothing that gives her a clue about where they are. She gets back in her car and sees that Pettibone has called her cell. She calls him back.

"We've got an indictment," he says.

"Without the other ID?"

"Apparently. But you should still get the affidavit."

"So do we have a deal?" she asks.

"I've been authorized to tell you we'll work with you provided you give us all of your information right away. Marvin Leach, the agent in charge of this case, has come out of retirement to bring her in. I'll send him out to apprehend her."

"Just a minute," Janey says. "Get more specific on the deal for me, will you, Bob?"

He makes a habitual noise that sounds as if he's dragging snot down into his throat.

"Maybe I can get a judge to agree to a lesser sentence."

She stares at the dashboard. "No good, Bob. It's not enough."

"Maybe they'll reduce it to thirteen. He's already served eight. With good behavior he can maybe be out in three."

She glances at the empty house. Pettibone doesn't know they're gone.

"Nope. He gets probation now or forget it."

Pettibone sighs histrionically. "That's not going to happen, and you know it, Janey."

She waits. She can feel him squirming.

"I'll try for you, but I can't promise anything," he says.

She can tell by his voice that he means it. He wants Lucy and he'll do what he can, but he can't say, 100 percent, that he can get Jack out right now. She can feel herself beginning to accept it even though she would like to force Pettibone to promise.

He says, "You're just going to have to trust me now. Give me her location and I'll do my best for you."

She hesitates, but she's already decided to take the deal. She knows that this is as much as she can get from Pettibone. This is her one shot. There won't be another.

"Done," she says. "Just give me a couple more days before I give up the location."

"You have forty-eight hours," Pettibone says.

She hangs up and considers what she must do next. The girl at the dentist's office said Doreen was away on a family emergency. Janey is sure Lucy's gone home. The question is, when will she be back?

chapter 29

IN THE end Doreen decides that she and Adam can't risk going to the funeral. Miles agrees. It would be madness to get caught now, when she's planning on giving herself up as soon as she's back in Denver. Miles and Ian go in their car and Augusta rides alone in the mortuary limousine. At the cemetery they stand in the back and Augusta occupies the one lone seat for family. She sits with her hooded eyes at half-mast, her short white hair breezed back, her back straight.

Miles feels self-conscious pretending to look like a distant relative of Ed and Augusta Johansson's. He suspects that he's failing miserably. As instructed by Doreen, Miles and Ian leave the grave before the burial is complete. Miles realizes now that what he has always believed to be Doreen's natural reticence was actually a skill she developed as a fugitive. She's always late to movies, preferring to walk in after the lights go down, while the previews are playing. At the end, she's the first one to jump up, even before the credits roll. It's something that's always bugged him, and they've had arguments about it. He would like to watch the credits to the end sometimes, and maybe sit together for a moment, like other people do, enjoying the afterglow of a movie, but Doreen will not linger. In restaurants, she insists on a corner table in the back, and must sit facing the door. Now he knows why she has the irritating habit of pulling the shades in the house at the first ashy sign of evening and even, sometimes, in the daytime. And her lack of friends and avoidance of social occasions, he can see, come from being a fugitive. All her little paranoias? It turns out she had good reason.

There are two men at the funeral, standing in the back. One is wearing sunglasses, the other isn't. They look disconnected from the rest of the group. He wonders if they're federal agents.

On the way back to the house, while they're still on the other side of town, he stops at a post office to mail the letter Doreen gave him. Before today the name on the envelope, Wilmia Nilon, would have meant nothing to him, but today he knows who that is and he understands that Doreen is sending her money, as she has many times over the years.

Back at the house, they hide their car with the telltale Colorado plates back in the garage before people come over. Adam and Doreen stay in their rooms, but Miles and Ian mingle, having decided that their story will be that they are Ed's nephew and great-nephew from Boston. And in case anybody starts asking them about Boston, they'll use their old life there as the basic story, changing their names, of course, and leaving Adam and Doreen out of it.

He's fascinated with Augusta, this formidable matriarch whose children are both fugitives and whose husband is gone now. She doesn't say much, but lets the neighbors and friends hold her hand and pat her shoulder. She accepts the casseroles and pies and fruit salads people hand her, and her face never changes expression.

A birdlike woman with a puff of dandelion hair introduces herself as Agnes DeVries. She holds out her trembling hand and looks up at Miles out of wrinkled lids spackled with mannequin-colored makeup that, as far as he can tell, does nothing to camouflage the dark veins on her upper lids and the sizable pouches underneath.

"Now, my eyes aren't so good for distance anymore, but didn't I see you at the cemetery?" she says, looking up at him intently.

"Yes, I was there with my son, Buck. My wife stayed home in Boston." Too much. He realizes he's saying too much.

"Your name?" she prompts.

"John Pelter," he says, as rehearsed, mentally crossing his fingers and thanking his colleague, the real John Pelter, for the temporary use of his name. He immediately feels shabby, lying about something so basic as his name. He wonders what thirty-four years of this would be like. "And this is my son Buck." Now he's repeating himself.

Ian shakes the woman's hand with an odd expression on his face. He hadn't wanted to use Buck Pelter's name. "I hate that name," he'd said, of John Pelter's sixteen-year-old son. "That kid's a dick." But Miles insisted they use it, just for the funeral, to keep their story straight.

"I've known Ed and Augusta since 1961. I don't recall ever meeting you before but I'm glad to see that Aggie has some family here," says Mrs. DeVries. Her sharp eyes take in every detail. "After what happened with the son and daughter, you know. And now she's all alone. She's had more than her share of hardship. But you'd never know it. Aggie never complains about her lot in life. You'd be hard pressed to find a more decent person than Augusta Johansson anywhere."

"I'm sure that's true," says Miles.

"But didn't you know the children? Lucy and Adam, I mean, growing up?" Out of the corner of his eye he's aware of Ian drifting away from the conversation. It is surreal to hear this old lady talk about Doreen and Adam as kids. He's starting to get disoriented. Wouldn't Lucy and Adam have met their cousins from Boston?

"No, I didn't really know them, Mrs. DeVries. We were in Boston and they were here. If we ever met, it was maybe only once, when they came to Boston on a trip."

"Oh, that's nice. I think I remember them taking a driving trip to New England way back when. We never had any idea they would go so wrong, you know. Well, how could anybody predict a thing like that? I always thought they were good kids. My husband, bless him, used to say that the boy wasn't quite right, if you know what I mean. I couldn't see it myself, but Bill was right. Of course, Ed and Augusta were the best parents you can imagine. They didn't deserve the terrible time those kids put them through."

He excuses himself and goes into the kitchen, where Augusta is cutting gingerbread and putting it on small glass plates.

"How're you holding up?" she asks.

"Agnes DeVries just took me apart," he says. "But otherwise, I'm okay."

Augusta snorts almost exactly the way Doreen does. "Ed used to say that Agnes ate his liver every time he had to talk to her. Do me a favor and serve these to people, will you?"

So he takes plates of gingerbread, two by two, out to Ed and Augusta's friends. While he has this task to keep him busy and give him reason to avoid conversation, he can delude himself that this is an ordinary thing he's doing, a commonplace occurrence, assisting his mother-in-law by handing out gingerbread on the occasion of the funeral of his father-in-law. But he can't get over the strange disconnect that he never knew his father-in-law and he's known his mother-in-law for less than twenty-four hours.

Later, after the guests are gone and Adam and Doreen have come out of their rooms, they sit around the kitchen table, in the dwindling light. The screen doors are closed to keep the bugs off, providing an effective blurring of the backyard. He watches Augusta leaning in to try Ian's iPod, the earphones in her ears, learning how to adjust the volume and selection on it, and suddenly Miles is furious at Doreen all over again. For blowing up the building, for denying them the knowledge of her parents, for keeping the most bedrock truth of her life a secret from him all these years. The light is dusty and soon the tiny green screen of Ian's iPod illuminates the faces.

"Do you have any opera on that?" Adam asks. What he means,

Miles knows, is does Ian have any music that Aaron would like, if he were here.

"Actually, I have some Aaron Star," Ian says. He must have translated the old recordings to CD and put them on his iPod.

"You do?" Adam says incredulously.

Miles can hardly bear how much he loves his kid right now. Adam takes the iPod and scans the dial, blinking rapidly and swinging his head like a wounded bison to see it properly, selects what he wants. Indicating to his mother to keep the earphones in her ears, he pushes PLAY.

They all watch Augusta listen to Aaron. Adam knows every nuance of the song playing in Augusta's ears now, and he is watching it play across Augusta's face. She listens with eyes closed for a while and then she looks up and her eyes spill over. She takes Adam's hand and holds it to the side of her face while the song plays out.

chapter 30

IT'S DARK and they haven't turned on any lights yet but Adam knows that isn't what's wrong with his vision. All of a sudden he can't see anything in the center again and his peripheral vision is blurry. It's as bad or worse than it's ever been.

In addition to the usual surge of adrenaline that goes through him whenever something new goes wrong with his body, he realizes that he's sick of it. Sick and tired. He's tired of losing one function and learning to accommodate, just to lose another. He's tired of being a good sport. He can't imagine losing much more and still living. He tries to ignore sudden near-blindness by thinking of other things.

His mother likes Aaron. She likes Aaron's voice. Adam thinks hard for a minute, trying to remember exactly why Aaron isn't here. He has the sensation of falling again, as though he were being dropped out of a helicopter. Aaron was just singing. Adam heard him. His head bounces up with the realization that he's sitting at the table in the house where he grew up. He can't remember getting here. It's strangely familiar and alien all at once. He wonders if he's been here a long time. It feels that way.

He stands up. Miles hands him his cane. Adam assumes it's his because Miles hands it to him. He wishes he could stay in the delusion that Aaron is here with him, that he can go to bed and soon Aaron will come to him.

———

Adam got to Boston the day after Lucy. He took a cab from Logan to Chinatown but the taxi driver wouldn't take him all the way to the address. He would only go within sight of the green arch that indicated Chinatown.

"That's the combat zone, there," he said. "I ain't going in there, man. You'll have to walk from here."

Adam got out. It didn't seem so dangerous, just poor and foreign. He walked past a pool hall where some tough guys were hanging around the stoop looking too bored to cause trouble, and down a main street until he found the side street. The apartment was in a stone and wood building above a food market where live fish swam in the window and chickens beat their wings in cages. Next door was an adult bookshop where round Chinese girls peeked from the covers of magazines. The wooden steps up to the apartment were on the outside, ending at a covered porch at the front. He knocked. He didn't know Aaron that well; they'd only been together a few weeks in San Francisco. It was a huge leap to ask him to take in Lucy.

Aaron came to the door in jeans with a short kimono over his bare chest. He kissed Adam on the cheek. Lucy emerged from the gloom of the apartment with buzz-cut hair dyed nut brown. She looked like a boy in Chinese pants and a blue denim work shirt, with black Chinese shoes on her feet.

He'd heard, just before he got on the plane, about the bomb at Columbia. Fishbone had been identified, but the Feds weren't yet releasing the names of individuals involved. He hoped Lucy wasn't one of them, but from the careful expression on Aaron's face and the shell-shocked look on Lucy's, he guessed she might be.

"Look at you," he said, running his hand over the bristle of her hair.

"Isn't she cute?" Aaron said. "We decided that she could pass as a boy. What do you think?"

Adam could see it. Lucy had always had that strong nose. Her hair had been her most feminine feature. Put long white-blond hair on an unremarkable face and body and people thought they were looking at beauty. And Lucy had always played it that way. But now, shorn and scared, the uncertainty and guilt shining out of her eyes, she might be taken for a thoughtful, delicate boy.

Aaron took Adam's bag and pulled him into the shotgun apartment. The place unfolded as they moved into it. The dark front hallway had one tiny bedroom to the side, Lucy's, he supposed. The hall opened to a good-sized living room with the surprise of a large industrial skylight in the ceiling giving the room natural light. Behind that was another room that Aaron used as his bedroom, and finally at the rear end of the apartment a small kitchen with a fire escape out the window.

Lucy dropped into a chair in the kitchen. She startled every time a noise came from downstairs in the grocery store. Adam tried to think when he'd last seen her: it must have been a couple of weeks ago in Berkeley. She hadn't told him then that she was coming east or how deeply she was involved in Fishbone. Now, she stared at the painted boards beneath her feet. The misery coming out of her was almost visible, like zigzag hurt lines in a cartoon. She wouldn't look up.

"I finally got her to eat something a little while ago," Aaron said. He stood with his hand on her shoulder. "I think she might be tired." Lucy got up, slowly, like an old woman, and shuffled off to her bed.

Later, after he and Aaron had eaten, Adam looked in on her. She slept as if it were work, her face concentrated on her dreams. Her arms were wrapped around her skinny body and her knees curled up to her chest. She looked like the Vietnamese children he'd seen sleeping on the street, always in the position of last resort.

At first he was just visiting. And Lucy was staying there to hide and marshal her strength before she made her next move, whatever it might be. She said very little, those first few weeks. She didn't leave the apartment, but stayed curled on the narrow bed in her dark room. Adam sat with her and listened when she wanted to talk. He made her rice and vegetables. He treated her as if she were recovering from a serious illness, and she was: the abrupt severing of her past and future, family, friends, name, Social Security number, parents, appearance, ideas, loss of hair, and even, now that she was a boy, her sex.

A week became a month, and then two, and then he was building stone walls for an old guy named Stebbins Moranghesy. He liked the hard labor, the quiet, honest lifting and placing of rock and being paid off the books, no questions asked. Lucy's picture was all over the news. She was wanted for conspiracy and murder. It became clear that Adam was in hiding, too, was a criminal, too. When he flew to Boston he'd tossed in his lot with her, and tossed in Aaron's, too.

Aaron took it in stride. Like most of the people he worked with, the drag queens and club performers, Aaron used aliases and created new personas for himself both on stage and off. None of his friends paid taxes or voted or were fully accountable to the straight world. Mrs. Chen, his landlady and the owner of the two shops downstairs, only accepted cash and didn't care who stayed with him so long as he paid the rent and didn't notice the numbers operation she ran.

And then there was the surprise of love. The unexpected and rare love he and Aaron had. With Aaron, Adam knew he'd gotten another chance. In going underground with Lucy he'd traded a shit job and a couple of casual lovers in San Francisco for a mate and a good reason to start over.

chapter 31

DOREEN AND Miles and Ian sit outside in the dark while Augusta helps Adam to his room. Doreen has come to love the dark. Dark is safe. Dark is where she can hide. Even though she knows what she's going to do when they get home, she likes the sensation of hiding here, in the dark, for another moment. Ever since yesterday (was it only yesterday?) Miles and Ian defer to her needs for food and drink, staying or going, light or dark. It's heartbreaking, how they won't challenge her about anything now.

"We'll need to get up early in the morning," she says. "It's a long drive back."

Ian taps his fingers on the iPod dial. "What happens after that?"

It's odd not having to hide this part of herself anymore. She hates what she has to say next, but she's past caring how it feels to herself. It's how this is going to feel to Ian and Miles that matters.

"I'm going to start talking to lawyers. Right away. I want to find out what happens if I surrender."

Ian tucks his lower lip in and nods. This is hard for him.

"It may get nasty. That's why I think you should go to Costa Rica exactly as planned."

Ian tilts his head. It means, We'll see. It's a gesture he learned from his father. "Do you think the Feds or whoever will deal with you?"

That's the question. Will the Feds make a deal? Will they reduce the charges based on thirty-four years of good behavior? Will she be seen as a medical person, a doctor of dentistry, a wife and mother and law-abiding citizen for the last thirty-four years who made one bad mistake when she was still a child? Will she, possibly, be able to pay her debt with community service and a fine, a period of house arrest? Or will she be seen as a terrorist?

"I don't know," she says.

"Didn't the Weathermen turn themselves in and get off?" Miles asks.

She nods. "In the early eighties. A bunch of them came forward banking on the belief that the FBI evidence was illegally gathered. It worked. Most of them were acquitted or did minimal prison time."

Ian perks up. "So you can do the same thing, right?"

"That's where my case is different. I didn't go underground within the radical network. That's how I disappeared so successfully. Instead of meeting up with student radical friends and depending on them to hide and help me, I called Adam. I lived with Adam and Aaron in Chinatown and the FBI never knew anything about it." She's still proud of this, that she slipped the FBI immediately and completely. She knows they don't have a single verifiable location or identity for her in thirty-four years.

"So it's ironic, in a way, that going underground the way I did and staying away from the rest of them both saved me and wrecked my chances to come forward when everyone else did."

Augusta brings vodka and limes and tonic water and pours drinks.

"Adam's in terrible shape," she says. Doreen tries not to hear the accusation in her voice.

"It goes up and down," says Miles. "This trip is stressing him and making everything worse. He may regain it once he's home again."

"I wish you could leave him here with me," Augusta says. "But I'm afraid that once people figured out who he is, and, believe me, it wouldn't take long, we couldn't keep the police away."

"Would they really arrest him?" Ian says.

Augusta turns to Doreen for the answer.

"They would," Doreen says. "Whether they'd win at trial would be another thing."

"Well, it's going to happen sooner or later that he'll end up in a hospital," says Augusta, fiercely. "Surely you've thought about that?"

Miles answers. "He's been there before. He uses Adam MacFadden, not Adam Johansson, doesn't give a Social Security number, and pays cash. He pays cash for his drugs." What he should have said is that Doreen and Miles pay cash for Adam's drugs, but Miles is too polite for that.

Augusta says, "Wouldn't he be able to get some real help if he could get in some kind of program?"

"He's in a program," Doreen says, as gently as she can. "He sees doctors, a physical therapist. He's on a drug that gives him some relief." Seeing Adam must be an incredible shock for Augusta. Still, it's annoying how she assumes Adam's been neglected.

Augusta blinks her hooded lids rapidly and drinks some vodka and tonic.

"Lucy, you must talk to someone about sparing him. You must. Look at what he did for you. You owe him that much, for God's sake, so that he can come out of hiding and I can take care of him."

Doreen is stung. Not because it's untrue. It's true. And she agrees with Augusta, but it stings because in the nearly twenty-four hours they've been here Augusta has not once expressed concern for Doreen's safety or well-being. Only Adam's. What surprises Doreen even more is that her mother's attention still matters. She can't believe that it still hurts.

"I'm going to begin the conversation on Wednesday, Mother. Believe me, Adam is at the top of my list of concerns."

"Good, because, you know, he was only helping you. He wouldn't have got into this if not for you."

Doreen tries to think of what to say, how to respond, when the phone rings. Her mother goes into the kitchen and turns the light on before she answers.

"Hello?" she says. "Oh, hello, Jane."

Doreen jumps up and runs into the kitchen, signaling to her mother not to say anything about their being there. Augusta nods. Her posture, the set of her jaw, says she's tired of humoring Doreen's paranoia.

"Oh, he passed away on Friday, Jane. The funeral was today." She looks up at Doreen and performs another exaggerated nod. She speaks a little too loudly.

"What? No, neither of my children came. I haven't heard from either of them. I've been without them for so long it hardly matters anymore." And now Augusta lowers her voice conspiratorially. "*But Jane, all of my out-of-town guests are leaving tomorrow. Do you understand me?*"

Augusta looks up at Doreen to see if her words hit a nerve. "Thank you, Jane. I'll keep that in mind. Thank you for calling, dear."

THE WEATHER TURNED BITTER IN THE FIRST FEW DAYS SHE was in Boston with Aaron and Adam. There were record low temperatures for March and snow on the ground. Like an invalid, she didn't leave her little room much and the apartment not at all. Adam brought her stories about people ice-skating on the pond on the Common and shoveling out parking spaces and then reserving them with folding lawn furniture. It sounded to Lucy like something he made up to entertain her.

She slept more than she was awake. She tumbled into pitch-black sleep at night and napped, curled in fetal position, several times during the day. It was as though she were sleeping through the winter, waiting for true spring, when she would emerge as the person who belonged to the short brown hair and androgynous Chinese clothing. The person who may or may not be a boy. The person who didn't have a name.

Adam and Aaron tried calling her various names, agreeing that using Lucy was a bad idea. Enamored of the idea of her as a boy, they tried: David, Lawrence, James, Percy. None of them stuck. Eventually they always came back to calling her, simply, Lou. She didn't care. She wanted to forget everything. She wanted to forget she ever had a name.

Sometime in April, on a day when Adam was working on a stone job all day and Aaron was at the theater rehearsing, she got up and started moving around the apartment. The day was so warm and sweet that she tried to open the window in her room. It opened onto an internal air shaft that brought the smell of rotting fish and garbage into the apartment. She quickly closed it. Out the window of the front door she could see the WELCOME TO CHINATOWN sign painted on the side of a building a few blocks away. She opened the door a crack. A highway somewhere far off roared its endless soft wave of sound. A seagull cried, and she realized that water was close by, though she wasn't sure exactly where. She was a thin, white, nocturnal creature blinking at the light, sniffing at the sky and the smells of the grocery downstairs.

As the spring wore on, she ventured farther out onto the porch until, by May 1, she sat on a chair at the rail and watched the people come and go downstairs. She studied tops of heads, some with hats, most with straight black hair, one or two with no hair at all. She liked the rhythms of their language. She liked it that she didn't have to bother to understand. It comforted her, how foreign it all was. It made her feel as though she was a long way from Lucy Johansson and the men who hunted her.

Mrs. Chen, the woman who owned the building, had a voice like a crow and she cawed from deep inside the store. There was a skinny delivery boy who rode a heavy black bicycle fitted with a basket on the handlebars. He seemed to be about fourteen years old and never spoke or smiled. He entered the store looking down at his feet. Mrs. Chen's voice always gained volume and speed when he came in and she didn't let up until he emerged with his delivery and mounted the bicycle. Mrs. Chen followed him out to the curb sometimes, haranguing him in rapid-fire Chinese and flapping her black sleeves at him as he pedaled away from her abuse, the delivery item in the basket. Usually he carried something wrapped in paper. Fish, Lucy supposed. Sometimes he carried boxes of packaged foods and greens of a sort Lucy had never seen before. Once he came back with two live chickens, their feet tied together. Mrs. Chen ran out to meet him, her hoarse voice competing with the squawks of the flapping birds.

The evenings grew long. Now Adam sat with her, covered in stone dust after his workday, and they watched the sky turn gradually darker over the highway until the neon lights of Chinatown and the combat zone buzzed on. On the rare nights that Aaron didn't have a show he joined them, drinking glasses of red wine that stained his mouth.

One day, when Adam and Aaron were both at work and Lucy was inside, lying in bed, not thinking, not doing, someone knocked hard on the door. She froze, afraid it was the police, until she heard Mrs. Chen's abrasive voice call through the door, "Sick boy. You take soup. Very, very good for you." Then her footsteps clumped back down the stairs.

Lucy waited as long as she could stand it and then opened the door. A round metal box with a lid sat on the peeling boards. She picked it up by the handle. The heat of the soup nearly scalded her hand. It gave off a wonderful smell.

The soup tasted spicy and strong. She ate it fast, sucking the noodles in and gobbling the chicken. She tried not to think of the two birds on the delivery boy's bike. Adam and Aaron cooked vegetarian things: tofu, brown rice, steamed vegetables, and it had been months since she'd had meat. It had been longer than that since she had anything that tasted so good. She drained every drop of broth and then washed the metal box.

When Aaron and Adam got home later, she showed them the box. "She knows I'm here."

"What did you expect?" Aaron said. "You're out there watching them every day."

Lucy was astonished. "But she never looks up. How did she see me?"

Aaron shrugged. "She knows. She knows exactly how many people live here. She asked me the other day who you were. I told her you were Adam's sick brother."

Lucy handed him the box. "Will you thank her for me?"

Adam said, "You should return the box yourself and say thank you. If you build an identity as my little brother here in Chinatown, it's going to keep people from getting suspicious."

The thought of speaking to anyone but Aaron and Adam was terrifying. She had convinced herself, without really thinking it through, that she would never go out, never speak to a stranger again. Her life had been funneled narrower and narrower until it consisted of the apartment, Aaron and Adam, and watching the comings and goings at Mrs. Chen's grocery store. She was surviving by staying inside that magic circle, it didn't matter that the circle was small. But Adam and Aaron insisted, so the next morning when the store was quiet and Mrs. Chen's voice had come to a stop, Lucy crept down the stairs to the grocery door. Cement steps led down into a room painted bright yellow-green, illuminated by a bare bulb. Shelves on the walls were packed with food, floor to ceiling. The live chicken cage sat next to the plucked dead chickens and skinned pigs in the window. A carp swam lazily in the brown water of the window tank.

Lucy made her way down the narrow center aisle to the back

of the store where Mrs. Chen was cutting open cartons of boxed noodles with a long, ivory-handled razor.

"You like soup?"

Lucy nodded. "Thank you." She held the soup box out at arm's length.

Mrs. Chen's eyes moved over her from top to bottom and back up again as she accepted the box.

"Betta now?"

"Yes, thank you," Lucy said.

"Hand," said Mrs. Chen, and held out her own.

"Pardon?"

"Hand," Mrs. Chen said impatiently, pointing at Lucy's hand.

Lucy extended it. Mrs. Chen squinted at the palm, stroking the skin.

After looking for a long time, Mrs. Chen said, "Many little pigs and fishes. Hard, hard to catch. Never together. But you must. Fix nets and fences and bring together."

chapter 32

"I'M GOING to bed," Doreen says. She kisses her mother's cheek coldly, Ian's with affection. She trails her hand along Miles's shoulders on the way into the house. It's an invitation, Miles can tell, for him to join her. He wants to. The thought of slipping into bed with Doreen sounds better than anything. Even so, he hesitates, and stays with Augusta and Ian.

"I'll be up in a minute," he says to Doreen's retreating form.

Augusta strikes a match and lights the citronella candles on the table. The flames illuminate the deep lines and hollows of her face and the smooth, healthy strength of Ian's.

"She's always been like that," Augusta says.

"Like what?" Miles asks, though he thinks he knows what she means. He expects that she's going to say that Doreen has always kept things to herself; has always licked her wounds in private; has never been one to cry in public and expect someone else to make it better.

"Aloof. Bitter. Arrogant."

He sits back, stung. "I don't see her that way. I see strength and the opposite of self-pity. The secrecy always bothered me, but now I know why she was that way. I see concern for all of us. She might seem arrogant but she's not."

Augusta takes a deep drink. "She always thought she knew what was best. When she was in grade school she didn't like it that the girls had to wear skirts. So she wore blue jeans to school and got sent home. Next day, I couldn't talk her into wearing a skirt, so she wore her blue jeans and got sent home again. It went on that way until the principal finally called me. What a mess that was."

Ian stirs in his seat. "Mom was an advocate for girls' rights in grade school? Cool."

"She had a troublemaker streak. She went off to college so sure the war was wrong and so sure the young people were going to change it. I knew she was going to get into trouble somehow. She ruined her life. And Adam's. And yours."

"I don't think our lives are ruined," Miles says. "And the Vietnam War *was* wrong. Everybody knows that now."

Augusta leans her face into her arthritic hand and looks at him.

"She ruined her father's life," she says, levelly. "And mine."

"But you were so happy to see her yesterday," Miles says.

"Of course I was. I'm happy to see both of my children and to meet you. I never stopped loving her all these years. But that doesn't change the damage she's caused."

He doesn't know what to say. It's true and yet not. He would like to see Augusta proud of her daughter's accomplishments in spite of the trouble in her past. He hasn't heard Augusta say anything positive about Doreen's career or marriage. Augusta hasn't expressed to Doreen her pleasure in the discovery of a grandson. Miles notices that Augusta's anger acts like a bucket of water on his own. It all seems so silly, so stupid, really, to be mad at Doreen for something she did before he knew her. He wants to defend Doreen, but this is old, old anger of Augusta's and she buried her husband today. So he will leave it for another time.

He stands up. "I'm going to say good night," he says, formally. And to Ian: "Don't stay up too late." Then he climbs up the old staircase and lets himself into Doreen's childhood bedroom.

The windows are open, causing the curtains to rise on sweet-smelling Kansas breezes. He takes off his clothes and gets into the small bed. Last night they bumped into each other every time one of them turned. Now he has to wrap himself around the sleeping Doreen to keep his ass from hanging over the edge. He pulls her to him so that her bum fits in the curl of his lap. He enjoys the erection that results. He'd be happy just to hold her while she sleeps, but her breathing changes and he knows she's awake and aware of the presence of the boner between them.

"Sorry to wake you," he whispers.

"It's okay," she whispers back.

He brushes his hand along the length of her stomach. She's sleeping in a T-shirt and underpants. Something she never does at home. He puts a finger under the elastic of the underpants and snaps it, gently.

"What are these?"

She laughs. "I forgot to pack a nightgown."

"Why don't you take them off? It's too hot to wear all of that to bed."

She hesitates. "You mean sleep naked in my parents' house?"

"Yes."

"I can't."

She's quiet for so long that he thinks she's fallen asleep. He's content with holding her, though his erection loses some starch. He's closed his eyes when her hand reaches back and curls around him. He smiles. It's almost like being teenagers, doing this in her mother's house.

"What are you doing?" he whispers.

"Nothing," she says, manipulating him so that her hand and the silky material of her underpants stroke him together. He's about to take it further when the thought of Doreen not being in the bed, not being in the house, not being in his world and Ian's world, grabs him like a seizure. All of a sudden the playfulness is gone and he is desperate not to lose her. He holds her tight, so that her hand stops. Hot tears run out of his eyes into her hair. He needs to see her face.

She turns over and now they are front to front, both lying on their sides. She takes his face in her hands. He can see her blue eyes even in the dark and they are wide with fear and sadness and something else: Shame? Regret?

"Are you afraid?" she says. "I am."

He holds her to him like she's a newborn. He cradles her head to his chest. "We're going to do the best we can," he says.

He strokes her hair, rubs her back for what seems like a long time. All the nights together, all the mornings, are contained in this moment. He's aware of the painful and precious understanding that this night could be the last one. Or one of the last.

The Feds. He imagines them as the two men at the funeral. They could come and take her away tomorrow; be waiting when they wake up. Or they could arrest her when they get home. The thought of her giving herself up, admitting a crime to the world, hurts only a little less than the FBI scenario.

He holds her and wills the moments to stretch. He wants lifetimes with Doreen to fill each one. He wants to lie here with her head on his chest, her breath coming slow and deep as she labors through the dark valleys of her dreams. He wishes he could help, wishes he could change what will happen tomorrow or the next day, or the next. But in the end all he can do is hold her and keep watch.

chapter 33

ADAM GREETS the creature who hovers near the ceiling. He's caught sight of a wing or a tail several times before but here she is, entirely, and she is magnificent. The face is alien with huge black eyes and smooth skin. She has long, pale, greenish blue wings worked through with burgundy veins, an insect waist made of tarnished silver with patches of black fur. She is almost human, or beyond human, in her capacity for compassion and wisdom. She makes him know she is wise and loving without saying a word. And he can see all of her as if his eyes and brain weren't failing.

Her breath is a rough purr. She floats above, infusing him with something akin to gladness. Being in her great cooling presence, drinking her in, seeing her complete form makes him whole in a way he hasn't been in years. He soaks it up, crying with gratitude, content to lie here and do nothing else.

But the door to the room, somewhere outside of his narrow field of vision, opens and yellow electric light spills in, sending the creature spinning into the corner of the ceiling and then disappearing.

"Don't go," he cries.

An old woman, followed by someone else, comes into the room. And he's aware that the disease is causing some dementia because suddenly he seems to be in his childhood room in Kansas City, a place he never wanted to go to again. But the disease has put him here for some devious purpose of its own.

The old woman takes his hand and sits on the bed, causing him to have to rearrange himself. It's a major expenditure of energy to move his limbs to accommodate the weight of another person on this narrow, soft bed.

"Adam dear, you've had a bad dream," the fiendish old woman says, just the way his mother did when he'd wake sweating and afraid as a child. It's devilish and terrifying the way this old woman has his mother's voice. It's monstrous. Surely this is the nightmare. He wills the creature to come back and scare it away.

The yellow light of the doorway is blocked by another large figure.

"Who's there?" he calls out.

"It's Ian." And, indeed, it is his nephew's voice, but he can't trust that the body is Ian's. It's huge and hulking there in the doorway. And what would Ian be doing accompanying the crone with his mother's voice?

Terror makes him weak. "Go away," he says with all the force he can muster. He has found that with these apparitions he can sometimes send them away. And sure enough, the hulking figure with Ian's voice turns and leaves. But the crone lifts his head and rearranges the pillows behind him. She holds a glass to his lips and implores him to drink. He touches his lips to the liquid but doesn't swallow. He knows that if he drinks it he'll be lost.

The crone whispers with his mother's voice. "Adam, don't worry. Lucy's promised me that she'll make sure you don't go to jail. She'll sacrifice herself, if need be, to keep you free. And as soon as she does, I'll come and get you and bring you here where I can take care of you. Don't worry, Adam. Mother's here."

Adam goes still. Like small owls or rabbits, his only chance is to freeze and pray that the monster will leave and that the creature will return.

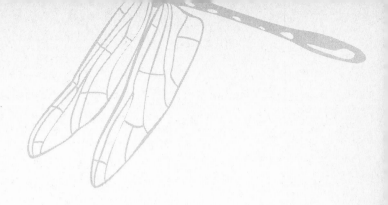

tuesday

chapter 34

THEY SHOULD have been on the road by
now. Especially given her mother's lack of control last night with
Janey, they should have been an hour or two closer to Denver and
the phone call she must make to Raymond Rhodes. Though Doreen has purposely, over the years, avoided any news about Fishbone
members, she has kept herself informed about lawyers and cases.
She reads the newspapers and notes defense attorneys the way other
people keep track of celebrities. Long ago she decided that Raymond
Rhodes was the lawyer she wanted, and the reasons are simple: He
takes difficult cases he believes in and he tends to win.

The car is packed. Everybody is up and dressed and ready to go,
but Augusta insists on giving them breakfast. She's made coffee and
set the table on the back porch. She's made blueberry pancake batter
and her old-fashioned griddle is heating on the stove. Doreen takes a
seat, trying to control the urge to bolt.

Miles is willing to stay or go according to what Doreen needs,
and Ian follows his dad's lead. Adam seems to be deep in his interior
world. He looks worn out. She wonders how much of what's going
on he's keeping up with. Several times while waiting for Augusta to
serve pancakes Adam turns his head sharply to the right, as if something has surprised him.

Augusta finally deems her griddle hot enough and starts flipping
the pancakes. In minutes that seem to take months she cooks enough
to fill a large platter and places it in the center of the table.

"Dig in," she says. She pours maple syrup on Adam's pancakes and then passes the jug around. She takes a seat and tries to feed a forkful of pancake into his mouth but he stops her.

"What are you doing?" he says, taking the fork from her. His expression is guarded and flat. Doreen can tell he's confused.

"Mom always did make the best blueberry pancakes," she says to him, as a prompt. He twitches and looks at Augusta out of the sides of his eyes. Then he smiles an awkward smile, which, Doreen knows, is meant to cover up that he had forgotten where they are and that this woman feeding him is his mother. She's wondering if she should recap the trip from Denver to Kansas City and their father's death, when she hears the sound of the yard gate coming unlatched. Doreen is half out of her chair when she sees the white puff of hair and wrinkled face of Agnes DeVries coming up the back steps.

"Yoo hoo," says Mrs. DeVries, shading her eyes with her free hand.

Doreen sits back down. Mrs. DeVries has seen her. Adam is oblivious, staring at his own thoughts as Augusta puts more pancakes on Ian's plate.

"Hello, Lucy," Mrs. DeVries says slyly, clearly delighted with her discovery. "And Adam, too. Oh my."

Augusta goes on eating. "Agnes, you startled us," she says.

"I can see that," says Mrs. DeVries. She turns to Miles and wags a finger at him. "You told me a fib yesterday, didn't you? You're not a cousin."

Miles immediately looks guilty. Augusta presses both hands to the table as though she were going to get up, but doesn't. "Now see here, Agnes. These are Ed's relatives from Boston."

Mrs. DeVries tucks her chin in and smiles. "Of course they are, dear. Don't worry, your secret is safe with me. I won't tell a soul. I'm glad you're here for your poor mother," she says to Doreen. She puts a plate of brownies on the table. "I only dropped by to bring you these. A lady in my bridge club made them."

She retreats the way she came in and Doreen hears the metallic sound of the gate latching. The five of them sit in stunned silence for a moment. Ian looks at Doreen to see how serious the breach is. Doreen is the first to speak.

"Well, that's it. We've got to go. Now," she says, standing up.

Augusta sits back in her chair. She won't be roused. "Agnes DeVries is a busybody but she's not going to turn you in. I suspect she guessed you were here and just wanted to take a peek. She's harmless, Lucy."

Doreen can't believe her mother thinks the danger is minor. "Really, Mother? How do you know that?"

"I just do. She's a very loyal friend to me, and for that reason alone, she wouldn't do anything stupid."

Doreen tries to give her mother a hard stare. She tries to pretend, just for the moment, that her mother is a difficult patient, a "green-stripe," as Fern would say, who must be managed. She can't do it.

"You want me to risk everything based on Agnes DeVries's loyalty to you?"

Augusta's eyebrows go up and she stares back at Doreen until Doreen breaks away and turns to the three men at the table. She does not wish to be caught here, of all places, flushed out by Agnes DeVries. She will call Raymond Rhodes as soon as they get to Denver. Maybe it's putting off the inevitable for as long as possible but she wants to be in her own house, in her own life, before she makes that call. But she will call and she'll do it as Doreen Woods, *not* as Lucy Johansson.

"Move it, guys," she says. "We're out of here in three minutes."

LUCY STARTED DROPPING IN ON MRS. CHEN. AT FIRST SHE made up errands for herself. She went down to the store to buy fruit, orange soda, carrots. She always stopped near the door to watch the huge carp in the tank churn lazily in his brown water, bending his muscular body nose to tail to execute turns that never brought him freedom. The third time she came in, Mrs. Chen called to her from the back of the store where she sat cutting the ends off cabbages with her ivory-handled knife.

"What is your name, sick boy?"

Lucy provided the name Aaron and Adam were using. "Lou."

Mrs. Chen seemed to approve of the name. "Lu. You betta now."

The bicycle delivery boy and a man came into the store. The boy stood by, hanging his head, while the man argued loudly with Mrs. Chen. Then the boy followed the man out of the store. Mrs. Chen flicked her knife and a rusty cabbage stump landed on the pile at her feet. She picked up another.

"He is bad boy. He thinks he will make lotta money delivering for other people on my bike. Bah! I have no need for that boy." She flicked the knife and the stump of the next cabbage landed on the pile. She eyed Lucy.

"You know how to ride a bike, Lu?"

"Sure," Lucy said, tentatively. From the front of the store one of the hens twisted its head and Lucy could see its hard button eye.

Mrs. Chen's eyes narrowed. "Okay, you be my delivery boy. I pay you two dollar for delivery in Chinatown, three dollar central Boston, and five dollar if you go on T."

Lucy was amazed that anyone would believe she could do something useful. She wondered if she was capable of pedaling a bike and making deliveries or if she had become too insubstantial, too ephemeral, for that much contact with the world. But Aaron and Adam were always saying she needed to get outside more. And even Lucy was beginning to see that she couldn't hide in the apartment for the rest of her life.

Mrs. Chen went on. "I pay cash. No tax. Regular delivery every morning, every evening. In between, you stay upstairs, and if I need you, I call you." Mrs. Chen smiled so that Lucy could see that only the front teeth were the color of her knife handle. All the rest were gold.

DRIVING THROUGH THE SUNNY FARMLAND OF CENTRAL KAN-sas, passing cars and truck stops and farmhouses, she fusses and worries. It's hard to believe that anybody will think much of her sur-render. Will it matter to the people who own and work this land? Will they care when a student radical from the Vietnam era turns herself in? Will it touch their lives even a little bit? The crime was long ago. She has made herself into another person. Surely a jury and judge will understand that she has rejected her past and under-taken her own rehabilitation. She passes through several moments of near-tranquillity in which she feels herself to be a small organism in a world teeming with organisms. In this light her crime and her punishment make barely a ripple.

But the golden moment doesn't last. The next moment she's think-ing about Wilmia Nilon. She wonders if Mrs. Nilon will be at the trial, if she'll sit and watch as justice is meted out for her husband's killer. It's the thought of vengeance on Wilmia Nilon's face, a hard, condemn-ing look in her eyes that shakes Doreen. Her self-imposed penitence and rehabilitation aren't going to bring Wilmia Nilon's husband home again. Doreen's exemplary life won't make up for the hardships Mrs. Nilon has endured. Doreen feels that Wilmia Nilon would be justi-fied in wanting Doreen to go to prison. And she would be entitled to her vengeance. But it's not going to be up to Wilmia Nilon. Doreen knows that. It will be up to a handful of people, the individuals the lottery of the justice system appoints to her case, whether they are old enough to remember Vietnam and have an opinion about that, or born since then and ignorant of it. They will decide her fate.

———

Riding Mrs. Chen's delivery bike suited Lucy. She rattled it over cobblestones and pavement throughout Boston and Cambridge. She liked to keep moving and made it a challenge to herself to avoid stopping for any reason until she got to the next delivery. She loved speeding through logjams of traffic, snaking around idling cars. She loved bumping onto the sidewalk, dodging pedestrians in order to keep going. She grew strong from the exercise and earned enough money to help with the food and rent.

It was while riding the bike for Mrs. Chen that she started making up scenarios about Louis Nilon. Since she didn't know anything about him, she imagined him a lot of ways: he was a young man working at Columbia at night to pay his way through school; he was an old man whose life was almost over, just keeping himself busy; he was a middle-aged man who worked two jobs to keep a house, wife, and kids afloat. About the only thing she didn't imagine about his life was the night he died. In her daydreams she could make him be alive. He'd been safe at home the night of the bomb. He cleaned other buildings at Columbia now.

She delivered Mrs. Chen's groceries to homes and restaurants, picked up envelopes from businessmen and housewives and brought them back to the grocery. She worked through the summer and into the winter, when riding a bike was sometimes dangerous and often impossible. On the days when it was too slick or snowy to ride, Mrs. Chen had a man with a car make the deliveries.

Among the people Aaron worked with in the clubs and theaters there were masters of disguise, artists of switched gender and forged documents. He asked a few discreet questions and was given the name of a man on Broad Street, an A. R. Addison, who, for five thousand dollars, a huge amount of money at that time, would obtain a new identity for Lucy. Aaron and Adam came up with the money and arranged the appointment.

On an icy day in January, Lucy walked to the address on Broad

Street. The building was old and narrow, with dark, cramped stairs. At the top were three doors lit by a dim bulb. One had a red star on it; one a mélange of photos pasted over every square inch; the third, typed on a piece of white paper inserted into a small brass holder, read, simply, A. R. Addison, Esq.

Inside, A. R. Addison sat with his back to an eyebrow window that looked out onto the structure underneath Interstate 93. His desk was an old wooden library table with neat stacks of paper and an upright black typewriter on it. Filing cabinets lined one wall, books the other. A. R. Addison, himself, was a small man with rimless glasses, wearing a shirt that bore the creases from being boxed at the laundry. His vermilion bow tie was the only spot of color in the room. With his startled expression and habit of muscular tension, A. R. Addison gave the impression that he was perched there only briefly; that with the next strong wind he would be off, leaving this tidy room behind.

"May I help you?" he said, unsmiling.

She hesitated. Aaron said this guy was okay and that he knew she was coming. "I have an appointment," she said.

"Yes?" He stared impassively at her. She had a flattening moment of extreme anxiety. Maybe this was a trick. Maybe this was some kind of a trap.

"Yes," she said, and her voice quivered. "Weren't you expecting me?"

"Your name?"

Now she understood. Aaron had given her the name to use.

"Terry Wilson," she said. She stayed near the door, her ears trained on the narrow stairway. If police came up the stairs she would be trapped in here. Still, she had her hand on the doorknob because it felt like the safest place to be. A. R. Addison abruptly swung his desk chair to a nearby file cabinet and pulled out a khaki green file folder.

"Sit down, Miss Wilson."

So he didn't buy the Chinese boy clothes and the butch haircut. She sat in the chair facing him, her back to the door. Since Columbia she hadn't been able to keep her back to a door. She turned the chair sideways.

"Your year of birth?"

"1952."

"Very well," he said, as though he didn't approve of the year. He printed something onto a piece of paper and handed it to her. "Go next door to the photographer." He cocked his head in mild dismay at her hesitation. "Come back next week, same day, same time."

She took the paper and left the office. Out on the tiny landing she knocked on the door with the photographs. No one answered. She knocked again and the third door, the one with the red star, opened.

"In here," said the woman. She was huge and wheezed like a broken accordion. She had a nice smile. She stepped back to let Lucy in.

"Sorry," Lucy said, squeezing past.

"Not at all. I'm Wren."

Lucy handed her the paper. Wren arranged Lucy on a stool in front of a blue backdrop and took three pictures. She had Lucy change into a shirt that Wren provided and took more pictures of her in front of a gray backdrop. On the walls were large black-and-white photographs that looked like rock or cloud formations. They had all the majesty of nature but somehow didn't seem to be land-scapes. There weren't any reference points for size or location, so she couldn't be sure. They induced a serenity she liked, though, as if she could fall down the vortex of one of the pictures and come out on the other side a different person.

"What are those of?" she asked as Wren worked.

Wren looked up from the camera. "Oh, just some shots I'm working on." She pointed at the smallest of the lot. It swirled and whirled to a dark center. "That one is the inside of an ear. I've got every orifice of the human body here and some animals, too."

Lucy looked at the photos again. She could see what she thought was the back of a throat in one. The branching vessels of the back of a retina in another. "How do you do that?"

Wren shrugged. "I'm working with some guys over at MIT. They've got cameras that are so small they can go into the body."

Wren turned off the hot lights. "You're all set. I'll give these to Mr. Addison when they're ready."

A week later Lucy went back to the Broad Street building. A. R. Addison greeted her with slightly more warmth.

"Come in, please." He swung around to a cabinet and pulled out a file.

"Here we are." He spread out the documents on the table. Lucy came forward to see them. There was a birth certificate with a genuine-looking stamp and signatures, an ID with her picture for the University of Massachusetts, a high school diploma and transcript, and a Social Security card. She sat in the chair and looked closer. The name on all five documents was Doreen MacFadden.

"The Social Security number is absolutely solid. So is the card. That's the most important piece of your new identity. Come up with a signature and sign the card. Memorize the number, it's yours now. Keep the card somewhere safe, don't carry it on you. Doreen MacFadden was born on July 6, 1952. That's your new birthday. The real Doreen Mac-Fadden died a week later. This birth certificate is a good fake, but don't depend on it as much as the Social. The UMass ID is only good for a photo, don't try to use it at UMass. The high school stuff is fake."

He looked up. "Do you know how to drive a car?"

"Yes," Lucy said.

"Good. You take the birth certificate, the UMass ID, and the Social Security card and you apply for a driver's license. A legitimate driver's license. Once you have that, you start building the identity.

You get a library card. You open a bank account. You get a job with pay on the books. You start paying income tax. Apply for a credit card or buy something on credit. Get a Filene's card. You build the credit. Now that you're Doreen MacFadden, you don't do anything sneaky or on the sly. You do everything legit. You go in daylight and show your face. You don't hide. You become Doreen MacFadden. Do you understand?"

Lucy nodded. A. R. Addison handed her the documents and watched her put them in her bag. He stood up and nodded curtly.

"All right, then, Miss MacFadden."

At the door, nearly out on the landing, she turned. "Thank you," she said.

He nodded again and sat down.

She ran down the confining stairs, burst into the tepid January day, whispering her new name to herself. For the first time since Columbia she felt she had a chance. With the name and the documents in her possession she would begin again. She would be Doreen MacFadden, a girl with a Filene's card, a driver's license, and a job on the books. She would take no interest in politics and the war in Vietnam. Maybe she would be able to go back to college. She wouldn't major in political science like she had at Berkeley. She would major in biology, and forget about governments in favor of the tyranny of organisms.

She borrowed a car from a friend of Aaron's and got the driver's license. She quit making deliveries for Mrs. Chen and started a series of jobs in restaurants. Aaron kept dying her hair, but she let it grow and allowed herself to look like a girl again. Mrs. Chen still called her Lu, and seemed to take it in stride when Doreen started wearing skirts.

She took the college boards and did well. A year and a half after she'd gone underground, she got into Northeastern University. In her second undergraduate year, having become, even to herself,

Doreen MacFadden, she was flipping through a *Newsweek* at a magazine stand when she came across an article about the victims of student radical crimes. The article devoted considerable space to Louis Nilon and his family. She bought the magazine, took it home, and shut herself in her little room to read it.

At the top of the article was a photo of herself that she'd never seen before. It was taken at the Berkeley ROTC protest. Her face was contorted with effort, her blond hair flying as she shouted what seemed to be angry words at a stony-faced cop. The picture they printed of Louis Nilon was his wedding picture. He was tall and serious in his dark suit. His young bride wore a white dress with a ballerina skirt and carried a small nosegay. Her name was Wilmia. They were both lively in the eyes. She leaned into him, ever so slightly.

The article featured school pictures of their kids from the year their father died. Yvonne was a senior in high school, James a sophomore, Cheryl a shy-looking eighth grader, and Harriet a laughing fourth grader. The story told of the support from her community that Wilmia Nilon received after her husband was killed, how she went from having one job to three. In the three years since their father's death the oldest girl, Yvonne, a straight-A student and valedictorian of her class, didn't go to college in order to help her mother raise the other three. James enlisted in the army and went to Vietnam. He came back six months later with a purple heart, and missing his left hand. Cheryl dropped out of high school. Harriet was about to enter seventh grade and had a hard time remembering her father's face.

Mrs. Nilon was photographed sitting at her kitchen table. She was middle-aged and would have been beautiful if she weren't so worn. She was wearing a uniform, maid or waitress, and the crisp collar and jaunty pocket detail were at direct odds with the suffering earthiness of her face. When asked what she felt for her husband's killer (Doreen flinched at the word), Mrs. Nilon said it was up to God to forgive, but that she, Mrs. Nilon, couldn't.

Doreen threw the magazine in a construction dumpster on her way to work the next day, sickened and ashamed, and afraid that Adam or Aaron would see the article. She knew her parents in Kansas City would see it. And having lost both their children, now they would see the other family Lucy had destroyed.

NEBRASKA IS ENDLESS. THE ROAD IS A SERIES OF OVERLAPPING mirages in the sun. Doreen fidgets behind the wheel. Miles dozes in the passenger seat. Adam sits in his own open-eyed nightmare in back while Ian is alert next to him. Doreen turns on the radio and hits the seek button until she gets a station with a strong signal. The voice is clipped and hard. Sardonic.

"We're talking about the mother of an American soldier slain in Iraq who is camped out at President Bush's ranch in Crawford, Texas. She says that she's not leaving until the president comes out and explains why her son's death, and this war, is justified. It's turned into a spontaneous antiwar sit-in. Hundreds of people are camping out in the ditches along the road. We'll take comments from callers. Next caller, you're on the air."

The caller clears her throat.

"You're on the air," says the host impatiently.

"Yes, I just wanted to say that I'm glad that finally the peace movement for the Iraq War is gaining some momentum. She's getting a lot of press and it makes people think, so I think it's a good thing."

"Okay, you're delusional but you're entitled to your opinion. Next caller."

The next voice is male; oily and pugnacious. "Who does the woman think she is? She's using her son's honorable death in service to his country to get attention for herself and her misinformed little cause. I heard she already had a meeting with the president. Why does she feel she's entitled to another? Her son enlisted. He died and that's sad for her, but this is war. He died to protect America from terrorists and to keep his unpatriotic mother safe from Saddam's nuclear and biological weapons."

"The caller brings up an interesting issue," says the radio host, smoothly. "In fact, every American citizen has the right to petition the president for a private audience. Many do. But this woman thinks she has the right to cut ahead of all the other people waiting for face time with the president."

The next caller identifies herself as Sherry. Her voice is soft and sweet with a Midwestern accent. "But she wants to stop other mothers' sons from getting killed. The president lied. There aren't any weapons of mass destruction and Iraq isn't connected to Al Qaeda. And that—"

The host breaks in. "I'm gonna jump in here. How do you know the president lied? Do you have a direct line to the White House? Are you privy to everything that goes on in the Oval Office? Don't you get it? In war the president can't spill state secrets."

Doreen catches Ian's disgusted look in the rearview mirror and changes the station to one with music.

"Are you tired, Mom?" Ian says. "Do you want me to drive for a little bit?"

She realizes that she's exhausted. Her arms and eyelids are heavy. Her face feels as though it will fall onto her chest any moment. She pulls the car over and there is a general reshuffling of seat positions amid the sudden blast of hot, dry air as the doors open. Doreen moves to the passenger seat in front. Adam and Miles are in back. Adam seems agitated even when he's dozing. It will be good to get him home and back into Miranda's capable hands. Ian pulls the car onto the highway and the droning sound of the tires almost puts her to sleep.

"Mom?"

She leaves her eyes closed. "Yes?"

"Why did you do it? I mean, I know it was a long time ago and you're not that person anymore. And the Vietnam War was wrong. But still, why did you do it?"

If she could just zone out and not think about it, she would be happy. What a luxury it would be to ride along and go to sleep. She leaves her eyes closed to answer.

"For a long time I told myself that the reason I did it was because I was influenced by a bad group of people. In the last few years, though, I've been able to admit to myself what the deeper reasons were."

Ian keeps his eyes on the road and the car at the speed limit. He's a good driver. She feels safe with him at the wheel. She makes the effort to dredge up all the words, all the emotions of the time, and distill them into an understandable explanation for her son.

"When I saw the current administration send kids to fight and die in Iraq and start to bankrupt the country to pay for it, I remembered the way I felt in 1970 and '71. It was the same feeling of being hoodwinked by the government.

"I was frustrated and furious about Vietnam. I was heartsick at what my country was doing to itself and to the people in Southeast Asia. Most of America had bought Nixon's lies, but in Berkeley we thought we had the moral responsibility to fight against the Establishment."

The story sounds pretty good up to here. It's the next part that starts to veer off into questionable territory.

"We knew that nobody was going to listen to us unless we grabbed attention. That meant we had to be in the news. So we decided to destroy things, symbolic things, to send the message that what the government was doing was wrong and we, the young generation, weren't going to take it. Other groups were doing the same thing. We made ourselves the conscience of the country and we thought that every action brought mainstream America closer to our way of thinking. We were sure that kids all over the country would join us and demand change."

Telling it exhausts her. She's already sick of saying it out loud and this is only the beginning. Her eyes threaten to close, she could easily drift off into sleep and stop all thoughts, what a pleasure that would be, but she will tell it. First to Ian and Miles. Then to lawyers and judges.

"The group I was in, Fishbone, burned down the ROTC building at Berkeley. Nobody got hurt. The University of California got the message that the people didn't want officer training on campus. They stopped the ROTC program at Berkeley because of what we did. The bombs at Columbia and NYU were supposed to be the same. Nobody was going to get hurt. That was our first concern. We wanted to take a shot at the draft, the war, the administration, and the colleges that allowed the selective service to propagandize. But none of that changes what happened. I didn't know Louis Nilon was going to come into the building that night. I'd made extra sure that no one was ever in there after six o'clock on Monday nights. But he was there somehow, so I'm responsible for his death. My comrades, if they hadn't all scattered like cockroaches, would have said he was a casualty of war. But it doesn't matter what you call it. A death is a death, and his is on my head."

The three men in the car are the three most important people in her life. She has the distinct sense that she is hurtling with them at a fantastic speed toward a membrane they will be propelled to break through. Once on the other side, they will be in another world where even the air will weigh differently in the lungs and smells will sit differently in the nose. It will be an alien world where they will all have to learn everything from scratch because the membrane is one-way-only and none of them will ever be coming back.

chapter 35

ADAM WAITS for the creature. It's as though he is caught in a paralyzing dream. His body is unbearably heavy. The vibration of the moving car lulls but also makes his vision that much more erratic. The creature, in all her glowing green-white radiance, hovers just out of sight. Whether his eyes are open or not, each time the car hits a bump in the road he sees the creature, flitting around the edge of sight. He wonders, if his eyes weren't wrecked, would he see her all the time? Or not at all?

SOMETIME BEFORE CHRISTMAS, HE KNOWS IT WAS CHRISTMAS because there was a pathetic twig decorated with a few strands of tinsel in the mess at the base, they went out on another battalion sweep, trying to take out the hot spots command had identified. The battalion officer was Lieutenant Colonel George Bowman. He was choppered in to give them a pep talk before they hit the bush.

Bowman was a short, dark man with a patrician nose. He'd been in 'Nam since '63, and though he had the reputation of being a by-the-book Marine officer, the men all knew he was starting to lose it. His eyes were *sampaku*; they had a rim of white above them. His forehead shone and his jaw was stubbled. His uniform looked decidedly unclean, as if he had been sweating in it for months. The rumor among the men was that he was shooting smack, that he had both a gook wife in Saigon and a mistress in Da Nang, and the wife had paid thugs to cut the mistress's face from mouth to ear, destroying her beauty and therefore her value, which drove Bowman insane with rage.

On the morning of the sweep Bowman's eyes were bloodshot. The bags underneath were a shade of blue verging on black. He got to the point. "We have to clean up these known areas of enemy activity. The VC are slipping through." He made a strange weak gesture with his hands open, fingers spread, the gesture of a supplicant, not a commanding officer. Adam realized the lieutenant colonel was afraid. "Division wants a higher enemy body count. So, as a special incentive, the squad that makes the most kills today gets forty-eight hours R&R in China Beach." He waited. Was he hoping for enthusiastic cheers from the men? It took a moment before the men stirred and shifted, and finally, dutifully, broke into halfhearted cheers. But Adam could feel the drive building, overtaking the doubts, as the men contemplated an unheard-of two days off from the war. Seeing that they were sufficiently inspired, the lieutenant colonel got back in his chopper, saluted with a shaky hand, and took off.

Adam's squad NCO was a sergeant major named Gunny Belsky. He was a hotheaded Polish kid from Wilkes-Barre, Pennsylvania, with slanted-in teeth and small eyes that missed nothing. He wore a silver ring worked into the shape of a Chinese character, and a string of beads tight around his neck that made the veins above it bulge. He had an annoying habit of referring to himself using the royal "we." He assigned women's names to the men under him and used them with malicious delight. Tom Poole was Patty. Adam Johansson was Johanna.

"Okay, ladies," he said as they moved into the bush. "Make us proud. We are *going* to China Beach. Therefore, anything that's moving is a VC. Anything else? Shoot it anyway. Get ears for the count."

Adam looked at Tom. "Ears?" he said, under his breath.

The set of Tom's jaw was grim but carefully neutral. "I've heard of ears for beers before, but this is ears for R&R."

Gunny whirled on them. "You got a problem, Patty?"

"No sir."

Gunny's small dilated eyes skittered all over Adam. He looked like he was on speed. He seemed to be deliberating something but then he turned to the group. "We didn't pick this squad. You were assigned. But you will behave like marines and follow orders. Anybody showing cowardice or questioning orders will be dealt with. We don't have time to tolerate bleeding hearts. Do you know how we deal with cowards and homos, Johanna?"

Adam held Gunny's stare. He knew better than to weaken when he was being challenged. "No sir," he said.

"They never finish their tour. We don't bother with conduct unbecoming. We make sure they die heroic marine deaths so that their mamas can feel proud that their son died a man. But they never finish their tour. It's a service the marines provide. We call it fag fragging."

Gunny stared at Adam a minute more. "We'll be watching you, Johanna," he said.

The squad moved west for three kilometers and encountered no VC. The terrain became hilly. They found VC holes and spent considerable time gassing them but flushed out nothing. Gunny's agitation increased as the hours passed. All the time Adam could hear bursts of fire to the north and answering AK-47s.

"Goddamn," Gunny said. "They're getting all the action over there."

He grew petulant and reckless, crashing through the bush looking for VC. All around were abandoned holes. They passed through burned-out villages with Gunny pushing them, not bothering to check every hole, not always putting guys on point. Adam and the other grunts were getting nervous. They could sense the presence of Viet Cong, but none was visible.

They came to another burnt village. Clearly Americans had been here, maybe yesterday or the day before. There was only one hooch standing, but no bodies. Adam and Tom were crouching in the bush, watching the gaps in walls, when Adam saw a dark shape move just beyond the hooch.

Gunny opened fire. The other men followed suit. Adam aimed his M16 at the shape and sprayed the trees, the hooch. When it was quiet again, they ran in, a dozen brave marines, to kick open the door of the hooch. There was nobody inside. Beyond the hooch, where Adam had seen the dark moving shape, there was one Vietnamese boy, maybe twelve years old, wearing the loose black pajamas and coolie hat of a farmer, dead in the dirt. He had an ancient .22 in his hands.

"Is this it?" Gunny shouted, still breathing hard, as they all were, from the adrenaline. "One fuckin' gook? That's all?" He swiveled, his gun at the hip, looking for others, and then, realizing there weren't any, kicked the body, screaming, "I hate this fuckin' war." When he had kicked it enough, his knife was in his hand and with one quick, smooth flash he cut off the boy's ear and stuffed it into a cloth drawstring bag he wore at his waist.

"Let's go," he said.

They kept moving west, heading for the ridgeline. They climbed the slope to the ridge, all of them slow and despondent now, having spent their adrenaline. Adam followed behind Gunny, unable to take his eyes off the bag with its bloody prize. The point man at the ridge signaled that there were VC beyond. The squad moved forward, each man a quiet stalker, sliding through the green until they were all just below the ridge. Gunny risked a look over and came back to the squad, his carnivore's teeth bared.

"There's a bunch of 'em down there. Maybe twenty or so. We can pick 'em off like ducks at the fair."

They formed a line along the ridge. Adam and Tom Poole were among the last to move into position. When he looked over the ridge and down into the shallow dip below, Adam saw black-clad people standing around an open pit. He saw women. Some were holding babies or small children. He saw old people leaning on sticks. The few men were digging in the pit using marine-issue E-tools. Bodies, maybe fifteen or twenty of them, some of them shrouded but most of them not, lay in a line next to the grave.

Gunny held up his hand, ready to give the order to shoot. Adam turned to him. "But they're burying their dead," he whispered. As if somehow Gunny had missed that fact.

Gunny turned his head slowly, smoothly. He was a doorknob turning and Adam had no choice but to wait and see what was on the other side of the door. Tom leaned in and whispered past him to Gunny, "And we can pick 'em off like target practice, just like you said. Waiting for your order, sir."

Gunny made the neck-cutting gesture for him to shut up. He took aim. Adam followed Tom's lead and aimed down into the funeral. He didn't think he'd be able to pull the trigger, but when Gunny gave the order he aimed and killed exactly as the men on both sides of him did. He emptied his gun at every moving, living being in the gully until the battle silence came over him. It was so silent while the guns were spraying down and the people were dying that when the people had stopped moving and the guns stopped shooting, the noise that rushed in nearly deafened him.

The marines ran down to the dead Vietnamese to claim proof of the kill. Tom dragged Adam to his feet and forced him down the hill, too. Marines were cutting ears off the newly dead, as well as off the bodies laid out next to the grave. Tom pulled his knife and began cutting, moving faster than Adam had ever seen him move. He cut and cut and cut, his face fierce and intent on his task, his hands covered in gore. Adam vomited on the ground and Tom was suddenly next to him talking over the noise in his ears. His bloody hand was on Adam's back.

"They were already dead," he said. "Even if you had sacrificed yourself, you couldn't have stopped it. Now make it look like you're doing it or your ears will end up in Gunny's bag. Here, take these."

In a stupor, Adam took the bloody cloth bag Tom gave him. Then, at Tom's prompting, he moved to the next body and drew his knife. It was a young woman. Her black eyes were open and staring through him. Her teeth were small and pointed and bared as if to bite. She had strange, small, dark blue marks, crude tattoos, he realized, running across her browline that gave her the aspect of a warrior. She was thin and muscular in her unisex clothes, and in her fierce death pose, achingly beautiful.

He reached over and closed her eyes gently. Then he made the cut, surprised at how easy it was.

His squad didn't win the two-day R&R at China Beach but they came in second and so each man got an extra beer at the end of the day.

"Drink it," Tom said. "Gunny's watching."

Adam did.

HE SENSES THE MOTION OF THE CAR, FEELS THE PULL OF speed on his body. He feels the engine beneath him and the road below that. The creature hovers to his right. Her green legs and arms are folded into acute angles. Her face turns to him. The black eyes and pointed teeth are terrifying. But he can tell, somehow he knows, that the chimera is not evil. She's only waiting.

chapter 36

MILES DRIVES from the Kansas border into Colorado over prairie that gives way to refineries and factories, and finally, to Denver itself, spread out along the front range as far he can see. Night has fallen but the sky still holds enough light to keep it a deep dusty purple, and with the mountains muted and dark behind it the city looks like a huge ship in full running lights heading north along a hilly shore.

Miles turns on the radio and finds NPR. They're playing the BBC news.

Miles loves the BBC, especially the female announcer with her clipped enunciation and dry reporting. He imagines her, sexy and dark, in a small recording room in London where it is four o'clock Greenwich Mean Time, drinking coffee and reading out the news while England sleeps.

"In Iraq," she says, "there have been a string of major attacks and ambushes on U.S. forces in the last three weeks, including the killing of fourteen marines in the town of Haditha yesterday. At least forty U.S. personnel have lost their lives in the attacks. Violence has intensified ahead of a deadline for drafting a constitution. U.S. Defense Secretary Donald Rumsfeld said the new constitution will be one of the most powerful weapons against insurgents."

Miles chuckles to himself. The BBC commentator's deadpan delivery makes the idea of Iraqi rebels brought to heel by a U.S.-directed constitution sound ridiculous. It's the Iraqization of Iraq.

Just like the Vietnamization of Vietnam. He remembers how well Vietnamization worked.

He met Doreen in '79. The war was long over, Watergate was even over by then. It was spring. It rained constantly. He and Doreen were together every moment they weren't working. They slept together the first night and every night after that, and everywhere, in the papers and on the radio, it was all about the Vietnamese boat people, leaving their devastated country. He remembers seeing them on the news constantly, starving and half drowned, being turned away at ports in Asia, begging to be taken in. But nobody would. So they went to prison or perished at sea.

BY THE TIME THEY'VE SETTLED ADAM IN HIS HOUSE AND PULL up in front of their own, the sky is smooth and black. Trees whisper and a silky cool meets them when they open the car doors. They are home. The place of shelter and refuge. The place to recharge before they have to put on their game faces and do the next, unimaginable, task.

The three of them silently unpack the car. Doreen goes up to the bedroom. Ian calls his girlfriend. Miles escapes to the backyard and puts the sprinkler on the cherry trees. He stands in the dark, not wanting to think about what comes next, instead placing all his attention on the hypnotic oscillation of the water on trees and dry earth. The cherry tree leaves are shiny and wet. It reassures him that they never close their leaves, never turn away from water. Unlike human beings, plants never shun the thing they crave.

He's just beginning to pull shades and turn off lights inside, waiting until the last minute to turn off the sprinkler in the orchard, when there's a knock at the door. He looks out, dreading what he will see. He's sure that it will be G-men in black suits, but it's a skinny woman with wild red-gray hair standing on the front porch.

A taxi waits at the curb. He hesitates, not sure if he should open it or not. Doreen appears at the bottom of the staircase with Ian close behind her.

"Who is it?" she says. She takes a look and immediately opens the door.

The woman on the porch seems startled and a little confused. Her eyes have that slightly poached quality of the old or ill.

"Lucy," she says.

Doreen opens her arms and embraces the woman. "Adrienne," she says, and brings her inside.

"Oh, it's good to see you," says Adrienne, her anxious eyes bouncing from Doreen and Miles to Ian.

"What are you doing here?" asks Doreen. Her voice sounds like it's coming from somewhere deep inside of her. She asks the question as if she doesn't want to know the answer but can't help herself.

"Janey said you knew about it. She said it was a little reunion. I should have known better than to trust her, but I was hoping it was true. Then she stole the picture."

"Picture?" Doreen and Miles say at the same time.

Adrienne's mouth twitches to one side. She's even more uncomfortable now and she speaks in a jumbled rush. "We came to see you the other day. Janey found the key and came inside. I thought you were friends. Then she took a picture. I'm sorry, Lucy. I thought, I hoped, we really were going to have a reunion. I didn't realize until she came inside and took it. I'm so sorry. I came to warn you. The Feds will be here tomorrow or the next day, I think. Maybe you should leave tonight."

Doreen smiles a sad, sweet smile. She puts her hand on Adrienne's cheek. Just a quick, soft touch. Miles realizes that here is someone his wife knew and liked, that she has thought about this woman and wondered about her and he never knew she existed. "Don't worry," Doreen says. "I'm turning myself in anyway."

A small, dark figure walks up the sidewalk with the agility of youth. Selima slips through the door and tucks herself into the shelter of Ian's arm so that the top of her head rests at his shoulder. They stand as if they were made to fit together this way, as if this is their most natural and authentic position. It is as clear as a billboard that they are completely comfortable presenting themselves as a couple, that they are, in fact, a solid couple.

To a stranger who doesn't know them, this meeting with Adrienne could be the happy reunion of two friends who haven't seen each other since college, but from the strain on Doreen's face he can tell she's feeling that every minute the FBI are getting closer. Doreen introduces Adrienne. To Miles, Adrienne seems pathologically spacey, like some homeless people or people with Alzheimer's. He wonders what she was like thirty-five years ago, if she was always like this.

He's relieved when Adrienne finally says good-bye and gets back in the taxi. He shuts the door and locks it, a hopeless gesture, he knows, to keep out the forces that are already beginning to creep into his home. He gazes at the faces of his family, including the young woman who is the new but perfect addition, and asks, "What do we do now?"

Instead of answering, Doreen takes Miles by the hand and leads him up the stairs, leaving Ian and Selima in the kitchen. Miles is beset by a strange unreal feeling, as if all of his senses have gone synthetic. The couch in the living room, the sound of the clock ringing the hour, the color of Selima's hair are all distorted a shade or two beyond what his nervous system has registered as normal. The stairwell is wider and much brighter than he has ever noticed it to be before. It's as if this is an imagined alternative life he's stepped into. He has the embarrassing and incongruous feeling that he and Ian are two guys about to go off and get laid by their respective girlfriends.

Upstairs, Doreen shuts the bedroom door behind them and kisses him. The kiss is long and slow. Her eyes are open and looking at him, but he knows he's probably as fuzzy to her as she is to him, given that they've both been in reading glasses for a few years. It grips him then, the sense of coming to the end. Is it their marriage, their life together, that's ending, along with the identity of his wife, as he always knew her? She may go to prison. He read something, somewhere, about the statistics on marriages when one or the other is in prison. They're not very good. A vast, cold space opens beneath him. It's the same feeling he gets when he tries to think of distances between planets, or when he tries to contemplate the atomic or sub-atomic world.

The kids in his class at school ask him, sometimes, how old the earth is. He has a riff that he does to try to give them an idea. He tells them to spread their arms as wide as they can. He tells them that this is the area of time we know anything about at all and it is only one hair on a large dog, a needle in a haystack, of all time. Starting from their left hand, he tells the students to look at their left wrist. This is when one-celled life-forms appeared and the earth started to form landmasses. At the left shoulder the atmosphere becomes oxygen-ated. Past the head, the right shoulder, just above the elbow on the right arm is when two-celled organisms developed hard parts like bones, teeth, and shells which could be preserved as fossils. Traveling on to the top knuckles of the right hand is where the dinosaurs came and went. And humankind? He tells them to imagine a speck of dust on the very tip of the fingernail on their right hand. Here, he says, is all of human history.

But when he thinks about it for himself, his mind can follow such threads only so far. He'll be fumbling along trying to understand how many a million years is, and then struggling to conceive of what ten million years are, but when he tries to grasp what one hundred million or a trillion is, the cold emptiness opens up, vertigo takes over, and his mind backs away from the edge. If he's lucky he might catch a glimpse of something vast beyond words before his mind shuts down.

That's how it feels to know that tomorrow, or very soon, Doreen, who isn't really Doreen it turns out, is going to confess to killing a man. Things will start happening but he can't conceive of what they will be or how it will go. She'll stand trial, he knows that much. She may go to jail. She may never come back. His mind can't accept that she may never come back. On that thought his mind shudders to a stop.

He tries to get a grip on himself as they get into bed and hold each other beneath the odd chandelier that Doreen loves so much. He tells himself not to jump ahead. He tries to talk to himself as he would talk to a fifth grader or anyone, really, who came to him for guidance. Tomorrow will be hard. But tomorrow they will know more than they do today. Tomorrow they will meet with the attorney and start to assess the situation. They will begin to learn what they need to do. And then they'll do it.

chapter 37

DOREEN WAITS until Miles has fallen into a fitful sleep. She pulls herself out of the safety and comfort of their bed. She puts on a T-shirt and a pair of shorts and slips downstairs into the kitchen, awake but surprisingly calm. Outside the trees are shifting in a soft breeze. The temperature is lower than it's been in two months. She wonders if the hot spell has broken or if it will ratchet up again tomorrow. For now, she doesn't care. She drinks in the cool and the dark the way Ian used to drink water when he was little, gulping and so desirous of it that he forgot to breathe and ended up gasping for air once his glass was drained.

She looks at the photos on the refrigerator door. There are hundreds of pictures. Some are cut to the shape of the subject, some are full-frame, some overlap, three or four deep. She has always kept the fridge door as a kind of constantly changing record of their lives. She's always added or subtracted according to her whims, rearranging pictures whenever the mood strikes her.

There's a hole where the one Janey took used to be. The violation is as real and palpable as if it were in her body. The thought that Janey Marks was in her kitchen and stole a photo of her family sets her teeth on edge.

She has to fix it. She has to repair the breach. She takes all the photos off until the fridge is a clean slate. She goes to her desk drawer in the room off the kitchen they use as a home office and pulls out a manila envelope full of shots she's been saving. Then she goes to work putting up old photos with newer ones, and using lots of shots of Ian as a newborn. Over and over again, Ian, in her arms, on his first day.

She needs more magnets to stick them to the fridge. She rummages in the junk drawer, running her hand through fuses, old birthday candles, flashlight batteries, wire, and tape. Here are several packets of nasturtium seeds from two or three years ago. She'd meant to plant them, had envisioned them growing thick and lustrous, their edible orange blossoms a nice garnish to new and unusual dishes she intended to cook. But then People's Dental got under way and she was working twelve-hour days. She never planted the seeds. She never cooked the wonderful new dishes.

She finds the magnets and finishes putting the photos up on the fridge door. She opens it and leans into its light. Eggs, milk, cheese, vegetables, vinegar, butter. All the staples are here. And a bag full of overripe peaches that Miles must have bought before they left for Kansas City. What did her mother say? When disaster strikes, people empty out their refrigerators and make food?

She takes out the peaches and runs them under cool water. She sets them on a clean dish towel to dry while she tries to remember how to make a pie crust. Augusta showed her a thousand years ago. She finds the flour and puts a cup in a large bowl, hesitates and then puts in another cup. She adds a pinch of salt, wondering, as she does every time on those rare occasions when she bakes something, why there has to be salt in sweet things. Just a pinch. In all that sweetness there has to be a little pinch of salt to make the sweet better.

She takes two sticks of butter out of the fridge and cuts one of them up into small pieces that she drops into the flour. She has no idea how much butter she'll need, but this is at least a start. Miles has most of the kitchen tools but she can't find a pastry cutter. She won't be deterred. People made pie long before that wired contraption on a handle was invented. What did they use? Knives, of course. She takes two sharp knives out of the drawer and with one in each hand begins to cut through the butter in the flour. The knives rasp together. She chops and chops, enjoying the repetitive effort of it.

Everything she told Ian and Miles in the car was true. She did join Fishbone because of her strong political and patriotic views. But what she didn't say very well was that equal to the pull of the ideology was the pull of the group. That ragtag little band of revolutionaries was as irresistible as movie pirates or Robin Hood. Peter Pan or Butch Cassidy. They made it clear to all who cared to listen that they were special, an elite force and a new kind of patriot, dedicated to overturning the established government. Mojo, Jack, Janey, and Adrienne were intoxicating to an eighteen-year-old Lucy Johansson. They made revolution look sexy and heroic. And she wanted to believe it. She did believe it. She believed it so much that she moved out in front and planted that bomb.

Augusta used to say that the butter and flour should look like half sand and half peas. The first stick of butter is cut in so that it looks like coarse sand. She cuts up the other stick of butter and chops it in, crossing her knives again and again until it forms pea-sized clumps in the flour. Now, theoretically, the dough will hold together, though it needs water. She remembers that Augusta drizzled water over the dough as she formed it into a ball. "The water has to be cold!" Augusta used to scold. "Put it in the freezer." Doreen lets the tap run on her wrist until the cold is as cold as it will get, which in this heat is just barely cool. But the butter and flour receive it and she works at it, adding drops of water now and then, until she has a cohesive ball of pie dough.

The rest is easier. As a girl she helped Augusta roll out pie crust many times. She sprinkles flour on a board and takes half of her ball of dough and flattens it in the flour, turns it over and flattens it again. Then she finds the rolling pin and begins to roll the dough out to a thin flat piece. She finds a glass pie dish on a high shelf in the pantry and she cuts the dough to fit and drapes it in the pie plate. Then she rolls out the other piece the same way, cuts it into a circle the size of the dish, and folds it loosely in half and half again.

Now she can turn her attention to the peaches. She circumvents each one with her knife, pulls it open to reveal the pit and the peach flesh. She digs out the pits and then cuts the peach into thin slices. These she puts into a bowl and covers them with sugar and, of course, adds a pinch of salt. There was something else her mother used to add to fruit pies. Something unexpected. A secret ingredient. What was it?

She picks up the phone for the second time in three days and dials her mother's number. A simple and odd luxury.

"Mom? What is the last ingredient in peach pie?" Doreen says.

"Oh, good," her mother says. "You made it home. How's Adam?"

"He's at home, sleeping. Miranda will be there early."

"Good."

The silence on the line between them is almost companionable. It's the most ordinary thing in the world, to call up your mother. But for Doreen it's like setting foot on forbidden soil. Rare and unsettling.

"Well, okay, then," her mother says. And Doreen realizes she can't remember why she was calling.

As soon as she hangs up she remembers. The last ingredient. She holds the phone, debating about calling back. Then it comes to her. She sees her mother shaking it out of a red and white box into the fruit. The last ingredient is tapioca.

She finds a box in the pantry and folds three tablespoons of it into the peach and sugar mixture. She slides the fruit into the lower pie crust and dots butter on it before she puts the top crust on. She works around the edge, folding the two crusts under and crimping them with her fingers. Finally, she does the last thing. It was the thing her mother let her do as a child. With a fork she pierces the pie crust, all over, several times until it is riddled with little lines of four holes. The result is a passable pie. Not a pie that would come out of a bakery, not a special or extraordinary pie, but a pie made by somebody at home. An ordinary pie.

wednesday

chapter 38

ADAM WAKES in-country again. He
doesn't have to open his failing eyes to know. The bilious green jungle smell snakes its way over and under the smoke of breakfast fires,
rot, and human shit. Not even the diesel exhaust of ten thousand
motorbikes and trucks can overcome it.

The creature, herself a jungle thing, is still sleeping, one long
insect leg extended into the black field of his closed-eye vision. She
doesn't flicker, she merely pulses like a heartbeat. Good. He feels
much too exhausted to put up with her spastic jumping just yet. Perhaps if he lies perfectly still and tries not to move his eyes behind
his closed lids, he can keep her quiet for a while yet. He practices
mindful breathing. Slowly and deeply, in and out. It is the meditation
practice of a monk.

AS THE YEAR WORE ON, TOM POOLE GREW MORE SILENT, MORE
obsessed with writing the names of the immolated monks and nuns
in his little book. At night on the base in Da Nang, when everybody else was asleep in their cots, Tom Poole would light a stub of a
candle, sit on the floor and close his eyes, his back straight, his hands
holding the little book of names. He got to where he could recite
the names without looking, but he held the book anyway. He always
recited it the same way, this catechism of martyrs, starting with the
monks. "Thich Quang Duc, Thich Nguyen Huong, Thich Thank

Thuc," he would chant. Adam counted fifty-three monks before Tom moved on to the nuns. "Dien Quang," he chanted, "Nhat Chi Mai." And with every name his upper body would rock forward from the waist in a kind of bow. As he learned of more immolators, his list grew. And when he had said the names of the more than two dozen nuns, he would start all over again with the monks.

On the night before their last patrol together Adam lay awake listening. This time, at the end of the nuns, Tom whispered three new names. "Alice Herz," he said. "Norman Morrison, Roger LaPorte."

"Hey," Adam whispered, rising up on his elbow. "Who's that you tacked on the end? Americans?"

Tom turned. His profile was illuminated in the candlelight. He spoke matter-of-factly. "A guy in the news service gave me those. I guess Americans are doing it too. In front of the Pentagon. At the UN. The government keeps it quiet. Just like here. No one knows exactly how many have burned."

Adam dropped back and stared up at the peak of the tent, the standard "GP medium" that was paradise on earth compared to sleeping in the bush. How could people be burning themselves in the U.S., dying that horrible death for peace, and no one cared enough to do something about it, or even report it? What a waste, he thought then, to believe something was so wrong that you set yourself on fire and died and nobody knew. Or maybe nobody cared. He thought of the nun in Da Nang. How her burnt body was taken away and in a few minutes traffic resumed as if she had never been there. Even the ashy dark spot was walked on until it blended in, once again, with the ordinary dirt of the street. The holy people, the martyrs of the war, had only Tom Poole to stay up late and remember their names.

The next day they were back in the bush on mop-up. The only thing worse than being in a firefight was mopping up after one. Their squad's job was to carry out the dead GIs, strip them of packs, helmets, pocket contents, put them in body bags, and load them onto choppers. They tossed enemy dead onto trucks where access was possible, to be taken away to a mass grave somewhere. When access wasn't possible, the mop-up crew had to dig a grave and bury them where they found them.

But this day, in the late afternoon, they came on a blown bunker full of dead GIs blackened with smoke and jungle paint and grit. Their bodies lay in the intimate postures of death. One soldier was on his back, his arms upraised dramatically in rigor mortis. The guy next to him had fallen across his legs. Two other men had taken the hit more directly, their blood and brains mixed as they held each other in death.

They carried the four men back to the chopper and went in again, to another hole in the ground, and this one, too, was deathly still. The body on the ground next to it was Vietnamese. They approached.

"No uniform," Adam whispered.

"VC," Tom Poole answered, his eyes skittering around the fragged trees, looking for motion. "I wonder how deep this hole is. I suppose we should look." He lit a match and dropped it in the hole. In the brief light before the match hissed out in the water standing at the bottom, Adam saw something moving.

"Shit! What was that?" Tom said.

"Rats?" They'd both been in bunkers that crawled with rats.

Tom fired a round into the hole. They heard shouting in Vietnamese. A hand waved a scrap of cloth. It wasn't white cloth but it was meant to be a surrender. Two men, one middle-aged and one quite old with white hair, emerged supporting the weight of a younger wounded man. He was certainly a VC soldier. Tom pulled him out of the hole while Adam stood guard. The young man's leg was shot into hash and a sharp white bone poked through the bloody meat of his calf. He was weak, nearly unconscious from pain and loss of blood. Tom and Adam held their guns on the three, who dropped to the ground. The two unwounded older men knelt and put their hands behind their heads.

"We're not supposed to bring back prisoners," Adam said.

"I know it," Tom said. "You want to kill 'em?"

Adam pointed his weapon at the backs of the older men and then put it up.

"Shit," he said. "I can't."

"Well, we can't let 'em go, can we?"

Adam looked around. No sign of anybody. Gunny and the rest were out at the choppers. Tom walked around to where the two old men could see him. He indicated that they should get up. They did, staring at him with eyes that have already resigned themselves to imminent death. He motioned for them to pick up the wounded man. They did it, one on each side of him, the way Adam remembered kids making a seat out of their arms and carrying another kid on it in the playground. Tom waved them away, to the north, anywhere, just away. The injured man had passed out. The other two registered no gratitude or thanks. They set off in that direction and didn't look back.

"They won't get far," Tom said as he and Adam moved off in the other direction, "but at least we didn't have to shoot 'em."

They found two dead marines in a low marshy area near the perimeter where the water stood six inches deep and the mosquitoes swarmed like filings to a magnet. One of the dead men had tourniquetted his hand, which was missing three fingers. It was blue-black and in the gaps where the fingers had been Adam could see maggots, like white grains of rice, moving in the wounds. Adam and Tom brought him out first, then went back for the second man, who was lying facedown in the water. They bagged him and carried him out. Adam wasn't aware of much except the mosquitoes feeding on his face while both hands were occupied with the body. It was all he could do not to drop the dead man and slap at the bloodsucking insects. He blinked hard and shook his head at several on his eyelids, trying to move them off. They stayed and drank, preferring the living to the dead.

He never saw the sniper. Later, he realized that he had been too consumed with the mosquitoes and his own misery while hauling the heavy body through the bush to have seen any sign of VC. He heard the shot, but it sounded like it was far away. He didn't realize Tom had been hit until he dropped his end of the dead soldier and fell.

There was no cover, no place for Adam to drag Tom to be safe, so Adam knelt where he was and took Tom in his arms, oblivious to possible sniper fire. The single bullet had made a neat hole above Tom's ear. Adam rocked on his knees and tenderly held his friend. Adam picked him up and for the first time realized just how small Tom was.

He carried Tom out. Gunny and the other guys still had another area to mop up and they agreed to finish without him. Gunny didn't make Adam put Tom in a body bag. He let him get on the chopper with Tom in his arms.

Adam sat among the body bags holding his friend. His mind jammed. He was aware of the chopper, its pilot, and the blade whomping above, but he couldn't articulate a thought or a word or even move his eyes. He held Tom throughout the day, as other marines, some he recognized and some he didn't, loaded more body bags onto the Huey. The light was starting to soften and the bird was about to fly, when a sergeant with the name "Bird Dog" inked onto his helmet pushed the two old Vietnamese men from the morning, their hands bound behind their backs, onto the chopper and jumped in behind them. There was no sign of the younger wounded man.

"Get them outta here," yelled the pilot from his seat. "We ain't taking no prisoners."

"Just fly the fuckin' bird," yelled Bird Dog. He outranked the pilot.

Swearing, the pilot turned around. Bird Dog sat near the door with the prisoners. The Huey lifted, hesitated, regained equilibrium, and took off for Da Nang. It was dusk and the hills were hazy with pinkish smoke and golden light. On another day, a day when Tom was alive and sitting next to him, Adam might have been able to appreciate the beauty. From here, skimming along above the canopy, where the protracted gang rape of this land and her people wasn't so apparent, you could see the grace of the hills and the gift of water everywhere. If you wanted.

Normally, Adam would have been concerned about the breach of procedure, bringing Vietnamese on the chopper. He would have been wary of the crazed sergeant, Bird Dog, sitting in the door. But as it was he could barely breathe. He could do nothing but hold Tom's stiffening body.

The pilot took the chopper higher. The canopy gave way to fields.

"Want to have some fun?" yelled Bird Dog. The Vietnamese men stared at their feet.

Adam didn't respond. He looked at Tom's face. It was as peaceful, serene, and smooth as a buddha's. Adam eased the little book on its thong from inside Tom's shirt and opened it. Each tiny page held the name of a monk or nun who had self-immolated, written in Tom's square handwriting.

Bird Dog stood up, a manic grin on his dirty face. His eyes were crazed and jumping as he pulled the two Vietnamese men to standing. Adam realized the guy was stoned out of his mind. Now he could see that their hands were bound with copper wire that cut into their flesh. Blood oozed from the wounds. Bird Dog pushed the older man toward the open door of the chopper. Below, the smoky hills ran gray and the sky was bright vermilion.

Bird Dog turned and grinned at Adam.

"Don't," Adam said. But his voice was so weak that the word was torn from his mouth in the chopper wind and Bird Dog never heard it. It was as though Adam was nailed to the deck of the chopper; as though Tom's body suddenly weighed as much as a jeep. Adam couldn't move. He could see that Bird Dog, whoever he was, was a berserker. Tom would have talked to him. Maybe could have talked him down enough to keep him from doing what he was about to do. But Adam was frozen to the deck.

Bird Dog faked sending the old man out the door, and when the man's legs scrabbled against the chopper deck he hauled him back by the wire. The man's wrists bled heavily now. His mouth was moving and distorted and he was probably weeping, though the chopper wind blew any tears away before they could run. He was clearly begging, looking over his shoulder at Bird Dog. The other man sat huddled in the door opening.

Bird Dog laughed. He glanced over at Adam, making sure he was watching, then he turned the old man around and made him walk backward toward the open door. He pushed the man in the chest and the man took another tiny step backward. When he was poised on the lip of the door opening Bird Dog made him stand there, balancing with his bleeding hands bound behind him. Any turn, dip, or sway of the chopper would have sent him out the door.

"That's enough," Adam yelled.

Bird Dog laughed with glee. This was what he wanted, to get a rise out of Adam. He grabbed the old man by his shirt and pushed him backward so that the only thing keeping him on the chopper were his bare feet at the door and Bird Dog's grip, holding him above the fields below.

"You think I'm going to drop him? You think anybody cares?"

Adam tried to do what Tom would have done. He moved Tom's body to the side and stood up. Bird Dog was bigger and stronger than Adam, he could see that, so he dropped to the floor and held on to the Vietnamese man by the foot.

"I'll send you out there with him," Bird Dog yelled down at him. "Don't think I won't be happy to kill a faggot."

For a minute Adam thought he *would* go out the chopper door with the old man. They would float together for a few seconds and then it would be over. It would be a relief, almost, finally to know his fate, to know that this was the end. He could imagine relaxing, welcoming the darkening ground coming up to meet him.

Bird Dog pulled the old Vietnamese man up so that his face was close. He gazed almost tenderly into his eyes. He shushed the old man, he held his eyes and smiled. Without changing his grip, Bird Dog stepped on Adam's elbow. He stepped down hard so that Adam felt the bone give and his hand open.

Bird Dog stood on Adam's broken arm while he let go of the old man's shirt. The man wobbled a moment, his mouth open with the effort of balance, his eyes on Bird Dog's as if he could hold on to his life by holding the gaze of his killer. Bird Dog gave him a nudge in the chest with one finger. The man dropped like a wing-shot bird.

Bird Dog grabbed the other Vietnamese man by the throat and hustled him to the door. This time he didn't pause; he just held Adam's gaze while he extended his arm and dropped the man overboard.

"There," Bird Dog said. "No more prisoners." He stepped off Adam to sit in the chopper door and clean his nails with his knife.

THE CREATURE IS LOUNGING NEXT TO ADAM ON THE BED. SHE is stretched out on her long prothorax with her head on the pillow. The celadon green body mottled with rose and black markings looks like a dressy kimono. Her bent legs splay at all joints, but her forearms, with the sharp spines, are folded primly in front of her chest, like two pocketknives.

From somewhere near yet unreachable, like a dream bleeding into daylight hours, he hears the bright clatter, the insistent vulgarity of a TV commercial. Is it used cars or is it furniture? He's aware for a moment that it must be Miranda's TV in the kitchen. Another voice, a grave, male voice talks.

"Welcome back. We're talking with our guests First Lieutenant Brian Berger and Sergeant John Racine of the First Marine Battalion about suicide bombers in Iraq. Gentlemen, this seems to be the most difficult thing to deal with in the entire war on terror, these suicide bombers. Both of you have witnessed suicide bomb attacks, but tell us, what's the attitude over there? Do troops live in fear and suspicion of every Iraqi on the street?"

The creature listens and masticates. She rubs her forearms together, gently, causing the tiny knife blades on each to sweep the other with a sound like metal rasping on stone.

"That's just how insidious this cowardly way of fighting is," says one of the soldiers. He's been coached about what to say. He's delivering lines.

"Our orders are to keep civilians safe, and we do that, but sometimes it's really hard to tell who they are because civilians turn out to be these suicide bombers. You never know when one of them has decided to guarantee his place in paradise by taking sixteen lives with his own. It's a diabolical tactic but we'll find a way to fight it. I'm sure of that."

Adam drifts while the newsman talks to the soldiers. Restaurants and cars were blown up in Vietnam. Firefights broke out in occupied cities and VC grenades were lobbed into markets. The VC were like these Iraqi insurgents, impossible to find, impossible to engage by conventional methods. To fight them you had to get creative. You had to get paranoid. You had to see VC under every bush and in the face of every friendly. That was the only way you were going to survive. And coupled with whatever opium or weed you were smoking, everywhere you went there were things that blew your mind: the flayed body of the dead American soldier left by the VC, the answering disembowelment of a female said to be a VC operative, the canopies of trees turned into machine-gun salad, and the smoking hills laid bare by chemical agents. The body bags swarming with flies. All of it, to catch Victor Charlie, whoever he was. You could work up a pretty good freak-out.

But they weren't doing it for the Vietnamese people, in spite of what the president said. Vietnam wasn't the front line for freedom, or the thumb in the dike of communism, or any of that bullshit. Once you'd been in-country for a week or two you realized that in Vietnam there weren't any fronts. The only reason you had a gun and were there humping those hills for gooks was because Command wished it. And the only way you were going to survive it was to do whatever you had to do and stay as high as possible.

Everybody saw pictures of the first immolator in 1963. The image went around the world as fast as the new satellite TV transmissions could send it. The image of the monk sitting in lotus while his body burned was like nothing seen on TV before then, and it seared the collective mind of the world. After his act, governments froze in their steps, then moved quickly to squelch reporting of the others who copied the act. In America and Europe, where self-sacrifice had supposedly been eradicated long ago, governments moved to nip in the bud anything that might be a Western version of the monk's act.

Now, in 2005, Adam hears about suicide bombers every day on the news. But there the similarity ends. Unlike the monks of Vietnam, the goal of the suicide bombers in Iraq is to kill the wearer and others. The message is war, not peace. Not one of them sacrifices himself singularly, without risk to others, in a ritual as old as sand, with the goal of shocking open the mind of the world. In Vietnam no one called the immolating monks and nuns terrorists. He wonders if they would be called terrorists now.

THE CREATURE FLEXES HER BACK LEGS AND WAKES UP. SHE maneuvers her sticklike body around and faces him. The pale oval human face still gives him a shock. The dead eyes and bloodred mouth are terrifying and magnificent. She looks at him, cocking her head to the side and rubbing her shorter front legs together. She masticates continually, the powerful jaw and sharp white teeth moving rhythmically as she stares. She seems to want him to do something. He can't avoid her, she's fully in his vision now. Whether his eyes are closed or open, it's the same. She beckons.

He moves his legs to the edge of the bed and finds that they've regained some of their strength during his sleep. He gropes his way to the dresser and searches with his hands, hoping to find a pen or a pencil. He knocks over a glass of water, soaking books, change, medicines. He moves into the rest of the house. His hand trails the wall, the doorjamb, the back of the settee. For a second the room lights up and Aaron is there, stretched out long on it, well again, his skin smooth and unblemished. He's there and yet not. But Adam doesn't care. Reality has become so relative that he'll take any glimpse of Aaron, no matter where it comes from. He can even smell Aaron, the way he always smelled like sweet bread.

The creature waits patiently until the last glow is gone. Then she urges him to move. He stays in his diaper and T-shirt, and furniture-walks through the sitting room, out to the kitchen. Miranda isn't here, but she has left a list for herself, written in Spanish, and a pen next to it. He takes up Tom Poole's book from where it hangs below his heart. He thumbs through the pages, fragile as insect wings now. The ink is faded. One day it will disappear. He says the names as he has so many times, turning the tiny pages as he recites. When he comes to the last names, the American names on the last pages, he picks up Miranda's pen and, leaning against the counter for stability, adds his name, Adam MacFadden, at the bottom.

The creature prods him toward the garden. She faces forward, giving him a break from her devastating face, but only so long as he keeps moving. Outside he takes a rest on a chair in the yard and consolidates strength while she stares at him and rubs her front feet together. He makes it to his truck, the one that Derek and the boys use for the rock jobs, and opens the door. It's become much heavier since the last time he opened it. He gets in, and the creature folds herself into the passenger side. Her long, stiff body only fits by wedging it in until her neck is bent at a sharp angle against the ceiling of the cab while the end of her body is on the floor. Her back legs are folded up against her abdomen and then splay out on the dashboard at the lower joint.

Adam takes the keys from the visor and starts the truck. The gas pedal feels far away beneath his bare foot, but at least he can feel it. A very good sign that he's doing the right thing. He blesses Doreen for making him buy an automatic.

He drives down the alley and onto the street. He finds that he can hold tight to the steering wheel and let his right foot and leg devote themselves to the gas pedal. His left foot and leg are in charge of the brake. That way he doesn't have to move back and forth between the two. With the creature in the truck with him, he can see well enough. Somehow he knows that she's giving him strength.

He drives slowly through the morning-washed streets. He realizes that he must act as soon as possible. Doreen may be up at this hour, she probably is, but it makes him feel better knowing she won't be able to call her lawyer for hours yet.

He makes his way across town until he comes to the state Capitol building. He drives up the hill and around the back to the service and office entrances. The front side is where the steps are. It's the most public, most obvious place. He parks as close as he can, but doesn't leave the truck. He must conserve his strength. The creature watches through the windshield and rubs her praying hands together.

"Is this it?" he asks.

She gnashes her teeth.

It has to be a public place, a political place. It has to be a place where he can be seen. Like the White House. It used to be that the White House was the place to protest. After Vietnam he went there and stood at the fence in a howling pack with other veterans. These days it's an armed fortress. No one can go near it. Not so the Colorado Capitol building.

He puts the truck in reverse and backs up. Looking over his shoulder is easier than driving forward, because his peripheral is stronger than his central vision. He manages to turn the truck around and drives slowly to a busier street where there are two gas stations, Shamrock and Shell. He chooses Shell in honor of the Shell station in Hue.

He and Tom went there once. It was before Tet and Hue was still a university town. There were white houses, a park, sampans on the river, and people who weren't refugees. Young men walked on the streets holding hands, in the Vietnamese style. It was where most of the monks and nuns who immolated came from. They would have bought their gas and diesel at the Shell before they went to Saigon or Da Nang.

Adam wobbles inside, leaning on the creature, and buys two cans, one for diesel and one for gas. He pays at the counter. The teenage attendant stares at his bare legs and feet, and the diaper, but doesn't seem to see the creature standing with him. Most likely he's never seen the effects of Willy Peter mortars, either, how the white phosphorous hits human flesh and burns and burns, and there's no way to put it out. He probably doesn't know that a person thrown out the door of a chopper at eight hundred feet falls like a trussed bird and there isn't any sound at all when he hits the ground. But the kid's eyes telegraph his own pain. He knows. He knows in his own DNA all of the unspeakable acts taking place, now and forever. Whether it's in Iraq or Afghanistan. Korea or Iran or America.

Adam fills the cans at the pump and puts them in the back of the truck. Then he and the creature get in and make their slow, difficult way home.

chapter 39

DOREEN IS in the shower, shampooing her hair, planning what she'll say to the lawyer. The heat has broken and after catching some sleep in her own bed she's pretty sure she can do this.

It's important to present herself the right way. She's a dentist, a mother, a solid member of the community. She's sane. She's rational. She made a terrible mistake as a kid and now she's coming forward. There will be that moment when she's said all that she can say and Raymond Rhodes will make his own silent judgment of her before he agrees to take the case. Just as, later, she'll have to wait and hope for the compassion of jury and judge. She will be throwing herself on their mercy, because that's the only way to do this. You have to take the posture of a penitent, a supplicant. Absolute contrition is essential to show you know the difference between right and wrong. You apologize. You mean it. You show how this has ripped you up for thirty-four years, and you've been suffering all along and your family is suffering now, too, but you also show that you understand that your suffering can't be compared to the suffering of the family of Louis Nilon. And then it's out of your hands. That will be the terrifying part. As long as she can persuade, explain, and convince, she'll be all right. Coming in on her own terms lets her have that for as long as possible.

She's conditioned her hair and is shaving her legs when Miles comes into the bathroom and stands outside the shower.

"What?" she says.

"Dorie," he says, standing there with his arms hanging awkwardly at his side. It's the helplessness of Miles's arms that gets to her. She opens the door to the shower, not caring that the water splashes out onto the floor. She sees his face and she knows.

"FBI?" she asks.

He nods. His eyes are full of fear and something else: sorrow. She's never seen him look so sad. He puts his hands on either side of her wet face and kisses her mouth. The shower soaks his shirt.

After he leaves she puts her head under the spray, rinsing off conditioner. Her legs have gone to jelly, her hands are all needles and pins. This isn't the way it's supposed to go. She was going to turn herself in. That was the plan. But Janey must have gotten through to them.

When she opens her eyes she realizes that someone else is in the bathroom. She turns off the water and opens the shower door a crack to get her towel. There's a stocky woman in navy blue pants and a blazer standing next to the door, looking apologetic but firm.

"Please step out of the shower, ma'am."

Doreen dries off quickly and wraps the towel around her before she steps out.

The woman shows her the badge, tells her she's under arrest. She reads the Miranda rights. She's got handcuffs and she means business.

"Just let me put on some clothes," Doreen says. "I won't give you any trouble."

The officer nods and follows Doreen into her bedroom.

Homicide. Conspiracy. Destruction of federal property. They're calling her a terrorist.

The officer stands where she can see everything, her hand resting lightly on her gun. She isn't taking any chances. And why should she? From her point of view, Doreen is a violent felon with those terrible crimes against her. She could have a gun in her closet or tucked into her underwear drawer.

Doreen tries to focus. It's important that she keep her wits about her. Getting dressed is the first thing. She puts on a pair of khakis and a white sleeveless blouse. She combs her hair and puts on a little lipstick. It's important to maintain her dignity. It's important to be Dr. Doreen Woods; she must fend off the return of Lucy Johansson. She grabs a light jacket thinking there might be air-conditioning where she's going.

"Am I allowed to take anything with me?" she asks the agent. "A book? A cell phone? I'm going to need to make some calls."

"I'm sorry, you can't bring anything with you. You can request of the magistrate when you're admitted that they keep essential items for you such as prescribed medications and your address book. You'll be allowed to make a call once you're inducted."

Miles comes into the room. He's pale and the wrinkles around his eyes have gained new depth. They're really quite cavernous.

He says, "Ian's up. We'll be right behind you."

The things that must be done whirl in her mind. There are things he must do right away. She says, "Call Raymond Rhodes and explain the situation. Tell him to get down to the Denver county jail right away." She makes quick eye contact with the female agent, confirming that this is right. "Call my office. Get my Rolodex from Nikki and my address book from upstairs and keep them where you can get at them. The lawyer will tell you what to do next."

Once she's dressed, the agent handcuffs her. She's imagined this moment many times, but now that it's here she feels strangely flat about it. Of far more concern to her is her son, probably waiting out in the hall or downstairs with the other agents. She will be led out like a criminal in cuffs and he will see it. Infuriating tears prick her eyes but she won't let them spill. She breathes through her nose and calms down. She won't cry from humiliation. That's a waste. She must reassure Ian. She must tell him she loves him.

She walks downstairs in front of the FBI agent. Another agent sits on the couch in her living room. He's an older man with thin hair combed over and dark spots of sun damage on his face. He looks almost apologetic. Ian is in the chair across from him. Both stand up. She goes to Ian and stands on her toes to kiss his cheek. He puts his arms around her and she wishes that she could put her own around him. She looks into his eyes and smiles. It's not hard. He's so beautiful. He's turned out so well.

"Help Dad call the lawyer and sort things out, okay?" As if this is something that can be, that will be, sorted out. As if this is a mix-up that will get fixed. She didn't mean to make it like that, to patronize him, or to paint a rosy picture to save him from the truth. "There'll be some kind of hearing today or tomorrow and I'll see you there. Are you okay, Ian?"

He looks like he might cry. "I'm okay," he says.

The big FBI agent takes her by the arm and walks her outside. She felt something like this when she went into surgery for the C-section that produced Ian. It's that same feeling of not knowing, of giving your body over to others. Only this time there's no anesthetic and she doesn't get to reassure herself that when she wakes up it will be over and she'll have a new baby. She looks for Miles, cranes her head to hold his eyes as long as she can. They put her in the car and she has no choice but to face forward.

chapter 40

As soon as the black sedan is rolling down the street, Miles goes straight into the kitchen and pulls out the phone book. He sits on the stool at the counter to make the call. As the phone on the other end rings, he notices in a distracted way that there is a pie in front of him on the counter, a homemade golden brown pie, in all its wholesome, fragrant splendor. It's peach, from the looks of it. It's the kind of pie, with top crust and vents, that oozes with buttery, fruity goodness. He doesn't know where the pie came from, but right now, it is no more surprising than anything else that's happened this morning. He stares at it, uncomprehending.

Ian sits on the other stool. His knee touches his father's. Miles is absurdly grateful for that touch right now. Ian stares at the pie, too. Miles glances at the clock over the kitchen sink window. It's only seven o'clock. He finds a number for Raymond Rhodes, atty., and dials it without hesitation. He explains the situation to the lawyer.

"Things could move pretty fast," Raymond Rhodes says, after he's heard it all. He speaks quickly but calmly as if he has a lot to catch up on but doesn't ever go in for panic. "Since the crime occurred in New York and this is a federal case, the first thing that will happen is there will be a removal proceeding so that she can be charged and moved to New York. At the removal proceeding she's entitled to an identity hearing and a bail hearing. We'll waive bail. Of course we could do the identity hearing in Denver, but if federal agents came for her they've got proof that she's the one they're looking for."

"Why waive bail?" Miles asks. "Whatever it is, we'll raise it."

The lawyer pauses. "It would be denied right now. It's better to ask the court to release her on bail in New York. After I talk with Dr. Woods I'm pretty sure we'll be trying to get her to New York as soon as possible, arraigned there, and out on bail. So, to that end, I'll call you as soon as I know when the Denver hearing is going to be. Hopefully sometime today. Meanwhile, get character references in writing from professionals, upstanding people in the community, any charities or good works she does. Get as many as fast as you can. Organize friends or employees to help. Also, if you can do it, line up a couple of the best character references to stand by to go to New York for the bail hearing. That's important. Sympathetic references in the flesh go a long way. Also call your bank and give them a heads-up that criminal proceedings are under way and that you'll need access to a large amount of cash for bail sometime in the next few days."

When he's off the phone with Rhodes, Miles pulls a yellow pad out of the drawer and starts a list. He moves the pie an inch or two to make room. It's still warm. It smells of sugar and peaches and butter.

It's immensely comforting to have Ian hunker over the list with him, suggesting things and making half of the calls from his cell. They call Dorie's office and explain to the staff. It's awkward, but he realizes that he's got to get used to it. He calls the bank and the other dentists with whom Dorie started the homeless project. Ian calls Kumar's parents, Brad and Mitra Pearson, and a teacher friend from Ian's middle school. Miles goes to the neighbors on each side and asks them to help.

At ten-fifteen the cell rings. "I just met with your wife," Rhodes says quickly, and moves on to an account of the legal details.

Miles interrupts him. "How is she?" It seems like days since seven this morning when they took her away. How could it be only three hours?

Rhodes pauses just long enough to take a breath. "She's calm and in good spirits. Things are moving along. There's already been a grand jury indictment in New York. I spoke with the prosecution and, just as I suspected, the U.S. attorney in New York says to hold her without bail while she's out of that jurisdiction. It's in our best interests to get her moved to New York as soon as possible. She will appear before the magistrate here in Denver at eleven o'clock today to hear the reading of the indictment and start the removal proceedings. I will be with her at that hearing. The prosecutor's agreed that speedy removal is essential and he's willing to cooperate. He's arranging for a Justice Department jet to take her to New York immediately after the hearing."

"Ian and I will come to the hearing," Miles says.

Rhodes pauses. Miles is beginning to understand that his pauses signal disagreement.

"Actually, since you need to be in New York for the arraignment, probably by tomorrow, along with character witnesses, it might be better if you get busy with those arrangements."

"Can we fly with her?"

Pause. "I'm afraid not. You'll need to make commercial arrangements. Dr. Woods will be escorted by the federal agents you met this morning. And, of course, after she leaves Colorado she'll need a criminal lawyer in New York. I know some good defense attorneys there. I'll make that call now. Someone will be waiting to meet her plane. I can't stress how important it is that you and two character witnesses get to New York. Today."

Miles holds the phone, but he can't say anything. It all seems too bleak.

Rhodes clears his throat and his voice softens. "You have to expect the worst but hope for the best. Assume she's going to trial but understand that there's a chance they'll offer a plea deal. We don't know yet how much they have. It happened a long time ago. It may turn out that the case is stale."

Miles hangs up the phone in a daze. The flurry of tasks and new information and the pressure of the next round suddenly give way to devastation. A granular, gritty pain has set in somewhere that he can't exactly place, maybe in the hard calcium of his bones. He must make the arrangements. Adam must be told. And Augusta. The weight of it, the overwhelming hugeness of the situation, renders him weak as a kitten. He needs a minute to not think, to not act. He sits on his stool, his hands slack in his lap, studying the refrigerator door where Doreen keeps a continually changing photo record of their lives. He has always enjoyed the door's cycles and molting.

She's been here, working on a new arrangement, since he last noticed the fridge door. Ian as a newborn in his mother's arms is repeated over and over, showing up through a series of baby pictures, toddler and childhood pictures arranged in chronological order. Like the same staccato note repeating here and here and here, is the shot of Doreen, still exhausted from giving birth, holding new Ian with a fierce gleam of victory and accomplishment in her eyes and endless love in the curve of her arm and in her breast that perfectly echoes the curve of the baby's head.

There's so much to do and he must do it, but tears fill his eyes and fall. He can't stop. He sits, his hands useless in his lap, and cries. He should save it for later, when all the tasks are done and he and Ian are on an airplane for New York, but he can't stop. His shoulders shake, his face contorts, and he can't make it stop. Ian's arms are around him.

"Dad. It's all right. We'll save her, Dad. I know we will," Ian says. And Miles clings to him, leans, really leans his weight into his son's arms, and tries to believe the impossible words. His attention lands on the peach pie.

"Ian, who made that pie?"

Ian looks at it. "I thought you did."

"I don't bake pies." He touches the warm crust. "It's still warm."

Ian touches it, too. They're like archaeologists with a rare finding.

"She must have made it," Ian says. Miles nods. They both watch the pie the way new parents watch a baby.

And then Brad and Mitra and Kumar are there with new energy and hope and can-do attitude. Mitra gets on the phone and makes the airline reservations for the five of them. Brad puts a sandwich and a cup of coffee in front of Miles. Before Miles can do anything he cuts the pie and puts a piece on a plate for Miles.

"Eat," he says gruffly. "You look like shit."

Miles obediently takes a bite of the sandwich. He's grateful to have somebody else make decisions for a few minutes. The food absorbs some of the terror and helplessness. The coffee begins to do its work. Now he takes a bite of Doreen's peach pie. It's like eating mouthfuls of sunshine the way the peaches dissolve in his mouth. Suddenly he's ravenous. He devours the rest of the sandwich, drinks the coffee, and eats every crumb of the piece of pie.

He notices that Kumar and Selima are in the other room writing character essays for Doreen. Somehow, in all the flurry, Derek has arrived without Miles knowing it and is quietly making calls from his cell phone.

Ian is on his phone talking to Augusta. "It's the Southern District of New York," he's saying. How did he know that? Miles doesn't remember anybody specifying the Southern District of New York.

"We don't know how long she'll be there. We're hoping she'll be granted bail and can come home until her trial."

How did Ian get so capable, so adult, all of a sudden? When did he learn to comprehend and articulate a situation so well that he makes it easier for his newfound grandmother to understand? Hell, he makes it easier for Miles to understand. He watches Ian talk to Augusta, calming her and helping her figure out what she should do.

"Do you want me to call you from New York as soon as we know?" Ian catches his father's eye, meaning: Is this right? Is this what he should say? Miles nods. But Augusta is talking loudly, Miles can hear her voice buzzing, insect-like, through Ian's phone.

"Well, of course you can come to New York if you want to," Ian says. Again, he seeks approval from Miles and gets it.

"Our flight leaves at six. We'll reserve a room for you at the same hotel as us. Are you okay with taking a cab from the airport to the hotel? The hearing probably won't be until tomorrow at the earliest, so anytime today that you can get into New York."

Mitra is tapping frantically on her laptop.

"Here is a flight from Kansas City leaving at two-thirty today non-stop to LaGuardia," she says. "Ask Doreen's mother if I can book that for her."

Ian does. Augusta agrees. Mitra clicks a few more times and it's done. It's set. They're all going.

Mitra and Brad take over the character references, making phone calls, arranging for letters to be picked up or dropped off before they leave for the airport. Miles's eyes won't stop running. It's chronic now. Ian drives him over to Adam's. Somehow Miles is sure that this is going to be the most difficult part of the day.

They park in the alley and let themselves in through the kitchen door.

Miranda is stirring oatmeal on the stove. Her smile is huge. Miles, for a moment, thinks she knows about Doreen and is perversely pleased with her arrest. Then he realizes that she knows nothing about that. She's probably happy because the weather broke and she doesn't have to cook oatmeal in a sweltering kitchen today.

"Come in, come in," she says. "Mr. Adam is awake. You can go in and see him, if you want."

They pass through the oppressively dark sitting room with its gaudy decoration. He and Ian are both like mules at Belmont in here, he thinks, as he always does, whenever he sees the peacock settee and the decorated ceiling.

Adam is sitting up in bed, staring vacantly at the wall in front of him. He's got something in his hand. At first Miles thinks it's a bracelet or some kind of jewelry, but it's only five or six dark beads, strung together. He's worrying and working them between his fingers. Around his neck he's wearing a leather strap with a tiny moth-eaten book hanging from it. Adam turns his head slowly, like a wasting elk.

"They arrested Dorie this morning," Miles says.

Adam's eyes are aimed at Miles and Ian but it doesn't feel as if he sees them.

"She's been indicted. They're going to take her to New York today."

Adam doesn't seem to be paying attention.

"Adam?"

"Sir?"

Miles ignores the odd response. He hands the paper with Raymond Rhodes's name and phone number on it to Adam.

"This guy is Dorie's lawyer. You're going to need one, too. This guy will help you find one. Doreen is going to do everything she can to make sure you aren't prosecuted, but you should talk to the lawyer anyway. I'll help as soon as I'm back from New York. In the meantime I'll see if Miranda can be here a little more."

Adam holds the paper as though it just happened to float down into his hand and it's no business of his if it sits there. With the other hand he fidgets with the short string of beads.

Adam speaks to someone just over Miles's right shoulder. "They were just kids, sir."

Miles looks at Ian, who has an expression of dread and pity on his face.

"No reason to grease 'em," Adam says.

Miles approaches Adam and puts his hand on his shoulder.

"Adam?" Summoning him from the depths, he shakes the shoulder a little. It's important that Adam understands what he's saying.

Adam looks out of the sides of his eyes and Miles knows that now Adam is seeing him.

"Did you hear me? I said they've indicted Doreen. They're taking her to New York. Ian and I have to go, too. You must call the lawyer on that paper. We'll be back in a few days. With Doreen, I hope."

"Doreen?" Adam says, with the thin voice of an old man. "They got her?"

Miles nods. "Yes, they did."

Adam seems to take the information in and process it.

"Well," he says at last, "it's a body-count war. We've always known that."

chapter 41

F<small>ROM ABOVE</small>, in the Justice Department jet, the American farmland is drought-burned, scored by roads and mysteriously marked by ubiquitous, perfect geometric circles. What are they? Doreen has always meant to find out. Every time she's flown somewhere she's meant to, and then, back on the ground, she forgets about it.

The brown land below is the same land she has crossed many times. She and Adam drove from Kansas City to Washington the summer of 1970 and then out to Berkeley. She and Mojo drove all the way back across the belly of the country, from Berkeley to New York to set the bombs. And she and her family, Adam, Miles, and Ian, just yesterday drove back to Denver from Kansas City. This land *is* her land. She's given everything for it.

Marvin Leach, the big FBI man, sits stiffly in the seat next to her. The female agent is behind them. Leach doesn't read or doze, he stares at the cabin wall ahead. Every now and then he shifts uncomfortably and emits a sigh that is almost a moan.

"Are you all right?" Doreen asks.

"Sciatica," he says.

"Oh. I'm sorry."

He's an older man. His hands are gnarly and spotted. He has an overbite with malocclusion which probably gives him chronic head-aches or jaw pain. He would have been well served by good ortho-dontics when he was a child, but from his blue-collar manner and hillbilly accent Doreen suspects that orthodontics were never an option for Marvin Leach.

"I came out of retirement to come for you," he says, conversationally.

If it weren't for the handcuffs it would be easy to mistake this trip in the private jet for something to do with business or pleasure. And this affable old fellow could be her guide. In reality he has been hunting her.

She says, "How long were you on the case?"

He turns to her now. His eyes, surprisingly, are cornflower blue with dark lashes, quite friendly, and magnified by his thick glasses. "Thirty-four years and five months. Almost to the day. I have the dubious distinction of being the agent in charge of the longest fugitive search with the fewest leads my office has ever seen. I retired thinking for sure we'd never solve your case and I'd go to my grave with it unfinished."

"Well," she says dryly, "glad I could help."

He chuckles and shifts in his seat.

She watches the ground below. Now that it's happening, she can stop dreading it, anticipating it, and making up scenarios about it. In the moments when she's not worried for her family she can see that a weight has lifted. She even dozes for a while.

When she wakes they've begun to circle over Manhattan in the clear, bright afternoon. The architects of the tall buildings must have had just such a day in mind when they dreamed up these towers. The city looks vibrant and healthy. From this height, all shabbiness and street-level effluvia are rendered nonexistent.

True to his word, Raymond Rhodes has arranged for a lawyer to meet her. Paula Stein, a delicate, dark-haired woman, accompanies her through the mug shot and the fingerprints, waits while she's searched and changes into the mandatory blue jumpsuit. They meet for what feels like hours and hours, going through everything about tomorrow's hearing until Doreen nearly falls asleep at the table.

And then she's walked through locked doors and down corridors of other locked doors. The place smells of industrial cleaning products that haven't quite eliminated the body smells that lurk beneath. She has a sudden memory of the DeVrieses' basement freezer in Kansas City where they kept frozen elk and venison. She stood behind Mrs. DeVries as she opened the door. Inside the freezer was as clean as could be with all its white paper parcels, but she caught a whiff of something raw and rank just the same.

Finally the matron stops in front of one particular door. She unlocks it and they walk down a corridor of cells with metal bars. The fluorescent lights in their cages high above emit a buzzing noise.

The matron unlocks the cell and Doreen walks in. The bars lock. She's aware of the many layers of locks behind her. A cold dampness lingers in the room. She is disoriented, she doesn't know if she's aboveground or in some kind of basement. She reminds herself that this is temporary. Tomorrow she will see the judge, and even if she isn't allowed to go home until the trial, she probably won't be staying here. It helps, somehow, to know that this room is only a temporary lodging. You can put up with anything, temporarily.

The cell is narrow, with a toilet and sink at the far end. The top bunk is occupied but the woman in it doesn't speak or move. Doreen sits hunched over on the hard bottom shelf that is her bunk, unable to sit up straight without bumping her head on the upper, so she lies down. From here the flickering yellowish lights shine into her eyes. She closes them. She hears footsteps on metal. They stop at her cell, then walk on. The person on the top bunk mumbles and turns over, kicking the metal shelf in the process. From far away, beyond layers of bars and doors, someone cries out loud, "Ai! ai! ai!" "Shut up!" yells another voice. And another, "Whore!" The footsteps return and pass, quicker, harder this time.

Now Doreen is wide awake. She hugs herself, cold to the bone, and stares at the underside of the shelf above. It is smooth metal, designed to be tamperproof, yet in the uppermost corner near the wall, in a place that can't be seen unless you're lying on the bottom bunk, there is something scratched into the metal. Someone found something sharp, smuggled it in and worked on this. Doreen moves in as close as she can, lifts her arm and touches the rough scratches.

"LaVon was here."

A simple declaration. Given a sharp tool and the time and the inclination, LaVon decided to scratch her name and insist on being known. Her name and the fact of her occupation of the bunk are what LaVon, whoever she was, wanted the next occupant to remember about her. And it was important enough that she scratched it into a metal surface.

Doreen wishes she had a sharp object. In here, a sharp object would be the ticket to certain freedoms. It could be used as a weapon. It could be traded for something of equal value. It could be used to open a vein and leave the premises immediately, one way or the other. Or it could be used to write your name on the metal underside of the bunk.

If Doreen had a sharp object she would add her name under LaVon's. She would lie here on this bunk and scratch her existence into metal for the next and the next and the next woman who came after her.

D-o-r-e-e-n, she would spell. Doreen was here.

thursday

chapter 42

Adam has retained some of the strength he gained yesterday. The creature is still here next to him, magnificent and whole, the folded knife blades of her forelegs clicking in anticipation. He doesn't fool himself that she's given him this reprieve for his own sake. She has an agenda.

He's not sure if Doreen has been arrested or not. Yesterday Miles and Ian stood here and told him so, but their story has the tinny quality of one of his hallucinations, one of his waking dreams. Whether it has happened yet or not, he has very few choices left, he knows that, and they are diminishing every day. Once Doreen is arrested he won't have any more choices. Either he'll be arrested too or he'll be put into the care of his mother. He decides to exercise his free will while he still can.

He stands up and so does the creature. He holds the nun's beads, Tom's beads, in his hand. He feels their bumpy surfaces and thinks of her nearly wasted death. He leaves the book, Tom's book, with its recent addition, on his night table.

They sent him home from Vietnam to Walter Reed Hospital, where he had two surgeries in three weeks before he was honorably discharged and sent home to Kansas City. Weak as he was, with his arm in a cast and his mind as devastated as the hills of Vietnam, he drove to Douglas, Wyoming, with Tom Poole's letter to Marjorie in his pocket.

Though the first sweet green of spring lay on the banks of the twisting Platte, the hills outside of Douglas were remarkably restrained compared to the hills of Vietnam. He knew there had been wars here, Indian wars, back when this was frontier, but there was no lingering trace of death now. Animals grazed, cows and calves, on new grass under a high, clear sky. Maybe in a hundred years, he thought, the acid viridian hills of Vietnam would have this same clean feeling.

Tom's family had been notified of his death in the usual way, but there was still the matter of the letter for Marjorie. Whoever she was. Tom never talked about her. He never said if they were married or engaged or what. For all Adam knew, Marjorie was Tom's sister. He didn't have an address or a last name for her, but the town was small, laid out on a simple grid, and he had Tom's parents' address, so he made his way there.

The Pooles lived in a small white house one street off the main drag. The roses next to the porch were just starting to leaf out. Bright sparks of forsythia lined the walkway. Mrs. Poole answered the door. Her unblinking eyes in their crepey pouches took in his cast and sling; they searched his drawn face before she stepped back to let him in.

She brought him hot percolator coffee with cream and sugar in a pink melamine cup. Up until that day he took his coffee black, but Tom's mother didn't offer it. He drank the pale mixture slowly, not sure he'd like it at first, but after one sip wanting to prolong the flavor as long as possible. Nothing had ever tasted that good. Nothing ever would again. After that he always took cream and sugar, but never quite recaptured the flavor of Mrs. Poole's Maxwell House.

"Tom wrote to me about you," she said. "He said you looked out for him over there."

He concentrated on the coffee but its sweetness only encouraged the tears backing up behind his eyes. He put the cup down and reached into his shirt to bring out Tom's book of names on the leather thong around his neck. He took it off and handed it to Mrs. Poole. She held it on the flat of her hand, turned the sheer pages with one finger. He dug into his chest pocket, behind the letter to Marjorie, and brought out the partial string of beads Tom had collected from the immolated nun. He handed that over, too. He felt bereft, giving up these two last bits of his friend, but it was right that Tom's mother should have them.

"He was never without these," Adam said. He explained who the names belonged to and how Tom collected and recited them.

She held the book in one hand, the beads in the other. She put one and then the other to her cheek as if to impress them there, then she offered them back to Adam.

"You keep them," she said.

He shook his head. "It's okay, ma'am," he said. "While I was at Walter Reed I wrote down all the names. I don't need them."

She stood and brought them over to him. "My Tom is the boy who hasn't gone to war yet. He's a 4-H boy who has never been hurt." She gestured to the narrow staircase that led up to a shadowy landing. "I have a whole room full of his things. *Your* Tom is the soldier who memorized those monks' names." She put them in his hand and closed his fingers around them. "You keep them, dear."

He accepted. He put the thong around his neck again, the beads back in his pocket. He showed her the envelope.

"This is for someone named Marjorie."

She put her hand to her mouth. "Marjorie Polk. Her folks own a place out east of town," she said, wiping her eyes on her sleeve. She took his empty coffee cup. She told him how to get to the Polk ranch, then she walked him to the door.

"Thank you for coming," she said. "I'm real glad to know you."

And then she opened the door and patted him on the back as he walked over the threshold. He had the distinct feeling that he was being hustled out the door. As he got back into his car he could see through the living room window that Mrs. Poole hurried up the stairs as if she'd kept someone waiting up there.

The meeting with Tom's mother had taken it out of him and he was trembling with weakness by the time he got to the Polk ranch. His arm ached. The cast felt heavy, hanging in the sling from his neck, but even so he could see that the place was fortuitously situated with a creek running near the barn and cottonwoods towering overhead.

A pigtailed girl about ten or eleven told him that Marjorie was "out with the ponies." He walked in the direction she was pointing until he came to a corral where a young woman rode a bareback horse. She brought the horse around to the gate where Adam stood. Now that she was closer he could see that she was tan and lean with a face that would be stern in a few years but now looked pensive. She wore beat-up cowboy boots and blue jeans and a snap-front cowboy shirt that the sleeves had been cut out of. A long scar like a crudely drawn zipper ran down the inside of her muscular arm from shoulder to elbow crease. The athletic body and acne-scarred face made a startling contrast with her hair. Most of the girls Adam knew had stopped curling and styling their hair in favor of a straight, natural look. Marjorie's hair was curled and stiffened. A small velvet bow sat just behind the roll of her bangs, and a hill of teased hair mounded behind that, which all came to a curved stop behind her ears. It was hair made to imitate the hair of girl groups from ten years before. It was 1960, not 1970. And it was completely misplaced on the clear-eyed horsewoman beneath it.

"I'm Adam," he said.

"I know it," she said. She stayed on the horse but she leaned over its neck to shake his hand.

He pulled Tom's letter out of his pocket and handed it up to her. Her hand came slower this time, hesitating before she took the envelope. She glanced at her name in his handwriting before she unsnapped her breast pocket and tucked it in.

"Look," she said, not making any move to get off the horse. "Do you want to come up to the house? Have a cup of coffee?"

Suddenly he was beyond exhaustion. All he wanted to do was get a motel room and sleep until he could drive back to Kansas City. The idea of another cup of coffee and another tearful woman who knew Tom, whose eyes conveyed that Adam had failed to keep Tom alive, was too much for him.

"I really need to be getting back," he said.

Her horse stepped sideways and tossed its head. She made him turn in a tight circle and brought him around to face Adam again.

"Look," she said. "Tom and I were going to get married." She gestured to the land, the barn, the corral, the river. "All this was going to be ours. Tom's and mine. But he wanted to go to the war. He wanted to go to college. I was third. I was always at least three down on his list. So while he was away I met somebody else." She held out her left hand where a single small diamond sparkled on her ring finger. Her eyes glittered with angry tears. "I'm going to marry him. I wrote to Tom and told him that. That was my last letter to him. Did he get it?"

"I don't know. He never mentioned it."

She looked bitter. "No, of course," she said. "He wouldn't."

ADAM WALKS THROUGH HIS HOUSE, AND THOUGH HIS FEET ARE rubbery, he can feel the floor. The creature follows behind like a huge, angular dog. He sees that Miranda left a basket of folded laundry on one of the chairs. In it are a pair of khaki pants and a T-shirt. He puts them on before he goes outside.

He and the creature get into the truck, as before, and with her help, her sharp eyes, he drives through the liquid sun of the new day, over the shimmering pavements, until he's at the Capitol.

IN THE COURTROOM THE LIGHT IS BLUE-GRAY COMPARED TO the fluorescent yellow of the women's facility. Every seat in the place is occupied. Who are these people? She doesn't recognize any of them except those in the first row. Miles and Ian, Mitra and Brad. Her mother is here, too. She looks for Adam. Of course not Adam. She wishes he were here.

Her lawyer, Paula Stein, addresses the judge, and so does the prosecutor. Doreen is unable to hear most of the words for the roaring in her ears. Marvin Leach and Janey Marks sit behind the prosecutor, with his ostentatiously shabby briefcase. Janey is flanked by two Sewell, Smith & Marks lawyers. She is relaxed and confident, and gazing forward. She doesn't look at Doreen. Her expensive black blazer and the thick gold bracelet on her wrist say all that needs to be said about her influence and affluence. Doreen's linen dress looks weak by comparison. Even graceful Paula Stein, in her tea-colored suit, looks watered-down next to Janey.

"We're here to read the indictment of Lucianne Johansson, also known as Lucy Johansson, Doreen Woods, Doreen MacFadden, and Patricia Wolfer."

Janey stands up and identifies Doreen as Lucy Johansson. All eyes turn, briefly, to look at Doreen and then away again. Her ears start to ring. She feels faint.

"Will the accused confirm identification?"

Doreen's lawyer stands up. "Your honor, my client confirms the identification. We move for her to be identified as and referred to as Dr. Doreen Woods."

"Granted."

The roaring in her ears takes over and she can only watch Paula

Stein speak for her and then the prosecutor, whose jowls jiggle as he frowns and shakes his head. She's cold to the bone and trembling. She wishes she could turn around and see the people who are here for her. She wishes she could look at Miles and Ian and see them smile at her. The distance between them is maybe five feet but it seems very far right now. It's been twenty-four hours since she was home.

At this hour maybe a dozen people are on the Capitol steps in Denver already, including an old woman who shakes her head as if she can't believe what she's seeing and then shakes it again.

With the creature at his side, Adam lifts the cans of gas and diesel out of the back. He soaks his clothing, coughing from the fumes. The creature observes with calm approval. When he's thoroughly doused, they leave the truck. He carries the half-empty gas can with him. The fumes swirl around his head. The Capitol lawn, green nearly to the point of synthetic, forms a moiré pattern that bleeds into the ultramarine sky. The creature stays close. She helps him to the center of the top step.

He sits with some difficulty but finally manages to cross his legs. Instantly a flock of dove gray nuns and more than a hundred monks in marigold robes appear. They all assume the position of the Buddha. Adam pours the last of the gas from the can over his head and on the ground around him. A magic circle. He sees people walking below but they can't see him yet. The creature wraps her legs around him, the folded-knife forelegs cross in front of his chest with a resounding metal click.

In New York the prosecutor stands up and smooths his tie. "Due to the flight risk and the grave nature of the crimes, the prosecution seeks pretrial detention."

Paula Stein stands, too. "Your honor, the defendant has lived for thirty-four years as a respectable, law-abiding citizen. She is a legitimate, established dentist with her own practice. She founded People's Dental, a nonprofit organization that benefits the homeless in Denver. Dr. Woods is a loving mother, wife, and daughter. She has friends in her community who vouch for her and are willing to put up their property and life savings in order to make her bail. She was preparing to surrender of her own free will at the time of her arrest."

"Your honor," says the prosecutor, "Lucy Johansson, excuse me, *Dr.* Woods, has been a fugitive for thirty-four years. She is comfortable with running and hiding. Why wouldn't she do so again?"

"Because," says Paula Stein, patiently, "she has a family, a practice, friends, and community who are behind her. She's thirty-four years older. She's made a respectable life for herself in that time. And she wishes to stand trial."

The judge speaks. "Bail is set at one million dollars. The defendant will be limited to the state of New York. She will surrender her passport and report to pretrial services for electronic monitoring."

Paula Stein stands again. "Your honor, we request that the geographical limitations be extended to the defendant's home in Colorado with permission to travel between Colorado and New York for trial preparation."

The roaring in Doreen's ears takes over. She gathers that it's over because the room comes alive with people moving toward the door. Miles and Ian, her mom, Brad and Mitra all enfold her. She finds Miles. She finds Ian. It feels like a victory though she knows the fight, if it can be called that, has only just begun. Paula Stein tells her she has won the right to go home and prepare for her trial. She's won the legal right to use her own name, Doreen Woods, instead of Lucy Johansson. She's won the right to leave this place. For now.

———

AT THE TOP OF THE STEPS IN DENVER, ADAM SITS WITH THE monks and nuns. The creature hunkers behind him. In his right hand is the kitchen match. In his left are the beads. His mother used to say, "The world is round." She meant that everything comes around again and a person can get a chance to do better. This is his chance.

He remembers watching Tom Poole recite the names of the immolators. At the time and for years after, he thought that their self-sacrifice was only meaningful because Tom Poole remembered them. And after Tom died, Adam did his best to read the names every now and then.

But now, sitting with them, their many bald heads shining in the twenty-first-century sun, he understands that being remembered was only a by-product of their immolations. Doused in gas and diesel and holding the match, he understands, finally, that it is the act itself, not the remembering of it, that matters. The act itself is enough. The act is the price of admission. Even when, especially when, nobody is watching.

AT THE FAR EASTERN EDGE OF THE CONTINENT, DOREEN, PAULA Stein, Miles, and Ian walk down the cool gray hallway. Augusta and the Pearsons follow. Ahead the big doors open and close, letting in wedges of light. Only a little more than twenty-four hours in custody and Doreen craves to get out of cold gray buildings and cold gray air like she's never craved anything else.

The doors open and she feels the warmth of sun on her face. It temporarily blinds her, but she can sense a great crowd of people. She shades her eyes with her hand. People with microphones and TV cameras are trained on a man speaking at the top of the courthouse steps. It seems that they've stumbled onto some news event, that they've walked into a press conference about some important trial.

The politician speaking is a man whose face she's seen in newspapers since the beginning of the current administration. Paula Stein takes her arm and steers her away and toward the street, but she hears what the politician says into the microphones and cameras.

"This is a great day," he says. The breeze ruffles his hair and the sun shines benevolently on his head. "A fugitive terrorist we've been hunting for many, many years has been pulled from hiding and indicted by a grand jury. Using all the technology and manpower we have to bring to such a case, we have succeeded in arresting Lucy Johansson, a dangerous radical terrorist at large for three and a half decades. Make no mistake about it, justice will be done."

IN THE CENTER OF THE CONTINENT, IN THE CENTER OF THE world, Adam holds the match in his right hand. In his left, the beads. His vision clears and he knows exactly what he's doing. He could stop now, having taken himself to the edge and peered over. He could go home and strip off his gasoline-and-diesel-soaked clothes, let Miranda give him a bath. He could stop this and die with his family around him. It won't take much longer at the rate his mind is degrading. He can stop now, or he can drop his arm and strike the match.

Adam wishes to pay. He's happy to. He lets his arm fall.

The sulfur head of the match strikes stone.

"THIS IS HOW WE'RE GOING TO WIN THE WAR ON TERROR," says the politician on the other steps. "Hunt them down and arrest them, one by one. Whether they are domestic terrorists from the time of Vietnam or foreign terrorists now, they're terrorists if they commit acts of violence against our country and our people, and we will root out each and every one of them and bring them to justice. I'm proud that the Southern District of New York has set this example for the country and the world. No stone has been left unturned, and as a result, the wheels of justice are turning today."

The microphones and cameras suddenly swarm around Doreen. Paula keeps a firm hold on her arm. "Don't answer any questions. If you have to say something, say, 'No comment.'"

She is hustled toward the street and the line of waiting cabs and cars. Miles and Ian flank her. Reporters shout "Lucy" and "Doreen" to try to get her attention. "Are you sorry?" someone yells. But she's whisked away and into a car before she can answer.

ADAM SEES PEOPLE RUNNING TOWARD HIM ON THE OTHER SIDE of the fire. They worry and suffer, but they must stay outside his circle. His body is anchored by a singular sensation poised at the base of the neck, pouring upward through his ears, jaw, eyes, brain, and skull. He feels again, for one last second, the weight and pain of his ruined body. He lets it go with a tiny movement of his chin. He moults it off.

He rises with the creature until he can see the city and its human-encrusted outskirts. And then the eruption of mountains from the vast brown plain. As he rises he sees how round the world really is, and that the virus of humanity, so far, only affects the skin. The deeper regions, the integrity of the whole, has not been infected yet. A vast sense of relief fills him and gives him lift.

The creature is huge, she is above and below. She is wild and fierce, released into her element. And suddenly, effortlessly, the earth is only a blue-green agate swinging back and forth on her neck.

friday

chapter 43

THE BURN unit is a place of sterile sur-
faces. Doreen, Miles, Ian, and Augusta wear yellow paper gowns,
booties, and masks to keep their germs from infecting Adam.

Adam's body is wrapped. Only his nose and mouth are visible.
The skin around them is black and cracked and oozing. He's still
alive, though the doctors say his kidney function has shut down. Augusta sits at his left side. Miles and Ian stand with Doreen at his right.
Doreen touches his hand, a clublike appendage underneath the layers of wrapping. She hopes her touch doesn't hurt him.

There's no way to know, but she suspects that Adam isn't in there
anymore. He did this to himself. He wanted to die. She senses that
this lingering, this breath and heartbeat, are residual. But, of course,
she doesn't know. She didn't know he was planning this. She knew
he had a long obsession with that little book of monks' names, but
she didn't think he'd ever add his own to it. She knew his dementia
had been on the rise, but she had no idea it would go this far. If,
indeed, this was the work of his dementia and not the work of his
more rational mind, deciding to get out while he could still make the
decision for himself. But to burn himself? To copy the immolators
from decades ago?

All she can do is watch his body labor to breathe its last breaths
and commit herself to be with him for each one.

She wonders if he thought that alive, he would be a bargaining
chip for the forces against her. She hopes he didn't think his life was

a liability to her. That he might have done it for her, thinking that he would save her one last time, threatens to tear her into pieces.

The grief, the mourning keening, is already rising. Adam is gone. She knows he is. He has left this world, left her, and she can't imagine it without him. He's always been here. He has been the one constant in her life.

She reminds herself that he chose this. He chose this ending. She squeezes her eyes shut and hopes he was lucid enough when he did it that it really was his choice.

The machines beep and record his vitals. The nurse comes in to check on him but there is very little to do. They aren't treating him for the burns beyond pain medication. The decision has been made to let him die, that he is beyond saving. The truth is that most of him was already gone before he did this. Adam has been leaving little by little for a year or more. That his body is still technically alive is a fluke, or possibly a last consideration.

Augusta takes full advantage of the lingering life. She whispers into the wrappings over Adam's ear. Her tears drip onto his bandages. The nurse comes in again and adjusts his medication. After she leaves he takes a breath and lets it go. He takes another breath and keeps it. The monitor goes off and the nurse comes back. Doreen waits for the exhalation but it never comes. And then even the unrecognizable charred husk of his body is dead.

chapter 44

AT HOME, much later, they sit close in the light of a single lamp. Ian and Selima sit on the couch talking quietly, their legs entwined, pretzel-like. Mitra, Brad, and Kumar bring chicken and potato salad. Mitra puts out plates and napkins. She turns on more lights before she fixes a plate for Augusta and sits next to her.

Nikki, Joan, Avery, and Fern from the office come in and each of them hugs Doreen, tells her how sorry they are about Adam. None of them mentions her arrest but she knows it's included with the sympathy about Adam. Fern flits around the room with her dramatic eyes done up, clearly trying to observe some kind of proper decorum, but forgetting and letting a high, silvery laugh escape. It sounds good to Doreen. It sounds like life. She looks down at the unfamiliar weight and bulk of the electronic bracelet on her bare ankle. Everyone can see it. She doesn't care. She's unashamed. There is nothing left to hide.

People keep coming in, neighbors, patients, other dentists, friends of Ian and colleagues of Miles. People who knew Adam and people who didn't. The house fills up with people who want her to know that they care about her, about Adam. They bring food. They bring life.

Derek stops in. His eyes are red and he starts crying when he hugs her. Miranda and her family come to pay their respects. Miranda leaves a pan of something in the kitchen and takes Doreen in her arms and rocks her the way she might rock a child. Doreen closes her eyes and lets her head rest on Miranda's shoulder. She will accept this love. She will accept this life.

This is where she and Adam were always different. Or at least since Vietnam they have been. After the war Adam didn't care if he lived or died. Meeting Aaron gave him another shot at it, but after Aaron died Adam drifted along, indifferent to his life. Doreen has always chosen to live, on whatever terms life presented. After she set the bomb and it killed Louis Nilon, she ran and hid, but in Mrs. Chen's grocery she chose to live. She chose again when she took the name Doreen MacFadden. And again when she married Miles. When Ian was born it was fixed forever that, come what may, she would always choose to live.

It feels stuffy indoors. Now that she can't leave it, even her own house feels restricting. She steps out the back door. The ankle bracelet won't let her go as far as the orchard, even, but she can stay on the flagstones next to the house.

She breathes the cool night air. Inside, the others continue talking and milling about, eating and smiling. She watches. She has chosen to live but she has also chosen to pay. She will pay for Louis Nilon's life and the last thirty-four years. She will take these weeks or months, if she's lucky, with her family and hope that the case won't go to trial. She'll hope for a plea bargain. Paula Stein says it's possible even though the prosecution will go after her with a vengeance. But even if she gets a deal, she'll certainly do time. Paula Stein says the most she can hope for is a short sentence, a year or two if she's lucky. It could be more. Much more. She could get twenty-five to life. She could die an old woman in prison.

Inside, Ian stands to hand his father a tamale from Miranda's dish. Ian will be fine, he's got his future, college, interesting work, Selima. It's Miles she's worried about. Not Adam anymore, but Miles. Though she has chosen to live, the life they created together will end. There *will* be a kind of death, a second death for her. She wonders if

Miles will experience it that way. As his first. And then a whole new life. For her it will be the third. But this time she is legitimately Doreen Woods. In that, in just that, she has gained something. Because of that, she's not the person with blurry edges and a rotting secret at her core that she's been for thirty-four years. She's no longer who she was, but who she will become, exactly, remains to be seen.

acknowledgments

THE AUTHOR is grateful to the following people and organizations: The MacDowell Colony, Abby Lester and Jocelyn Wilk at the Columbia University archives, David Farrell at the Bancroft Library at UC Berkeley, Linda Williams and Paul Fitzgerald, Sam Green, Sara Jane Olson, Vicki and Wah Peterson, Ed Huston, Dr. James Marquardt, Dr. Stu Brown, Marc Leepson, the Vietnam veteran at the Boulder Vet Center who wishes to remain anonymous, the Boulder Arts Commission, Leslie Fields, Barry Schwartz, Charlie Szekely, Alex Sierck, Erin Koenen, Carl Sheola, Martha Stone, Elizabeth Bouvier, Nika and Dave Haas, Dr. Mike Carry at University of Colorado Health Sciences, Dr. Heidi Winquist, D.D.S., Spring Alexander, Maya Turner, Jonathon Holden, Gayle Mylander, Sheera Boris, Jeff Kocar, Larry Wright, Kim and Brad Keech, Kate and Mark Villareal, Lisa Jones, Julene Blair, Marilyn Krysl, Gail Storey, Elizabeth Hyde, Peter Heller, Rebecca Rowe, David Grinspoon, Helen Thorpe, Tory Read, and Steven Mascaro.

The following books, articles, films, and reference materials were invaluable research materials for the writing of this book:

Books: *The Portable Sixties Reader* by Ann Charters; *Rolling*

Stone: The Seventies, edited by Ashley Kahn, Holly George-Warren, and Shawn Dahl; *Dispatches* by Michael Herr; *Achilles in Vietnam* by Jonathan Shay

Films: *The Weather Underground*, directed by Sam Green; *Winter Soldier*, documented by the Winterfilm group; *The Cockettes*, directed by David Weissman and Bill Weber; *The Nomi Song*, directed by Andrew Horn

Other materials: John Kerry's testimony before the Senate Foreign Relations Committee on April 22, 1971; the journalism of David Halberstam; "Through the Flames" by Kent Chadwick; 1970–71 issues of *Berkeley Barb*